Hadrian's Trader

Richard Yeo

Winchester, UK
Washington, USA

First published by Roundfire Books, 2013
Roundfire Books is an imprint of John Hunt Publishing Ltd., Laurel House, Station Approach, Alresford, Hants, SO24 9JH, UK
office1@jhpbooks.net
www.johnhuntpublishing.com
www.roundfire-books.com

For distributor details and how to order please visit the 'Ordering' section on our website.

A CIP catalogue record for this book is available from the British Library.

Design: Stuart Davies

Printed and bound by CPI Group (UK) Ltd, Croydon, CR0 4YY

We operate a distinctive and ethical publishing philosophy in all areas of our business, from our global network of authors to production and worldwide distribution.

Prologue

Trista tiptoes through the night-damp grass. Goose pimples thrill her limbs not from cold – it is a fine, summer's night – but from the joy of adventure.

The window made her do it. It was wide open, inviting her, and nurse was so fast asleep, snoring like a hog. Trista bends to squeeze through the gap in the hedge. The orchard is dark but the stars light her path. She stops and gazes up into old Granfer Apple Tree. Tonight she will see them, she is sure she will.

Without thinking she kilts up her nightdress. Her hands reach for the branches above her head. Her foot finds the bump of a lost branch. She climbs up and up towards the stars. Because she is light she can go way up among the leaves until she is hidden from the ground. She finds her favourite seat, straddling a branch with another making a backrest, and settles to wait.

Father has told her all about *strix otus*, the Long-eared Owl. Lying wakeful in the summer night she has heard the *hoo* of the male sometimes answered by the rasping buzz of his mate. There are nights when they duet for long minutes. She so wants to see them.

She waits. The night is warm with hardly any breeze. She can see ever such a long way from here, all the way to Aurelianum where a few lights sparkle in the dark. She has been to Aurelianum lots of times, riding with Father, up in front of his saddle. They were there just last week when mother had her measured for her birthday dress. It will be a dreamy, bluey-green. She can't wait to try it on. She knows it will make her look very grown up but, then, ten *is* grown up; much more grown up than Marcus her little brother.

There! She jerks out of her reverie. The owl cries, *hoo hoo*. He's out on her left; not far. Father says he can fly through even quite dense branches. She cranes round, willing him to show himself. Yes! Here he comes: gliding through the branches, his great wings tipping this way and then that. He is only just lower than her. Oh, if only his mate joins him. If only they will sing together.

But no: he is sheering away abruptly into the dark. Something has startled him. Then she hears it: harness jingling and muffled hoof beats. She clings to the branch and looks down. Round at the front of the house someone is pounding at the door. What is going on? She must return to her room before they discover she is out. As she shifts her weight, ready for the descent, she freezes. Someone is creeping through the orchard – not just someone but several people. Noiselessly, she settles back. What is going on?

Just then – uproar at the front of the house. There is the clash of arms. She has heard it before from the practice grounds where Father exercises with Wulf, his bodyguard. There is shouting and then a scream. A voice below her. "Spread out. Be ready for any of them that has come out the back."

Now she can see figures in the backwash of starlight. They have pushed through the hedge into the garden. She sees half a dozen shapes spreading out across the lawn. The metallic clangour becomes louder with shouts, oaths and screams.

A door opens. There is lamplight. Mother is silhouetted. She is carrying Marcus, turning to speak to the nurse who follows her with a bundle. They step out onto the lawn. Trista tries to shout, to warn her but her mouth is dry.

"Mother." It comes out as a whisper, too quiet and, in any case, too late to sound the alarm.

The black shapes surround Mother and the nurse. She hears Mother's voice, imperious, not at all afraid.

"What is this? Explain yourselves or by Jupiter ..."

Her voice ends in a bubbling groan. The nurse is shrieking, turning to run back into the house. In the light from the door Trista sees the woman stabbed and cut down. The figures gather around something on the ground. "Mama," she hears then heart-breaking sobs. They too are cut off. She hears a throaty laugh.

"Get them inside." The men are dragging Mother, the nurse

and little Marcus in through the door. Trista hangs on blindly to the branch. Her bladder releases its contents down her leg. She lays her head against the rough bark. For a while she loses consciousness.

She awakes to flames. The house is burning. "Mother! Father!" she moans to herself, shaking her head from side to side in disbelief. Should she go to them? She doesn't know. She doubts she can move anyway so she clings on to the branch and watches her life turn to smoke and ashes.

After a while men come around the corner of the house. There is plenty of light now from the flames. She can see their leather jerkins and their long swords but she knows instinctively they aren't tribesmen. She has spent her young lives around soldiers. These hold themselves too straight for Gaulish warriors. Two of them come to the gap in the hedge and pass through.

"She certainly didn't come out the back. We had all the doors and windows covered in good time," says one. He is speaking Latin with the accent of Germany. She has heard it often enough in her uncle's Legion.

"Well, we must find her," says the other. "She can't have gone far. She'll likely be frightened and hiding in a ditch. Spread out. Search the orchard with your men. We'll do the front. When you find the brat, kill her and chuck her in the fire. Fifteen minutes, mind; no more. Beyond that the countryside will be up in arms and Sertorius won't thank us for getting caught. Rendezvous at the horses."

"Sir," barks the first man, saluting, fist on breast.

"Apollo's Crutch, you're a tribesman, not a fucking soldier. Remember that or we're all up the Styx."

The second man wheels and stalks away.

"Right, you lot," shouts the first. "Into the orchard. Spread out. Beat the whole place flat and the wood beyond. I want spears in bushes, the lot. Fifteen minutes an' then we're out of here. Small girl, black hair. If you find her, spit her. Then we'll roast her."

The men laugh. Trista shivers. Her teeth chatter. She holds onto the rough bark even tighter.

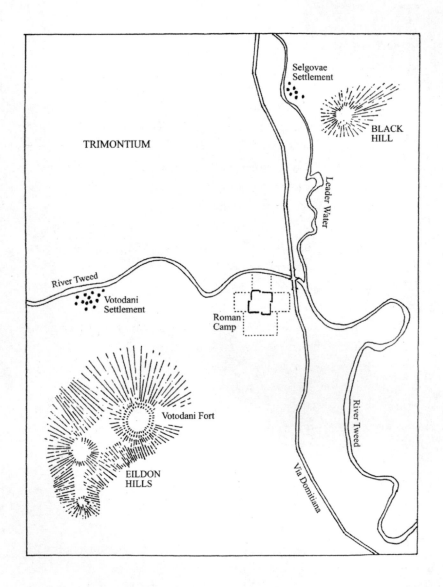

Part 1

Chapter I

(Eboracum)

Lucius Terentius Aquilina, Centurion of the Fifth Century, Second Cohort, Sixth (*Victrix*) Legion, screamed with agony, then slumped backwards, tasting blood.

"Just as I thought: quite rotten. Look here and here." The surgeon, a dispassionate Greek, held out the bloody remains of the molar, jabbing with his finger. "You young men will *not* clean your teeth and this is what happens."

Lucius groaned, swallowing gore. The diatribe continued.

"I shall prescribe dentifricium with myrrh and hartshorn but it will be of *no* use, no use at *all*, unless you use it, do you understand? Find yourself a cleaning twig and use the dentifricium at least twice a day."

Lucius nodded weakly. The surgeon turned to a slave and took from him a large bolus.

"Open," ordered the surgeon. He thrust the bolus into the empty socket. "Close."

Lucius closed.

"You will hold that in the wound for one hour or until the bleeding has stopped. Afterwards you will wash your mouth every six hours with salt water for two days. Now, unless you wish to waste my time with more self-inflicted wounds, I have a crushed foot and three hernias to attend. Good *day* to you."

The Centurion rose to his feet and fumbled for some coins. Accepting a small jar of powder from the slave, he made his unsteady way towards the door.

Outside Marcus Gracchus Naso, Optio, second-in-command of the Fifth leant against a wall, idly swinging a wine skin from one finger. He waited for his leader, his broad, freckled face set in a wary frown. Toothache made a poor companion and the march from Eboracum had become a trial for all concerned.

The tall figure of the Centurion appeared at the top of the steps of the sick quarters. He looked left and right then, spotting his Optio, descended to the street.

Marcus pushed himself upright. Lucius waited for a bullock cart loaded with stone to pass then strode across to his deputy. Marcus handed him his helmet with the tall, red crest.

"Feeling better, sir?" he ventured.

The Centurion growled, spat out the bolus and said, "Give me wine."

The Optio lifted the wineskin and uncorked it. Lucius swigged, spat and swigged again. Wiping blood from his mouth, he handed back the skin.

"Everything ready, Marcus?" he asked.

"Yes, sir. Formed up outside the north gate."

"Let's get on, then. Either we're in Habitancum by nightfall or we'll be building camp."

Corstopinum bustled. Bullock carts hauling building materials for the Great Wall drew sparks from the cobbles. Squads of auxiliaries and mule trains filled the roads. An imperial messenger on a black stallion forced a path through the crowds. The two soldiers passed under the shadow of the north gate to where the Fifth waited on the verge of the Via Domitiana. Legionnaires straightened, tightening harness and shouldering packs, as they passed.

"Any problems overnight?" asked the Centurion as they walked to the head of the formation.

"A couple of brawls with the Ninth. The usual thing."

The unhappy Ninth (*Hispania*) had been used piecemeal to reinforce other Legions. Consequently a rumour had started that they didn't know where their Eagle was. From there – no one knew how – came the myth that the Ninth had marched into the mists of Caledonia and disappeared along with their Eagle. Thus, where it met other Legions, the Ninth heard bird calls and offers of chickens. They had, perforce, become first-class brawlers. Now the Sixth was relieving the few remaining cohorts of the Ninth in northern Britannia and the Centurion would be heartily glad when they were gone.

"I'll see them this evening. Any previous offenders?"

"Bracchus and Grotius," replied Marcus. Not for the first time Lucius thought what a fine world it would be if Bracchus and Grotius could be locked away until needed for battle. "Grotius was laid out by the guard," continued the Optio, "and Bracchus was cornered on the roof of the Prefecture."

The Centurion sighed. "No point in flogging them again. I'll give them a fair hearing then we'll put them on latrine duty for a week."

As they passed the baggage train the Optio pointed. "We've picked up a couple of merchants, sir. Hope that's alright."

It was normal for traders to travel with military formations when they could. The southern marches of Caledonia had only been reclaimed by the Legions in the last two years. They were quiet enough but no one took unnecessary risks in the lonely tracts of heather and oak.

"Do they understand about keeping the pace?"

"Yes, sir; briefed them myself."

"Fine; I hope they're fit."

The Century would accomplish the twenty miles to Habitancum in eight hours allowing a five-minute rest each hour and a forty minutes break at noon. Each legionary carried his personal gear, tools and weapons – around ninety pounds weight.

The two drew abreast the head of the line where the Signifer carried the Century's signum with its five bronze discs. "Keep the signum out until we've passed through the Wall then cover it," ordered the Centurion.

"Marcus," this to his Optio. "Take point and keep the pace. I'll be up and down the line." He swallowed, tasting blood. "Oh, and get word to my body slave. Tell him to prepare me a flask of salt water."

He moved to the centre of the Via Domitiana and halted, looking up and down the line. For a long moment he took in the details of his command. Individually they might be the sweepings of the Empire but seen in formation, wearing full harness, the Century epitomized a small part of Roman power. One or two hangovers, he thought; nothing that couldn't be sweated away by noon. Then, taking a deep breath, he commanded, "Fifth Century make ready."

Legionaries braced; mule drivers raised their whips.

"Fifth Century, advance."

Eighty-seven steel-shod sandals met the paving slabs of the trunk road in unison and took up the day's cadence. Whips cracked, wheels creaked and mules brayed. The Century was on the move.

Lucius stood by the roadside and watched them pass. First came the advanced guard of twenty behind its screen of scouts; next, the baggage train consisting of six bullock carts and two strings of mules plus traders and their animals. For tactical deployments the century carried everything on its back but now it was moving home, heading for Trimontium, military headquarters of Caledonia, for an indefinite stay.

Among the baggage train walked camp followers – wives, children and the few sutlers who made the Fifth their preserve. Then there were the itinerant traders. The Centurion made a mental note to speak with them later. Traders usually had a good grasp of current events and places. Behind the baggage train marched the main body, some forty legionaries and finally, twenty paces behind them, the rearguard, a further twenty.

As the last of the rearguard came abreast he moved off beside them. Some centurions marched at the head of their commands. Lucius preferred to move up and down the line of march. It was a trick taught him by his mentor, old Centurion Appius. "Keeps them on the 'op," he'd said. "More to the point, though, you can see 'ow they are – even talk to them, heavens help you, if you must. Wouldn't do too much of that though," he'd added, scratching reflectively.

Now, unencumbered by kit, he moved ahead, steadily overhauling the line. The legionaries eyed him surreptitiously. Ol' Lucy had been a right bastard these last few days. Word was the tooth had been pulled but no one felt like checking the hypothesis.

Abreast the baggage train, he beckoned his body slave who jumped from a cart and jogged over. Lucius removed his bronze helmet and gave it to the slave. The slave gave him a flask of salt water then Lucius waved him away.

Among the traders walked an imposing man; tall, with a hooked nose and swarthy complexion. He was followed by two slaves, each leading a string of heavily laden mules. The man caught the Centurion's eye and called, "My thanks, Centurion." He slapped the pack on the nearest mule. "Valuable stock," he continued, "and the writ of law runs thin this far north."

"Glad to be of help," replied Lucius, "just as long as you can keep up."

The man laughed. "Be assured of that, Centurion. One learns many lessons on the road. Taking protection when it is offered is one of them." He placed a hand on his breast. "Josephus, Josephus of Arbela. "

"Terentius," replied Lucius. "You're a long way from home, sir."

Josephus shrugged. "Ah, young sir; it is the road you see. After a while it becomes a drug. You think you travel for the profit but then it becomes a matter of horizons: always horizons. I cannot tell you how many horizons I have crossed these long years."

A messenger came running down the line and saluted. "Optio's compliments, sir, and the Wall's in sight."

"Tell him I'll come," replied the Centurion; then, to the trader, "I would speak with you more, Josephus, but for now excuse me." His body slave appeared at his elbow with his helmet. Putting it on he strode towards the head of the line.

* * *

"It was a bad time: Legions recalled: Trimontium abandoned: effectively everything north of Eboracum gone too."

It was evening. The Centurion shared a glass of Marsala with Josephus in the trader's tent. Josephus was recalling memories from fifteen years before when the Emperor Trajan had stripped northern Britannia of Legions in order to expand the bounds of the Empire.

"I continued to trade for a season or two but it was risky. Picts would always rather steal than trade. I got by. Usually I can charm the honey from the comb with my tongue but the third season my luck ran out. A war band took my mules on the southern shores of the Great Firth. They beat me and killed my slaves; valuable slaves they were too."

Josephus held his hand out to the small charcoal brazier, the glow of the coals accentuating his aquiline features. He was silent.

"Did you cease trading then," prompted Lucius.

Josephus laughed, slapping a knee with his free hand. "Nay, trading's in the blood, my friend. The goods I lost represented but a tithe of my wealth. I limped back to Corstopinum – took me three weeks. They still kept a garrison there then. Got fit again and thought a lot."

He took the crystal-cut wine flask and refilled both goblets. A slave entered noiselessly and placed a tray of sweetmeats on a small table beside the brazier.

"Trade follows the Legions, Centurion: no Legions, no trade. The Emperor Trajan was expanding into Dacia and Persia. The only decision was which one to choose. I returned to my home in Syria for the first time in twelve years – followed the armies into

Persia. To be honest I longed for good, dry heat."

The Centurion marvelled at the self-sufficiency of this man, travelling the length of the Empire, living on his wits.

"So why have you returned?" he asked.

Josephus gazed into the heart of the coals. "You ask a pertinent question, my friend; why indeed when the whole Empire is my plaything? Why would I return to the wet, the cold and the mud?"

He looked up, smiling wryly. "If I knew that I would be wise indeed: I, Josephus, born to the hot winds of Syria, longing for wet bracken and mists. In truth I cannot answer you except to say that if you were to travel north from here, fourteen days' march, you would see a land of such piercing beauty – mountains, torrents and snowfields – that your soul would never again know rest. I long to see it once more; to cross the mountains, mayhap."

There came a tapping on the tent post and the Optio poked his head through the flap.

"Will you be inspecting the sentries, sir, or would you like me to do it?"

"I'll come," said the Centurion, gathering his helmet and standing. To Josephus he said, "My thanks, friend, for the wine and the company. If you will forgive me I have many more questions but they will wait until tomorrow."

"And answers have I in great abundance. Goodnight, Centurion," said Josephus, rising from his cushion, hands pressed together. "May the stars and moon grant you a quiet night."

* * *

North of Habitancum gangs of tribesman, under the supervision of auxiliary troops, were clearing trees and scrub to a bow's shot either side of the road. Where woods still came down to the verge the Centurion doubled the scouting screen. He had spears distributed and ordered helmets worn. As Appius, his mentor, had put it, "There are bold centurions and old centurions but there ain't no old, bold centurions."

Today's was a short journey, just twelve miles to the fort at Bremenium. There he could allow most of his men to relax for the night in the wine shops and brothels. The pay-off would be a long march on the morrow to Cappuck followed by the final march into Trimontium. The Centurion walked again with Josephus.

"Have you been to Trimontium," asked the trader.

"No," answered Lucius, "but my father served there. He told me much about it. 'Three Hills of the Legions' he called it."

High above them to the left, white smoke rose from the signal station on Great Moor, one of the chain, which paralleled the length of the trunk road. Strange to imagine that, within minutes, headquarters at Trimontium would know where they were.

"I doubt your father would find it greatly changed," said Josephus. "It needed much cleaning and clearing but little in the way of repair. In truth, the local tribes shunned the camp because of the ghosts."

"Ghosts?" asked the Centurion.

"Nothing you wouldn't find in any Celtic mind. They fear the souls of those they slay which is strange," reflected Josephus, "when you consider that they spend much of their lives killing."

The conversation ceased as the Centurion went ahead to supervise the fording of a burn. One of the ox carts lost a wheel in mid-stream and it was some time before he sought out Josephus again.

"Tell me of the camp's situation," he said.

Josephus gathered his thoughts. "Well, tomorrow you will see for the first time the three hills which lend their name to Trimontium. You can see the Eildons for thirty miles or more across these borderlands. The Celts love them. Whoever has control up there looks down on everyone else and gains much face. The Votodani have a great camp on top of the northernmost."

"But your military camp is north again a mile, on a promontory bounded on two sides by the River Tweed. The valley is deep and the river fast. The Via Domitiana crosses the river on a tall bridge just beyond the camp."

"It is a big place; perhaps one hundred and fifty double paces each side with tall earthen walls. And that is not all. Outside each gate is a vicus, an annex, bigger than the camp itself. But you will see all this the day after tomorrow. If you will I shall point out the details as we approach."

* * *

The next day was the most arduous. For six miles beyond Bremenium the engineers had maintained straight alignments. Beyond that they had been forced to follow ever-deeper valleys climbing through the Cheviot Hills, winding along stream banks. Higher and higher the century climbed between bare hillsides and screes. They passed below the signal station on the dizzy height of Brownhart Law. Lucius shuddered to think what such a place of duty would mean in winter.

Noon saw them huddled under cloaks in a fine drizzle, eating hard tack and dried meat. In early afternoon they forded the Kale Water and climbed past the fort at Pennymuir. Men who had overindulged the night before gazed longingly at the camp but four days was the standard march allowed from Corstopinum to Trimontium. That meant camping at Cappuck tonight and Lucius led them onwards.

There had been no time for conversation today as he passed up and down the line, encouraging and chivvying, lending his weight where necessary. As the day began to wane, they came out of the hills and the rain stopped. Lucius, mud-stained and wet moved forward past the baggage train for the twentieth time that day. Josephus left the line of march, touched him on his arm and pointed. Far to the west the setting sun had broken through the clouds. Three steep hills were crowned with golden light.

* * *

On the final day the Via Domitiana sped straight as an arrow towards the northernmost of the Eildon Hills. By noon the hills filled much of the northwestern horizon. It was possible to make out the earthen banks and stone dykes surrounding the top of Eildon North.

"Tell me of the tribes," said the Centurion, resting barefoot on a rock while his body slave cleaned his sandals.

It was noon. The Century was halted beside a burn, cleaning away the worst effects of the journey. Helmets were being burnished, tunics sponged. The Signifer, clad now in his ceremonial leopard skin, uncovered the signum. He raised it and the pale sun struck highlights from its discs.

Josephus pointed towards the hill fort. "Up there are the Votodani." He gestured at the low ground. "Down here are the Selgovae. That's about all you need to know, really. It hasn't always been so but for now the Selgovae are the underdogs. They plot and they steal cattle but that's about the end of it."

"You'll find the Votodani relatively civilized. They pay their tributes and maintain the trunk road across the Tweed valley. Because they control trade, they've got most to lose if war ever breaks out. From your point of view the Selgovae are unpredictable but then," he waved his hand, "they're Celts. They make an art out of being unpredictable."

Josephus paused to bite into a bannock. He chewed thoughtfully and took a swig of wine.

"Of course both of them have an eye to the north where the Picts live. They're the real problem. They've never known the

Pax Romanum; wouldn't know what to do with it if they found it lying in the road."

The body slave stooped to buckle the sandals onto the Centurion's feet. Josephus rose and stretched, twisting to left and right.

"There are fortunes to be made here," he said. "The country is rich in everything from cattle to metal ores. The people are avid for trade goods. For now it is good quality cloth and metal tools they want but as they become richer it will be more valuable, easily portable goods such as glassware and jewellery. And mark this, Centurion: trade makes for peace. Accustom these tribes to luxury and you won't find them rebelling."

Lucius stamped his feet to bed in his sandals then said, "Time to be moving. Josephus, would you join me at the head of the line? I'd appreciate your pointing out the sights to me."

Now the road ran more to the north, skirting the foot of the hills. The valley of the Tweed began to open up ahead of them. Smoke rose in the foreground to their left.

"The Southern Vicus," said Josephus. "Every industry you can think of – tanners, blacksmiths, brewers, bakers – everything necessary to support a Legion."

As they crossed a low crest, an enormous enclosure became visible. It was covered with low sheds and chimneys and sloped gently downwards to the walls of the fort. He studied the walls. Thirty feet high and turf-covered they rose from a deep ditch forming a rectangle with wooden towers at the corners. In the middle of each wall stood a gatehouse. The same design could be found all over the Empire. The difference in this case was one of scale. It was huge.

Josephus touched his arm and pointed to the left towards the foot of Eildon North.

"You can just make out an aqueduct there, Centurion. Do you see?"

He saw fresh stone arches cutting across a deep valley.

"That carries water from a spring to the bath houses. They're in the Western Vicus along with the civilian administrative buildings and the official lodge." He pointed again. "You can just make them out behind their own earth bank beyond the western wall of the camp."

The bass note of a cornu echoed across the valley from the southern gatehouse. Their approach had been formally noted. The Centurion ordered his cornicen to reply. The road began to slope downwards.

"You'll find a spur road leading off the Via opposite the eastern gate," said Josephus. "That will take you into the transit area where you will probably be invited to camp for the moment. Be warned: between that and the gatehouse lies a sump of iniquity, the Eastern Vicus. That's where the ale houses and brothels lie. I have no doubt that your men will want to try them out. And now," the old trader sketched a slight bow, "it is probably best if I leave you to your martial affairs."

"Thank you, my friend," said Lucius, taking his hand. "It has been a delight to travel with you. I trust that we will meet again once the Century is settled in."

"As do I, Centurion; as do I." The old trader smiled, touched his breast then turned and made his way back to the baggage train.

Chapter 2

(Adrift)

Trista huddles under a hedge, shivering. Her clothes are in rags and the piece of sacking wrapped around her shoulders is soaked through. Her teeth chatter. Cramps twist her empty stomach. Her burnt hands sting. She nods into a fitful doze, only to wake with a start as the same awful dream unfolds.

"Mother," she murmurs and then the tears return. Sobs rack her slender frame. Mucus runs from her nose. The rain lashes down, uncaring.

She wishes she was dead.

The food the villagers gave her ran out yesterday. They had been kind enough but terribly afraid. Men sent by the headman had found her standing in the orchard, stiff with shock. It was clear that she had been pulling at smouldering timbers. They carried her to the village where women put salves on her burnt hands, washed her and dressed her in homespun clothes.

She was aware of hurried conferences; that the villagers feared for themselves as well as for her. She heard the name 'Sertorius' whispered and saw fingers making furtive Horns.

In the morning they gave her a satchel of food and a bottle of water. They told her she was being taken to Aurelianum; that she should speak with the Præfect there, tell him what had happened. She set out with one of the field hands but after a couple of miles they heard galloping hooves coming towards them. The field hand had bundled her over a ditch and through a hedge, telling her to stay there and be quiet.

She'd stayed there for over an hour because she was a good girl but when she had timorously poked her head through the hedge, the field hand had gone. She was alone.

Everything became a blur after that. She'd taken to the fields, being too frightened to use the roads, and she never found

Aurelianum. The weather broke and it rained. She didn't know it but she was lucky it was high summer because, although frequently soaked, she was seldom cold. Until tonight.

She might have died during that awful night. She might have done but she doesn't. As dawn lights a louring sky, the rain stops. Far in the east the sun rises beneath the layer of cloud, sending its rays out to the west. Trista raises her head. Across the field the sun's first rays have turned a tall elm tree to gold. She thinks that she has never seen anything so beautiful in her life.

Deep within her a tiny flame ignites, a spark of that universal defiance granted to all things small and helpless which finally turn at bay.

She knows that she isn't going to die; that Mother wouldn't want her to die. Little though she is, her upbringing has been patrician and she knows that she simply *has* to go on because that's what patricians do.

Trista takes stock. She knows she needs food and warm clothing but she has no money and she doesn't know whom to trust. In the growing light across the valley, she sees smoke coming from the chimney of a substantial steading. There will be food there and clothing. But there will be people and dogs there too. Maybe bad people.

With the pragmatic simplicity of a child Trista decides that she will become a thief. She is a good girl, yes; but it seems that goodness goes with warm villas and loving families, not wet fields and lonely nights under hedges. Trista stands, stretches her aching limbs, wraps her sack around her and sets off, bending low, to start her new career.

Chapter 3

(Trimontium)

Trimontium: in years to come he would look back on it with the fondness of a first love. There was an innocence and a freshness about it all. Lucius had served on the borders of the Empire before. There was Syria: unbearable heat by day and curved daggers by night, the whole overlain by endless grit and flies. There was the awful deep dankness of the German forests, the howling ferocity of enormous warriors striking without warning, driven on by bestial gods.

Here in Caledonia was a gentleness, a peace not found on other borders. Certainly there were fractious tribes. The Selgovae were as cross-grained and vicious as most while the occasional full-scale Pictish incursion called for rapid and effective military response.

And yet...and yet...

There was a lilting score underlying it all: a feeling of – what could one say – playfulness? The Celts would fight but for them it was an art, not a science and they would rather strike poses and sing of their deeds than take to arms – unless honour was involved. And even though a Pictish spear in the guts would kill you as surely as a German war club, there was a strange under-standing (at least on the part of the Picts) that it was all a game and not at all personal.

Beyond the cleared ground of the security zone, endless vistas of rounded hills, purpled with heather, led the eye upwards. There were scrub oak forests on the lee slopes, brilliant green in spring and summer. The sky was an ever-changing panorama from dawn to dusk and from day to day. Only the skylarks remained constant. Extremes of heat or cold were few nor, thought Lucius, sardonically, was there any danger of drought. Cloudburst followed drizzle but, in a way, the bad weather accentuated those days of soft sunlight that followed.

Ever present were the Eildons, the three hills after which the camp was named. From the camp itself only Eildon North was visible, its bulk blocking out the other two. The hill seemed to fill half the sky, its flanks painted in muted shades of brown. Below the skyline ran the mighty earthwork guarding the Votodani camp.

* * *

The Fifth had settled into their new garrison with little fuss. Initially they occupied one of the temporary camps in the transit area, setting up their tents as they would on the march. There was little hardship in this for legionaries who spent much of their time in these conditions. The rain, for these men inured to the Britannic climate, was part of the way of life and, anyway, just a stone's throw away was the Eastern Vicus where a man could slake his thirst and stretch his feet before a roaring fire.

In the vicus were stalls selling meats, fruit and native artefacts. Booths offered cheap wine, heather beer and the peculiarly ardent native spirit distilled from grain. Here you could have your hair cut, your boots resoled and a letter written to your mother. Here too were the brothels promising earthly delights for the tired soldier.

If the excesses of the first nights created headaches for the ranks they produced as many for their officers.

"How many today, Marcus?" Lucius asked his Optio, as he buckled on his helmet in front of his tent.

"Seven drunk, two woundings and one urinating in an improper place to whit the guard commander's helmet, sir," the Optio replied with a straight face.

The Centurion raised an eyebrow.

The Optio rolled his eyes.

"Don't ask, sir," he said.

It was the morning of the third day. A crapulous line of defaulters swayed, bracketed by the spears of two burly military policemen. Lucius observed the rank of miscreants with a jaundiced eye. Rain began to spot his cloak. He hefted his vine staff.

"The sooner we get this lot into barracks and regular training the better," he said.

For three days Lucius had spent long hours attempting to take over the barrack block from the century they were to relieve. He had not expected it to go smoothly and it hadn't. Even though they were only two years old, the barrack blocks and latrines he was being offered were far from clean and suffered from a backlog of damage. Lucius had no intention of taking over a shambles whereas the outgoing centurion of the Ninth had little incentive to put anything right at this stage. He would trade upon the fact that Lucius would want to get his men settled as soon as possible.

Then there was the matter of the permanent loan list. The barracks should come complete with everything from oil lamps to latrine sponges, but it didn't. A whole host of items were missing including an entire stove from one block. Someone would have to pay for all the missing gear and the outgoing century was currently involved in trying to make good the shortfall by theft. This, in turn, was causing ill-will throughout the camp and it certainly wasn't smoothing the arrival of the Fifth.

Lucius sighed. For this they paid him the extra denarii.

"Right, Optio: let's get this over with," he growled.

* * *

Trimontium was a wild frontier where, as Josephus had said, the writ of law ran thin. There were fortunes to be made in the wilds of Caledonia by those with the courage or naked greed required.

Many such entrepreneurs earned their living supplying comforts to the garrison and to troops in transit passing up and down the Via Domitiana, the great trunk road that ran the length of Britannia from Dubris in the south to Devana in the far north.

As Josephus had told him, the camp occupied nearly twenty acres of flat land on a plateau sitting high above the River Tweed. Outside all four gates of the camp was a vicus or annex, each with its own purpose. To the west were the bathhouse and civilian administrative buildings; to the north, the residences of senior officers. The Southern Vicus was an industrial zone while the Eastern Vicus provided for trading and off-duty entertainment.

The camp was the hub of Southern Hibernia and, as such, of prime strategic importance. An experienced Tribune ("Not one of them spotty kids," to quote legionary Grotius), seconded from Eboracum, was in charge of military operations. The camp itself was commanded by a Camp Præfect, the highest rank available to a non-patrician. He was a former centurion of immense experience and standing.

Almost by default the Roman army, wedded as it was to the notion of class as a prerequisite for command, understood the need for experience to underpin breeding. Thus the Camp Præfect of Trimontium acted not only as the administrator of the garrison but also as an intelligence co-ordinator and, at needs, a diplomat, smoothing ruffled tribal feathers and generally maintaining the Pax Romanum.

The camp was home to fifteen hundred troops including an ala of Gaulish cavalry. In addition there were hundreds of artisans, camp-followers and traders whose livelihood depended upon the military.

* * *

It took a week before the men could move into their barrack

blocks and another week before the Centurion was happy with the condition of the buildings. Eight men – a tent group – occupied each room, just as they would occupy a tent in the field. Under Lucius's supervision the officers of the Fifth worked tirelessly to ensure that the quarters were clean and weatherproof.

As soon as they were settled the Tribune sent for him.

"Right, Centurion: next two weeks weapons drills, tactical formations and so on," said the Tribune. He was a tall, spare man, not terribly intelligent as the world measures these things, but a staff officer of considerable experience.

"At the end of that time we'll inspect them. Præfect'll go over their kit and the barrack block. He'll want to see your punishment returns, accounts and so forth. I'll take the ceremonial inspection and then watch you put 'em through their paces. Prepare yourself for century attack, defence – you know the sort of thing. Meantime we'll send you and your officers out, a couple at a time, with patrols from other units. Let you see the lie of the land."

He selected a map scroll from a rack behind his desk and beckoned Lucius forward as he unrolled it on his desk.

"We're here." He tapped the map with a stylus. "Main east-west feature is the river valley; north-south is the trunk road and they cross here by the camp." He looked up with a wintry smile. "Military planners got something right for once."

Lucius smiled back.

"North and west, lots of hills with deep valleys mostly running north-south – Gala Water here, Leader Water and so on. Difficult country. We try to keep the trees cleared back from the tracks but even so the whole area's ripe for ambush."

He looked up, frowning.

"You'll have to get used to it. Treat it as enemy territory. Keep your guard up. The Selgovae'll have you, given half a chance, and as for the Picts…Well, we don't see them that often but when we do it's usually a minor war."

He paused, looking down at the map, stroking his moustache.

"That's about all you need to know to start with." He swept his hand to the right. "Sea's out there to the east a long day's march. We have a sub-fort at the mouth of the Tweed. You'll get to patrol there from time to time."

"Off to the west," he gestured with his left hand, "Yarrow Water runs into the Tweed: another big valley running southwest. Questions?"

Lucius sat back already thinking of the best way to use infantry in such an enclosed environment.

"What are our main roles, sir?" he asked.

"Just coming to that."

The Tribune rose, walked to the window and peered out for a moment.

"Main thing's protection of the trunk road." He turned back into the room. "If that goes, we're all in trouble. Second one's maintaining the peace. Most of that's policing – making sure the cattle raiding's kept in bounds, that sort of thing – but as I say, every now and then the Picts put in an appearance and then it's serious soldiering. Main thing is showing a front. Never let the natives get away with anything."

He scratched his chin.

"A lot of it's about good intelligence. That's the Præfect's province. He's got the brain for it. Try the patience of a magus, sorting out the lies from the truth when the Celts are telling tales about each other."

He nodded reflectively.

"Downy bird, the Præfect," he concluded.

* * *

By the time the year began to turn, the Fifth had fallen into the routine of the place and found it to their liking. They took their turn guarding the camp and the great bridge that carried the trunk road over the Tweed. They cleared culverts and dug ditches, for all Roman legionaries were trained as basic engineers. Best of all they patrolled the valleys, sometimes in force, sometimes in numbers as small as ten under the charge of a decurion for Lucius believed in delegating command as low as possible. Although, on occasion, this led to problems, in general it worked and paid huge dividends in building trust and confidence.

After the first couple of months Lucius took advantage of a local practise that allowed Centurions to live outside barracks. With the help of Josephus, he rented a small villa in the Northern Vicus and bought a slave girl to cook his food and warm his bed. The rest of his domestic staff consisted of his body slave.

There was a thriving centurions' club within the camp where he frequently took his ease, drinking, dicing and telling stories. At first his youth had been a cause of more or less well-humoured ragging by the older men. Lucius accepted this with a good grace. He held his own in the inevitable drinking competitions and arm wrestling, winning his fair share and smiling ruefully when he lost. He made a number of friends, notably Quintus Fabricius. Quintus was a serious young engineer who saw the world as something to be measured. A close friendship, based on mutual esteem, grew up between the two men.

* * *

As autumn became winter the Fifth became wise in the ways of the Borderlands. They learnt, as close as one could, whom they could trust and whom they could not.

Of the Celts, the Votodani were, broadly speaking, friendly. They occupied the best land and regarded the Romans as a stabilizing force. Since they were the dominant tribe, it was to them that profits from trade went and they regarded the Pax Romanum as a good thing.

The Selgovae, on the other hand, bitterly resented their position as underdogs. It had not always been thus and the core of their belief was that, one day, positions would be reversed and woe betide the oppressors at that point. Because there was no doubt that the Votodani oppressed their client tribe with a careless disregard for justice and, as far as the Selgovae were concerned, the Romans were tarred with the same brush.

"The big difference is religion."

Lucius and the Camp Præfect leant on their hunting spears in a clearing by the Tweed. Drifting down from the woods came distant shouts and the rattling of spears on shields as native beaters drove wild boar toward them. While they waited, the Præfect was holding forth on his pet subject: the Celts. After twenty years in Britannia he was something of an expert and Lucius was keen to pick his brain.

"The Votodani worship their version of Apollo. They call him Bel. It's a relatively new religion in these islands. It's masculine and pragmatic. Because we're talking Sun-worship it's out there in the open and we can do business with it."

He glanced at Lucius to see that he understood. Lucius nodded and turned back to the woods. A distant crashing was coming closer. The Præfect scanned the forest's edge.

"The Selgovae, on the other hand, are mostly still worshipping Luna or, more properly, the Moon in her third phase – Hecate. It's a deep, dark business, very much centred on Hag-culture. They don't name their goddess, by the way – just call her the Goddess and generally what they do is called the Old Religion. It's inward-looking and secretive."

A young sow burst from the trees, checked for a moment, then turned and ran towards the left of the line of spears. For a while the men were fully engaged as more boars charged into the open. Later as the natives skinned the kill, the Præfect watched Lucius washing blood from his arms in the river. He had known the young man's father years ago but he hadn't told Lucius. Old Metellus had done something right, he reflected as he tilted his wine flask.

The Præfect had never married but had he done so he would have wanted a son like this. The rank of centurion was won by merit and Lucius was the youngest in the *Victrix*. More to the point he was a second-degree initiate in the Cult of Mithras. The Præfect knew this because he was Magus of the Trimontium shrine. There were centurions who were never invited to join the Cult. Of those that did, many did not progress beyond first degree in an entire career so someone somewhere had noted strong potential in this young man.

The Præfect belched quietly. Naturally no written records were kept but sooner or later word would reach him through the Mithraic network that permeated the Roman army. As it was, the young Centurion had sung the pæon of praise faultlessly at the last initiation, chanting as the dying bull thrashed and the blood pumped and splashed onto the upturned face of the novice.

"Yes", he nodded to himself, "definitely a young man to watch."

Chapter 4

(Treachery)

A man prepares to die.

His mind flutters between terror of the Darkness and dread of what will happen first. Perhaps worse than either is the knowledge of his degradation, he, a proud man, a Roman Tribune, yet lying face down in the pine needles and mud of this forest clearing. His wrists are tied to his ankles behind his back. His nose is broken and probably at least one rib. He has been kicked, spat and urinated on in revenge for the one he knifed before they clubbed him down.

The German chief and the enormously fat Roman patrician still talk. The man doesn't know which he fears more. The chief incites more physical fear. He is slightly smaller than his hulking body guard but big enough for all that. It is his scarred face and air of ruthless cruelty that mark him out as leader. His men swagger, as do all German warriors, yet they defer to him without demur.

And yet the fat Roman instils in him a soul-deep repugnance, even from a distance of twenty feet. He feels soiled from within as if death itself will hold no escape from the man. He is dressed in a black toga. His head is totally bald, nor does he appear to have eyebrows or lashes.

Ironically the Tribune now holds the secret for which he has crossed the Rhenus, into the forest. The patrician is selling out his own people. He is offering weapons to the German tribes in return for their support. If only there were some means of escape. This information must get to the Legate of the Twenty Second. It must but it won't.

The German warriors have been busy hammering sharpened stakes into the ground and building a rough table. And it is not for a feast. But there will be a sacrifice to cement the unholy alliance being negotiated. The sacrifice will be him. Silently he prays to Mithras for a speedy death but has no impression of being heard.

A pair of fur-trimmed buskins appear before him. A meaty hand grasps his chin and twists it upwards. The warrior, face framed by greasy, yellow war braids is offering him a clay dish. The Tribune abides silently, in agony, unwilling to give his tormentors satisfaction. The warrior slams the dish into the ruin of his nose and rubs it round and round. Excrement. Howls of mirth from the others. The man blacks out briefly from the pain.

A snarl cuts across the laughter and there is silence. The leader speaks. He doesn't raise his voice.

"Place the filth on the altar."

A knife is drawn and his bonds are cut. He attempts to kick out but his limbs are cramped and weak from hours of confinement. Big hands grasp his arms and legs, lift him like a child and dump him face up on the altar. His limbs are tied to the uprights leaving him spread-eagled.

The moon-face of the obese Roman looms over him, carious teeth exposed in a smile. His breath is rank.

"Bare his breast," he lisps.

Big hands grasp his tunic and rip it from top to bottom. From within the folds of his toga the fat man withdraws a long, curved knife. He bends closer, the better to whisper.

"It would be good if you were to pray to Mithras, my child," he says. "It will not help you but it will greatly increase the efficacy of the sacrifice when I cut out your heart."

He stands back, raises both arms and starts an incantation.

Chapter 5

(Meeting)

The Prefect's Chief Clerk and the Chieftain's Advisor – old adversaries – were arguing a point of precedence, oblivious to the Centurion. For a precious moment he was just a young man on a spring morning standing in sunlight.

Casually he gazed to his right where a small vegetable garden sheltered at the foot of the inner earthwork. There, half stooped, a pot of seedlings in one hand and a planting stick in the other, was a young woman. For the space of two heartbeats their eyes met and for a moment his world consisted of blue eyes framed by red-blonde hair.

A cloud winged across the sun. The girl, blushing, turned away to kneel among her plants. The Chief Clerk coughed. "Centurion, the matter is settled. We may proceed."

With an effort he tore his gaze away from the woman and turned to the Chief Clerk. There was an embarrassed hiatus. Everyone was looking at him expectantly and he had not the slightest idea what had been said. Training took over.

"Ah…yes…carry on, Chief Clerk."

* * *

It had been yesterday that the Camp Prefect had sent for him.

"Lucius, my boy; come in and sit down. Have a splash of wine – good stuff – Gaulish."

He poured the wine.

"What's the Fifth on tomorrow?" he asked, taking up his glass.

"Guard duty all week, sir, plus weapon training by groups. Two tent groups detached on bridge repair detail," the Centurion replied.

"Good; nothing your Optio can't handle then." The Prefect eased his ample body back in his chair and picked up a wax tablet. "Seems we need to have a chat with Belinus. The old fox has just moved back up to his summer quarters on the Hill. Got to nail him down on levels of tribute this year – grain, meat and so forth. He's also been slacking on road repairs – nothing too serious but it doesn't do to let him get too out of hand."

He took another sip of wine and looked at the Centurion benevolently.

"Not met him have you?"

The Centurion's year at Trimontium had been one of patrols, policing and the occasional skirmish. Such Votodani as he had met had been farmers and traders.

"No sir," he said. "I've heard a lot about him though."

The Prefect smiled. "Doubt if half of it's true. Typical Celt: bags of swank: lots of aggressive posturing with neighbours but deep down he wants a quiet life. Speaks our lingo well. Quite educated under the bluff exterior. Thing is Celts are impressed by show so I want you to go up there tomorrow – full fig: ceremonial armour: best plume: the lot. Chief Clerk'll handle negotiations with his opposite number. Just want you to show a presence; drink beer; loads of compliments."

The sound of a marching squad drifted in from the parade ground. The distant voice of an Optio poured scorn on a group of recruits. Well, it would make a welcome break from garrison duties, a chance to try out his command of the Votodani dialect. He'd been learning it from Flòraidh, his slave girl, nightly for several months.

"That's fine, sir," he said. "Is there anything particular you want me to speak to him about?"

The Prefect pursed his lips. "No; just remind him how well off he is with us here – subtly, of course. And take up a dozen flasks of Valerian – keep 'em here in stores for these occasions. Old fool would murder for the stuff. See the Chief Clerk. Get him to indent for them and a couple of mules. You'll be going up with the relief crew for the signal station. Get them to mount an honour guard. You know the sort of thing."

And so it had started.

* * *

Later, in the smoky fastness of the Chieftain's great roundhouse, when the heather beer had been drunk, the honey cakes eaten and the gifts exchanged, the advisors huddled in a corner to conduct the formal business. The Centurion sat in the place of honour.

Belinus, the Chieftain, was retelling, with boundless mirth, how his father had been attacked by a wild boar while relieving himself against a tree. His warriors, who had heard the story many times, laughed uproariously at the appropriate places. The Centurion, who heard not a word, laughed with them.

The story finished. The warriors howled with mirth then, duty done, resumed their noisy conversations. Belinus wiped tears from his eyes and drained his drinking horn. Choosing his moment the Centurion leaned across and said confidentially, "Those are very fine vegetables you grow in the plot within the gate."

For a moment Belinus swayed slightly, his glaucous eyes unfocused. Then light visibly dawned through the beer fumes. "You mean Aithne's little garden!"

He chuckled indulgently, a fond smile touching the corners of his full lips. Then, remembering his dignity, he nodding sagely. "It would be true to say that we grow the biggest bagies, neeps and...and, er...bagies in all of Caledonia," he announced weightily. "I, myself, gave orders for the finest topsoil to be carried up from the river valley. It is to my own daughter, Aithne, that I have given charge of this vital, er, logistical resource."

He blinked sagely, evidently satisfied with this piece of

extempore boasting.

Aithne! Here was the first piece of intelligence.

Seizing the moment the Centurion made his move. "When I lived in Hispania, I was counted a gardener of some repute yet never have I seen such abundance, such huge er, bagiels, such magnificent sneeps. I wonder, while our advisors dispute, might I view this logistical resource, the better to learn a little of your, ah, advanced planting methods?"

Belinus gazed at him blankly again, evidently pondering why any red-blooded man would choose to view a miserable collection of weeds when he could be quaffing ale and boasting. Then the thought, 'Ah, but he's Roman' fell into place. Belinus composed his face in a superior smile.

"But of course, Centurion: my garden is your garden," he said grandly. "It is ever our aim and, indeed, delight, to share our skills with our Roman brothers in a spirit of fraternal co-operation that our two peoples may move forward in...in..." He looked around, owlishly, for inspiration. Finding none he rose ponderously, followed closely by his bodyguards.

This was no part of the Centurion's plan.

"My Lord Belinus," he protested, "there is no need at all for you to inconvenience yourself. I can find my own way easily."

Belinus, however, was not to be put off. "Your Excellency, it is my great honour to escort you the better to expound upon the, er, detailed planning and, er, intriguing detail of this justly renowned, er..."

* * *

Fuming inwardly the Centurion arrived with the small cavalcade at the vegetable plot. Fresh air had wreaked it work upon Belinus who was being judiciously supported by his bodyguards. Aithne rose, a look of wary resignation on her face.

"Ah, Daughter," Belinus began, escaping his bodyguards and

crushing a patch of marjoram with a large boot. "It seems that His Excellency the Centurion is an expert, er, vegetable, er, person from far off, er…and I have undertaken to show him the finer point of our plant…er…veg…er."

At this point, to the relief of nearly all present, Belinus fell forward into the parsley. Without a word the bodyguards, with the ease of long practice, grasped the fallen chieftain under his arms, hoisted him between them and set off trudging back to the huts.

Aithne stood, stoop-shouldered, head bowed, her left hand tucked under her right arm. The Centurion felt ashamed. Without looking at him, she knelt and tried, forlornly, to straighten up the broken parsley seedlings. Not knowing what else to do, the Centurion put aside his helmet, removed his cloak and knelt with her, attempting to help.

Then Aithne spoke to him, words he was to remember for the rest of his life. "Your Excellency, if renowned plants-man you be, do me the inestimable favour of not crushing the ever-loving thyme to death as well!" The Centurion tried to move both of his feet at once in an attempt to identify thyme, overbalanced and went sprawling. In the ensuing silence he suddenly heard peels of laughter. Looking up he saw Aithne, face transformed with mirth, rocking back and forwards on her haunches and pointing at him with her planting stick.

"You look so funny!" she choked.

Suddenly the spring sunshine, the freedom of the day and the hilarity of his position burst upon him. He laughed, at first ruefully and then with whole-hearted delight and when the laughter was done the young man and the young woman gazed at each other in surprised wonder, there on the summit of Eildon.

* * *

The signallers who had formed the Centurion's escort were

taking over from the previous week's garrison at the signal station, high on the western rampart of Eildon. In the wooden storeroom at the base of the tower the two decurions were mustering stores.

"Watch him, Titus," said the first, counting sacks of grain. "Got the wind under his tail good and proper this morning. Sent the clerk and the mules up the main path then had us sweating our way up the west face and you know how steep that is. No bloody path; bollox-deep in heather and us in full fucking armour. And him like a fucking mountain goat, leaping about, telling us to get a move on, yelling that if we couldn't do better than this the fucking Celts would have us next time out."

"Bloody officers," said the other, marking his tally stick. "You know ol' Sextus, don't you; Cornicen over in the Fifth? Well he says that yer man's always like this. Gets these bees in his bonnet and there's no holding him back. Mind you," he added reflectively, "that's not to say that they don't rate him over there 'cos they do. Came out of that fight up the Via last month with all his men and that was a pretty nasty business. Outnumbered three to one, they said, and the ground against them."

"Yer, well," ruminated the first, "that's all well an' good but I ain't in the fucking Fifth. This is just a poxy routine change of duty. And another thing: we gets to the top and he expects us to form an honour guard. Had us stopped in the dead ground below the walls polishing our fucking armour then marched us up to the gate like a squad of fucking Praetorians. So, all I'm saying is this, mate: I'd get your lot proper squared away. He'll want you all nicely lined up and gleaming by the time he's finished swilling beer with the natives down the camp."

* * *

A muscular woman with long red braids, strode down the path from the Great Hut, the Chief Advisor panting at her elbow. As the wife of a Celtic chieftain The Lady Innogen's status was equal to if slightly different from her husband. Thus when word had arrived of Belinus' minor indisposition ("Snoring like a hog, m'lady") it was natural for her to take his place seeing off the departing guest. What he was doing in the vegetable garden was a mystery but, then, he was a Roman.

Passing through the shadow of the inner gate she stopped abruptly. There in the pale spring sunlight at the foot of the inner wall knelt the Centurion, his helmet and cloak piled neatly to one side on the grass. It was evident to the Lady Innogen that, of all things, the Roman was busy planting seedlings under the tutelage of her daughter. Both were oblivious to her presence.

She gazed at the two young people as they knelt, heads together; took in their relaxed posture and heard the rise and fall of their murmured conversation. This would not do. She coughed loudly and stepped forward. "Ah, Centurion. I am so sorry that you have been left to your own devices but I see that Aithne has been entertaining you. I trust that you have not been too bored. Vegetables are not, as it were, to everyone's taste."

The Centurion rose, dusting earth from his hands and knees. The Lady looked for signs of guilt but he seemed to be supremely at ease. The same could not be said of Aithne whose downcast face and curtain of hair failed to hide flushed cheeks. She fidgeted with the planting stick.

"My Lady; how good to see you," said the Centurion. "No indeed; I begged the Lord Belinus' favour to be allowed to view the vegetable garden. In my youth I too grew vegetables and the Lady Aithne has been explaining how it is that she is able to grow such fine plants here. She has been kind enough to offer to show me the nursery beds in the valley from which these seedlings came."

'Has she, indeed,' thought Innogen, looking intently at her daughter. Aithne looked up, caught her mother's eye and quickly looked down again.

"How kind of her," said the mother, "but you must not let her distract you from your military duties, Centurion. If Aithne has a fault it is that she gets carried away with her little projects and fails to appreciate that they are of little interest to others. It is to be hoped that her imminent betrothal to Lord Callum of the Selgovae will be a steadying influence upon her."

The Centurion's smile faded for a moment. 'Ah', she thought, 'I was right'.

"And now perhaps I may escort you to the gate. I see that your soldiers await you."

Outside the gate the decurion had drawn up his ten men in two lines, facing inwards. Sun winked off burnished harness. The legionaries radiated an air of studious military competence.

The Centurion picked up his helmet and cloak and put them on. He turned to Lady Innogen. "My thanks for your hospitality, my Lady. Please convey my compliments too, to Lord Belinus."

Then he turned to where Aithne stood, downcast. "And my thanks to you, my Lady Aithne, for your time." He saluted both women then turned and marched out of the gate.

The decurion called his men to attention and saluted with an expectant flourish. "Carry on, Decurion," said the Centurion in a preoccupied voice. "Report back to camp. I shall make my own way."

"Sah!" barked the decurion but he might as well not have bothered. The Centurion was already striding off alone through the heather. 'Fucking officers!' he thought.

Chapter 6

(Josephus)

Josephus of Arbela sits by the fire, warming his hands. It is winter. Firelight plays on the walls and hangings of his living quarters. Outside a winter storm throws fistfuls of rain at the walls.

The small villa stands in the Northern Vicus at Trimontium, part of a speculative development by a Catuvellauni magnate. The land here falls steeply to the Tweed. In winter little sun touches this side of the valley but the tall river cliff opposite shelters the vicus from northerly winds and for this Josephus is glad.

A life of travelling has left him fitter than he has any right to expect yet the damp pain seldom leaves his joints now. It is worst of all on these long, dark nights filled with storm and rain. He draws his thick, woollen robe tighter round him and holds his hands out to the flaring logs. Not for the first time he chuckles inwardly at the irony of his life. Son of the Desert; Syrian Jew: what is he really doing here?

Wealth is not an issue. He could retire tomorrow, take ship and within a time see the morning sun gilding the turrets of Latakia. He closes his eyes and imagines the gentle roll of the ship as it glides eastwards to the shore on the swell of the Central Sea. The scent of cedars drifts from the land – yes…

Yes, one day, maybe, but not yet. For now life is too interesting out here on the frontier. The cut and thrust of trading at the edge of the Empire is simply too stimulating and there are still corners of this haunting land that he has never seen.

'Horizons': he remembers the last journey north and his conversation with Centurion Terentius, Lucius, as he now knows him. Yes, of course, it is a matter of horizons not profit, but one does not easily allow others to see beyond the professional mask of the trader. Such things are bad for business. Yet he has never regretted allowing Lucius into his confidence. When he meets one of that small number who can understand and be trusted, he knows immediately.

Philip, his Greek slave, comes through the curtain with a tray of food. He places it on a small table which he draws near to his master.

"A wild night, Josephus," he says as he rebuilds the fire with apple logs from the basket. Josephus has never seen a need for ceremony between himself and his people. Each knows the strengths of the others. Often their lives depend on those strengths. Rigid hierarchy achieves little, willing co-operation everything.

"Wild indeed, Philip. I doubt not that the roads will be blocked in the morning."

"May I bring you anything else?" the slave asks.

"Nay, Philip; off you go to your bed. Keep warm."

"Goodnight, then, Josephus."

Left alone again, the Syrian rejoins his thoughts.

Lucius has been a frequent visitor to the villa and Josephus, in turn, a guest at various legionary feasts. He has watched the young man with interest. Perhaps eight years younger than the average centurion, he bears himself with complete self-assurance. Nor, after early attempts to discomfit the new boy, do his peers now patronize him. He is simply too competent.

Josephus studies the Roman military. His safety often depends on it. On paper it is an irresistible, seamless machine but everything depends on personalities. There are camps where he would not willingly stay and centuries with which he will not travel. Even here at Trimontium it is possible to make comparisons.

The Seventh is commanded by a bully who uses his vine staff to thrash his men. The Centurion of the Third is a lackadaisical greybeard who should have been retired years ago. In the wine shops of the Eastern Vicus one can hear the character and faults of every officer dissected and discussed with a stunning degree of accuracy.

Josephus selects a date and bites into it. He gazes into the heart of the fire.

But if one accepts that all soldiers complain about their officers, it is clear that Lucius is appreciated as a strict but fair leader. More than that: Josephus has heard the odd rueful comment indicating that the Centurion is often way ahead of his troops. More than one soldier has been caught flat-footed in the commission of a crime. Under these circumstances Lucius would be well within his rights to punish with the lash but he seldom does.

Most officers regard their men as a barely subjugated under-class: a rebellion waiting to break out. Common wisdom says that sparing the lash shows weakness. Lucius, however, seems to operate on a different level. Josephus can only liken it to the way he treats his own small group of specialists where he values each individual for what he can contribute. Lucius manages to do this on a much larger scale and with a group of men, many of whom could be seen as the sweepings of the Empire.

Unconventional or not, it works. The Fifth are good. In tactical exercises and in sporting competitions they frequently win. It isn't so much that they are smartly turned out, although they are. A legionary of the Fifth seems to walk taller than others. An exceptional young man, Lucius. Well worth the watching.

Josephus reaches for a roll of hide. He unrolls it in the light from an oil lamp. It is a map of northern Britannia. He traces with his finger the route of the Via Domitiana as it curves north to Devana. Much of the map, especially to the west, is specu-lative. At one time, before the legions left, he had added to it bit by bit. He looks now at the mountains and lakes to the north of Strathclyde.

One of the military roads follows the north bank of the Western River until the waters become salt. He could turn north just there. He places a finger on the map where the deep valley of a small river drains the Great Loch. From there he knows of a track that follows the western shore for many miles, deep into the heart of the mountains. If he started in early spring, who knows where he might journey. There are tales of monsters and giants and gold, not that he believes them.

For a while he nods drowsily in the warmth seeing mountains capped with snow and torrents stained brown with peat. Beyond the mountains lies the sea. Dark islands march rank on rank towards the horizon. Horizons...

He jerks awake, yawning. He rolls his map. Time to think of the details as the days lengthen. There are many details: who and what to take, what to trade for, which tribes he can more or less trust. He wonders whether an amphora of the right Falerian might tempt the Tribune into sending the Fifth on extended patrol to that isolated fort on the Western River. He smiles gently to himself. Yes, it would be good to march with Lucius again. He places a screen in front of the fire then, rising, unhooks the lamp and makes his way to bed.

Chapter 7

(Second Meeting)

The days that followed were busy ones. The Selgovae had been raiding cattle from the Votodani. Rather than risk a tribal war, the Prefect despatched the Centurion with fifty men up the valley of the Gala Water to search and punish. One week turned into two as they chased rumours across heather hillsides. Summer advanced and nights in the open became a pleasure rather than a penance.

In the end he sent for a detachment of Vocontii auxiliary cavalry to surround and cut off the raiders' corral, hidden deep in a wooded side valley. Cattle were seized, identified and returned. Selgovae men were chained and marched back to Trimontium where due process of law would lead to their deaths. The Pax Romanum was restored.

The Camp Prefect received his verbal report and praised him for a job well done. "Have yourself two days off, young Lucius. I'm sure the Legion can manage without you."

After seeking out his Optio and confirming that all was well with the Century, he scraped off the dust of the campaign in the bathhouse, immersing himself in the warm waters for half an hour. Dressed in clean clothes, he ate his first fresh meal for two weeks and then slept for nine hours.

He awoke early to the scent of overnight rain. A song thrush exalted the new day. Flòraidh was already up, quietly clattering dishes. Yawning, the Centurion flung aside his blanket, stretched and rose. He padded barefoot across his sleeping quarters pushing aside the curtain into the tiny space where Flòraidh prepared breakfast. The servant girl looked up fondly at her master. Still yawning he caressed her shoulder briefly as he made his way outside to the latrine.

As he scrubbed himself with cold water he thought about his

two free days. The air was already warming. Early sunlight and distant haze promised a peerless day for doing very little. Such luxury was rarely his and he reviewed his options carefully.

Back in the kitchen he told Flòraidh to put up a bundle of cheese, bread and dried fruit then dressed in worn, comfortable breeks and tunic. Humming quietly to himself he rummaged in a curtained corner behind his weapons stand and brought forth a long fishing cane and a reel of thin catgut.

Flòraidh, coming noiselessly through the curtain with his breakfast, heard the humming and saw her master, tousled head bent in concentration. She treasured these unguarded moments when her master seemed to her like a large boy, full of enthusiasms. The Centurion turned with a smile as she placed the platter and cup on the table. "Fresh brown trout this evening, Flòraidh, unless I've lost my touch."

She smiled in her turn. "Then I shall gather fennel and parsley, my Lord, and I'll go to the market and buy fresh butter and leeks. I'll make you a feast fit for the Emperor himself."

Anxious now not to miss any more of the day, the Centurion wolfed his breakfast – oat bread, cold mutton, honeycomb and watered wine. Flòraidh gave him a knapsack containing enough food for a week and with his fishing cane over his shoulder, he set out up the path to the North Gate. The sentries came to attention but he waved them back to quiescence. He cut across and out of the East Gate turned left and picked up a path which ran through a scattering of small villas to the camp's amphitheatre. From there he turned steeply downhill towards the river.

In the shadowed depth of the valley it was cool. After its winter spate the Tweed was summer-lazy but it's clear, brown waters still humped over hidden boulders. The Centurion set off westwards beside the river, winding in and out of hazel coppice. His goal was the still pool below the native settlement where fat brown trout rose, especially in the cool of the morning.

After half an hour a bright thread of conversation announced the washing place of the village woman. Through leaves of willow he saw them, a round dozen, squatting on a wide rock shelf, homespun gowns kilted to the waist, pounding garments. Talk ended abruptly as he emerged into the sunlight.

"Hello," he called. One young girl with chestnut braids gave a cheery wave but was instantly quelled by outraged looks. Not for the first time the Centurion missed the open ways of his mountain village

Around another bend the river widened, its waters becoming placid in the shadow of oak and willow. The Centurion sat and removed his heavy sandals. From the knapsack he took a fold of canvas. Inside was a selection of hooks. He selected one, disguised with two small feathers bound with red wool, and carefully tied it to the end of his line. Then, toes feeling for grip on water-smoothed stones, he entered the river.

The next hour passed in sublime peace as he cast and recast into the shadows near the north bank. There were rises and ripples but the fish were lazy. Then, just as he debated breaking for a mouthful of wine, the juniper cane bent and twitched. Carefully he struck and was rewarded by a strong pull. The next minutes called for full concentration as he fought the fish. Little by little he gathered handfuls of line and brought the trout to him until it lay gasping in the shallows. He took a short gaff from his belt, deftly hooked the fish through its gills and turned for the bank.

His absorption was shattered by the sound of applause. "Bravo, my Lord." He looked up. Before him on the bank sat a small figure. He saw it was Aithne wearing a green tunic and cross-gartered trews, her long braids falling over her shoulders.

"My Lady," he called, "how came you here?"

"Well, my Lord," Aithne seemed to ponder deeply, "we must all of us be somewhere, must we not?"

The Centurion laughed. "Indeed we must, my Lady, but this

is a big valley and I thought to make my approach unnoticed."

Aithne arose and came to the water's edge. "Then, my Lord, thou hast much to learn in the art of stalking and even more about the tongues of women. No sooner had thou passed the washerwomen than word sprang from tree to tree. 'A dark, curly-headed young foreigner, well-muscled and tall – making his way up-river – up to no good for sure'. As my father's daughter I could do nought but spy on this trespasser, selling my life dearly in defence of the tribe if I must."

The Centurion, smiling broadly, waded ashore, carrying the trout by its gills. "And now that you have seen the invader what do you intend?"

Aithne seemed to consider, finger on dimpled chin. "Well that would depend, my Lord. It seems that the foreign devil has been poaching our fish. If he were willing to make recompense for his theft – perhaps a share of his catch – then I might allow him to live."

He looked at his one trout doubtfully. "Then it seems, O Warrior Princess of the Votodani, that I must needs poach another fish for there is little enough here to share."

"It is agreed, then, Foreigner," said Aithne, "but only if thou wilt show me thy devilish method of catching fish. We civilized folk use the net and spear and I would learn how foreign devils charm the fish from the water."

The bargain struck, they returned barefoot to the river. Even when the water, no deeper than mid-thigh on the Centurion, came up to her waist, Aithne did not pause. Finally established on a shallow gravel bank, he initiated her into the secrets of fly-fishing as practised in the mountain streams of Tarraconesis.

Her first attempts at casting were clumsy so the Centurion stood behind her and controlled the movement of her forearms with his hands. The morning was now well advanced and the trout lazier than ever. However, by exerting his fishing guile, it was not long before there was another strike. Now he quietly schooled her in the subtleties of tiring the fish without breaking the line, her small fist guided by his large, brown hand.

Eventually the trout lay exhausted, flapping weakly at their feet. The Centurion gaffed it and removed the hook from its mouth. He then threaded a piece of catgut through its gills and, with a flourish, presented it to Aithne. "Just tribute to the Queen of the Celts," he said.

Aithne clapped her hands and skipped before gravely accepting the fish with a small bow. "Giving due consideration to thy abject tribute we decree that thy miserable life shall be spared." Then, bending, she scooped a handful of water into his face and splashed off towards the shore shouting over her shoulder, "Come: let us cook them."

* * *

Later, their appetites satisfied with succulent fish and bannocks from the knapsack, they lay on either side of their small cooking fire talking. The Centurion spoke of the mountains and torrents of his childhood home; of climbing and fishing and hunting. He spoke of the deep snows and bitter colds of winter. She saw the fond, faraway look in his eyes as he spoke of his village and his family.

"My father was a centurion of the Ninth. That is why I have Roman citizenship. After he retired he took up a grant of land in his home village. My mother went with him. She was born in the mountains of Thrace. They grow grapes and olives and make cheese. It is a simple life but good."

She spoke of long, dark winters and the joy of spring; of endless summer twilights; of Samhain and Beltane; of driving the herds through the fires to make them fertile; of young couples leaping the flames together. Her zest for life was strong.

"Nearly everyone thinks of Father as a great, brutal bear but I tell thee I can tame him at will. It is Mother of whom thou should'st beware. She is a daughter of the Brigantes. She had hopes of marrying into the Catuvellauni and sees poor Father as second best. So she organizes him and pushes him. I tell thee, I would not want to meet her in battle."

After a lazy, companionable pause she asked, "Knowst thou how to tickle trout?"

The Centurion, who had been tickling trout since his fourth summer said, "No; will you show me?"

Aithne leapt to her feet and beckoned imperiously. "Come," she said. She led the way to a place where the river undercut its bank and stopped some way from the edge.

"Thou must be very quiet," she whispered. "Lie down in the grass here and wriggle slowly to the edge there."

They crept together towards the bank. She touched his arm and leant close to whisper, tickling his hair. "I go there," she pointed. "Thou creep round there and lie along the bank with thy head towards mine. But be thou ever so quiet and slow or thou wilt frighten the trout."

They settled, lying along the bank, faces inches apart. "Now watch," breathed Aithne, "and make no sudden movements."

With glacial slowness she eased her right arm over the bank into a clump of weed below the surface, her face taut with concentration. A small pulse beat in her temples. The breeze toyed with the hair at her brow. Silence fell.

Brown trout enjoyed the tickle of the water weed in the shadow of the bank. With infinite patience Aithne drifted her hand across to the fattest until her fingertips were under its belly. She began to stroke. Inasmuch as piscine features may display emotion, the trout looked ecstatic. Then, with brutal suddenness, it was out of its element, flying in a glittering arc of drops to land flapping hopelessly in the grass.

Aithne leapt up with a whoop of triumph and stood over her catch.

"Well," said the Centurion, with a fair attempt at sincerity, "I would not have believed it had I not seen it. Would you have me kill it for you, my Lady?"

Aithne considered. "Art hungry?" she asked.

"No," he replied.

"Then let us put him back for he gave us good sport and I would not have him die needlessly."

While she placed the fish back in the river the Centurion thought rapidly. The day had scarce passed noon and he longed to spend more of it with Aithne. Yet her mother's words had not been lost on him: this girl was spoken for. There were ramifications to this which he could not ignore. Perhaps now was the time to make his excuses and leave.

All of which came to nought as Aithne, radiant with the joy of the day, wiping fish scales on a handful of grass said, "Come, fetch thy fishing pole. I promised to show thee my plant nursery and it is just up there beyond the village."

"My Lady..." he began.

"And thou mayst call me Aithne and what may I call thee?"

The Centurion wondered how much of the mother resided in the daughter. "Lucius," he said. "You may call me Lucius."

* * *

It was late. Flòraidh added another small branch to the embers. She wondered where her master could be. The fennel and parsley had long been chopped and mixed with the butter. The leeks lay simmering in a savoury broth. Apple pasties warmed on the oven's top. The meal lacked but a trout and someone to eat it.

Faint, at first, she heard footsteps. She rose. The outer curtain was pushed aside and the Centurion, fishing rod in hand, ducked to enter.

"Hello, Flòraidh," he said, handing her the knapsack. "My thanks for waiting up for me."

"It was no trouble, my Lord." She waited, expectantly, but he moved towards the inner door.

"My Lord, what of the trout? Didst thou catch many? I will have them cooked and ready for thee while thou wash."

"The trout?" he said. "Oh, the trout: I ate them at noon, Flòraidh. And I ate at the village this evening." He thought she looked a little put out and sought to make amends. "But those apple pasties smell good. I will have one before I go to bed."

Catching up a pasty he slipped through the curtain to his sleeping quarters.

He did not call for her that night.

* * *

"He's off again, then," the sentry muttered from the side of his mouth, his face immobile.

"Wonder where he's going," muttered his mate.

It was well before sunrise and the Centurion clad in old clothes had just left the East Gate again heading for the valley.

"Quintus reckons he's on one of these 'ere clandestine assignments," said the first. "Says he's infiltrating the Selgovae – finding out their war plans."

The second sentry thought for a few moments then spat. "Ain't fooling no one, not in them flaming great 'obnail sandals," he said.

* * *

Once again the Centurion trod the dawn shadows but this morning his feelings were mixed. Aithne was a force to be reckoned with yet there was a sweet pleasure in surrender. In truth, he knew that he should not be doing this but...

The sun's first rays topped Bemersyde's heights, striking through the trees and evaporating his introspection.

Yesterday was a pastiche of memories: Aithne scampering through the woods: the two of them creeping silently round the margins of the settlement: the nursery, hidden behind hurdles of woven hazel. She had proudly shown him her domain: annual seedlings ready for planting out: fruit bushes and canes: the composting enclosure: the woven covers put aside after the last frosts. She showed him the herb garden. Some of the herbs he knew – parsley, marjoram and fennel. Others were new to him – sweet woodruff, golden seal and dragon's blood.

"With these a skilled person may ease pain, draw disease or make the barren fertile."

He had asked her if she possessed these skills.

"Nay, not more than a little. But I will learn. I will be a healer. For now I supply the midwives and wise women of the valleys with herbs that do not grow in the wild. In return they teach me."

They had worked in close companionship as afternoon drew towards evening, planting and pruning, watering and grafting. Stories were shared: tales of triumph and sadness, of noontide and evening. Many more were spoken without words. Hand brushing hand and smile meeting smile, magic distilled from the very air. As twilight fell they stood close and surveyed their work; content.

She turned and touched his hand. "My thanks, Lucius; it has been a wonderful day. Now I would feed thee for thou must be hungry."

He had begun to protest gently but she had insisted. She had a small lean-to nearby where she slept on summer evenings and in it a store of food. From this she made them a meal of unleavened oatcakes and vegetable stew over a small fire. They lingered long beyond nightfall and then she led him by narrow ways, dappled with moonlight, around the village to the riverside path.

There he had held her for long moments her head upon his

chest while the sounds of the night echoed in the woods. He stroked her hair then raised her chin with one finger. "I must go, Aithne." He hesitated, not knowing what more to say.

"Lucius, listen:" she whispered, "tomorrow I go to Black Hill across the river. I have herbs to deliver to the wise woman of the Selgovae. Wouldst come with me? We could take food and...and I could show thee badgers in the woods yonder and there are caves in the cliffs ..."

The Centurion struggled with his conscience. Nothing prevented him from visiting a Selgovae village but it would mean telling the Prefect and there would be checks crossing the bridge. He tried to explain this to Aithne.

"Nay," she said. "Come here at dawn and I will ferry thee across in my skiff. No one need know." She gazed up at him, more girl than woman, and he found that he could not deny her.

And so, here he was. He waited beneath the trees and before long a small skiff, such as the Votodani used for salmon fishing, cut through the river mist, Aithne sculling over the stern. She peered over her shoulder then deftly turned the boat towards the shore, grounding in the shallows. Grasping the gunwales, Lucius pushed the boat into the stream again and stepped aboard.

Aithne smiled, all mischief. "Welcome, my Lord," she said.

* * *

"What foolishness is this, child?" hissed the Old One.

Aithne was taken aback by the old woman's disapproval. What had started as fun was rapidly turning sour. They had left the skiff on a gravel bank and climbed the steep northern slope above the river through beech trees and hazel coppice, baskets of herbs on their shoulders. Where the bridge guard might have seen them near the skyline they had passed with care before running and laughing down the rear slope. The journey had taken an hour following native tracks, mostly in sight of the trunk road. Now she sat outside the Old One's hut in the morning sunshine.

The old woman gestured with her sharp chin to where, at some distance, the Centurion sat on a tree stump, apparently at ease. Selgovae, mainly women, went about their village business but always with one eye on the Roman.

"Who is he, child, and what is he to thee?"

Aithne swallowed. She was used to a degree of equality with the wise woman; a relationship founded on mutual esteem.

"He is a friend, Old One, just a friend."

The Old One spat then turned her penetrating gaze on the younger woman.

"Think not to cozen me, child. I see much and know more. It is in thy walk and thy face. Thou wouldst have this man and he thee. He is a foreigner, child." The Old One spoke with disdain. "His ways are not thine. He will stay for a while and then go. He is not for you."

Aithne raised her chin defiantly. "We are friends, Old One, and that is my business and mine alone."

The Old One sat back and rummaged in one of the baskets, crooning quietly to herself. Aithne relaxed thinking the interrogation finished. She looked about her at the round houses, smoke rising through their thatch. The sound of sawing came from the woods.

"And what of the Lord Callum, child?" The Old One spoke conversationally, still examining the contents of the basket. "Thinkest thou that he will hear nought of this? Thinkest thou that he will be content to know that thou flaunt this Roman in a village of his tribe?"

Anger flared in Aithne's breast. "The Lord Callum is a pig. I would sooner die than marry him."

The Old One slowly raised her eyes from the basket, her face grave. She pointed a claw-like finger at Aithne. "Take care, child. Tempt not the gods for they hear all. Now go, for I cannot teach thee today and thou cannot learn." With that the old woman rose painfully to her feet with the aid of a stick and hobbled into the dark door of her hut.

Aithne rose and went to the Centurion. He looked up. "Are you finished so soon?"

"Aye," said Aithne. "The Old One feels the pain in her bones today. She is for her bed. Come Lucius; I promised thee badgers, did I not?"

* * *

The summer day unfolded: strands of sunlight and birdsong woven with the scent of wildflowers. The young couple climbed through woods of scrub oak on the slopes above the Leader Water. They lay in long grass and watched an old badger boar clearing winter bedding from his sett, grunting all the while to himself. Aithne took Lucius into deep caves and showed him where water had formed sword-like formations with the rock. They traced a beeline to a wild hive and Lucius showed Aithne how to use smoke to steal pieces of the comb.

After their noontide meal they rested in a grassy pocket beside a spring facing southwards towards Eildon. Lucius lay on his back, his head on his knapsack, eyes closed. Aithne lay beside him propped up on an elbow, preparing to tickle his nose with a grass stalk.

"Art asleep, Roman?"

Lucius lay silent, pretending to snore. The grass touched his nose, making it twitch.

"Speak to me, Roman."

Lucius sighed and opened his eyes. "Of what would you have me speak, O Pest?" he asked wearily. Aithne pretended to think deeply.

"Tell me of thy women," she said.

Lucius rolled onto his elbow, facing her. "We do not have the time," he said, "for I must return to camp before tomorrow morning."

Aithne hit him across the head with her grass stem. "Pig!" she said. She thought for a while, tracing patterns on his chin with the grass. Then: "Were they all very beautiful?" she asked.

Lucius was silent, brow furrowed in concentration, ticking off the fingers of both hands twice. "Yes," he replied at length. "Yes, every single one."

"More beautiful than me?"

Lucius looked up at her, ready to continue the banter but his eyes met hers and neither looked away. Without thought he leaned across the inches that separated them and gently kissed one corner of her mouth, then the other. "No one is more beautiful than you, Aithne," he heard himself say.

Then they were together, stroking, holding, feeling the length of each other's body. Their kisses were gentle at first, then urgent. Tongues touched and probed, learning each what the other knew; seeking, teaching...

Neither knew how long it was until they drew apart. Lucius looked down at this woman child. He saw the tumbled hair and the colour in her cheeks. The outline of her face was soft, slightly blurred to the eye.

* * *

Aithne watched as he took in every detail of her face. She saw him smile gently and shake his head, a look of wonder in his eyes. "Aithne," he said, "you are so very lovely." Then he bent down and kissed her with infinite care and time stopped again.

Much later, as the sun moved westward, she lay in his arms and saw that he was troubled. She smoothed his hair and said, "What ails thee, Lucius? Tell me."

He turned to her and ran a finger slowly down the side of her face. He did not know how to start. She reached up and drew his head onto her breast. "Come, beloved; whatever it is thou must tell me, otherwise I shall worry."

He withdrew from her embrace and looking down at her again said, "Aithne, my love. This is wrong. You are betrothed. We cannot allow this."

Aithne placed a small finger on his lips. "Hush, dear one. Listen to me."

She knelt and took his hands.

"Beloved," she said, "my mother, the Lady Innogen, spends her waking hours scheming. She would have our tribe tied to those around us by marriage. She believes that this will bring us peace and for the sake of quiet my father does not say her nay."

"Andraste she hath married into the Carvetii and Arianrhod the Damnonii. That leaves me and little else but the Selgovae. Mother thinks that Callum, a lumpish, uncouth fool, would suit me. Father laughed when he heard – said he would rather welcome a rutting boar into the family than some inbred by-blow of a minor tribe. And there it stands. Art content?"

Lucius raised first one of her hands to his mouth and kissed it, then the other. Still he looked troubled. "But…" he faltered then started again. "But does Callum know of your mother's plans?"

"Ha!" Aithne stood, pulling Lucius to his feet with her. She put her arms around him and buried her head in his leather tunic. "He may have heard something but I tell thee this: I shall marry whom I will and it won't be a foul-smelling idiot whose only skill is killing," she looked up, impishly, "saving thy presence, of course."

* * *

Late that evening Aithne ferried Lucius back across the Tweed. She tied the skiff to a willow and together they walked slowly, arms around each other, along the path towards the camp. An owl hooted from the far bank.

"When will I see thee again, Lucius?" asked Aithne.

"It is difficult," he said. "I will not know until I return to duty tomorrow. It may be that I will be sent on patrol but that isn't certain. Is there somewhere I can leave a message for you?"

Aithne thought. "Aye; Ula, mother of the blacksmith. She lives alone in the village near the river. She can be trusted. Tell her when thou art able to come and I will meet thee by the willow where we tied the boat."

"Then I will send one of my servants but you must not worry if I cannot get away for some while," he replied.

She stopped and turned, looking up at him, her face a blur in the backwash of starlight. "Thou wilt come to me as soon as thou may, though, Lucius?"

He smoothed the hair from her temple then bent and kissed her. "I will come from the far end of the Empire if I must," he murmured. They held each other for long minutes then, gently, he disengaged himself. "I must go, loved one." Holding her by the shoulders he kissed her on the brow then turned and was gone into the darkness.

$$* * *$$

Thus it was that the next day around noon the Centurion pushed aside the kitchen curtain as Flòraidh ground corn. He leaned in the doorway and said, "Flòraidh, will you run down to the village for me. Find a woman named Ula. She lives near the river. Tell her, 'Tomorrow at dusk'."

Flòraidh dusted floury hands on her apron. "Of course, my Lord." She tried to smile but her heart ached.

Chapter 8

(Aithne)

Aithne hums to herself. She makes a hole with her planting stick and drapes a tiny leek plant into it. The sun is now high enough each day to peer over the outer earthwork quite early and warm her back. It causes her to stretch with pleasure, feeling the heat through her felt jerkin. She loves this time of day. Nights in the roundhouse are noisy with snores and lovemaking; the air foetid with smoke and body odour. The escape into dawn freshness is bliss.

Lucius, ever present in the back of her mind, steps forward. What will he be doing now, this moment? Perhaps stripped to the waist, washing? She imagines the sheen of his brown skin. The warmth of it under her hand is real to her just as on the day when, greatly daring, she had first run her hand down his chest and felt the reality of its contours.

He'd been gone four days now, which meant – she ticks off on her fingers – that he would be back in three. It seems forever. She still finds it difficult to believe that he will come back although he has reassured her often enough. As the youngest daughter Aithne has gone generally unregarded, especially by her mother. Father, she knows, dotes on her but only in the infrequent moments when his mind is not full of hunting, feasting and affairs of state.

In truth, after seventeen summers of insignificance, she is unused to the gift of uncritical regard. That such regard should come from someone as wonderful as Lucius is magical. She feels like a small plant which has been denied rain and is suddenly watered. Lucius: Lucius of the black, curly hair and the deep, brown eyes: Lucius who draws her body like a magnet...

"Child!"

Her daydreams are cruelly shattered. The Lady Innogen looms over her, blocking the warmth.

"I wish, I truly wish that you would find a pastime more suited to a chieftain's daughter than growing vegetables. It is unseemly."

Aithne bows her head so that her mother shall not see her frown. She says nothing. Both know that this battle has been fought and won. It was one of the rare occasions when Belinus had put his foot down.

"What could be better for a young woman than being a healer?" he had asked with uncharacteristic directness. "And you can't heal without herbs so if she wants to grow them, let her. She's got to do something until she marries."

To make the point, he had had his ox wains drag topsoil from the valley bottom for three laborious days so that his daughter might have her garden. Later, when she had urged the need for a sheltered nursery for seedlings, he had had his coppicers fence off an enclosure in the valley. Thus had Aithne spent a happy and productive two years alternating between her high and low gardens. The Lady Innogen is aware that her daughter uses this as a device to avoid her and misses no opportunity to pounce.

"I need to speak with you, child. Come with me." The Lady Innogen sets sail for the outer gate of the fort. Aithne, swearing quite vilely under her breath, rises and follows her. The warriors on guard knuckle their forelocks in a perfunctory manner as the two women pass.

Out on the hillside among the heather and far from prying ears, Innogen stops, looking out over the wide lands to the south-east. Larks breast a fresh southerly breeze. Aithne comes to stand at her mother's shoulder. For a long moment both survey the view. Aithne's stomach is tense. In her eyes, her mother is a force of Nature.

"Child," Innogen never uses her daughter's name, "this land," she waves a beringed hand at the view, "belongs to the Votodani. It is ours by right, earned by our fathers' blood."

'It is our birthright...' thinks Aithne.

"It is our birthright," says Innogen.

Sometimes as she gardens, Aithne rehearses this speech in her head. '…willed to us by the Great God Bel for all time, against all enemies, perfidious and grasping. They shall not prevail! Ne'er shall this Fair Land fall whilst yet a single Votodani, glorious and slave to none, can yet raise a sword, whilst one drop of the true blood remains in our veins to be shed. O Alba! O great and glorious Land. Stand forth, I say…' Usually by this stage Aithne dissolves into laughter.

Innogen continues. "It is meet that we hand it down to our children intact. While men," she invests the word with scorn, "see fit to kill for it, we women play another and more subtle role."

'Oh no,' thinks Aithne with alarm. 'Not the marriage speech.'

Innogen turns to her daughter. "Thanks to your sisters we have peace with the Carvetii and Damnonii. Andraste is with child and Arianrhod…well no doubt Arianrhod soon will be too."

'Not unless that Damnonii idiot finds out how babies are made,' thinks Aithne.

"There remain yet the Selgovae, child." Innogen's voice rises as she warms to her theme. "The Selgovae are the worm in the apple, the viper in our breast. We women have a solemn duty to bind that viper to us." Innogen ploughs on, mixing metaphors as she goes. "Child, the time has come for you to put away your childhood. The moment for greatness calls you. You must go to the Lord Callum and make of our two nations one!"

In the silence that follows it seems to Aithne that the very larks are stunned. She gazes unseeing to the south. Tears prick her eyes.

"I won't."

It is difficult to say which woman is the more surprised. For a moment Aithne doesn't know where the words have come from. Innogen, on the other hand, knows full well.

"What did you say?" she asks, her voice dangerously soft.

Aithne draws a shuddering breath. "I said no; I won't marry Callum. If you should try to make me I will kill myself."

Innogen draws herself to her full height, her massive breasts adding to the effect of towering majesty. "I knew it," she hisses. "I warned your father but he wouldn't listen. It is this Roman, isn't it? You have lost your reason, girl. Romans want only one thing. And when they get it they turn away and find another fool. What do they care for us; for our ancient culture: Romans with their straight lines, their laws and their precious trade!"

Hearing Lucius so maligned, Aithne knows a blinding fury. Small and young though she is, her mother's blood runs in her veins.

"How dare you?" she begins breathlessly then shouts, "How dare you? You ... you great *cow*!"

Innogen recoils. Her face blanches.

"You know *nothing* about Lucius; nothing of his gentleness and kindness. You have never met anyone like him you shrivelled-up, dried-up, old bully. If you had you wouldn't be so... so...so *nasty*!"

With that Aithne dissolves into tears.

Assuming that tears mean victory, Innogen lets her daughter cry for a while. Then she says loftily, "For your sake and the sake of the tribe I will overlook what you have just said. We shall announce your betrothal before Yule and you will leap the Beltane fires with Lord Callum."

Cuffing the tears from her eyes, Aithne looks up at her mother, a small animal at bay. Hectic red spots mark either cheek. All the years of neglect and criticism, all the carping and bullying she has had to endure fuel her anger. Controlling her sobbing as best she can she speaks in a low trembling voice, "If you dare to even try that, Mother, then Father will hear what took place between you and Uncle Alaunus last Yule."

Innogen flinches as though she has been slapped. She takes a step backwards. "What are you saying, girl? What lies are you telling about me?"

Aithne advances a step, committed now and reckless. "Lies, Mother? Lies about the shepherd's hut yonder?" She points to the east where the land falls steeply into the valley. "The shepherd's hut above the river, Mother. The one which cannot be seen from the beacon fire even by day when everyone is sober; certainly not on Yule Eve when the fire flares and the celebration is at its height."

The Lady Innogen gulps. "You…you followed us?"

"Aye, Mother; just out of curiosity. I wished at the time that I hadn't but now…"

For perhaps the first time in her life the Lady Innogen is lost for words. Her mouth opens and closes like that of a stranded fish. Then she regains some control. She steps forward threateningly and towers over her daughter. "You may think you've won this time, girl," she breathes, "but there will be other times. You won't win them all."

With that she turns on her heel and stalks back to the camp.

Chapter 9

(Summer)

The Lady Innogen strode into the gloom of the Chieftain's hut. "Belinus," she boomed, "we need to talk."

Belinus, who had been replacing the leather thongs on his boar spear in preparation for a day's hunting groaned inwardly. His wife's need to talk made his head hurt but, from long years of experience, he knew the futility of attempted delay. Nevertheless, he wished he were already free in the woods. He wished that last night's heather beer had not been off. He gestured for his warriors to leave.

Assuming a grave, attentive smile he said, "Certainly, my dear; what do you want to talk about?"

"Aithne," announced Innogen, arranging herself with dignity upon a wooden bench. "What are we going to do about her?"

A large part of the agony associated with these periodic talks was the fact that his wife inhabited a world bereft of hunting and feasting. Thus Belinus was inevitably at a disadvantage. The Lady Innogen exploited her advantage mercilessly.

"Aithne, my dear?" he hazarded.

"Yes, Aithne," she snapped, "your daughter. You cannot be unaware that she is spending time with a Roman, Belinus. It must stop."

Belinus had a vague memory of vegetables and wondered why.

"Ah, a Roman," he tried.

"Belinus!" Her voice would hone iron, he thought. "You have no idea what I am talking about, do you? Must I always be the one to think of the future of this tribe? Do you care at all about your family?"

Belinus felt the start of a familiar misery. He glanced at the doorway where a shaft of sun promised a perfect day for hunting. Anger stirred. A small germ of rebellion was born.

The Lady Innogen continued in full flow.

"It may have escaped your attention but your daughter, the one who is betrothed to Lord Callum of the Selgovae, has for the last several weeks been gadding about with a Roman soldier. You should know about this because it was *you* who introduced them in the first place."

She paused and glared at her husband. Belinus began to remember. He felt the injustice of the accusation. His anger grew. Deliberately he turned, lifted his drinking horn and took a great draught. Then, putting it down, he turned back to his wife.

"Well?" she said.

He wiped his lips with the back of his hand.

"In the first place, wife, Aithne is not betrothed to that third-rate fool Callum. *You* suggested it and *I* told you that I was not having the bloodline of this tribe sullied by an inbred by-blow from a family of thieves and cretins. In the second place as far as I am concerned Aithne is welcome to walk out with a Roman. In case you are unaware, wife, the Romans own this country now. I go further: it would be to our great advantage if one of our daughters married a Roman."

They glared at one another.

"Are you saying that you will do nothing about this situation?" asked the Lady Innogen, icily.

Outside, one of the warriors experimentally wound a hunting horn. Belinus' head came up like that of an old hound. He climbed to his feet, hefting his boar spear.

"Innogen," he said, "you had your way with Andraste and Arianrhod. The Carvetii boy I can just about stomach but the Damnonii is a half-wit. Do you think either of the girls is happy? Do you care?"

He took a step towards the door, turned and pointed at her.

"You leave Aithne alone, wife. Let at least one of our daughters have a little happiness."

With that he strode towards the daylight.

* * *

That summer was remembered for many a year. Gentle breezes tempered days of sun. Rain came and went with a just sufficiency. Crops grew in abundance. In the sheltered water meadows of the valley bottoms, two harvests of hay were cut. Beasts were fertile and healthy. Samhain was celebrated joyfully with the knowledge that for this winter, at least, there would be no starvation.

For Aithne and Lucius it was a time of contented exhilaration, marred only by his absences on duty. The goodbyes were hard to bear but both agreed that the greetings made up for them. A disinterested observer might have wondered at their naivety. Obviously so much in love, they spent their time gardening, fishing and roaming the woods. They held hands and kissed and laughed a lot but of love making there was no sign.

In fact the couple had discussed the matter at an early stage. Whilst each longed for the other with a strength that hurt, they agreed that marriage was not a foregone conclusion. Aithne's parents and the Roman military authorities could not be relied upon to give their blessings. So, for the moment, they had agreed to rein in their desires.

As autumn advanced and the days began to draw in the Tribune in charge of military operations held his weekly meeting with the Camp Præfect. Military duties assigned, logistical problems sorted, they relaxed over a flask of wine.

"The Fifth seem to have their combined tails up," commented the Tribune. "Saw them in the amphitheatre last week. Won more than their fair share in the weapons competitions as well as the running."

The Præfect raised his glass to the light. "That's young Lucius for you. Got the golden touch that lad. Doesn't surprise me.

Knew his father back in the old days. Used to be the best in the Ninth." With his long years of service, the Præfect's knowledge of Legionary personalities was encyclopædic.

"Yes." The Tribune riffled through some files until he found the one he sought. "Report here on the last night field exercise. Umpires' opinion the Fifth wiped out the Eighth. Had their every move plotted from the outset. Ambushed them against Bemersyde Moss."

The Præfect chuckled. "That'll be his new reconnaissance decade. Put ten of his best together and given them a free rein. They melt into the night," the Prefect made a sliding motion with his free hand, "and see everything. Castor and Pollux, the two Numidians, are the key players."

The Tribune tapped his teeth with a fingernail, thinking. "Look, Præfect; I'd welcome your advice here. Suppose you know about him and the Votodani girl? Bit of an open secret really. Point is what do I do if he asks permission to marry, and I think he may? Under the new regulations it's not an administrative problem but I have to know what to recommend to the Legate."

The Præfect nodded. The Emperor Hadrian had recently liberalized Legionary law to make it easier for soldiers to marry local women. From henceforth the women as well as any children would become Roman citizens.

"But," the Tribune went on, "a bird tells me that the girl was promised to some Selgovae lordling. So tell me, Præfect, how do I square this circle?"

The Præfect, pursing his lips, said nothing for five seconds. He gazed in thought at the cohort's standards, crossed behind the Tribune's desk, then: "My opinion, for what it's worth, sir, nothing's going to keep them apart. Forbid it and the lad'll go downhill. So will the Fifth, and that," he took some more wine, "is assuming he doesn't continue slipping out of camp anyway."

"Other side of it is, who'd you rather insult – Votodani or Selgovae. If I know Belinus he'd be tickled pink to have a Roman son-in-law. Cement relations and all that. Marry her into the Selgovae," he shuddered theatrically, "fate worse than death. Wouldn't do us any good. Mucky lot," he added in an undertone.

"Right, Præfect; thanks for that." The Tribune made a note with his stylus. "May come to nothing, anyway. Who knows?"

* * *

In a dank, smoke-filled hut high above the Gala Water a warrior of the Selgovae gnawed on a bone his every move watched by a small dog. The man stank but, then, so did the warriors around him. Before him crouched an old, one-eyed man. A warrior stood over him with a spear. The old man looked frightened to death.

The Lord Callum, pointing the bone at the man. "Tell," he grunted.

The old man pulled his rags together across his thin chest. "My Lord, what I saw, they was gardening together and walking through the woods and she cooked for him and then he went home." He cringed closer to the earth.

Callum hawked and spat. "Did he have her then?" he growled.

"My Lord," the old man hesitated. "My Lord, I didn't see but he may have."

Callum glowered. "I say he had her. What do you say?"

The old man turned his face to the ground, visibly shaking. "He had her, my Lord. Yes, he had her."

Callum gave the bone to the small dog. It dragged it away into a dark corner, wagging its tail in anticipation. Callum fisted an earthenware pot of ale. "Throw him out," he snarled. He stared moodily into the fire. After a few moments a muffled yelp followed by a burst of deep laughter came from outside. Around him in the gloom his warriors waited. He was not very bright. He ruled by the strength of his arm but he knew that the loyalty of his warriors might not survive a loss of face.

"The Roman dies," he growled. A sigh went round the circle of faces. That would do for now, he thought.

Chapter 10

(Marriage)

Lucius and Aithne became lovers one autumn day of high cloud and slanting sunlight when the waning year spoke of loss and endings. In a grassy dell high above the Tweed they touched the ineffable bounds of eternity and became one.

As they lay naked with wonder, a small, ferret-faced man backed silently from his hide in a bramble thicket high above the dell. Once an intervening ridge blocked sight and sound, he turned to the west, broke into the hunter's lope, a pace he could maintain all day, and headed for a hill fort above the Gala Water.

* * *

"Attacks are up forty per centum this last month. Can't go on, Præfect."

It was the weekly conference.

"Thing is, spies say it's Callum. Sworn some kind of oath. No one's saying what it's about but seems to involve assaults on Romans." The Tribune absently tapped his dagger on the desk and stared out of the window at a louring sky. "We'll need to put an end to it before the weather breaks."

The Præfect considered his wine glass. It was a good vintage from the Tribune's own vineyards in Gallia Narbonensis, better than anything the wine shops sold by a long mile. He wondered if he might grow grapes when he retired, then sighed: there was a little distance to go yet. He brought his mind back to the present.

"Have you thought, sir, that this may have to do with the Centurion of the Fifth? Remember, we spoke of him and the Votodani girl. Could it be that's what ails Callum?"

The Tribune swung round in his chair and contemplated the older man. He tapped the dagger blade on his knuckles. He knew he wasn't the brightest disc on the signum; had come to terms with that years ago. That's why he'd learned to trust the Præfect's judgement. Præfect was a downy bird.

"Could be, Præfect, could be." He worked at his thoughts. "Seems to me that argues the Fifth leading the assault, what? Celts understand that sort of thing would you agree?"

The Præfect considered then said slowly, "Yes; yes that would do but may I suggest something else?"

The Tribune nodded.

"If you really wanted to rub Callum's nose in it then tell Lucius to marry the girl."

The Tribune looked mildly horrified. "I say, Præfect," he finally managed, "hardly my place to tell a fellow who to marry. I mean to say, there is a limit…"

The Præfect smiled quietly. He was starting to enjoy himself.

"Look at it this way sir: we know the lad's keen to wed her. Chances are she feels the same. As far as we know Belenus would be all for it. In Celtic terms, if Lucius takes her from under Callum's nose, we'll have won enough kudos over the Selgovae to last us years."

He sipped his wine while the Tribune nodded in bemused admiration, then he continued. "What I'm proposing is that you tell Lucius, unofficially of course, that you would look favourably upon any request from him to marry." He allowed himself a brief chuckle. "After all he should be grateful. Can't be getting much sleep what with all these midnight assignations."

And so it was that, returning from inspecting sentries one afternoon, Lucius was joined by the Tribune, apparently out for a stroll. The Centurion saluted.

"No need for that, Centurion," said the Tribune. "Just out for a stroll, what? All quite, ah, unofficial." There was an awkward pause then he continued, "Lovely weather." He seemed to run out of words.

Lucius agreed with his superior. They walked together in

silence for a while then the Tribune cleared his throat.

"Days like this should be shared," he ventured.

"Yes sir," said the Centurion, having no idea where this was going.

An embarrassed silence ensued. The Tribune's face was flushed. Finally, in a rush he said, "Dammit, Centurion, never was any good at this sort of thing. Leave that to the wife. And...and that's just my point – yes – just my point. Man needs a wife, Centurion. Damned good things, wives. Marry that Votodani girl if I were you. Damned fine filly. Do it soon."

The Tribune emphasised his last point by thumping his staff on the ground before stalking off towards the Headquarters building. He needed a drink.

* * *

High on Eildon, Belenus was closeted with his Chief Advisor.

"What d'you reckon then?" the Chieftain asked gloomily.

The Chief Advisor had been enumerating the taxes, tolls and tributes paid to the Romans over the last year. It seemed to Belenus that less than half of anything stayed in his treasury.

His advisor, who doubled up as High Priest of Bel and chief medical practitioner, wound a lock of greasy hair around his finger. Was this the moment to settle an old score? He thought it was. He sighed aloud.

"There is little to be done, my Lord. All the tribes groan under the yoke of the Oppressor. If there were but some way of exerting leverage, of patronage...Of course, if the Romans were just another tribe we would bind them to us by marriage..."

He looked sideways at Belenus to see if his words were having any effect. The Chieftain remained sunk in gloom. Raising his voice a little and speaking more slowly he went on, "If only there was a daughter of the blood, one who would be willing to marry a Roman of some standing."

Still nothing.

"If only the Lady Aithne…"

"Eh!" grunted Belenus. "What did you say?"

"I only wondered whether the Lady Aithne …"

"Yes! That's it! Aithne's seeing that Roman. Why didn't you think of this? You're meant to be my blasted chief advisor. We'll tell her she can marry with our blessing. And," he added as an afterthought, "damn the Lady Innogen."

"Masterly, my Lord," said the Chief Advisor. And to himself, 'Yes, let's damn the Lady Innogen'.

So it was that as Aithne dug compost into the vegetable beds the next morning, her father appeared beside her, leaning on his spear.

"Fine bagies you have there," was his opening gambit.

Aithne knew better than to point out that the bagies were already lifted and stored for the winter. She contented herself with thanking her father.

Belenus asked, "Are you still seeing that, what's his name, that Roman fella?"

Aithne, blushing, allowed that she was.

"Think you might marry him then?" he plunged on, rather more loudly than necessary. "Only if you are, your mother and I would be all for it."

With that he turned and stomped off towards the gate leaving his daughter bemused and not a little perplexed.

When next the lovers met they could only marvel together at the ways of Fate.

* * *

Lucius and Aithne were married in the early spring of the Roman year 965.

There was a Roman wedding held in the Temple of Jupiter at Trimontium and a Celtic ceremony in the Chieftain's hut on

Eildon North. The Lady Innogen was indisposed for the former. For the latter she glowered beside her husband, leaving before the feasting had properly started.

* * *

Callum's fort was reduced and overwhelmed a week before the first of the great winter storms swept across the Borderlands. Roman artillery showered the defences with rocks and spears. In the ensuing confusion legionaries hurled fascines, basketwork bolsters, into the outer ditch to make a footing. Finally five centuries led by the Fifth attacked the walls, scaling them with ladders carried within their *testudos*. From that moment, despite death, wounds and desperate fighting on both sides, the outcome was never in doubt.

Tactical plans seldom unfold as they should, however. Lucius saluted the Tribune, with a blood-stained arm.

"Seems Callum wasn't there, sir. Word is he was out hunting. Still, the place is taken. We lost thirteen outright. Another eight won't last the night. Their body count so far stands at eighty-six. Forty-seven are still standing plus women and children. Do you want prisoners, sir?"

The Tribune considered. "Yes. Finish off the wounded. Keep the able-bodied for slaves. That'll settle Callum's hash. We'll spend the night here. Tomorrow, burn the huts. Carry off livestock and grain; the usual stuff. After that, let's get back to camp and close up shop for the winter."

* * *

Deep in a dripping wood of stunted oaks, the Lord Callum huddled by a fire with his few remaining warriors. Absently, he stroked the small dog, curled in his lap. Black hatred filled his heart.

* * *

As the sun, moving northwards, reached mid-Taurus, a fire was lit at evening twilight on the high saddle between Eildon North and Eildon Mid Hill. All over Britannia similar scenes were enacted as the first of the spring stars appeared. Now began the great ceremony of Beltane where the people called down Bel's blessing on another growing season.

The huge heap of bracken and wood soaked in oil broke into ready flame, fanned by a warm, westerly breeze. Sparks streamed off into the gulfs of air to the east causing the penned livestock to bellow and bleat. Their time would come later when they were driven through the embers to assure their fertility and health in the coming summer. Then, too, couples wed or betrothed since last Beltane would leap the flames, for Bel embraced all.

For now, though, the night was given to feasting. Through the growing dark, torch-lit serpents of Votodani carrying baskets of food left the gates of the fort for the feasting ground. Barrels of mead and heather beer were rolled down the slope. The plaintive rhythm of native pipes and drums filled the air. Here and there figures began to caper and dance.

High on the walls of Eildon, Aithne and Lucius stood, arms around each other's waists. They gazed into the growing dark, pointing out Beltane fires to one another. There, near at hand, Black Hill sprang to life. Out to the east grew a pinpoint of light: Sandyknowe; then further still, Peniel Heugh. Soon, in the arc of clear air, there seemed as many lights upon earth as in the heavens.

Aithne turned towards Lucius and gazed up at him, her eyes large and solemn. "You will take care, won't you Lucius?"

Tonight they would leap the Beltane flames. Tomorrow the Centurion would leave with the Fifth on an extended patrol to Strathclyde. Josephus was to travel with them. The speculative amphora of Falerian gifted to the Tribune had done its trick.

Lucius gazed down into his wife's eyes, overcome with tenderness. He pulled her to him and she nestled her head on his breast. Bending to her ear he whispered, "I have always been careful, beloved, but now I have someone to be careful for."

He felt her begin to sob gently. Reaching down he raised her chin with one finger.

"Beloved, we've been apart before. Think of my return. Think how that first night will be."

The muted glow of firelight sparkled in the tear tracks marking her cheeks. Aithne tried to swallow her sobs. "But it's never been so long before," she managed, cuffing at the tears. "What am I going to do?"

Lucius pulled her to him again and held her tight, rocking her gently from side to side. "It will only be two months, my love." He searched for comforting words but, "You have the villa to furnish," was all he could find to say.

"Nay, I will not stay at the villa while you are gone. Flòraidh resents me. I will stay up here and work the garden."

Argue though he might, Lucius could not shift her resolve. He was disappointed that his new wife could not love the small villa they had rented. He had assumed that she would accede to all his wishes. It was hard to discover that she wouldn't.

Much later they jumped the Beltane flames. Hours of feasting and dancing had passed and the main fire had burned down to a great glowing bed. Two slaves armed with long rakes were put to dragging embers. With these they formed a fiery peninsula over which the couples could leap and through which the herds would be driven. As the embers were raked so they burst into renewed flame.

A young tribesman grasped the hand of his betrothed. She made a brief play of resistance then, laughing and shrieking, the two of them ran pell mell down the slope and leapt the fire. A cheer went up from the onlookers as the smiling couple emerged unscathed from behind the flames.

A second couple made the leap and then another. Lucius turned to Aithne and raised his eyebrows questioningly. Laughing she grasped his hand and they took their turn in the line. Renewed cheering rang out as they began their run. They were a popular couple and the Celts approved of a Roman joining in the ancient ceremony.

As he leapt, Lucius felt Aithne stumble. He tightened his grip on her hand. The brief heat of the flames passed and he landed but Aithne had fallen with her feet still in the embers. Quick as a cat he turned, grasped her shoulders and hauled her clear. There were flames at the hem of her skirt which he beat out before dragging her further from the flames.

He lay her down in the bracken. "Are you hurt, my love?" he asked anxiously.

Aithne sat up. She was shaking. She felt her lower legs. "Only a little scorched I think, Lucius." A crowd was forming round them now, some holding torches. "It must have been a bracken root," she said. "I twisted my ankle."

People were gabbling now, some about salves for burns, others about what such an augury could mean. Certain now that she was not badly hurt, Lucius scooped her into his arms and started back towards the fort. The last thing she heard as they left the circle of fire was an ancient female voice proclaiming, "No good will come of it, you mark my words. She'll be barren or worse."

* * *

The cornu sounded, conjuring echoes from the river cliff. Wood pigeons clattered into flight. Moments later the diminished note returned from the flanks of Eildon. The East Gate creaked open and the Fifth Century marched.

Aithne stood with a group of wives, shivering in the dawn chill. Goodbyes had been said in the small, dark hours as menfolk, with varying degrees of fatalism, struggled into harness. The single men were to be envied. They simply rolled out of bed, dressed and walked to the mess hall for an early breakfast.

Aithne tried to ignore the soreness of her burns. Though not severe they smarted beneath the salve provided by the garrison doctor. She watched as Lucius exchanged a final word with the Tribune and the Præfect before saluting. He gazed in her direction briefly then turned away to join the marching century. Aithne knew that a final word or even a wave was unthinkable given the Legion's iron culture but still it hurt. Her man was a soldier once more. She felt lost, bereft.

Now the tall figure with the red plume was passing out of sight through the gate beside the main body. Now the rearguard was gone. Now the gates were creaking closed.

The small knot of women was dissolving. One or two quiet words were exchanged but mostly they left silently, alone with their thoughts and fears. Aithne turned towards the North Gate. As she turned she experienced a sharp stab of pain low down in her stomach. She gasped and staggered, holding her hands over the spot. Then it was gone and she wondered whether she had imagined it. Thoughtfully she started walking. The pain did not return. 'Just as well,' she thought. She had Flòraidh to deal with and then the removal to Eildon North.

* * *

Some miles up the trunk road, the century was halted, transforming itself for the journey. The signum was covered and stowed on a mule along with the officers' best helmets. Shields were slipped into cloth covers. Final adjustments were made to buckles and straps.

Lucius knew this moment of old. It was the low point of any venture when the essential spirit of the Century had yet to be reclaimed. A combination of leave-taking, hangovers and lack of sleep would be isolating each man in his own small misery. It was his job to carry them through but he had never had to do it with farewells of his own still raw in his mind. Nevertheless, it had to be done.

The Optio came bustling down the line. "They're as ready as they'll ever be, sir," he reported.

"Thanks, Marcus," he replied. "Tell Porcius we'll have a song as soon as we start out. Tell him there'll be five sestertii in it for him if he gets the others joining in."

Marcus saluted. Lucius tightened his helmet strap then marched to the far side of the road where all could see him. He gave the order to advance. Two charcoal burners working in woods to the east heard the clash of marching feet followed by a clear, soaring tenor voice.

"I had a girl in Dubris Town,
When first I crossed from Gaul
But now she's in the family way
And wants me pay an' all.

There followed a chorus. It was ragged at first but gathered confidence:

Sing thank the fuck for Roman roads
They let you travel fast
So debts an' crimes and babies too
Stay buried in the past.

The song faded into the distance.

* * *

Aithne lay on a bed of bracken in the foetid gloom of the Old One's hut. The wise woman mumbled to herself as she poked and prodded the bared belly. Finally she sat back on her haunches and gestured for Aithne to get dressed.

While the younger woman adjusted her clothes, the Old One

took a large swig from her flask. She coughed extravagantly before expectorating into her hand. She studied the result with evident interest and then flicked it into the fire. Aithne knew the Selgovae healer too well to be moved. "If you can't impress them, revolt them," was one of the Old One's mottos.

Wiping her mouth as she turned to Aithne she said, " Well, thou art two months gone at least."

A look of joy crossed the young woman's face. Seeing no answering emotion in the other she asked, "And is all well, Old One?"

The Old One did not answer at once, merely stared into the gloom of the hut working wrinkled lips over toothless gums. Finally she sighed and said, "All child bearing is un-chancy. Thou mayst do as well as any but mark me well: if thou feel ought strange – ought at all – bloody fluxes, fainting fits – thou must come here if thou can or send for me if not. Dost thou understand?"

Aithne searched the other's face but found only the usual mask of inscrutability. Falling into the patois of the Selgovae she asked, "Dost suspect ought?"

The Old One waved her hand in dismissal but did not meet her eyes. "Nay, child. It is but the vapouring of an old fool who has lived too long. Away with you back to your mighty hilltop."

Still unconvinced, Aithne made brief obeisance and left the gloomy interior for the spring morning.

Alone within the hut keen intelligence reclaimed the features of the old woman. Long ago the Old One had schooled herself not to love anyone in this transitory world, but, despite her resolve, Aithne had crept through her defences. Now she muttered to herself, "What will be will be, you old fool. Go not looking for troubles." She paused before ticking off on her fingers muttering beneath her breath, "Pennyroyal and mallow, parsley of course and buttercup root. Yes, some we have, some we'll find. There is time."

Chapter 11

(Picts)

Three weeks later Lucius sat outside his tent in the sun writing up notes on the journey. A copy of his report would go to the Legate in Eboracum. It was important that it was detailed and, as far as possible, objective.

He flexed his shoulders and gazed around him. To his left glinted the deep estuary of the Western River, the Clota Estuary, winding between half-exposed mudflats. Gulls wheeled and scolded where a group of tribesmen hauled nets. To his right a broad, fertile valley opened between low hills, framing a view of distant, cloud-capped mountains. The marching camp of the Fifth was built hard on the banks of the swift river that emerged from the valley.

"What about Camelon?"

Lucius regarded his companion. "What indeed?" he replied.

Quintus Fabricius, engineer and surveyor, peered earnestly at his friend. "Well, I wasn't impressed by the defences," he said. "I wondered what you made of the garrison."

Lucius considered. The Century had arrived unannounced at Camelon fort and found the auxiliary troops scruffy and ill equipped. "I'd say that the commander has an arrangement with the local chief. Even on Legion scales of building materials you don't get that kind of disrepair. As for the arms and uniforms…"

Yes, Camelon was in for a shock. There would be a surprise inspection and audit. Lucius would take no bets on the prospects of the indolent commander. The fort was of some strategic importance guarding, as it did, the broad ford where the Via Domitiana crossed the Eastern River. He wondered whether the appointment itself had been the result of corruption.

Lucius spied the tall figure of Josephus making his way towards them through the ordered lines of tents. He rose to meet the trader. "Good morning, Josephus. Are you ready?"

"Good morning, Lucius, and you too, Quintus." He touched his brow and breast. One of the special qualities of the Syrian was that he took time for courtesy. "Yes, the mules are loaded and the road, as ever, calls."

Lucius had volunteered to escort Josephus through the Vale of Leven, the wide valley leading to the Great Loch. This was not strictly necessary nor part of his duty but he was moved in equal parts by care for his friend and curiosity to see at least the edge of the Syrian's land of piercing beauty.

Leaving the report writing to Quintus, he walked with the trader to where Marcus was mustering the tent group which would accompany them.

"All present, correct and sober, sir," reported the Optio. The eight men carried full packs and weapons. No chances were taken in unfrequented areas such as these. The Centurion shrugged into his own equipment. Finally his body slave handed him the gilded helmet with the tall red plume.

"Keep the scouts and the survey parties at it," he told his deputy. "We'll be back by dusk. If we're not, no heroics. Wait two days and then head for Old Kilpatrick." He named the nearest manned fort.

"Very good, sir," the Optio replied, saluting.

Lucius thought, not for the first time, how lucky he was to have a competent deputy. If there were any justice, Marcus would soon have a century of his own. He raised his head, took in the sunlight and fresh breeze of the new morning then gave the order to march.

* * *

Two hours later he stood on the shore of the Great Loch gazing northwards. Before him, diminishing into distance, lay an enormous body of water bordered by steep slopes of purple and green. Far to the north the loch disappeared into mountains; range beyond range of mountains, their peaks capped with cloud.

Lucius turned and walked a small distance along the stony beach. Wind-driven waves broke at his feet. He looked aloft. Almost beyond sight a pair of eagles wove lazy circles in the blue. He tried to put his feelings into words but failed. Perhaps words could not express this sense of unspoilt continuity, this tugging at the soul. He noted from the corner of his eye that even his hard-bitten escort appeared lost in contemplation.

"Will you break bread with me before we part?" Josephus stood at his elbow.

"Gladly, my friend," he replied.

He gave orders to the legionaries to take their noon break then walked over to where the trader's slaves were laying out cold meats and preserved fruits. Josephus personally selected wine from his stock. "You'd best make the most of this before you return to your legionary vinegar," he said, smiling, as he poured the light, amber liquid into goblets.

As they ate, the Syrian sketched the journey before him.

"The path there," he waved a drumstick to the left of the water, "goes right the way to the head of the loch. That will take us the rest of today and tomorrow. From there you follow a series of valleys westwards to the coast; maybe a week's journey for the going is hard. When we arrive I shall start trading among the coastal settlements."

He took another mouthful of chicken and chewed thought-fully.

"After that I am reliant upon travellers' tales and the vagaries of trade. It seems that if you head up the coast – no easy task because it is riven with sea lochs – you come at last to a great valley running to the north-east. Follow it and you will eventually come to the Eastern Sea. We are talking some months of travel."

Military maps of Caledonia were rudimentary but Lucius could follow the logic of the journey. "That would leave you some weeks march north of Devana, would it not?

Josephus nodded. "Yes, it's fairly easy going either along the coast or through the coastal plain, I believe. Once in Devana it is a matter either of travelling south down the Via or, if the luck's in and the trading has been good, taking ship. Either way I would hope to return to Trimontium before the first snows."

Lucius watched a group of wading birds dipping in the shallows as he pondered what he had heard. At last he said, "It's hard to believe, Josephus. Shortly you will set off up that track with three slaves and six mules. Now, I know that you lack not courage but if I set off, like you, on the same track with a fully armed century, I would be afraid. I go further; I would not expect to survive more than three days. So tell me: from whence comes your assurance?"

Josephus laughed. "My friend," he said, "consider the flight line of bees, to and from their hive. If you walk into it feeling afraid or aggressive, the bees sense this and they will attack. Consider, now, the bee-keeper. He opens the hive, albeit wearing protective clothing, and the bees know him."

The trader laid his hand on his chest. "I am the bee-keeper. The Picts know that I trade and therefore offer me no harm. One village tells another that I am coming and my approach becomes an open secret. You will say that even the bee-keeper gets stung now and then and you are right. But manifest confidence counts for much and it is not in the interest of the Pictish nation to allow their rogue elements free rein. If too many traders are robbed or killed, they will cease coming to these parts. Men will be denied their iron tools and weapons but, more to the point, women will miss their ribbons and trinkets."

The slaves were now packing away the last of the dishes after washing them at the loch side. One brought a bowl of water and a towel to his master. Josephus rinsed his hands and wiped them on the towel. He offered the facility to the Centurion who shook his head, smiling. "Thank you, Josephus, but I may wish to lick my fingers on the return journey."

And so the goodbyes were said. Josephus embraced Lucius as a friend then, holding him at arm's length said, "Take care, won't you, my young friend. I may be wrong but my nose tells me that something is in the wind."

The Centurion smiled again at the thought of this old man, alone in the wilds with his slaves and mules telling him, the commander of a hardened fighting force, to take care. "You too, Josephus. May you walk before the wind. May the gods smile on your path. I will look for you before winter comes."

The small group of men and beasts dwindled rapidly until a spur of rock suddenly cut them off from view. Lucius turned to his men who were already buckling on their gear. He checked the westering sun. "Time for off, lads. If we time this right the evening meal will be cooking as we arrive."

* * *

It was a mile short of the camp with the sun throwing long shadows across the path that two small figures rose from the heather almost at their feet. The Centurion recognized them at once. They were Gwyn and Dafydd, the century's two British scouts.

"No go further," said Dafydd, holding up a small hand.

Lucius held up his own arm to stay his troops. He turned back to the scout. "Why, Dafydd; what's the matter?"

"Picts," the small, dark man hissed, sweeping his arm in an arc encompassing the surrounding hills.

There was no point in hurrying the Britons. Their sense of the dramatic was too strong and they loved a tale. Lucius squatted down while his men leaned on their spears. Bit by bit the story came out. The hills were suddenly lousy with Pictish war bands.

The scouts had seen one survey party taken and slaughtered. Pictish scouts, hidden from view, now surrounded the camp. Rather than attempt to warn the camp, the two men had used their initiative to seek out the Centurion and his isolated band. Lucius was thankful for that.

He shrugged off his pack as he turned to his men. "Bassus," he addressed the senior legionary, "take yourselves into the trees there." He indicated a large oak he knew he would recognize again. "Take my kit, post sentries, stay quiet and hidden. I'm going forward to take a look. I'll be back before dark. Password," he thought for a moment, "civis – answer Romanum. If I don't make it, try to warn the camp. If all else fails, head for Old Kilpatrick."

* * *

Lying in the baths; it's crowded; waves; bodies rocking together; Tribune wearing fur robes and bull's horns; "Up Centurion, wake up Centurion, wake…up Centurion." He wakes and lays still. "About an hour before dawn I reckon, sir," whispers Bracchus hoarsely.

The Centurion sits up slowly. He looks around, collecting himself. Thirteen of them crowded into the dell. He remembers the number although he cannot see the others. Just before dark the scouts brought in the other survey party. The four engineers were badly shaken.

He runs through the plan in his head.

The camp's warned. Gwyn slipped across the open ground to the gate in the dark. So Marcus knows what to do. With the Centurion are twelve fighting men. The engineers are lightly armed but have basic infantry training.

The dell is three hundred yards from the camp, looking across open ground to the gate. He had found it with Dafydd just before twilight. It is the closest cover to the camp. The scouts guided the others here in pairs after dark.

The two Britons had reported Picts massing in the woods half a mile to the east. His group could probably have made it to the camp but the plan is now set. He takes a sip from his canteen. "Wake the others quietly," he orders Bracchus then crawls to the lip of the dell beside one of the sentries.

"Anything?"

"Thought I saw some movement off to the left just now, sir, but can't be sure. It's black as Hades. The Brits are out there somewhere."

Lucius crawls back into the dell. He gathers his men around him where the sentries can hear and runs through the plan again. As he finishes he hears the whispered password and response. A small figure slips into the dell from the rear.

"Many Picts," whispers Gwyn, pointing to the east, "They short time. Come this way." He uses his hands to show them moving on the camp. Britons don't do numbers but the information is enough. There is a slight lessening of the dark.

"Right. Relieve yourselves. Eat, drink then make ready. Remember: swords, shields and spears. The packs stay here. We'll recover them if we can. You have fifteen minutes."

The packs are a sore point. Legionaries are as wedded to their packs as to their women – more so probably. But they won't move fast enough encumbered and that's an end of it.

Back on the rim of the dell he chews a hard biscuit. He can make out the skyline now. There is a flurry of movement. "Civis." "Romanum." Dafydd wriggles into the dell. "Picts stop. They round camp here to here." He indicates the three sides of the camp away from the river.

"Well done, Dafydd. You and Gwyn go up hill now. You know what to do?"

"Yes, Lord. We watch. We go."

The Britons will watch to see what happens then make their way to Old Kilpatrick whatever the outcome. It may make the difference for the beleaguered Fifth. They stand, bow and are gone.

"You can see 'em now, sir," breathes a sentry. Lucius squints, using the edge of his eyes. Yes: there is a darker mass against the heather. He hears his men crawl into position around him. Suddenly a horn sounds then another followed by a blood-curdling howl that splits the dawn hush. The dark mass is moving. From inside the camp comes an answering blast. The walls are suddenly alive with men.

"Steady lads: plenty of time."

Spears are flying; men are falling. The Picts are into the ditch, trying to climb the turf walls. Here and there one reaches the top, only to be hurled back. The growing light lends detail. Blood stains the grass. Individual figures crawl and stumble from the fray. The Picts are drawing back, re-grouping. The cornu sounds twice.

"Stand by lads; wait on my word."

The thorn bush gate is drawn aside. Two lines of legionaries – some forty men – emerge. They form in an arc across the gate, their flanks secured by the walls. A roar goes up from the Picts. They stream from all corners of the camp towards the gate like iron filings drawn to a magnet.

Taking his time the Centurion divides the crowd into squares, multiplies, adds: yes, around two hundred. He grunts with satis-faction. The Picts now form a milling crowd before the Roman shield wall. He sees the legionaries hurl their *pila*, spears with soft iron heads designed to lodge in shields, rendering them useless. Other spears are being hurled from the walls. The Picts are now committed. There is a clash of metal as the shield walls meet. Shouting and screaming rises to a crescendo.

"Form on me lads," he says, climbing from the dell. "Remember: keep my pace. Don't want you out of breath. *Pila* when I throw mine then yell and take them in the kidneys." He looks left and right. The engineers look pale. Grotius grins.

"Let's go!"

Running now, leaping heather and rocks, *pila* aloft. One man trips. He's up again. Two hundred yards...one hundred. He balances the *pilum*. Still no one's seen them. He marks out a naked, blue-painted back and throws, drawing his sword in the same movement. He bellows, "Fucking Picts," at the top of his voice; hears the others roaring. A big, bearded Pict begins to turn. Lucius takes him low in the back. The man screams and pitches forward.

Now it is point and shield. Still hardly any Picts have turned. More go down to the stabbing. Stamp with iron-shod sandals. Watch for wounded Celts stabbing from the ground. A small man, teeth bared in blue-painted face, lunges with a spear. Lucius knocks it aside with his shield and stabs upwards between the third and fourth rib, twists the blade and withdraws. Blood and gore fountain as the Pict goes down.

Watch for outflanking. This is the danger point. But no: Picts are streaming away, left and right. Nothing ahead now but piles of dead and the blood-drenched Roman shield wall. The air reeks of blood. Bracchus casually cuts the throat of a wounded Pict; cleans his blade between thumb and finger. "In you go, lads," he shouts as the shield wall opens. He counts as they pass him. Ten; one being supported. Better than he had a right to expect. He follows them through.

"Welcome home, sir." Marcus salutes. They clasp hands briefly.

"Onto the wall." The two rows of legionaries stay in place. Now comes the big decision.

From the top of the wall they take in the scene. Knots of Picts stream and stumble away in all directions. "Count the bodies, Marcus." No sign of any Pictish control yet.

"Around forty, sir, plus the ones in the ditch – probably sixty in all. Is it enough?"

Sixty means at least forty badly wounded too. The decision is stay or go. Stay for a lingering death if reinforcements don't show or make a fighting retreat towards Old Kilpatrick. The retreat is the less unattractive course. It'll be a day's hard march with wounded and battle-weary men tiring fast.

"We'll go. Get them out quickly. Defensive marching formation. Wounded on mules where we can. Fast march 'til we see the situation then forced march if they're up to it." A forced march is run, fast march, walk, twenty minutes each then repeat. It may not be possible.

"What about our packs, sir?"

'Bracchus', he thinks, 'why do you do this to me?'

"Optio, one tent group with Bracchus and pals to retrieve packs." He turns to Bracchus and Grotius. "Bloody run, all the way there and back, you hear me?" They grin.

"Yessir."

* * *

It took perhaps fifteen minutes for the Century to form up outside the fort in an elongated rectangle with the pack mules in the middle carrying three badly wounded men. Much of the time was taken up recovering the pila, essential for breaking up the expected attacks. The sun, now showing above the eastern hills, struck sparks from the dew, belying the scene of slaughter and the stench of blood. Here and there wounded Picts crabbed in agony towards the slope above the camp. The first crow alighted and tore at a corpse. Low moaning pervaded the scene, punctuated by occasional screams.

Lucius glanced up the slope. A scattering of Picts, mainly women, kept a wary distance. The main body had faded into the scrub oak. Marcus appeared at his shoulder, wiping his face with a rag.

"What do you reckon, sir," he asked. "The narrow bit by the crag?"

Lucius nodded.

"I believe so. They'll hope to pin us against the river. I'd reckon about an hour."

Marcus nodded.

"Can we bypass it?"

Lucius considered.

"No. The ground is likely broken and there is scrub oak up there for them to hide in. No, the path it is and we move quickly."

"Well, we're ready as we'll ever be, sir," said the Optio.

The two officers took post within the rectangle and Lucius gave the order to march.

To the Picts, watching from the hill, the formation was an alien thing of iron and sharp edges. They jeered as the Century set off. A few of the older boys ran down to the track and threw stones at the rearguard.

Lucius sorted his options. Three ranks of eight led the formation and the same made up the rearguard while single files of sixteen guarded each flank. In the middle were the officers and the mule strings. The Signifer held aloft the *signum* of the Fifth just behind the vanguard. The Century maintained a quick march. He wanted the men relatively fresh for the expected attack. Time enough for a forced march once they were through. Sunlight sparkled on the river. Gulls cried and a small breeze played with the wavelets. Canteens of water were passed from hand to hand.

"Listen to me," Lucius ordered, his voice pitched to carry.

"They will likely attack front and rear in the narrow place beneath the crag just up ahead. On my order you will halt. The vanguard will form a shield wall under my orders and rearguard under the Optio's. Flanks are the crag and the drop-off to the river. We will use *pila* only if there is time. Ranks two and three at both ends will form *testudo*. We can expect them to drop rocks."

The legionaries are listening intently as they march.

"Rearguard, after the initial shock I want you to withdraw under the Optio's orders to fifteen paces from the vanguard." He turned and Marcus waved acknowledgement. It would be necessary to concentrate the formation ready for the break-out.

"Right file," he indicated the flank nearest the river, "will guard the river flank. It's a steep drop-off but expect at least some of them to try it." The senior decurion nodded.

"Left file," he went on, "will act in reserve. Keep away from the rock face and that goes for the mule string and supernumeraries."

He drew breath.

"Once we have stopped them we will use our weight to push our way out into the open. Be ready to form square if they maintain the attack. We leave our dead."

A sigh went through the ranks. The top of the crag began to show above the swell of the left-hand slope.

"Make ready," he shouted. "Listen for my orders and kill the bastards."

Men hunched or straightened according to temperament. Here and there harnesses were tugged. The warmth of the day brought out the smell of sweat and leather.

The formation entered the shadow of the crag where water dripped and the footing became muddy. Four paces behind the front rank Lucius scanned the far end of the defile as it came closer. Marcus would be doing the same at the rear.

"Steady, lads," he growled. The formation advanced.

Then, wild shouting from the rear. Lucius glanced over his shoulder. A mass of Picts boiled around the far shoulder of the crag, some actually dropping from the rocks in an effort to take the rear guard in the flank.

"Century halt! Form shield wall," his voice pitched to carry over the din.

Marcus had turned the rear guard and inclined the two ranks to receive the shock face-on.

Turning back, Lucius was just in time to see the remainder of the Picts streaming around the eastern edge of the crag some fifty paces ahead. Taking a split-second decision he shouted, "Vanguard, prepare *pila*."

There was just enough space to make them worthwhile. The three ranks reached over their shoulders for the javelins.

"Vanguard, make ready!"

Right arms reached backwards, hefting the missiles. Thirty paces, twenty...

"Vanguard, throw!"

Twenty-four heavy spears flew and the front rank of the Picts went down in a welter of blood. With barely a pause those that followed were leaping and trampling over their fallen, screaming and shouting hate.

"Draw *scuta*. *Testudo*. Brace!"

With a roar and a wild crash, the two sides met. The shield wall was driven back a pace by the impact. Then the slaughter began. From between the shields the short swords of the legions, stabbed relentlessly, the rear ranks giving weight. Tribesmen in the front of the crowd found themselves held against the shield wall by the press behind, unable to use their swords and spears in the confined space. They fell. Some Romans also fell to the sheer ferocity of the attack and decurions hauled them clear, but the wall held.

Now a shower of rocks came bouncing down the crag face, smashing into shields and hitting one of the mules. The beast reared dislodging the wounded man on its back who fell to the ground with a scream. Two men from the reserves leapt for the mule's lead rein. One missed while the other was struck by a hoof and sent flying. The frightened animal dodged around the small space between the shield walls sending men sprawling and infecting the other mules with its fear. Finally, as a mule handler lunged for its halter, it turned and launched itself at the back of the vanguard, knocking the middle files to the ground and breaking the shield wall as it struggled forward. With a roar Picts began piling over the struggling mass of legionaries and mule.

"Reserves to me!" shouted the Centurion, leaping towards the gap.

The two halves of the shield wall were bent inwards. Legionaries still standing fought on but a dozen Picts were already inside the formation led by a large, tattooed warrior, laying about him with an axe. With a war cry of startling malevolence he scythed the axe at the Centurion's legs. Lucius leapt. The haft of the axe caught one of his feet and he fell smashing his shield into the warrior's face. Then they were down, Lucius on top. In the melee of feet he felt for the man's breast and thrust his *scutum* in up to its hilt just under the nipple, twisted the hilt and withdrew the blade. Blood fountained and the warrior died.

Lucius rolled onto his back and, covering himself with his shield, struggled to his feet. Marcus had left the rearguard and was organizing the defence, feeding reserves into either flank of the Pictish salient. Savage duels were taking place but the training of the Romans began to tell. Bracchus and Grotius, shoulder to shoulder and covered in blood, stood in the gap, stemming the flood of Picts. As more men scrambled to their feet and linked shields, the enemy was steadily forced back.

"My thanks, Marcus," shouted Lucius. "I'll take it now. Get ready to move out."

Marcus smiled, saluted and headed for the rear.

Lucius looked left and right. The shield wall was reformed and the Picts had pulled back a few feet, snarling defiance, winding themselves up to attack again although there were many fewer than before. At this moment the mule, which had been knocked over by the weight of the battle, staggered to its feet and barged into the Pictish line in an effort to escape. Several tribesmen went down before someone cut its throat but it had disorganized their line and Lucius grasped the moment – that instant upon which every battle hinges.

"Fifth Century will advance!"

With a roar the vanguard stepped forward, shields linked, rising over the ridge of bodies to their front. Lucius glanced over this shoulder to see the rearguard retreating steadily in the face of sporadic opposition. More rocks rained down but the Century was on the move. The Pictish war-band fell silent. They had already lost almost half their number since dawn. Their idea of fighting involved wild charges, acts of suicidal bravery and brutality. They were unmanned by the inhumanity with which the Romans fought.

At first they backed away. Then they walked. Finally, without a word spoken, individuals broke into a run and the band dispersed back up the side of the crag and into the scrub oak.

* * *

The day wore on. It was hot. The men were weary. Water was in short supply. A dozen wounded now limited their pace. There had been no forced march. Seven men had been lost. No major attack had developed. Instead there were haphazard attacks from the rear. Lucius judged them to be the work of young men wishing to prove themselves but, even so, they slowed the march as the Century was halted and the rearguard turned to beat off the attackers.

Twice the formation halted as wounded men died. One passed in a welter of blood, soaking the mule carrying him. The mule panicked, lashing out, evoking laughter and jeers from the Picts. The dead men were stripped of weapons and armour then left by the side of the road where the Picts hacked and stabbed at them, whooping with glee.

Lucius turned and gauged the height of the sun above the western hills. Three hours of daylight left he reckoned. At this rate they would be lucky to reach Old Kilpatrick before dark. A night in the open would be suicide. He found himself thinking of bees and bee-keepers. He smiled bitterly. Josephus had the right of it.

Screams rent the air as another attack developed. He gave the order to halt and joined the rearguard as they turned to face a crowd of thirty or so spear-wielding Picts. Then, for a moment, he thought he was hearing things. A *cornu* was sounding from somewhere to the east. The attack faltered. He turned. Coming over the nearest ridge at a run was a half-century, signum to the fore.

"Thank you, Mithras," he muttered under his breath.

The fresh troops streamed past the main body and halted abreast the rearguard. Lucius recognized the centurion as Julius from Old Kilpatrick. Julius saluted and shouted, "By your leave?" gesturing to a squad of Scythian archers. "With pleasure," shouted Lucius.

The first flight of arrows took the Picts by surprise. The second mostly fell short of their fleeing backs.

Chapter 12

(Eventide)

It was hot at the gate of the hill fort. There was no breeze. The humming of bees in the heather soothed the air. One of the guards yawned. At this rate he wouldn't make it through to the noon meal. He turned and stomped his feet, gazing back into the camp.

There was the Lady's vegetable patch – harmless work for one of the nobs, he supposed. Not much else to do with her bastard foreign husband away. No one around; she'd obviously gone up the huts. 'Tell you what,' he thought, 'a carrot would go down well right now.' His mate was leaning against his spear dozing. He wouldn't mind anyway.

The guard sidled across the turf, then – 'Funny,' he thought. The Lady was there but she was crashed out among the plants. Intrigued, he sidled closer. It was then that he saw the blood.

* * *

The pain is back. There was the buzzing and then nothing and now the pain is back. Aithne gasps and hunches into it. She feels stickiness down her legs.

What is the Chief Advisor doing here? Is this part of the same dream. She groans and rolls her head. What is he doing? Something with white feathers. He's chopping the air around her with feathers. They make a fluting noise.

Pain knifes at her stomach. Buzzing turns to roaring. She passes from consciousness.

* * *

Sweat beaded the brow of the Chief Advisor, sweat caused in

equal parts by the stuffy closeness of the hut and panic. He sliced the air above Aithne's head with the flight feathers of a swan.

"Thus we cut away the evil humours surrounding the stricken one," he told the Lady Innogen. In truth he had no idea what ailed the girl and wished the Lady would go away. At least then he could consult one of the women versed in midwifery. For the moment, however, it was more important to show complete control.

"Can you not do something for her evident pain?" asked Innogen.

The Chief Advisor consulted his internal medical lexicon. "Not for the moment, my Lady. For now it is essential that the patient remains as conscious as possible. Thus she will aid the therapeutic effects of the cleansing."

* * *

She is talking to the Old One. The old woman is looking up at her. "Come, please, Old One," she cries. "It hurts; it hurts terribly…"

…the pain. Oh! She doubles up and gasps. Her mother comes into view upside down. With the hand that is not holding her agony she gropes for her mother. She grasps her hand and whispers, "Please, Mother, send for the Old One. She knows what to do. Please…"

Innogen smooths her brow. "There, child; you don't know what you are saying. We don't want that dirty old woman interfering. The Chief Advisor knows what he is doing. He will make you well."

Aithne tries again. "Please, Mother…" but the pain and the buzzing take her away once more.

* * *

The Old One peered intently at the smoky rafters. She cocked her head, listening. Then, cursing, she stumbled to her feet using her stick. Going to the door she stuck her head out and shouted, "Boy!"

A Selgovae stripling peered from a lean-to.

"Get the donkey, boy, and quick about it."

Returning to the hut she fumbled among baskets and flasks. Not for the first time she cursed the degradation of sense and intellect inseparable from old age. There, she thought; she had it all. Flasks, leaves, roots and powders all packed into an old shoulder bag. She returned to the door.

"Come *on* boy; where art thou?"

The lad came into view leading the donkey, alternately tugging its bridle and beating its hindquarters. Two passing men were co-opted to hoist the old woman onto the animal's back while the lad held things steady.

"Now, boy, get me to the Votodani fort. Thou must go quickly without killing me. Canst do that?"

"Aye, Old One," the boy replied, carelessly, and so began the Old One's last journey, a journey which was to pass into Selgovae folklore.

* * *

High on the deck of the signal station, the decurion leaned on the railing.

"What'd they say?" Soutra Law had just been signalling.

"Fifth's on its way south. Should arrive tomorrow," replied the young signaller.

The decurion grunted. "Pass it on to the camp, then," he said.

* * *

The sun was well down the sky as the donkey stopped outside

the gates of the hill fort. The Old One all but fell from its back into the arms of the lad. For some time he held her upright. Then, recovering somewhat, the old woman beat at his hands.

"Let be, boy. I'm not so feeble yet I canna stand on my own."

The gate guards gawped at this visitation. Leaning heavily on her stick and followed anxiously by the lad, she made towards them. Automatically they crossed spears to bar her way.

"Out of the way, fools. I have business within," she cried, waving her stick. They wavered. She might have forced entry had not Eoghan, the chief's champion, been lounging within. Now, pushing upright from the wall with his foot, he strode forward. He brushed aside the spears and stood before the Old One, hands on hips.

"And what business might that be old woman?" he asked.

"None of yours," came the tart reply. "I am needed, that is all thou needst to know. Now stand aside."

She made to step around the big man but he moved to bar her way.

"Listen, hag," he began, "a civil tongue costs nothing and you are going nowhere without I say so."

Had time not pressed, the Old One would have indulged herself. As it was she hooded her gaze. Bowing her head she said in a humble voice, "I am but a poor old woman. I go where I must to help where I can. There is one within who needs that poor help. Wilt thou send within, sir, and ask that I may enter?"

Slightly mollified the champion turned to one of the guards. "Get within and tell the Lady Innogen that the Old One of Black Hill is here."

Some minutes later the Lady Innogen stormed from the inner gate.

She glowered down at the Old One. "What do you want, old woman?"

The Old One had her anger well in hand. "Thy daughter is dying from the unborn child within. The child must come out or both will die. I have here herbs which will accomplish this. Wilt let me through please?"

Innogen gazed down her nose at the Old One. "What need have we of your foul potions, witch? she spat. "We have a healer of stature, trained in the groves of Mona. He heals by the virtues of the Sun. Take thy moon-filthy nostrums and go hence."

The Old One looked up. Innogen felt the piercing gaze searching her soul. "Even thine own daughter," hissed the Old One. Then, defiantly, "I will stay here without thy gate, proud lady. Shouldst thou change thy mind before the end, send for me."

She turned and limped away.

* * *

Aithne awakes. It is dark. She is floating. The pain is all but gone. It is good. Soon she will be well again. She must get better because Lucius is coming home. "Lucius," she murmurs. She smiles and passes into sleep.

* * *

In the dawn, before the gate the Old One nods, dozing. The lad has persuaded the donkey to lie down and she is huddled against its warm flank. Suddenly she starts awake, staring into the darkness. "Ach no," she whispers. "Dear Arianrhod, no."

She looks over at the lad. He is sleeping soundly. She leaves him be. 'Time enough for the return journey when he wakes,' she thinks. 'All the time in the world.'

* * *

The signals decurion leans on the railing atop the signal station, taking in the sun. A gang of slaves, chattels of the Votodani, are passing faggots of wood up the open hatchway and stacking them around the foot of the fire basket.

"Here, Decurion." The signalman tasked with watching the south nudges his elbow and gestures with his chin. "There's a lucky man."

The decurion turns in time to see the Centurion of the Fifth striding through the gate of the fort far below. He turns to the signalman. "Whether he's lucky or not, my lad, if you don't keep your fucking eyes on Rubers Law, I'll have the skin off of your fucking back before sunset."

Chastened, the young soldier resumes his watch. The decurion returns his gaze to the Centurion. The lad's right, mind. That's a prime bit of Celtic crumpet he's got down there.

"Wouldn't have thought he's that lucky." One of the slaves has paused in his work, wiping his brow. The decurion considers another rebuke but curiosity overcomes his natural violence.

"What'd yer mean," he growls.

"Well, she snuffed it this morning, didn't she?"

The decurion grabs the slave by his arm. "What!"

The slave becomes flustered. "I thought everyone knew. She's been ill this last day or so. She just, like, died, somewhere round dawn."

Just then, from below, rises the howl of a man in agony. It resolves itself into the one word, "Aithne!" echoing around the walls of the fort then fleeing into the wastes of air.

"Hades!" mutters the decurion, flinging the slave's arm away. "Sentius!" he shouts. A signalman pokes his head up the hatch. "Get the other watch out of their pits and send them up here pronto. Tell them they've got the weight until I get back."

"You," he turns to the round-eyed South Watcher. "D'you understand what's happened?"

"Y-yes, Decurion."

"Then get the mule, get down the camp like a rat down a drainpipe an' tell the Præfect. Tell him I'm going down the fort

now. Tell him I think he better get up here quick." He turns to the
North Watcher. "You're with me Vibius. Let's go."

* * *

Aithne's cremation took place near the spot where she and Lucius
had jumped the Beltane flames. She was arrayed in her best green
gown, her favourite necklace of blue beads around her neck. The
womenfolk had washed and braided her hair. Offerings of grain
and wine stood around her in clay flasks. She looked tiny, lying
there on the pyre.

Stepping forward, Lucius unclasped the badge of the Sixth
(*Victrix*) Legion from his cloak and placed it tenderly in her left
hand. Then, impulsively, he laid his vine staff beside her too. He
leant and kissed her bloodless brow.

"Go well, dear one," he whispered, the tears beginning to
flow.

Straightening up he looked around him. Belenus had aged. He
had returned from a trip up river the night after the death, being
met on the road by messengers. The Lady Innogen stood tall and
defiant beside him.

At the Centurion's side were the Tribune, the Præfect, Quintus
Fabricius and Marcus, representing the Fifth. The signals
decurion and Signalman Vibius stood a little to the rear. It was
they who had arrived in time to prise the Centurion's hands from
the Chief Advisor's throat. They had sat with the distraught man
through the long hour it took for the Præfect to arrive and take
charge.

There were no longer any Druids in Britannia; the Romans
had seen to that. Neither was the Chief Advisor in attendance. He
had fled the camp in fear of Belenus. So an elderly greybeard
sang the incantations. At a nod from Belenus another stood forth
with the sacred torch. Lucius watched as the clear flames climbed
the hazel faggots but as the hem of the gown ignited he turned

away. He thought of Beltane. His mind raced like a squirrel in a cage, thinking of everything he might have done differently.

In due time the pyre was reduced to fine, grey ash. The skill of the pyre builders was such that the ashes of the deceased settled in the one spot. As soon as they were cool enough, they would be gathered in a funerary urn. In his grief, barely knowing what he said, Lucius had expressed the intention of burying them in a stone cist on the northern flank of Eildon. He wanted Aithne to look across to Trimontium. He couldn't bear to think of her being lonely.

Belenus and Innogen turned and made their slow way back to the fort followed by the Votodani contingent. There would be a funeral feast as tradition required. The Tribune and Præfect would attend as a matter of diplomatic etiquette. They came now and, each in turn, touched the Centurion's shoulder before turning to follow the Votodani. The rest of the Romans left, some bowing briefly but none speaking. Finally only Quintus and Marcus remained at his side.

"Will you come back to the camp now, Lucius?" Quintus asked quietly.

Lucius took a long, jerking breath. "No, my friend," he said. "I'll just find myself a spot out of the wind and think awhile." Putting on his helmet he set out, straight-backed, for the eastern flank of Eildon without looking back.

When, from afar, they had seen him settle in a sheltered nook, Marcus and Quintus stood watch over him for the rest of the day and the following night.

Chapter 13

(Moonrise)

The brass buckle of the heavy campaign cloak cut the slave's cheekbone deeply. The helmet he caught before it slammed into his chest.

"Get these boots off me, boy, and you, woman, bring me wine."

Flòraidh fled through the curtain while the body slave knelt at the Centurion's feet. Blood flowed down his cheek.

"One drop on my boots, boy, and I'll have the hide off your back."

The boy tilted his head to one side as he worked the heavy boot off his master's foot.

It felt good to be unreasonable and yet Lucius hated himself for it. The slave had given him good service. Unspoken between them was the threat of the lash if the slave responded. This made for poor sport.

Flòraidh returned with a tall flask of the thin British wine. She poured and offered the glass.

"Now get out, the two of you," he snarled.

The body slave touched his brow and scuttled out through the curtain. Flòraidh stood her ground, head down and trembling.

"Did you not hear me, woman? Get out."

Still looking down Flòraidh drew breath and, barely above a whisper, said, "My Lord, this woman would speak."

For a moment rage brought the lees of the afternoon's wine to his throat and he was tempted to lash out. Yet he held back. Before Aithne, before the world changed forever, this woman had shared his bed. They had known tenderness together. He knew her as a person. He owed her better than a thrashing.

"Speak, then."

She raised her head, eyes big with tears, fear writ large.

"My Lord..." Her voice failed her. With a visible effort she started again. "My Lord, the Old One would speak with thee."

A spark of curiosity ignited in his drink-dulled mind. Lucius had seen the Old One just the once in Aithne's company at the squalid Selgovae village of Black Hill, two miles north of the Trimontium. He had never spoken to her but was quite clear that she neither cared for him nor approved of his marriage to Aithne. The Old One could best be termed a spiritual leader of the Selgovae, that troublesome, unlovely tribe, and, as such, unlikely to seek anything from the military administration. And, even if she were to; why him? Why not the Camp Præfect or the Tribune?

He wanted nothing more this evening than to drink and fall into oblivion. However the Selgovae were showing signs of restlessness recently. If speaking with the Old One meant gleaning intelligence then he had a clear duty to receive her, tiresome though it might be.

With a sigh he said, "Send her in then."

Again Flòraidh stood her ground.

"My Lord," she whispered, "the Old One would have you see her alone at her hut this night."

"What?" he shouted. "Woman, are you mad? Do you expect me to walk two miles in the dark with the risk of death behind every tree at the whim of some deranged, old biddy? How came you by this message?"

The maid flinched, tears now filling her eyes. "It was given me at the market this morning, My Lord. I knew not the messenger but guessed him to be Selgovae. The message was very clear. My Lord, be not angry with me. I could do nothing more than pass the message and risk your anger. Had I not, the Old One...the Old One would..."

She choked on her tears, standing now in abject misery awaiting punishment. Indeed the Centurion was by now incandescent with unfocused anger which demanded release. Yet again, with great difficulty, he stayed his hand. His anger, seeking another outlet, seized upon the message. Its purpose was clear to him. The Selgovae wished an easy target for assassination and thought him fool enough to offer them one.

"Well, dammit," he muttered between his teeth, "why not?"

Flòraidh watched with mounting alarm. She loved this man although she could never tell him. Now she watched him spring to his feet and pace back and forth. Suddenly he stopped and shouted, "Boy, campaign cloak, boots, sword and long knife, now!"

Within moments the body slave blundered through the curtain, his arms full of equipment.

"Clothe me, boy, and hurry!" He flung himself into a chair, thrusting out a foot.

In two minutes he was shod and armed, his leather campaign cloak over all. Greatly daring the body slave ventured, "Would you have your helmet and shield, my Lord?" but he was speaking to the Centurion's back as he swept from the room.

Maid and slave looked at each other in mute anguish.

"Oh, Flòraidh, what have you done?" said the slave. "They'll kill him, and then what d'ye think will happen to us?"

The maid dissolved into tears of misery again and sank down on the hearthstone.

* * *

Lucius strode up the sloping path towards the North Gate. The last of the twilight lingered in the far west, palest ochre seen through a tunnel of storm clouds. Gusts, outriders of the coming storm, caught at the cressets on either side of the gate, causing them to flare.

The two sentries at the North Gate, veterans sharing a quiet duty, saw him at a distance and straightened up. As he approach they crashed to attention and executed perfectly co-ordinated salutes. The Centurion returned their salute with an air of distraction and strode on.

After a pause one of the sentries murmured from the corner of his mouth. "Old Man of the Fifth, wasn't it? What's eating him, then?"

"Dunno," said the other and then, after a moment's reflection, shrugged. "Officers!" he said, his voice heavy with world-weary disillusion.

Within the ramparts was ordered stillness. With the work of the garrison's day done, only a few duty personnel were to be seen. Even the wind made little disturbance as yet. Cressets tended by slaves throughout the night lit the roadway at regular intervals. Lucius skirted the headquarters' building and turned left onto the road towards the East Gate. The gate's watchtowers stood black against the cold, clear luminescence of the full moon, as yet hidden behind Bemersyde Hill. Closer to home, first the lights and then the sounds of the Eastern Vicus made themselves known.

Tonight two centuries in transit, one travelling in each direction, occupied temporary camps in the field between the vicus and the road. Early though it was, off-duty legionaries were already slaking the thirsts of a long march. As he approached the gate the guard, charged with keeping the peace, was parading. The Guard Commander, catching sight of him, called the guard to attention, whirled to the front and delivered his own crashing salute. Again the Centurion returned it automatically and strode on.

Much license was allowed troops in transit since Trimontium offered the only half-civilized comforts for miles along the trunk road. Troop commanders knew well the advantage of allowing their men to let off steam here, the better to have them in hand for the next section of their journey. Indeed, it would be a misguided tribune who tried to deny his men their wild night off. A centurion would never make that mistake. Legionaries, especially *en masse*, had their own ways of making their displeasure known.

Garrison guard commanders had specific orders not to arrest without strong provocation. Familiarity with their policing task had made diplomats of all but the most intransigent. Similarly, legionaries, except the most obtuse, knew within a whisker, even in their cups, where license ended and crime started. The threat of the lash was a great aid to memory. Thus the nightly mêlée of the Eastern Vicus, although threatening to an outsider, was generally harmless. Lucius was politely ignored as he passed through the crowds.

Beyond the last drinking booth lay darkness punctuated here and there by the watch fires of the transit camps. Scattered sentries peered over the ramparts with varying degrees of vigilance, cursing the luck that had made them duty on this of all nights. The Centurion followed a wide track that glimmered faintly in the backwash of light.

At the point where the track joined the trunk road stood a young sentry in a turf guard post, gazing nervously into the dark. Not for the first time he pondered his purpose here. Of everyone in Trimontium tonight, he was the most likely to have his throat cut by marauding Celts. He had just concluded that he was there to die noisily, thus alerting the camp, when he heard a footstep behind him.

Grasping his spear he spun round. "Vulpes," said a voice from the darkness. For a long moment he couldn't remember the reply; then it came. "Canis," he tried to shout, his voice rising to a squeak. As he did so he recognized the Centurion of the Fifth and tried to execute a salute with the wrong fist, dropping his spear in the process.

"Pay attention, lad. I could have killed you three times over," barked the Centurion. Then he was gone down the slope of the road into the valley. When he stopped shaking, the sentry picked up his spear and wondered why he was more frightened of his own officers than the enemy. Years later, himself a centurion, he would smile at his naivety.

The bridge over the River Tweed was of strategic importance. With unrest among the Selgovae, the guard had been reinforced to twenty men under an Optio. At the north end, behind a stout wooden barrier designed to obstruct an attack, four men in full combat gear gazed into the darkness, spears in hand. Six more were spaced three to a side along the bridge parapets, watching the banks and the river. The remainder waited at the southern end, ready to form a shield wall across the bridge if required. The night was full of the sound of rock and water.

The Optio, an experienced soldier, allowed no lights, preferring to depend upon full night vision. He also knew the value of checking behind him regularly. Thus it was that he caught movement out of the corner of his eye and had turned, hand on sword hilt, before Lucius arrived at the bridge.

"Vulpes."

"Canis."

"Approach friend."

The Optio recognized the Centurion of the Fifth but instinct told him that all was not well. The Fifth weren't on duty tonight and the Centurion was neither in full uniform nor accompanied, both of which he would be if he were making an inspection. He didn't know the Centurion well but camp gossip had it that the man had taken his wife's death badly. What he could see of his face in the faint backwash of moonlight disturbed him.

"Good evening, sir," he said. "May I be of service?"

Lucius was silent for a moment. In truth he had come this far without a plan for passing the bridge guard.

"A word in private, Optio," he said, moving away from the other men towards the verge of the road. The Optio followed him.

"Optio, this is just between the two of us. I have orders from the Legate, secret orders, to visit our agent at Black Hill tonight.

I will be gone four hours, no more than five. Warn your men to be alert for my return and to say nothing. Lives are at stake."

If they had an agent at Black Hill, it was news to the Optio but that meant nothing. This matter of secret orders though...It was not unknown for patrols to cross the bridge by night but the bridge guard commander was always warned in advance. The Optio decided to temporize.

"With respect, sir, I'm not happy to see you go out there alone. We've word of at least one war band on the loose. Let me send up to the camp for an escort for you."

An escort was the last thing Lucius wanted. With an effort he kept his voice even and reasonable.

"This has already been decided at a high level, Optio. An escort would draw attention to my mission. In any case this is not a matter for debate. I am merely informing you so that you'll be prepared for my return. Now I'm going."

With a swirl of his cloak the Centurion set off across the bridge. The Optio shrugged and followed him, shouting to the advanced guard to move the barrier. He stopped and watched the Centurion squeeze through the gap and disappear into the night. As he returned across the bridge he considered his options. If this became official, it could be very messy.

"Legionary Luca," he shouted.

"Sir." Luca was a bright lad with an enviable turn of speed.

"Strip off your armour and weapons then come here."

In less than a minute Luca stood before him dressed in tunic and breeks.

"I want you to run like the wind to the camp and find the Optio of the Fifth. He'll likely be at the sign of the Juniper Bush. Tell him there's something wrong with his Old Man. Tell him he just crossed the bridge heading out to Black Hill village alone. Repeat."

In the shorthand of the trained messenger Luca rapped out, "Run to camp. Find Optio Fifth. Juniper Bush. Old Man flipped.

Just crossed bridge. Heading Black Hill village alone, sir." He was already jogging from foot to foot.

"Good lad. Like the wind, mind."

"Sir." Luca turned and sprinted into the night.

Chapter 14

(The Old One)

"Well met, Roman."

Smoke, the scent of rancid, old body and worse assailed him. Inside was unclean darkness lit by embers. Dim, atop a bundle of rags, red-lit eye sockets and a hooked nose glowered. This was the Old One, High Priestess and Hag of this village and many of the surrounding Selgovae tribes.

Lucius entered, crouching, dignity impaired. Fear of dirt, darkness and magic twisted his gut.

"Old woman, know that you are dead if I do not return within the hour."

The Old One cackled. Talons clawed at rags exposing the base of her scrawny neck.

"Strike well and swift then Roman; I care not for death." She tapped the hollow between her collar bones. "But if thou wouldst hear something to thy good, aye, and perhaps to the good of others, then spare this poor old body." The singsong voice dripped sarcasm.

There was something magnificent about her lack of fear. The Centurion relaxed slightly and squatted, avoiding the filth of the floor.

"Then speak, oh Wise One. Throw the bones. Tell me how my life might be improved. That should not, indeed, tax your wisdom."

The Old One crowed with delight. "Such wit and from a foreigner."

She sat back. As his dark vision grew he marvelled at the bird-like dignity of the tiny body. Old and verminous she might be but her back was straight. Her filthy, grey hair lay forward over her shoulders in long braids. Her eyes, two points of light, held his without waver. When she spoke her voice was hard as flint.

"Listen, then, Roman. This I am charged to tell thee. Thou are not as others. There be the Many who live and die as ignorant pigs and there be the Few who know. For the Few there is this choice: to serve or to die unfulfilled. Foreigner though thou be, thou art one of these. Thou must choose"

There was silence between them. The wind moaned. The fire guttered and blazed. The hut creaked in the rising gale.

There had been one such as this in his village in the mountains of Tarraconesis when he was a lad – La Vieja. Although the village elders, all men, held council, discussing matters of weight and importance, it was La Vieja who tended the soul of the place. It was she to whom the men deferred in matters beyond grasp, beyond sight. "Women's things," they would say, dismissively, but never in her hearing and they would spit between their forked fingers.

From the age of six it was he who carried his family's tithe – a chicken; a bowl of chickpeas – to her hut at the edge of the village. This was his sacred duty, jealously guarded. La Vieja said little but watched him steadily from the shadows as he grew in stature and in wit. In his seventeenth summer, before he left on the long journey to the legionary depot at Leon, she had sent for him, looked him up and down in silence a full minute and then spat into the fire.

"It is good," she had said. "Thou wilt travel far and true. Go well, boy."

It was little enough but to the young man it had been praise indeed; a real possession. It had told him that he had passed a test beyond the boar-killing or the trial by rock and water. It had whispered of things numinous, things he had learnt from her with never a word spoken.

Here beyond time and distance the thing was spoken again.

He looked up at the Old One.

"You speak in riddles, old woman. I have no time for this. I grieve for she who has gone. My loss fills my mind and gnaws at my gut. This is no time to speak to me of choosing."

The Old One nodded to herself as if in confirmation then leant forward, the ruddy glow of the fire making a mask of her face. Reaching out a claw-like hand, she tapped upon his knee, emphasising her words.

"Mighty leader of pretty soldiers thou may be but thou art, alas, only a man after all with the ears of a sheep and naught in between. It is no part of my duty to cozen thee, Roman. If thou wouldst know more then ask. If thou wouldst not, then thou art free to leave for it is well said 'Strive not to make a bard of a pig for it wasteth thine effort and vexeth the pig.'"

It was rare for a Briton to speak to a Roman other than with subservience and yet this old crone from the occupied nation, to all intents his enemy, spoke with distain. He should have felt anger. He owed it to his rank to react instantly and with violence if necessary. And yet; and yet...

Out of nowhere, hot tears spilled down his face. Uncontrollable sobs racked his body. The Old One sat back in the shadows and watched impassively until the crisis had passed.

"It is well, Roman," she said. "Grief, even though it be grief for thyself, must be lanced ere it poison thee."

Lucius sat, his head bowed, and felt shame. Before his wife's death he had last wept over the body of Flavius, his friend, in the bloody aftermath of their first battle. The other legionaries hadn't jeered but had gone about their duties, dispatching the wounded enemy and gathering their own dead. It was their rough solicitude that had made him vow never to weep again. Yet here he was, respected commander of men, crying like a child. And yet, when he looked up, the face across the fire showed neither contempt nor compassion but rather a keen interest.

He spoke the first words that came to him. "Why do you say 'grief for thyself', old woman, as if I had not grief enough to fill the Heavens for she who is gone?"

She gazed at him, unwinking, for a long moment then spoke.

"Roman, I speak to thee now not as if thou wert a child. Thou may not like what thou hearest but I counsel thee listen and meditate upon it for thus wilt thou begin to learn."

She paused and rearranged her rags with the unconscious grace of an empress. When she was satisfied with the drape of her shawl, she began again.

"There be love between man and woman and it is a good love. It is for the raising of bairns and for when the terror catch thee in night's dark gullet and for when thou becomest feeble and must be tended. Aye, but this; mark this: such as look for happiness in another are ever damned. For there be the lesser agony when the one that holdeth thy happiness proveth untrue. And there be the greater agony when thy beloved departs this earth, leaving thee lost and alone and without solace.

"And this, mark this, Roman: all of us shall know the bite of death, every one; and the only wager is upon who will know it first."

She paused, looking for a moment at the embers, then continued.

"Aye, love between man and woman is a fine thing and with the blessing they may know long years with harvests in the barn and little ones snug in their arms. But also they will know the slow withering; the poignant dying of autumn distilled many times over and at the end but grief and loneliness. And this is all that the Many hope for and all that they receive."

She looked up now, the points of flame dancing in the black orbits of her eyes.

"But there is another love, Roman, one which withereth not; one which is as a blazing star to the candle glow of this earthly love. For although the smaller love holdeth back a little dark for a little, the great love lighteth the whole of Creation forever. There be few who are worthy to tend this blaze, Roman; few indeed. And those that there be must prove themselves worthy."

"For those that would become the true Fire-bearers must

leave behind human love; the solace of a warm body in the small hours. This doth ever daunt those who are called and there be many, indeed most, who creep back to the furs of the bed-space and the arms that they know."

A log shifted in the embers sending forth, for a moment, a jet of pure, green flame. The Old One's shadow, huge and dark, loomed upon the inner thatch before blending back into the darkness.

"But for those that do not, those who prove steadfast and true to the calling, there is a long path of bitter loneliness which slowly becomes the gentle road of solitude, such time as they leave behind their cravings.

The Old One gazed long, then, into the embers. For a while her eyes closed. He thought that she slept and in sleeping murmured, "Aye, for I too was young once."

Then her eyes were on his again, black and glittering.

"Tell me, Roman, of thy love. Tell me of thy woman and the little love that thou shared."

* * *

He was tempted to refuse the challenge, yet there was between them now an intimacy born of honesty and deep emotion. He would speak, for in speaking was solace. He gathered his thoughts. In the manner that he had been taught, the Centurion began with an appreciation, as if he were briefing his legate on the progress of a field exercise.

"We Romans fight without pity or quarter, Old One. That is why we are feared. That is how we rule the world. It is our magic. It is to this magic that I have given my life. As a leader I exercise my will to achieve an aim, nothing more and nothing less. I do this by focusing on what is and discarding what is not. It is the magic and strength of the legions but it comes at a cost. The only joys I knew before the coming of my woman were those of the soldier – drinking, gaming and whoring."

The Centurion was silent for a moment. The harsh planes of his face softened. A small smile of reminiscence came unbidden and for the first time the Old One saw, in place of the stern leader, the man. Unconsciously he selected a twig from the edge of the fire and began making patterns in the ashes which spilled from the hearth.

"On the day I first saw Aithne at the gates of Eildon, it was..." He paused. "I have not the words. Perhaps it was as if a spring of pure water burst from a rock. There was a tugging upon my soul. It was as if I fell into her and, falling, realized that I had been much alone. It was the same for her although she did not tell me for many a month."

"Her eyes held the grey of the Northern skies. Every plane and curve of her body was perfection and when she came into my arms there she fitted perfectly."

"With Aithne I danced again as I had danced in my home village. I sang, not the lewd songs of the Legion but the ballads of the mountains of my youth. She gave to me the beauty of the heather hills and the song of the lark. We found an orphaned fox cub and together we fostered it until it was strong and then returned it to its own."

He looked up from the ashes with a wry smile. "Trust me, Old One; in the old dispensation I would have dispatched it with my spear with never a thought."

"When we became bed mates, it was as though I was reborn. Colours were brighter, sounds and scents more vital. On summer nights, I would creep out of the Northern Vicus, down to the meadows beside the Tweed and there we would make love amongst the wild flowers until the dew of dawn fell. At Beltane, when we leapt the flames, I was the happiest man in the world. I lost my soul in her and she gave it back to me. The circle was completed. I was whole."

"We had a year, just one short year until the fever took her and now..."

He faltered to a stop, overwhelmed once more by grief. When he spoke again it was in a voice harsh with pain.

"Now she is gone and I am a walking corpse. I stagger through each day clinging to routine and as soon as I may I lose myself in drink."

He looked across the fire, his face haggard with anguish.

"Know this, woman; I came here tonight expecting an ambush. I hoped to fight and die for there is nothing left in life for me now. Instead I sit here and pour my heart out to a stranger."

The black eyes across the fire sparkled.

"A stranger am I, Roman? Think thou so? And if it be death that thou seekest..." She paused, seeming to scent the air. "Aye, there is death on the wind. Thou mayst yet have thy wish."

The Old One seemed to think for a moment then leant forward slightly. She spoke, her voice innocent with wonder. "But tell me, Roman, wilt thou really never dance again? Wilt thou no more sing the ballads of thy home?"

Lucius was taken off guard.

"What nonsense is this old woman? Do you mock my grief? She is dead. My Aithne is dead and I will never more dance or sing."

The Old One allowed silence to build for a few moments then in a gentle croon continued, "Nay, but it is a question worthy of an answer, Roman. Pretend that I am an old fool with no understanding. Give me reason, if thou would, why thou shouldst lock away that part of thee because Aithne is no more?"

His analytical brain was at a loss.

"Aithne made it possible for me to do these things," he faltered. "You do not understand..."

"Aye, Roman, but mayhap I do. Tell me this: if one of thy men took a soup wound, wouldst leave him by the side of the road and march on?"

He was immediately indignant. "Of course not. Every one of my men is a trained fighter and of value to Rome. He would be transported on a litter until he could be left with competent care."

"Aye, Roman," said the Old One, "but I said 'a soup wound' and thou knowest that none survive such. Wouldst still carry him with thee, even though he slow thee down; even though he be doomed to die?"

For the Centurion, steeped in the lore of the Legions, there was still no hesitation. "Again, yes, Old One. We do not leave our own by the roadside to die like animals."

"And when thy man came to the end, in pain and fear, wouldst mayhap stop the march? Wouldst hold his hand and smooth his brow? Wouldst speak to him words of comfort until he entered the Dark Portal?"

His mind went back to the bitter cold of a mountain pass in Dacia; to a dank forest path on the German border with the clash of battle a few yards to his rear; to a track by a river in the Caledonian hills . He wondered whether this fey old woman had the second-sight.

In his memory he saw the frightened eyes of a man dying in agony, the manic grip of a hand trying to hold onto this world. He remembered smoothing the brow and speaking the words. He knew how to calm them, to help them make the transition with some dignity. He thought he knew why.

"Old One, if this is what you would have me say, you cannot lead men unless you love them."

For the first time he saw the Old One taken off balance. She blinked. "Dost already know this, Roman? Then thy life has indeed not been in vain. Thou hast some wisdom. Listen, then, for I would give thee more."

She turned, rummaged in a dark recess and brought forth a dirty flask. She took a swig then offered it to him. With an inner shudder, he shook his head. She replaced the flask, belched with evident relish and continued.

"Thou art a man, strong and proud, in the prime of thy life yet I say to thee that there is within thee, as within all men, a small part which is woman. That is the part that would dance and sing. It is that part which soothes a dying comrade. The same is true of woman. She is in small part a man. If thou doubt this, watch thou a mother defending her child."

For Lucius this was new. He listened with critical wonder yet sensed a fundamental truth. If asked, he would have described the care of dying soldiers as a matter of military expediency but he instinctively knew that there was more to it. As for militant mothers, the scar on his left thigh bore mute testimony to the fighting prowess of a Judean woman who had thought her children threatened.

The Old One continued. "Thy leaders, thy Rome would have thee all man; fighting; commanding and giving no quarter yet the woman within goes not away.

"When the woman within awakens, thou seekest a mortal woman and in thy mind say to her, 'Here, woman; dance and sing and give me permission to do so also. In return I will love and protect thee'. And the woman, again without words, will reply, 'Aye, man, this I will do and thou, in thy turn, bring food for our bairns and kill the wolf that threatens our steading'.

"Thus is the pact made for at the last we are lazy and fearful creatures. We would have others do for us that which challenges us most."

A storm gust shook the hut. From somewhere outside came a muted shout and the baying of a dog which ended in a yelp. Lucius rubbed his leg to ease a cramp. Time seemed to have stopped in this isolated, dark hut yet the relentless voice continued.

"If thou wouldst be free of this thraldom then thou must needs make terms with the woman within. Make of her a friend and thou mayst dance and sing at will. Thou wilt not be less of a man thereby; indeed thou wilt find a new richness in thy life, a richness which others will remark and value. And there is this, Roman; although thou may then be content to live without another, thou wilt find thy dealings with women deeper and stronger since thou wilt approach them as companions, not as chattels."

The Centurion cleared his throat. "I hear you well, Old One, but are you then saying that the love Aithne and I bore one another was without worth?"

The Old One shook her head. "Nay Roman; never in life. It was a good love and will endure. Nay, I would never counsel thee forget thy Aithne. And this: grief must have its day. It is mayhap the greatest teacher of all and I would not have thee miss thy lessons.

"Yet there will come a day when, without any betrayal of the love thou bore her, thou wilt think again of these words for this is the message I would have thee carry with thee: if thou undertake to follow the path of the Fire-bearer then thy first task is to make of thyself one whole and balanced man, sufficient unto thyself."

Chapter 15

(Callum)

The Old One falls silent. Man and woman stare into the fire, alone with their thoughts. At length the woman bestirs herself and throws a handful of twigs onto the embers. She sighs.

"There, the message is given. My task is done."

Lucius comes back to himself, surprised that, for the first time in weeks, his gut is relaxed. Almost he feels warmth towards the one opposite.

"Nay, Roman: think it not. Thou and I art enemies and always will be on this earth." She has read his thoughts. "Yet remember: there is a higher life, the one which we see not, and there we are one."

He readies himself to leave but curiosity piques him.

"Tell me this, Old One; you are old and weak. I could break you with one hand and yet you have power. How is this?"

The Old One cackles.

"Tell me this, Roman. When thou standeth on the war meadow with thy pretty soldiers, is thy chin shaved of hair, doth thine armour shine, is thy crest combed?"

The Centurion gestures. "Yes all of these things."

"And dost stand straight and speak with the voice of the bull?"

He smiles at the imagery, "Yes, again."

"And why dost thou these things?"

The short answer is that this is just how the Legions do them but the Centurion thinks on for a moment. He remembers old Glaucus, centurion, retired to the baggage train when the drink got him. Old and paunchy, his uniform a disgrace, his men had scorned him until he had no authority left. Whether they had killed him in a convenient skirmish was a moot point but he was, in any case, long dead.

"I think thou understandeth, Roman." Again that uncanny sense of having his thoughts read. "In our tongue it is called the Glammer. But wait, Roman and I will show thee for thus wilt thou understand in thy belly."

Reaching within her rags she brings forth one claw, fingers tight together.

"Give me thy hand, Roman."

Unwillingly he stretches out his right hand. Into it she places a pinch of powder.

"Dost trust me now, Roman?"

Surprised, he realizes that he does.

"About as far as I could throw you, Old One, but yes."

The old woman nods and struggles to her feet.

"In five heartbeats, Roman, I shall leave the hut. As I sweep the door curtain aside, throw thou the powder on the fire. But mind me and mind me well; whatever happens, thou must then follow me directly."

She bends to the curtain, sweeps it aside. Feeling vaguely ridiculous, he throws the powder onto the fire. There is a blinding green flash. Deprived of sight but mindful of her instructions he feels for the curtain, crouches through it and stands erect.

At first he sees nothing. Then he hears her voice near at hand.

"I see thee, Callum, son of Callum. Dougal, how is thy father's leg? Earchie; is it hunting thou art going?"

Guttural murmurs emerge from the dark. Metal rings on metal. Someone spits noisily. His vision begins to return. Six paces ahead of him stands the Old One, drawn up to her tiny height. Facing her in a semi-circle, torches and spears in hand, are some ten warriors, their faces hideous with tattoos. Storm gusts catch streamers of sooty flame from guttering torches. Flickering torchlight and fitful moonlight combine to create an eerie effect of insubstantiality.

The Old One has left her last question hanging on the night

air. Now a young giant, naked to the waist, steps forward, confronting her. His long hair is plaited in a war braid. He sports a huge moustache. On either arm and at his throat gleam golden torques. In his right hand he holds a war spear, a wicked, functional tool of butchery. At his heel a small dog scratches itself.

"We have no quarrel with you, Old One. We want him," he growls, jabbing his finger at the Centurion.

The Old One gazes at the giant, slowly taking him in from head to toe and back again. The giant drops his gaze. A silence grows. At last she says, in a calm yet resonant voice, "It is well, Callum. It is well that thou hast no quarrel with me. This Roman has been my guest. He has graced my home and now he would depart. Stand aside then Callum that he may pass."

Callum looks left and right, seeking support. He seems to find it for he turns back to the Old One and says, "Nay, Old One: we don't leave until we've spoken with the foreigner. Now *you* stand aside."

Behind him he there is an exchange of nervous glances and an outbreak of shuffling among the war band.

The Old One leans now on her staff, seeming smaller, more fragile. She nods to herself several times as if recognizing a truth long-suspected. She looks up at Callum who now appears to loom over her. The little dog looks up at its master, whines then slinks into the darkness, its tail between its legs.

"It is well Callum son of Callum. It is well. But the Moon, now Callum. Look thou at the Moon. Seest thou anything strange?"

Callum looks up. Moonlight lights his face as storm clouds clears the Moon. An owl screeches near at hand. Lucius sees Callum's eyes widen, a look of horror spreading across his features. His jaw falls open. With a clatter his war spear falls from his hand. Foam appears at the corners of his mouth.

The Old One straightens to her full height. Black and menacing, her moon shadow engulfs Callum and reaches for his companions.

"What, Callum; hast thou nought to say?"

She turns to the others, now huddled in a tight group behind their leader.

"It seems that Callum has nought to say. Will anyone else speak for him? Dougal? Earchie, now? What, no one? Then Earchie, lad; wilt though see Callum home for me? Tell his women to put him to bed with heated stones at his feet and in the morning he will probably be well again. Or there again…It is an uncertain world and who can know what will be? Not a poor old woman such as I." Then briskly and in the matter-of-fact tone of a busy mother, "Now, my lads, stand thou aside and let the Roman go in peace."

She turns to the Centurion and gestures him forward.

"Go well, Roman. We shall not meet again in this world."

She holds his eyes and for a moment he thinks he knows her again across a thousand years and a million miles. Then she smiles with a sweetness that warms his soul. "Glammer," she murmurs.

He steps forward, bows to her, before walking towards the warriors, exuding a calm he almost feels. As he passes Callum he is aware that the Celt is surrounded by an aura of cold. From the corner of his eye he sees ropes of saliva spilling from the slack jaw. The little dog has come back. It is looking up at Callum, pawing at his leg, whining.

The warriors part silently as he approaches. Taking his tone from the Old One he walks slowly and deliberately between their ranks, looking neither to right nor left: Glammer. He passes the last of them and enters the dark grove of trees which leads to the river. Brief intervals of moonlight light his path. Branches toss restlessly in the wind.

As distance opens between him and the warriors he relaxes slightly. Then, as he approached the ford across the Leader Water, he glimpses shadows among the trees. Silently he eases his sword and long knife from their scabbards and begins to calculate angles and distances. If this is to be the fight he has sought, he will make it one to remember. The nearest one to the right will be first with a stab to the gut then he will...

"Good evening, Centurion. It's a fine night."

The nasal tones belong to Marcus, his Optio. Suddenly he knows that he wants to live.

He relaxes and slides his weapons home in their sheaths. Silently, armed figures emerge from the trees. Four kneel on the track facing back towards the village, *pila* butted on the ground, points towards the distant firelight. Two more take up position on either side of him facing the trees. On the fourth side, towards the river, he recognizes Castor and Pollux, the two giant Numidians.

The Centurion draws a deep breath. "I won't ask how you come to be here, Optio, but your arrival is timely."

Marcus looks his friend over. He is relieved to see no signs of madness or harm. Following the arrival of the bridge commander's message, Marcus has been worried sick for his leader.

"At your orders, sir," he says formally, "It's been an interesting night exercise you've set us but we're likely to have company any moment. Suggest we execute an unopposed retreat."

Lucius smiles a crooked smile.

"Carry on, Optio," he says.

Chapter 16

(Post Mortem)

The Legate leaned back in his chair. His black eye patch gave him a raffish look. In fact he was an austere, dedicated soldier, something of an anachronism in a ruling class where military service was seen as a necessary step towards a political career. Like Lucius he came from Hispania. Unlike him he had been born into wealth.

"Centurion, I worry about you," he began. "The Tribune tells me that you have been an effective leader; that the Fifth stands comparison with any in Trimontium. The Præfect bears this out. Yet the Tribune also says that in recent months you have lost your edge. I hear stories of excessive drinking and outbursts of anger."

The Legate commanded the Sixth (*Victrix*) Legion from Eboracum. He had come north with the Emperor who had been inspecting the Wall and was now at Trimontium. This was only the second time that Lucius had met the Legion Commander.

"It goes without saying that you have my sympathy over the death of your wife." The Legate's voice softened. "I've been there too, Centurion. It was years ago but you don't forget." He paused, then went on, in clipped tones. "However, I am concerned here with the good of the Legion first and your interests second."

He leaned back, picked up a wax tablet and examined it for some moments before replacing it.

"The Emperor has asked me to recommend an officer for detached duty. He has given me certain … parameters. I believe that you fit them. I also believe that your best interests would be served by leaving Trimontium. I am inclined to put your name forward. Your comments?"

Lucius was taken aback. Since Aithne's death his command of

the Fifth had been his anchor. To leave it was to be cast adrift. And to leave Aithne…no longer to visit the small grave on the flanks of Eildon, no longer to sit and talk with her…

"Legate," he started, unsure how to continue. He tried again. "Legate, if I have not given satisfactory service…"

The Legate shook his head. "Understand me, Centurion; I believe that you are an officer of exceptional talent. You are the youngest centurion in this Legion and that alone speaks volumes but no one is indispensable." He ran a hand through his thinning hair and leaned forward again, placing his elbows on the desk. "It is time to move on, Centurion. You will not serve Aithne by remaining here and grieving."

Hearing his wife's name on the lips of his austere commander Lucius felt a barrier break. The sense of things unseen moving slowly forward which had come to him in the hut of the Old One, returned with renewed force. Clearing his throat he heard himself say, "My Lord, if you think that I can best serve the Empire in this manner, then I am content."

"So be it," said the Legate. "I will arrange for you to meet the Emperor."

* * *

The Emperor Hadrian and his retinue had taken over the government lodge in the Western Vicus. The Praetorian Guard who protected him had annexed the entire enclosure within its earthen walls. The garrison was thus denied access to the bathhouses. Black jokes were doing the rounds about the increasingly bad smell.

Lucius waited in an anteroom with the Legate. He tried not to feel nervous but it was difficult. Meetings with emperors, so he had heard, were at best chancy. At worst they could be fatal. He tried to recall all he knew about Hadrian.

Unlike many of his class the Emperor had taken his soldiering seriously and fought in several campaigns. There had been talk after the death of Trajan, his predecessor; talk of murder – but, then, there almost always was, following a succession. After nearly five years of firm rule such talk had mostly died away.

Hadrian had secured his power base by scouring the civil service ruthlessly. Rome was now run by an efficient, loyal administration freeing the Emperor to travel. His priority was to stabilize frontiers that Trajan had over-extended. That was why the Wall was being built. It was a strategic device. Caledonia was still a Roman province beyond the Wall but if worst came to worst, it could be abandoned without the loss of the rest of Britannia.

The door to the inner room opened. "The Emperor will see you now," murmured a chamberlain. Together the soldiers entered, helmets beneath their arms. Behind a desk in a pool of lamplight the Emperor sat signing documents passed to him by a clerk. To his left a map of the Empire hung from a wooden frame. Lucius halted before the desk with his Legate and the two saluted. "Hail Caesar." For a moment Lucius felt a sense of unreality. He was in the presence of a man-god. Before him was the focus of Rome and therefore the entire Universe.

Hadrian signed a final document, waved away the clerk and looked up. "Sit," he said, gesturing with his stylus at a pair of folding campaign chairs. They sat. Lucius saw before him a handsome man of early middle years with dark, curly hair tending to grey. A short beard partially hid a prominent scar on his chin. Lucius sensed a firmness of resolve, a quiet competence.

"So, Metellus," Hadrian addressed the Legate, "this is the man?" He turned his gaze upon the Centurion. He saw a soldier like a thousand others, created in the mould of Rome. The Emperor noted the nervous movement of the soldier's laryngeal prominence, belying his composure. He trusted the Legate's judgement but had yet to be convinced that the Centurion was sufficiently stable to be of any use. An angry alcoholic pining for his wife was not what he sought.

"Centurion Lucius Terentius Aquilina, my Lord, Hastatus Prior, Fifth Century, Tenth Cohort," the Legate said. "I believe he fulfils your requirements. As ordered he has not been given details of the task."

"Thank you, Metellus. Would you be so good as to wait in the anteroom? I will speak with the Centurion alone."

The Legate stood, saluted and left the room.

Hadrian snapped his fingers and a slave entered silently with a crystal flask of wine and two glasses. While he poured, the Emperor tapped together his fingertips, studying the Centurion. The slave handed Lucius one of the glasses then left as silently as he had entered.

"Is your Optio ready for command?" The question was chosen to put the man off balance.

Without hesitation Lucius replied, "Yes, my Lord; he is a very able man." If he was going to be relieved of command, he would in no way prejudice the chances of his successor.

The Emperor nodded. So far was so good. The answer was free of prevarication. "You will understand, Centurion, that my first priority is to secure the frontiers. This can only be done with first class Legions. If by removing you I had weakened the Fifth, another way would have had to be found."

The Centurion relaxed a little. "My Lord," he said.

Hadrian turned in his chair and gestured at the map. "The Empire, Centurion, staggers on the edge of disaster." A thin smile touched the corners of his mouth. "Please don't quote me." He contemplated the map. "The Dacian expedition and the Persian venture achieved little but to bring dangerous tracts of land and disaffected populations within our boundaries."

The Emperor was speaking of his predecessor's expansionist policies. At the time the Legions had loved Trajan's successes but with hindsight it was clear that he had achieved little at great expense.

"In doing this," Hadrian continued, "we withdrew Legions

and therefore the rule of law from elsewhere. Caledonia is one such area. Trade was interrupted and, worse, subject races have learnt that we are not all-powerful. We also drained the treasury for little gain."

He reached out for the tall, crystal goblet on his desk and took a sip of wine. "Tell me, Centurion Terentius, if you were me, how would you proceed?"

Lucius met the Emperor's gaze then looked down. So…a test: but what was this about? Well, he had little to lose. What if he made of it a tactical exercise; pretend the enemy was the Selgovae and the Empire just the Tweed Valley? Then it could become just another military appreciation on a wider scale. Taking his time, as he had been taught, he revolved the factors in his mind. The aim; define the aim.

"The aim must be the continuance of the Empire, my Lord," he began slowly. "In essence that is a matter of finance under-pinned by politics and trade."

Hadrian nodded his approval. "Go on," he said.

Lucius spoke as he thought, finding the process easier as he continued. "If the treasury is depleted it must be refilled. Without it nothing functions. That means trade. Trade depends upon peace. Peace is a balance between diplomacy and military strength." He paused. "The Legions are over-extended. To raise more would need money which we don't currently have so the boundaries must be stabilized and that, my Lord, you are already doing."

The Emperor placed his elbow on the arm of his chair and propped his chin on his thumb. This was better than he had expected. Perhaps there was potential here. He took a sip of wine.

Lucius was now into his stride. He gazed at the map. "Simply abandoning our new territory is not an option. That would smack of weakness and we cannot afford to reinforce that perception. It would seem, my Lord," he looked at the Emperor, "that we have an inherent instability. The new territories must stay; indeed, we need to trade with them. Yet they are dangerous." A thought struck him. "That, of course, is why you are building the Wall behind Trimontium and Caledonia."

Hadrian gestured for Lucius to continue.

"So we trade and we fill the coffers." Steadily it was becoming clearer in his mind. "We achieve this by judicious use of diplomacy backed up by the threat of the military, always buying time. As trade flourishes and the treasury fills we expand the Legions until our military threat is an actuality. At that point we have stability."

Lucius frowned as he puzzled out the last strands. "It seems, my Lord, that the nub of the problem is how to manage the period of instability. If I were speaking of the local tribes, particularly the Selgovae, I would say that it all depends upon good intelligence."

Hadrian slapped a hand on his desk and chuckled quietly: perhaps this was no wife-grieving drunk after all. "Intelligence. Precisely. And since you have made the case for it so succinctly, I feel confident in telling you what I have in mind."

Hadrian stood and began to pace.

"What I envisage, Centurion Terentius, is a cadre of experienced soldiers who will travel the frontiers and beyond. They will be disguised as doctors, traders, travelling tradesmen, anything that allows them to move among the local populations without raising suspicions. They will be my eyes and ears."

He stopped behind his desk and leant forward on splayed fingertips. "Following your Legate's recommendation and what I have heard today I wish you to be one of these men."

He sat again, taking up his goblet. The night was quiet save for steel-shod footsteps on the ramparts. The Emperor studied his fingernails.

"There is a perception, Centurion, that Emperors, like officers, give orders which lesser mortals then leap to obey." He looked up slowly at the Centurion. "You and I know better though, don't we? If you are to be part of this cadre it is necessary that you both believe in the concept and that you embrace it whole-heartedly. This, then, is your opportunity to decline the offer. If you do, you will rejoin your century and nothing more will be said."

Silence weighed upon the room. Thoughts and feelings flooded Lucius' mind. Yet the sense of destiny that had started earlier in the Legate's quarters remained. A memory of a day in early summer rose unbidden to consciousness. Josephus, the old Syrian trader on the Via Domitiana had spoken of horizons, of a land of such piercing beauty that once you saw it your soul would never again know rest. Lucius yearned for that far land.

"My Lord," he said, "in life and death, I am your man."

Hadrian nodded, well-pleased.

"But, my Lord, may I ask one thing?"

The Emperor frowned. Much of his life was spent granting favours.

"Speak," he said.

Lucius picked up his new vine staff, the replacement for the one that had gone to the Underworld with Aithne. He held it before him in both hands.

"My Lord, may I ask that you keep my staff of office?"

Hadrian pursed his lips and nodded. He beckoned to Lucius to bring the vine staff to him. Lucius stood and placed it in his Emperor's hands. Hadrian examined it. He hefted it then looked at the Centurion.

"You understand, Centurion, that you may never live to reclaim this and, if you do, it may be another who returns it to you. Such is the fragility of life. However, within those constraints, it will be here waiting for you. You may go."

Lucius drew himself up.

"Thank you, my Lord."

He saluted.

"Hail Caesar!"

PART 2

Chapter 17

(Trader)

Trista observed the tall trader with the black hair from the shadows along the top of the wall. It was a tall wall; its upper reaches hidden by the leaves of a cypress. She leaned her arms along one of the tree's branches. Her chin rested on the backs of her hands while she took in every scrap of the scene before her.

She watched the trader come from behind his stall and limp to the middle of the square. He turned, considering his wares. As far as the girl could see the stall contained no food, however her practised eye busily assessed the goods. There were plenty of small pieces that could be converted into money readily enough.

A small wind, carrying the smell of new-baked bread, stirred the empty ache in her belly. She sighed, wriggling her bottom on the hard coping stones. There was nothing to be done until the square became more crowded. The food stalls would be on the lookout for her and the Market Reeve had made it plain that there would be more than a beating if she were caught again.

This was the first time she had seen the tall trader. His tunic was blue – some rich stuff, she thought. He favoured his right leg, leaning upon a black cane when he stopped. She wove stories around him to while away the time. He came from beyond the mountains. He had fought trolls in snow-choked passes, battling to bring rich bales of silk to the plains of Lugdunensis. He was a pirate selling cargoes of spice and camphor wood, rifled from the fleets of the Middle Sea.

Of course she had never seen mountains, far less the Middle Sea. They had been gifted to her upon her father's knee, a small child battling against sleep, desperate not to miss the next wonder. She cut off the memory with the ruthlessness of childhood. Thinking of Father would not help her now. She scratched herself absently. The boughs of the horse chestnuts surrounding the square cut dusty beams from the morning sunlight.

Now a knot of women entered the square from the bridge, bare feet stirring the white dust. In their black gowns and headscarves they looked like crows, she thought. They by-passed the new stall without a glance then broke up into smaller groups, their wrinkled faces set in expressions of dissatisfaction as they picked among the vegetables, breads and cheeses. The vintner decanted wine, pointedly ignoring the newcomers. He too knew the game.

A cock crowed. The murmur of voices grew as other groups arrived. On market day the best bargains might be made at the end but the best produce was to be had at the start.

Unaware of making a decision, knowing only that it was the right time, the girl slid from the wall, holding onto the branch. She dangled for a moment then dropped noiselessly into deep pine needles behind a bush. Bright brown eyes peered through the branches, measuring, assessing. From a battered basket among the pine needles she took a clean, homespun apron, someone's washing she had stolen earlier. She tied it around her waist, covering the worst of her rags. For a few moments she attacked the knots in her hair with hooked fingers, then gave the task up as hopeless. She would have to do.

* * *

The trader known as Aurelio of Tarraconensis (Purveyor of Fine Goods to the Discerning) picked up a small cedarwood jewellery box. With exaggerated care he breathed on it then polished its lid with a piece of velvet. He studied it closely, a slightly worried expression creasing his brow. Not by so much as a glance did he acknowledge the occasional look cast his way. At this stage the game required him to look totally self-absorbed and a little bemused.

Equally, for the moment, two of his slaves busied themselves around the wagon, moving bales and crates, apparently tallying stock. The third, Cadmus, who, with his thatch of blond hair, could pass as a Gaul, strolled the other stalls, sampling stock and keeping half an eye on Aurelio. He wore the clothes of a prosperous journeyman. Tadg, who had some skill as a tinker, had set out on a mule before dawn. He would be visiting the outlying farms making and mending while picking up news.

Aurelio settled the box into place on the stall, stood back then moved it a fraction of an inch. From the corner of his eye he glimpsed two women deep in conversation. They had looked at the stall briefly and one of them had pointed. Time to start. He caught Cadmus's eye, inclined his head slightly then continued adjusting stock. Cadmus sauntered by degrees over to the stall where he studied the wares intently, handling this and turning that. Having moved the length of the stall he pointed to the basket of ribbons and asked, "Do you have these in a darker blue?"

Aurelio looked up in apparent surprise. "A darker blue, young sir? Why, I believe we do. Marcello," he called, "bring me the ribbon samples, the Tyrenian ones."

He turned back to Cadmus. It was a fine day. Yes, business was good. The ribbons were for the young man's fiancée? To match her eyes? A wonderful idea! Ribbons arrived. The two men pored over them, held them up to the light. Comparisons were made; eye colourations known and remembered, shared.

Into this proprietorial vacuum drifted two women, shopping baskets held defensively, noses sniffing disapproval. They surveyed the stock at the far end of the stall through half-lidded eyes, exchanging brief, disparaging remarks. On cue, Marcello appeared behind the stall, carrying a crate. He put it down opposite the women and began to unpack it. Minutes passed. A woollen shawl was handled and dropped dismissively. Murmured words were exchanged then one of the women peered at Marcello and in a peremptory voice said, "You, boy; this shawl; where's it from?"

Marcello straightened, wiping his hands on his thighs. He gave a nervous smile. "Why, I believe it's from Britannia, mistress; woven from the wool of the finest mountain sheep."

"Tsk," said the woman. "Britannia, indeed. And I suppose because it's foreign you're asking the earth for it."

Marcello turned to Aurelio and raised his eyebrows helplessly. Excusing himself courteously from Cadmus, Aurelio came across to the women.

"It is indeed a fine article, is it not? The sheep of those parts grow long wool. It spins a heavy thread which, as you are aware, makes for the warmest cloth. Here," he said, picking up another shawl, "compare it to this Belgic weave. You will notice the difference right away."

The two women compared the weight of the shawls. Their faces gave nothing away.

* * *

From the shadow of the bush, Trista watched the play. Two more women had joined the original pair and Cadmus at the stall. Now three more drifted over, apparently comfortable with the anonymity assured by the growing crowd. Gesture and expostulation turned to pale smiles and self-congratulation as the shawl was wrapped and money exchanged. The proud owner was now showing it to friends and the crowd at the stall had grown to nine.

Trista picked up the basket she had won from the village midden and moved forward at a confident pace. Keeping the length of the crowded square between herself and the food stalls she drifted into the group around her target. She was careful not to barge or give offence. Because she was small for her age she was hardly remarked as she wormed her way to the stall's edge.

What to take?

A pair of soft leather gloves slipped off the stall and under the piece of sacking covering the basket; next, a copper brooch, inlaid with coloured enamel. Around her, conversation rose and fell. The trader and his slave were both fully engaged. She moved a few more steps before spying the glassware. There were goblets and dishes, flagons and cups. One flask, in particular fascinated her. It was tall and elegant. Its neck rose, fluted and thin, to a stopper fashioned in the shape of an eagle's head. The glass was of a delicate blue.

Trista thought she had never seen anything more beautiful. She knew she had to have it. This disturbed her. Her rule was only to steal items she could eat, use or convert easily into money. The flask fell into none of these categories. She just needed it desperately. A quick glance to left and right showed no one watching. She slid her hand forward and grasped the flask.

* * *

Cadmus put down the ribbons and made to turn away. The ruse had worked as it always did. 'Priming the pump' was what Aurelio called it. He would now saunter off into the crowd. Eventually he would make his way round to the back of the wagon where he would change into working clothes and prepare lunch. He took in the animated crowd around the stall, now grown to a round dozen. Just as he completed his turn, movement caught his eye. Halfway along the stall a grubby hand was dragging the Samanian flask across the black tablecloth. Moving forward to open his view he was in time to see a young girl struggling to lift a piece of sacking from her basket and slip the flask within.

"Thief!" shouted Cadmus. The girl looked up, brown eyes wide with shock. She turned, dodging between legs. The flask fell to the ground, shattering.

"Thief," shouted Cadmus again, pushing through the crowd. Heads turned; conversations ceased. The small figure was now in the clear, running for the bridge at the end of the square, the basket hugged to her breast. From the far side of the market the portly figure of the Reeve emerged, puffing and waving his staff but too slow and too late to intercept the fugitive.

She should have made it clean away. She would have but a pair of mongrels, caught up in the excitement of the chase, came rushing from separate cottages. Instinctively swerving from the snapping jaws of one, she fell headlong over the other, her basket rolling away, scattering its contents. Even then she might have scrambled up had not a young labourer, coming from the bridge, dropped his load of hay, run over and secured her by the scruff of her tunic.

"Young villain!" the Reeve, puce about the face, managed to gasp before bending over, hands on thighs, the better to heave air into his labouring lungs. After a period of extravagant breathing he wheezed, "I warned you, girl. You'll go into the stocks for this."

* * *

"Leave this to me." Aurelio patted Cadmus on the shoulder. "Back into the crowd. We may need to start again."

Loud noises and disturbances were the bane of market traders. They ended concentration; broke lines of thought. Aurelio was irritated. He could have done without this. Pushing his way through the crowd he came to where the Reeve was shaking a young girl with one hand while beating her about the back with his staff. The crowd was enjoying the spectacle.

He addressed the Reeve. "What has she stolen, master Reeve?"

The Reeve, jowls wobbling with indignation, pointed to the basket with his staff. Someone had set it upright beside its contents. "Are those your property?" he demanded.

Aurelio, stooping, picked up the gloves and brooch. "Yes, Reeve, they're from my stall."

The Reeve nodded with satisfaction. "Then she's for the stocks. I warned the young varmint; told her she was for it if I caught her again." He gave the child another thump with his staff to emphasise his point. The girl remained silent but big tears oozed down her cheeks.

Aurelio considered. There was little variety in the monotony of life in a place such as this. The stocks would draw a good crowd with little, if any, regulation. Sharp stones would be included amongst the filth. Disfigurement was almost certain, death a distinct possibility. Not worth it for a brooch and gloves, total value five sestertii, he thought, or even a Samanian flask. They could all be replaced.

"Reeve, I'm not minded to press charges. Can we let her go this time?"

A mumbling rose from the crowd at this radical idea. The Reeve, a brutal man in his own right, gauged the mood of the villagers. They wanted their revenge and quite right too. He turned a truculent eye on the foreign stallholder. "Nay, Master. This is a village matter. She's thieved before and look where leniency has got us. It's an example that's needed. Spare the rod and spoil the child," he added as an afterthought, hitting the girl again.

Aurelio too could read a crowd. Raising his voice so that all might hear he said, "You speak truth, Reeve. The girl should be punished. Yet I deem this one to be incorrigible. She is one who thrives on beatings."

There were nods among the crowd. "'tis true," muttered a greybeard, shaking his head. "Young people today – no respect." There were mutters of agreement.

Aurelio continued, allowing a thoughtful tone to enter his voice. "If you would let me, I would take on her long-term...rehabilitation," he drew out the word with a hint of the salacious, "and it is in my mind that she would learn more from me over time than she would from a day being pelted with rotten fruit."

Several throaty, male guffaws arose from the crowd. There was an outbreak of nudging. "Arr, he's got the right of it," opined one brawny farmer. "Go on, Reeve; let un have un," said another. The tension in the crowd relaxed as imaginations took cruel stock of the girl's likely fate.

The Reeve straightened, looking from the girl to the crowd. This was obviously a popular idea. Anyway, it would save him the trouble of guarding the girl overnight.

"Well, Master, I'm minded to agree but be clear," he said, wagging a finger, "she is your responsibility from this moment. When you leave here, you take her with you. If she comes back..." He shook his head portentously.

"I understand completely, Reeve," said Aurelio, taking a grip on the girl's collar. "And thank you for your...understanding." He pressed a coin into the official's hand then turned and marched the girl through the dispersing crowd, followed by knowing sniggers.

Back at the stall Adolphus was clearing up the shards of glass. A knot of people had drifted back to study the wares and more seemed likely to follow. Perhaps the interruption had been for the good after all. Aurelio took the girl behind the stall. "Marcellus," he called, "take over here. Bring in Cadmus if you don't need him. I'll be back in a minute."

He hoisted the girl into the bed of the wagon and climbed up after her. He cut a piece of bread and some sausage and gave them to her. Then he poured a splash of wine and, mixing it well with water, placed the cup beside her. He crouched down, wincing a little as his right leg bent. The girl held the food untouched. She gazed at him with suspicion.

"Listen, little one: you have nothing to fear here. Eat your bread and drink your wine in peace. If you decide to run away, I won't stop you. But understand this: the villagers will probably kill you if they catch you on your own again."

The girl sniffed and wiped her nose with the back of her free hand, never taking her eyes off him.

Aurelio went on. "If you decide to stay with us, then we will take you when we leave tomorrow. At the least we will find you another village."

He eased himself to his feet. "For now, stay here and don't worry. If you need more food, help yourself." He smiled down into the big brown eyes. "If you do decide to run, I would be grateful if you didn't take anything else."

He turned then, lowered himself to the ground and moved out of her sight.

Trista gave him a few seconds then, crawling quietly to the tailgate, peered round the corner. The man and his slaves were busy working the crowd at the stall. She retreated into the wagon, made herself comfortable among the bales and fell upon the food.

Chapter 18

(The Road)

The shadows of the horse chestnuts crept across the square. Aurelio placed his hands in the small of his back and stretched, yawning. It had been a good day. Marketing was not a precise science. For some reason the morning's fracas had brought people to his stall. He had a sneaking suspicion that many had come to see the foreign degenerate who was going to 'teach' the young thief.

Whatever: he could start relaxing. The slaves were making a show of packing up without actually removing anything. It was axiomatic that people would rush to make last-minute purchases as soon as a stall showed signs of closing. Adolphus, who was slow-witted, had taken a while to absorb this lesson. Now, however, his strong arms were busy shifting bales and boxes from one place to another. As Marcellus said, if only they could stop him winking, knowingly, as he did so, he would be perfect.

Aurelio took in the peaceful scene; the thatched houses, the mature trees. He looked around his prosperous stall, at the strong box brimming with the day's takings, hidden beneath the trestles. A chuckle rose, unbidden. Who would have thought – just three short years? And where now was Lucius?

He cast his mind back to that first brush with Hadrian's staff. Heliodoros, a Greek of doubtful gender, had taken him in hand, charged with devising a new persona.

"A blacksmith, perhaps," he had suggested, eyeing the Centurion's biceps. "We would supply you with a mobile forge and all the appurtenances." He minced slowly around the soldier, taking him in from every angle. "Or perhaps a tumbler? Are you athletic?" He made a moué and reached to feel the muscles of the soldier's thigh.

Lucius reached down and took the Greek's hand in his own.

Heliodoros glanced up, delighted but his rapture was short lived. As the Centurion's grip tightened, the Greek's expression changed to one of surprise and then agony. He found himself forced to his knees; felt the small bones in his hand grating against one another. He whimpered.

"It is not unheard of," began Lucius in a conversational voice, "for legionaries of a certain…conviction to make advances to one another. Not unheard of at all."

The Greek groaned.

"Equally it is understood under the Eagles that unwanted advances may be cut short using the sword. This makes them very cautious. Are you hearing me, Greek?"

Heliodoros nodded weakly. "Yes." A tear ran down his cheek.

"I merely mention this, Greek," continued Lucius, "to let you know how lucky you are not to be in the Legions."

He pushed the Greek away and let go his grip. Heliodoros went sprawling then scrabbled across the floor towards the door, cradling his injured hand. Using the doorframe for support he hauled himself to his feet then turned a hate-filled look towards the Centurion.

"You'll regret this!" he spat.

Lucius made to rise and the Greek scuttled from the room.

Subsequently Meridius, the Imperial spymaster, had taken over. "What do you do best?" he had asked.

Lucius could only answer honestly 'soldiering' and that didn't get them much further. However, he admitted a fascination with the business of trading. He mentioned Josephus. Meridius looked thoughtful.

"Now there's a name to conjure with. Many's the time we've tried to recruit him but he won't have it. Mind you, he's dropped the odd bit of information our way on his own terms – good information too. He's in Trimontium at the moment isn't he?"

Lucius said that he was. Indeed, the trader was currently gearing up for his spring departure.

"Well, how about this?" asked Meridius. "You resign your commission, become his bodyguard. Do this year's trip with him. Learn all you can then we'll set you up with what you need – mules, slaves, trade goods – and off you go on your own."

Lucius thought about this. "Can I tell him what I'm doing?" he asked.

The spymaster shook his head. "I'm afraid not, Centurion. If your cover is to be effective no one and I mean no one must know what you are about."

He studied the Centurion, thinking. The Emperor's plan for roving intelligence agents was a good one but Meridius doubted that soldiers were the answer. The trouble was their basic honesty; that and their tendency to look – well – military. Still, he had to try. He clasped his hands on his desk and leaned forward.

"Look, Centurion: you are going to hate much of what you will be doing, at least at first. You will be called upon to lie and cheat. Common legionaries who think you have failed will look down on you. Even your own parents cannot know the truth of what you are about. I shall expect you to wash and shave only occasionally. Your clothes will be grubby and you must, you really must lose that straight back."

He rose and paced to the window, his hands behind his back. He gazed out at the turf wall of the vicus then turned.

"The thing is, it's not just your effectiveness as an agent that will depend upon all this. Your very life will rest upon your ability to play a convincing part. Do you understand me?"

The lesson had been well learnt. As far as he was aware no one but he and Meridius knew that Lucius Terentius Aquilina and Aurelio Silvio Trio, prosperous itinerant trader from Tarraconensis, were one and the same.

Josephus had known at the end, of course; Josephus, his friend and mentor. Aurelio thought of the old Syrian Jew. There was a deep sadness still after three years; sadness and gratitude. He had gone with the Syrian to learn about trading but had learnt much else; about dignity and sacrifice among other things.

He sighed. "Start packing now, Marcellus," he called to the senior slave. "I think we're done for the day." Marcellus raised a hand in acknowledgement as Aurelio turned and limped over to the wagon. The girl was fast asleep in a nest of bales. So she hadn't run after all. Well, time enough to decide what to do with her after the evening meal. First things first: he would give the goodwife at the inn a sesterce to wash and delouse her as well as find her clean clothes.

There being little else to do for the moment he made his way to the bank of the river, downstream of the bridge where the water gate that controlled the mill leat made a comfortable seat. Green weed undulated below the surface. Coots and moorhens dipped and nibbled in the late afternoon light. Gratefully he breathed in the sweet fragrance of running water, revelling in the warmth of the summer. It was all so different, he thought, from that first journey with Josephus.

* * *

Infantry soldiers do not generally make good riders. Lucius had shifted his weight yet again only to find new areas of soreness. The steady rain penetrated everything and the surface of the mule's saddle rubbed relentlessly. He would much rather be walking but the day was drawing towards its dank end and the next inn was yet five miles across featureless moorland. 'Thank gods for proper roads,' he thought. The idea of floundering through mud rather than along good Roman stone setts appalled him.

Josephus eased his mule back until he rode alongside Lucius. "If we're going to have trouble it will be in the valley beyond yonder crest," he said, pointing to where the road disappeared into the mist over the near horizon. The road here, north of Channelkirk, was regularly patrolled but lawless bands still made occasional forays against unarmed travellers. "If they come, our best defence will be a bold front." Josephus smiled. "But I'm sure you know that better than I do."

Lucius wasn't so sure. It was one thing facing an enemy wearing armour and backed by overwhelming force; quite another to do so alone, armed with an unfamiliar sword. Still, time would tell. Ostensibly he was the hired guard protecting Josephus, his servants and his mules. He would do the job to the best of his ability. Nevertheless, he wondered whether he had chosen the right guise.

Here he was, rain-sodden cloak over leather jerkin and the whole smelling of wet sheep. His chin felt bristly. Hair tickled the nape of his neck. Saddle sores were a misery. All in all he felt thoroughly out of sorts and irritable. It was at this moment, as they breasted the rise, that three dark figures emerged from behind a rocky outcrop. Their appearance coincided with a peak of bloody-mindedness in Lucius. As the others stopped, he urged his mule forward, pulling it to a halt when he was some yards short of the largest of the three.

The plan he had in mind was suicidally dangerous – one of several he had idly pondered in preparation for this eventuality. Just at the moment he simply couldn't have cared less. Sliding from his mule he bellowed, "There you are!"

Holding his hands out palms up he marched towards the big man. "I'd given you up. Thought you'd never get here. Anyway," he said, "here they are all ripe for the plucking so nothing's lost." The strangers looked slightly bemused as Lucius swept aside the big man's spear.

"Just one thing though." He had lowered his voice, put his left arm around the man's shoulder and turned him away from his mates, as if about to impart confidential information. The big man lowered his head to catch the Centurion's words.

"Thing is there's a chest of jewels hidden..." At that point he slid the dagger concealed in his right sleeve into the big man's heart. The bandit's eyes opened wide. He gurgled. A bubble of blood burst from his lips. Letting him fall, Lucius reached over his shoulders and swept out the sword strapped to his back. It was a large weapon, totally unlike the *scutum* of the legions. It did not lend itself to science so he swept it in a wide arc as he leapt forward, roaring horribly.

The two men stood their ground for a moment, frozen in horror. Then they threw down their weapons and ran into the rain and growing dark. Lucius watched them out of sight before turning to the fallen man. Josephus came forward to join him as he studied the body.

"Selgovae," said Lucius, turning the body over with his foot. His companion was silent. Lucius looked up. "Are you alright, Josephus?" he asked.

The trader started slightly, as if waking from a dream. "What? Oh…yes. I'm sorry. I was just taken aback by the violence of the whole business." He was silent again, staring down at the body.

Feeling slightly put out Lucius explained. "I had to shorten the odds. I could not have taken on all three. That's why I used guile."

In the face of Josephus's continued silence Lucius began to feel irritation.

"What ails you, Josephus? They robbers are gone and we are safe. That is what you hired me for, was it not?"

Josephus searched his face with keen eyes for a long moment. Then he spoke. "I merely ask myself whether they were indeed robbers."

With that he turned and made his way back to the mules, leaving Lucius alone in the rain, looking down at the dead man.

* * *

The cave was all but invisible through the darkness and the tangle of wind-tossed branches. The merest hint of smoky orange gave away its entrance as the two men stumbled closer. Without warning a large figure sprang from the shadows. It lunged at them, growling, a spear blade flashing briefly orange.

"Let be!" shouted one of the men, stumbling back against his mate. "'tis Cadhir an' Tadg. Let be."

The dark figure growled again but lowered its spear. It gestured with the blade, beckoning the two forward. Tadg thrust Cadhir in front of him before his mate could do the same to him. It was not two weeks since Gol had skewered Gordan under similar circumstances. The guard peered at them from under massive brows then turned and shouted something unintelligible into the cave's interior. Apparently satisfied he turned back and gestured them in with a big thumb. The two men sidled carefully past him, never taking their eyes off the spear.

Instinctively they lowered their heads to avoid the sooty smoke roiling listlessly from the entrance. The cave opened out into a muddy interior, lit by sulky flames. A dozen men lolling around the fire turned expressions of bored indifference to the newcomers. Tadg sketched a salute towards the largest figure who gazed into the fire, scratching behind the ear of a small dog who nestled in his lap.

"We'm back, Callum," he said.

Callum continued to brood for a while then, turning his craggy brow he said, "Wot yer got, then? An' where's Laughlin?"

The two had debated their answer long and hard as they had journeyed through the night.

"Laughlin's dead, Callum. We woz ambushed. We didn't 'ave a chance." The words tumbled from Cadhir's mouth.

Callum hawked and spat. This was not good news. Laughlin had been stupid, true, but a doughty fighter. Their band was already small enough in all conscience. Callum's ire rose although he barely noticed. For him to breath was to be angry. But someone was going to suffer for this. He put the dog down. It padded into the shadows then turned to watch.

Tadg, who was no fool, read the signs. Wetting his lips he launched into their prepared mitigation.

"But Callum, hear me. The old trader 'as a new guard. 'e slit Laughlin's gizzard quicker than that then turned on us. 'e's huge an' there woz at least ten others."

A low growl began in Callum's throat. He was used to excuses. Excuses were all he ever heard. Tadg continued hurriedly.

"Thing is, Master; thing is this new guard, we knowd 'im. It's that Roman wot, wot..."

All at once Tadg was aware that he hadn't rehearsed his wording for this bit. Suddenly he felt exposed and vulnerable.

"Wot Roman?" growled Callum. "Wot fucking Roman?"

"'er...the one wot swived your woman, Callum."

With a speed unimaginable in such a big man, Callum was on his feet. His hand fastened on Tadg's throat and dragged the terrified man's face close. When Callum spoke, his voice was low and even, yet within it lurked sharp teeth of violence. Spittle fell on Tadg's face.

"No one swived no fucking woman of mine, d'ye hear me?" He shook Tadg violently. Tadg nodded as best he could. Lights exploded before his eyes. He couldn't breathe. "But just let's say that one did, what would he look like?"

He dropped Tadg who fell to the floor hacking and whooping. Callum's hand rose and a big, grimy finger pointed at Cadhir. The man gobbled in terror but managed to say, "Big bloke, black hair, used to be one of their high-ups with a red plume. Remember, we seed him at the Old One's ..." His voice trailed off. The events of that night were forbidden territory too. Cadhir's legs gave out and he fell to his knees, eyes closed and hands clasped before him.

When nothing happened immediately, he opened his eyes. To his immense relief he saw that Callum was gazing at the cavern roof, thumping a ham-like fist into the palm of his other hand. A horrible grin spread across his simian features.

"Right you lot. We're goin' huntin'," he growled. "Food an' weapons. We're goin' fast. An' you two," he pointed at Cadhir and aimed a vicious kick at Tadg, "are goin' to lead us." The smile exposed blackened teeth. "An' the Hag help you if you fail."

Chapter 19

(Essene)

The inn, when they arrived, proved to be comfortable enough as these things went. Its low, thatched buildings hunched in the lee of a crag to the west of the road. Having seen the slaves and animals fed and bedded down, Josephus joined Lucius at a table in the common room before a roaring peat fire. Inevitably the evening meal was mutton stew but the wine Josephus provided from his stock made it palatable. He said little at first, allowing the warmth of the fire and the wine to ease away the strain of the journey.

Lucius was clearly subdued and angry. This was their third day on the road and the first time he had been called upon to exercise his fighting prowess in defence of the company. Josephus understood that his friend believed he had acquitted himself well and could not understand his, Josephus', reticence. The message that he needed to impart must be given with sensitivity and care.

When the last of the gravy was mopped up and the plates removed by the pot boy, Josephus refilled their glasses and ease himself back against the wall. Looking into the fire rather than at Lucius, he allowed the silence to build for a while. Then, almost as if speaking to himself, he began.

"I was born in Arbela, a provincial town in southern Syria, lying to the east of the Jordan Valley. It was a good place to grow up. The desert was not far away but our hills were fertile with figs and olives, fields of grain and fat flocks. We paid tribute to Rome and, as Hassidic Jews, kept ourselves to ourselves. We led a life of study and business overlaid upon a cycle of religious observance."

Lucius relaxed and made himself comfortable, leaning back from the bench against the wall. In his mind's eye he called up the dusty wastes at the eastern edge of the Empire.

"My father was a leather worker," Josephus continued. "I grew up to the rich smell of animal skins. It was a joy to watch him at work. He could make the finest gloves from the skin of a kid or a camel saddle from the hide of a bull. From an early age he taught me his skill and I took pride in what I could do."

The old man paused. The ruddy glow from the fire caste his features in sharp relief. He sighed.

"Yet life was never entirely easy. Arbela is a microcosm of the East. On the face of it the town contained every sect and religion known to Man. Always, it seemed, there was trouble. Always there was someone willing to dispute our right to follow our way of life – to exist, even. Often I was chased home by other boys, gentiles and pagans, throwing rocks. Once or twice I was beaten."

"I remember my father taking me on his knee when I was hurt and crying. He told me that I must learn to be strong; that this was the life of a Jew. He told me that I should never fight back. The boys who chased me, he said, were people too, that God loved them and that while it was permissible to hate what they did, I must not hate them."

He half turned to his friend. "Have you heard of the Maccabees, Lucius?"

Lucius who, despite himself, was following the Syrian's discourse with interest, searched his memory. "Were they not Jews who held the Heights of Massada against the Tenth in the last Jewish revolt? Our engineers used slaves to build a great ramp from the plain to the top of the Heights. As I remember it, at the last, before we broke through, they killed each other rather than being captured."

The old man nodded gravely. "They were, in fact, Zealots but did indeed call themselves Maccabees. They were, however, using the name from a much earlier time. Old Rabbi Asher taught us about the Maccabees and I was a good scholar, avid for knowledge. He told us that some hundreds of years before, Syria and Judaea were ruled by a Greek dynasty, the Seleucids. They ordered Jews to worship the Greek gods. Judah Maccabee rose in revolt, the first Jew in modern times to do so. With his followers, he swept the Seleucids from the land and for a hundred years, until the coming of you Romans, we ruled ourselves."

Josephus leaned forward to select another peat brick from the box beside the hearth. He tossed it onto the fire making the sparks fly then dusted his hands together.

"Well, when I and my friends heard about Judah Maccabee," he continued, "we decided to fight back against our tormentors. We called ourselves Maccabees. We would arrange ambushes, using one of our number as bait. We were very successful. On several occasions we routed our enemies, beating them severely. Inevitably a day came when, after a fight, one of the gentiles did not get up. No one could say who killed him. To this day I do not know that it was not me."

Lucius gazed at the gaunt profile of his friend as he looked back over the years. He marvelled that the Syrian could have such a conscience about something that had happened so long ago. He wondered briefly when he had lost his own conscience about such things.

"Anyway, my father was appalled. I was now rising twelve. Although I was not big, I was strong and handy with my fists. More than that, though, I had the mind of a general. It was I who made our dispositions and the other boys listened when I spoke. Father and I argued for the first and only time. He asked me to promise to cease my violent ways. I said that I could not."

"There had long been a tradition in our family that the eldest son would be sent to study with the Essenes of Q'mran on the Dead Sea. Mattathias, my elder brother, had already been there for two years. I was expected to take over the running of the family business but Father deemed it more important to get me away from Arbela so I was sent south."

The Syrian sighed and shook his head. For a while he was

silent. Eager to hear more, Lucius prompted him. "Who are these Essenes? I have not heard of them."

Josephus did not answer the question directly. Instead he asked, "You are young, my friend, but can you look back on your life and discern moments when your life changed forever?"

Lucius thought of the day he had left his village to join the Legions then of the death of Aithne and his meeting with the Old One. He nodded. "Yes, Josephus."

"Just so with me the day I arrived at Q'mran. It was the end of a hot, dusty journey, the last leg with a group of pilgrims from Jerusalem. I was hungry, tired and frightened. More than anything I was filled with anger. At the age of twelve I knew I had discovered righteousness. Righteousness was the destruction of all who threatened we Jews. For this I had been banished to this awful, desolate spot."

"Q'mran is a high, dry plateau looking out across the deep valley of the Dead Sea."

Josephus took the wax tablet that always hung at his belt. With a stylus he sketched Judaea, the Middle Sea bordering it to the west. He marked Jerusalem and to the south of that the Dead Sea with the River Jordan running into it from the north. He made an 'x' to the west of the sea. "Here is Q'mran."

"The Essenes inhabit caves. They are an æsthetic people, bound through celibacy and common-ownership to a life of contemplation and prayer. To me, child of a busy, provincial town, they seemed bloodless and bland, a colourless people.

"There is much I could say about my three years at Q'mran. Suffice it to say that they changed my outlook utterly. I learned the lessons of quiet and meditation. I discovered that violence solves nothing, mastery of the emotions everything. True, the Essenes will carry arms against robbers, but Levi, my old master, showed me the tricks which in all but the most intransigent cases will allow one to dominate a situation by the projection of peace."

Again he was silent. Again Lucius prompted. "Why then did you leave?"

Josephus ran the heel of his hand across his eyes then rubbed the hand across his mouth. "Ah, my friend; how shall I answer you?" he said. "After three years the neophyte takes, if he will, an oath. He swears to practice piety towards the Deity and right-eousness towards humanity, to maintain a pure life-style, to abstain from criminal and immoral activities. There are other parts to the oath but you will excuse me if I do not speak them. The Mysteries ever keep their secrets. He must also decide at that point whether he will stay in the community or return to the wider world."

"I wrestled long and mightily with this decision. For a whole week I went into the barrens above the settlement, baking by day and freezing by night. In the end I took the oath but did not stay."

Josephus chuckled to himself and turned to Lucius with a wry smile. "Can you guess why I decided to go?"

Lucius shook his head.

"It was no more nor less than the bidding of my body. By then I was a healthy fifteen-year-old. I had never had a woman. I did not want to be celibate. More: I knew that I couldn't be. So I left, clad in an animal skin and carrying nothing but my scrip of food but I left infinitely richer than when I had arrived. Later, on the road to Jericho, I was confronted by two robbers. I spake them fair and shared with them my food. We left on the best of terms. For all I know my old teacher Levi was right and the pair gave up robbing from that day." Jospehus smiled. "All things are possible but whatever happened my conscience was clean."

There was silence between the two men for a space, each alone with his own thoughts. At the far end of the common room a group of local men were dicing noisily, watched by the landlord and his wife. The potboy replenished the fire then left again. It was Lucius who broke the silence.

"You have told me this because of what happened today,

haven't you Josephus?"

The old man nodded. "You must understand, Lucius, that I mean no criticism. What you did today was a brave act. Nor can I ask you to take on my philosophy or morals sight unseen. Yet it is my firmly held opinion that good seldom comes of violence. Fear and anger are powerful emotions. Often they are necessary to our survival. Yet often, too, they set in train cycles of hate and revenge which we cannot imagine."

He turned and looked fondly at Lucius.

"All I would ask of you, my young friend, is that you think on these things. I sense in you a great potential for good. If you will let me I would help you realize that potential."

* * *

That evening after supper, there came a tap at the door of Aurelio's room. "Come in," he called. The door opened and the goodwife propelled a newly washed Trista within.

"Here she is, your Honour," she said, her face carefully neutral.

The improvement upon the waif he had seen earlier was startling. Trista now wore a simple, homespun dress. Her hair, washed and braided, shone auburn in the lamplight, framing a heart-shaped face.

"Has she been fed?" he asked.

"Yes, your Honour. Ate like a hog she did. Wouldn't credit how much she put away."

Aurelio made a mental note to expect a few extra sestertii on the bill tomorrow.

"And where will she be sleeping?"

The goodwife, who had fed upon the gossip along with the rest of the village, had no answer to this.

"Well," she began slowly, "that will be as, your Honour..." Seeing her distinguished guest's face remain politely enquiring, she coughed and began again. "That is to say, in the hay loft, your Honour."

"Good," said Aurelio. "I will send her to you in half an hour or so. Please could you arrange for her to be ready to depart with us tomorrow at daybreak."

The goodwife allowed that she could and, thus dismissed, curtseyed and left the room.

Man and girl contemplated each other solemnly.

"Sit you down," said Aurelio, indicating a chair near the fire. The girl sat and looked around her.

"My name is Aurelio. What may I call you?"

The big, brown eyes came back to his face. Her first attempt was caught in a furred throat. She coughed, then started again, "Trista," she whispered.

"And how old are you, Trista?" he asked.

The girl thought. "I used to be ten," she hazarded.

Aurelio guessed that twelve would be nearer the mark. The accent was not uncultured. He noted her carriage and an air of curiosity, neither characteristic of a child born to thieving. He thought how to frame his next question.

"Trista, I would wager that you were born to a better life than you are currently living. Would you care to tell me how you came to be stealing in the market?"

The girl considered for a while, her eyes cast down towards Aurelio's feet. She shook her head.

"Alright," he said, "that's your affair but tell me: do you want to come with us tomorrow?"

Still with her eyes averted, the girl nodded. One of her braids fell forwards over her shoulder. She flicked it back.

"Well, we'll be starting early and travelling upriver about twenty miles. What I would ask of you, Trista, is to think what you want to do. We can leave you in the next village but if you return to thieving, sooner or later you are going to be caught and punished severely. It might be possible to persuade someone to take you on as, say, a serving girl but I can't promise anything."

He was pleased to see that the girl was now looking at him, apparently taking in his words.

"On the other hand you could travel with us. I haven't thought this through but it seems to me that there are jobs you could do – things like fetching water and perhaps cooking. If you proved an apt pupil I could teach you the business of trading. Don't say anything now. Think about it over the next day and we will talk again tomorrow evening."

The girl continued to gaze at him solemnly.

Aurelio coughed, slightly embarrassed. "That's all for now, Trista. You go and sleep and I'll see you in the morning."

Trista slipped from her chair and made her way across the room. As she opened the door she turned. "Thank you, Aurelio," she said in a small voice. Then she was gone.

Chapter 20

(Cher Valley)

Adolphus backed the second mule into the traces and held it steady while Cadmus buckled the harness. Tadg busied himself among the boxes and bales, making all secure. Marcellus made fast the load on one of the pack animals, whistling as he worked. The sun had just cleared the horizon, tinting the sky yellow. All around birds celebrated the new day. Aurelio, settling the bill with the landlord at the door of the inn, heard a muttered conversation from within.

"Now you just behave yourself, you hear? You do everything the man tells you to. No cheek an' keep yourself clean. The man likes clean girls." He smiled to himself as the goodwife led Trista through the door. The girl carried a small sack.

"I've given her some clothes and things that belonged to our daughter, your Honour," explained the goodwife. She paused then continued in a rush. "It's a good thing you're doing, your Honour. She'd 'ave come to a bad end if she'd stayed here. I've told her to mind her ps an' qs so I 'opes you has no trouble with her." Suddenly over come at her boldness, she curtseyed awkwardly and ducked behind her husband.

Thanking his hosts, Aurelio hoisted Trista into the back of the wagon beside Tadg. Cadmus climbed into his seat and took up the whip. Adolphus grasped the lead reins of the two pack strings. Marcellus finished checking the last load before calling across, "All ready, Aurelio."

"Let's go then," said the trader. Cadmus cracked his whip over the head of the team and with sundry creaks the wagon began to move. Adolphus leaned his weight into the lead reins while Marcellus dealt slaps to the rumps of the mules whose braying joined the noise of departure. As had always been his habit, Aurelio stood on the verge and watched his team pass, checking visually on harness and mood.

The wagon was in some senses a luxury. With it they could carry much more stock as well as a substantial stall. Of course it was only of use on paved roads. Once they passed beyond the frontiers, the wagon would have to be left behind and all the stock carried by mule. This should not be a problem. Aurelio had become adept at regulating stock levels to fit their itinerary. He could also leave stock in government warehouses at a cost.

The last of the mules passed, raising its small cloud of dust. Aurelio fell in beside Marcellus.

"A fine day for it," offered the slave.

Like Josephus, Aurelio stood on no ceremony with his team. There were many in the Empire who extracted work from their slaves with the whip. That was their business and perhaps said more about the master than the slave. Aurelio had long ago learnt the benefits of engaging the willing co-operation of men. It gave him access to their intelligence and other talents.

Marcellus, for instance, had originally been owned by a Thracian trader who had taken the time to teach him the business of selling. Marcellus had a deft touch in the display of goods which was unarguably better than that of Aurelio. Indeed, were he not a slave – an unfortunate result of an addiction to gambling – he could have been himself a successful trader.

"Yes, thank the gods for fine weather and good roads," replied Aurelio. "What are we short of after yesterday? he asked."

Marcellus didn't have to think. Ticking off on his fingers he said, "Leather wallets; we're down to half a dozen. Small linen tunics; there was a run on those – just three left. We could do with some more brooches too. There are plenty of opals and garnets in the copper settings but our selection of the other stones is getting thin. Oh, and more amphoræ of moderately priced wine. I imagine we can replenish all of those in Avaricon. Apart from that we are well enough supplied for the next week at least."

Aurelio nodded with satisfaction. They would be in Avaricon, a large, provincial city tomorrow evening. He planned to spend a couple of days there at the great market. It would give a good opportunity to rest as well as replenish stock. To a degree there was still an element of experimentation in all this.

Following his season with Josephus in Caledonia, he had made his first solo trading trip working south through Britannia. He still blushed to think of the mistakes he had made. The lessons he had learned were invaluable but he knew he would have gone bankrupt during that first year without the backing of the Imperial treasury.

The following winter he spent consolidating his stock and infrastructure in southern Britannia before taking ship in the spring to Gaul. That season he had toured Belgica and Germania Inferior, settled provinces opposite Britannia where conditions for a trader were as safe as anywhere in the Empire. His confidence had risen and to his delight he had turned his first profit.

Now, in accordance with his long-term instructions, he was embarking on the longest journey yet to Dacia. It would take two seasons to get there. At the moment, having over-wintered at Vindinium, they were two weeks into the trip, working their way up the valley of the Cher. Later the team would cross the hilly watershed to the Rhone. All being well they would over-winter somewhere in northern Italia.

Yes, it was good to be setting out again, chasing the horizon – always the same horizon, as Josephus had said, but in so many guises. As his feet took up the rhythm of the day his mind went back to that first journey.

* * *

After the damp and stress of their first days on the road, the weather had improved. A day's march beyond Channelkirk they had crested a rise and seen before them the sparkling waters of the great Eastern River. Far in the distance stood the blue hills of the northern shore. For a week, then, they made good progress across the fertile lowlands of Strathclyde, spending their nights mostly in legionary forts. All should have been well except that Lucius had a nagging intimation that they were being followed.

On the fourth day when the Eastern River had dwindled to little more than a stream to their right, he stood scanning the southward hills while the slaves cleared away the noonday meal. Josephus came and stood at his elbow.

"You look as if you expect to see something, Lucius," he said.

Lucius continued to scan, his hand shading his eyes.

"No, not really, but tell me, friend, do you ever have a fey feeling as if someone was watching you?"

Josephus nodded to himself. "So you feel it too?" he asked. "It seemed to me that I first felt it two days ago but I couldn't be sure."

Lucius gave up the search. If anyone was following them they were doing it with skill. Anyway, the heather and deep valleys could give cover to a small army. He turned to the trader. "What do you suggest?" he asked.

Josephus thought for a while. At last he spoke. "We are well enough for the next three days. There are plenty of patrols along the road and forts to shelter us at night. If we are talking about ordinary robbers, they will tire of following us and find easier prey."

Lucius waited for more. When it didn't come he said, "What if it is a war-band?"

Josephus gazed at his friend. He sighed, raising his hands palms upward as he shrugged. "If it is a war band then we must leave it to the military but why would a war-band bother itself to the extent of following us for two days?"

Lucius too shrugged. "Strange are the ways of the Celt, Josephus. We are a juicy enough target after all but it doesn't make sense to follow us without attacking – if, of course, our instincts are right."

"As to that," came the reply, "we have between us a wealth of instincts born of varied experience. Would you ignore them?"

* * *

From the shelter of a gorse brake in the southern hills, Callum looked out across the grassy lowland to the road. Clearly, from two miles, he could see the mules starting to move. He could also see the sun sparkle from twenty or so helmets approaching from the west. He grunted an oath then, "Tadg," he muttered. "You an' Cadhir follow them. We're goin' on to where the forts run out. One of yez get word to us when they're a day away. Got it?"

"Yes, Callum," replied a subdued Tadg. He didn't like the feel of this at all. It was one thing to plunder isolated travellers but this vengeance thing – well, it wasn't going to fill any bellies and his stomach was sticking to his backbone right now.

Callum backed his considerable bulk out of the gorse brake, hardly disturbing a leaf, as befitted a skilled hunter. Cabal, his little dog, crawled beside him on his belly. In the dead ground to the rear Callum stood and made his way at a lope back to his waiting band. Without a word he pointed up the slope. They stood and followed.

* * *

The weather remained kind to them, as did the Fates. On the fifth day they had joined a patrol heading west. For both men the feeling of being followed had lessened but neither was sure that this was not due to the presence of their armed escort.

Two days later, in mid-afternoon the gates of Old Kilpatrick had opened to welcome them. As the last outpost in the Strathclyde chain this was a large fort garrisoned by a reinforced century. Lucius recognized the hooked noses and swarthy features of the Scythian archers from their last visit. As luck would have it Julius was still the centurion in charge.

"Well met," he said as they were ushered into his quarters. "So you've learnt no sense since your last visit then?" His smile and firm handshake belied the words.

Lucius was relieved. Not all of his dealings with the military had been pleasant since he had resigned his rank. Meridius, the spymaster, had deemed it expedient for Lucius to exaggerate his drinking problems prior to resigning. Word had spread. Not only had he been patronized by some of his erstwhile friends but also, as Meridius had predicted, there were legionaries who had made plain their contempt for a fallen officer. Julius, however, was blessed with a sunny disposition, undimmed by service on this far frontier of Empire. Indeed he seemed to thrive on it.

After sending for food and drink, Julius asked them about their journey. Josephus explained that they would be following the same route as last year.

"So you made it through to the Long Lake unscathed?" asked Julius.

"Yes indeed," replied the trader, "and, the Deity be blessed, a further five months' journeying beyond, arriving at Devana from the west."

Julius shook his head in wonder. "Unless our scouts tell us it is safe we don't go through to the Lake. You must tell me how you do it. Indeed, Josephus, I would be honoured if both of you would share my evening meal and tell me of your journey. There is much I would know of the land that lies beyond the mountains."

Josephus told the Centurion that he would be delighted. Then it was Lucius's turn.

"Julius, have you heard ought about a war band loose in the hills, possibly not a Pictish one but from further afield?"

Julius slapped his hand on his desk and smiled. "How did

you know about that, you old fox? My scouts have been watching them these last two days. If I'm not mistaken the tattoos, not to mention the smell, indicate Selgovae – about a dozen. They're squatting in the woods up yonder." He extended his arm to the north west. "It seemed as if they were watching the valley through to the lake. As long as they stay there quietly I'll leave them to it. It'd cost lives to winkle them out and, anyway, if the Picts catch wind of them, they'll roast them for me."

Lucius and Josephus exchanged worried glances.

"Is there something here I ought to know about?" asked Julius.

Lucius explained their near certainty of being followed for at least four days. "We didn't think it was robbers," he said. "But now you tell us they're Selgovae…"

Lucius looked again at Josephus. "The one I killed on the road was Selgovae but surely it makes no sense that they would come this far to avenge one man?"

Josephus pursed his lips and shook his head. "It makes no sense but they are there none the less. I am no military man but it seems to me that the passage to the Lake will be impossible with them sitting on the slopes above. Even if we were to win through, what chance is there that they would not follow?"

For a while they discussed possibilities. Then Julius was called away. He told them to return for supper and that they would talk more then. Lucius went to stand on the northern rampart. He looked to the hills, remembering what he could of the terrain, gauging distances, worrying at the problem. After a while he wandered down to the riverside where a supply ship was unloading at the wharf. He sat upon a bollard, throwing stones into the water. The only complete answer would be to clear the war band out of the woods but he knew they could not reasonably ask Julius to do this. He would definitely lose men in the action, possibly start a small war if the Picts got involved. Julius was bound to refuse. Best not to ask then. No, there must be another way.

The answer, when it came, was simplicity itself. That evening Julius met them with a knowing smile but said nothing until food and wine had been served. Then, unable to contain himself any longer he said, "I've got it." He looked at the others, smiling, his brows raised, willing them to ask.

"What exactly have you got, Julius?" said Lucius.

The Centurion rose and selected a rolled map from a chest. Moving aside dishes he unrolled it on the table, anchoring it with cups. It was a sketch map covering the upper waters of the Western River. Julius leaned his hands on the table.

"See," he said, "here's the river." He swept his hand over the estuary of the Western River. "You'll note that it is shaped roughly like a hammer with the head lying north-south. We're here," he pointed, "right at the bottom of the hammer's haft. Now, follow my cunning and pretend you're sailors." Julius was clearly enjoying himself.

The others leaned closer, their food forgotten for the moment.

"So," continued Julius, "if you were, heavens forefend, making for the open ocean, you would sail down river and turn to the south." He traced the track with his finger. "But do you see here, the northern half of the head of the hammer? It is a long thin inlet biting deep into the hills. And see here, right at its very end, it almost meets the Long Lake. I am told that there is but an isolated hill set in a low saddle of land separating it from the track that runs up the western shore of the Lake."

He sat down with a look of triumph, raised his glass to his companions and took a long swallow. Had he been looking for applause, he was disappointed. Lucius and Josephus looked from the map to the smiling soldier with blank expressions. Then the ever-patient Josephus said, "That is truly interesting, Julius, but I have the feeling that you have missed out some part of your exposition."

"Ha!" came the response. "The supply ship! I have been

talking to the captain, a dour man; a man under command. His orders tell him to return to Deva as fast as wind and tide allow, staying for no man. Yet he tells me that wind and tide are fickle elements and none may tell how long the journey back across the trackless wastes will take." He paused looking fixedly at the trader, one eyebrow arched.

"And wind and tide," Josephus began slowly, "have an exemplary reaction to gold, perhaps?" He smiled and then Lucius caught on. Smiles turned to laughter, laughter to toasts drunk in the red wine of Gallia Narbonensis.

* * *

Shortly after first light the warrior on lookout called for Callum. When the chief arrived, he pointed to the Roman camp. In the clear air it was possible to see a mule being hoisted aboard the ship lying at the wharf.

"Wotcher reckon?" growled Callum.

"Dunno," replied the lookout. "Just fort you orter know, boss."

Callum gnawed on his breakfast thoughtfully. Tadg and Cadhir were down there somewhere, keeping an eye on things. They'd tell him soon enough. They'd better.

An hour later Cadhir came panting up the hill, making a pantomime of exhaustion as he fell at Callum's feet.

"They're loading them on the ship, Callum, the trader an' that," he panted. "Last of the mules just goin' on when I left."

Callum spat. "Where's Tadg?"

"'e's down by the quay. Goin' ter pick up any gossip then hotfoot it up 'ere."

All eyes were on Callum. Something needed to be said. His old dad had taught him that. 'Give 'em something to chew on', he'd said. Callum revolved his dad's Sayings in his mind. Finally he announce, "We'll wash in their fucking blood," then laughed so horribly that Cabal whined and grovelled. That'd keep 'em going for a while. The concept of washing in anything was novel enough.

* * *

Down at the wharf Tadg hefted a bale onto his shoulders then teetered up the brow. He was stripped to the waist. The sack that hung from his head, folded to make a pointed hat and short cloak, shaded his face so that he looked like any of the other slaves. So far he had learnt nothing except that the trader was taking ship. He was hindered by the fact that a slave couldn't speak directly to anyone so he kept his head down and his ears open.

His reward came as, the loading completed, the slaves were marshalled into a loose line on the jetty. One of the big nobs with a red plume strolled past with the trader and his mate. They stopped at the foot of the brow. Tadg's Latin was rudimentary but he managed to make out that the ship was heading for somewhere up the Long Lake.

Just one guard led the slaves away. They weren't even chained; after all, these were southern slaves who wouldn't last a day out here on their own. Thus it was easy enough for Tadg, from his position at the rear of the line, to roll into a ditch and lie doggo before worming his way into the clear.

* * *

Callum was watching the ship hoist its big sail when Tadg loped up to his hide.

"They're heading for somewhere up some long lake, Callum. I crep' right onto the boat an' listened.

No one would call Callum clever, at least behind his back. However his mind worked like a pair of heavy millstones. He had a tenacity of thought which, eventually, could render down most problems. When they had first arrived in the hills, he had climbed to the high peak above and seen the huge body of water, tapering off to the north. That would be the Long Lake.

Then, at a distance, he had traced the road from the fort; seen it dwindle from paving setts to rutted earth. What was clear was that it turned north at the river that drained the big lake, beside the abandoned Roman camp. It didn't go anywhere else. So that was the route the trader had intended to follow.

They must have realized his war band was here. So there was another way to get where they were going; somewhere the ship could take them. Big ship like that couldn't get up the river that drained the lake, could it?

"Bugger," said Callum.

He watched the ship pick up speed in the brisk wind. A modest arrow of wake extended from its bows. Callum gazed down river, trying to imagine what lay in the distance.

"Koun!" he shouted. A tall warrior, younger than most, jogged up from the dell. Koun was Callum's nephew. He was nack-all good at fighting but had the eyes of a hawk.

"Get yourself up the 'ill." Callum jerked a grubby thumb towards the summit behind them. "Watch that ship as long as you can see it. Tell me where it goes." Koun turned and jogged up the slope.

His dispositions made, Callum turned without a word and lumbered down to their camp in the dell.

* * *

Josephus stood in the bows of the ship enjoying the salt breeze. Lucius stood beside him, clinging to a rope. His last crossing of the Channel, although some years in the past, was fresh in his mind. The fact that the sheltered waters of the estuary were flat calm reassured him not a bit. He felt every slight heel of the close-hauled ship, every dip of the bow.

Josephus took a deep breath. "Makes you feel glad to be alive, doesn't it?" He gestured at the green hills surrounding the ship, the sun on the water and the gulls dipping in the wake. They had already passed one opening to the north but the captain had told them it was the next one they needed. A low headland was slipping by on their right. The ship's head seemed to be pointing towards a narrow break in the sheer hills ahead.

Suddenly there was a flurry of orders. Horny feet slapped on the deck. Lucius was elbowed aside by a sailor who began to undo the rope he had been holding.

"Best go stand back there," said the sailor, jerking his head towards the back of the ship.

The two men made their way aft, Josephus with a confident step, Lucius staggering to every movement of the hull. Just as they reached a point abaft the mast there was another flurry of orders. Sails flapped and banged while sailors hauled on ropes and shouted. The hull lurched to port sending Lucius cannoning into Josephus. The Jew grasped his elbow, steadying him.

"Gods, what a way to travel," muttered Lucius as his friend led him to the comparative safety of the poop.

* * *

High above them and twenty miles behind, Koun caught a flicker of white. Wiping his eyes, he cupped them with both hands. Yes, the distant speck was getting very slightly bigger. It was turning. Now it was moving away from the sun. Koun watched it for another twenty minutes until it disappeared behind the land. Catching up his spear he set off down the hill.

* * *

It was late afternoon as the ship came to anchor. The southerly wind had speeded her up the narrow arm of the sea and now she lay a hundred yards off the beach. The steep hills on either side looked close enough to touch. Only to the north east, beyond the beach, was there any view. In that quarter stood a rounded hill surrounded by grassland and beyond it the hint of more water.

"Mules'll have to swim for it," the captain had announced. The first was already floundering shore wards, to where two of Josephus's slaves waited on the beach. A second mule, complaining loudly, now hung from its slings, descending jerkily towards the water. Meanwhile the ship's boat, piled high with bales, made its way inshore towards the lead slave with his wax tablets and tally stick.

"You're welcome to stay aboard the night," said the captain grudgingly. He had no intention of running the loch in the darkness but equally was loth to see any of his profit lost on extra provisions.

"You are very kind," said Josephus, "but if the landing can be accomplished before nightfall we had best camp ashore, ready for an early start."

"Suit yoursel'" said the mariner, leaning on the tiller bar. "Bloody bandit country, you ask me. Why'd yer want to go there anyway?"

Josephus smiled blandly. "Profit, my dear fellow, just profit."

"Ar," said the captain, nodding knowledgably. He understood profit.

Chapter 21

(Lomondside)

"You challenging me?"

Callum stood, massive and louring, his big hands curled at his side. Cabal sat at his feet, growling deep in his throat.

Rhodri, the nearest the chieftain had to a Number Two, stood his ground, thumbs hooked in his belt. The others watched and waited.

"No I ain't, Callum," he said firmly. "You goes in there," he nodded towards the valley leading to the Long Lake, "I'll follow. But you knows as well as me that it'll be crawling wiv Picts like as not. Wot I'm saying, we goes in, there'll be less of us comes out, that's all."

Callum held the big man's eye then turned aside and deliberately spat on the ground. He looked slowly round his band of warriors holding the eye of each one in turn. Callum was at ease with this situation. He could break any man here with his bare hands and they knew it. Briefly he considered killing Rhodri but discarded the idea. They were a long way from home and he needed every spear. Later, though…He couldn't let a challenge go unanswered.

Raising his voice so all could hear he said, "We goes in there fast, after dark. We legs it up by the lake. Daylight we hides up, see wot's wot. Tadg an' Cadhir'll do a bit of scouting. If there's nuffin' to see, we comes back tomorrer night."

He paused, raking the group once again with his eyes. "Nah, if any of yer's too lily-livered ter fancy that, yer can stay 'ere." One or two eyes flickered. He noted whose they were. He let the silence grow. A cruel grin crept across his face, exposing blackened stumps of teeth. "Just don't fucking well be 'ere when I gets back, that's all."

No one spoke. One or two looked at their feet. The wisest

gazed back stonily at their leader.

"Right." This time the sharp edges were gone from his voice. "Eat. Sleep. Art, take guard. Wake us at moonrise."

He turned, picked up a stick and hurled it into the heather. Cabal bounded after it, barking. Rhodri stood for a moment longer then nodded, turned and set about stirring up the fire.

* * *

Dawn. Josephus and Lucius watched as the ship won her anchor. The sweeps were out, five a side. Painfully, like a wounded spider, she turned away from the shore. The two men waved. "Thank you, my friend. May fair winds attend you," Josephus called. Lucius marvelled. Gold was what had brought them here, pure and simple. He had found the captain to be surly and barely civil. He wouldn't have wasted his breath on the man. Yet as he watched, the old sailor came to the ship's side and raised his hand.

"Go well, friend. Earn lots of profit. Yer a braver man than me."

Josephus chuckled. The two turned and trudged up the shingle to where the slaves waited with the pack train. "Is all ready, Marcellus?" the trader asked his lead slave.

"Aye, Josephus," came the reply.

"Then let us make as much ground to the north as we may. I'll be happier when we've put the Lake behind us."

* * *

Tadg and Cadhir crept through the margins of the scrub oak along the lakeside. Both were fearful, jumping at their own shadows. They had heard about Picts; knew what they did to prisoners. The steep hillside to their left came to an end a little way ahead. It seemed to Tadg that there was an opening here, perhaps a side valley.

Cadhir, a little further ahead, stopped and raised his hand. He turned his head, his finger to his lips, then beckoned his partner to join him. Tadg crept forward. At first he heard nothing. Then, clearly on the still morning air, came the clink of harness. Together the two moved a few more paces to where a screen of alder edged the trees.

Yes! From their left, some hundreds of yards ahead, the figures of the trader in his long cloak and the Roman, came into view from the left. Behind them followed three slaves, each leading two mules. Despite himself Tadg was impressed. Callum had actually known. He crouched down, pulling Cadhir with him. He put his mouth to his mate's ear and said in a low tone, "Right, I'm back to the others. You follow them."

Cadhir protested as a matter of course. In fact, as both knew, neither staying nor going were any longer safe. Tadg rose and made his way silently back through the woods. When he was sure that he was far enough away he broke into a run.

* * *

Lucius gazed around him, enthralled by the scenery. The Long Lake reflected the blue of the sky in broken wavelets. Far across the water lay a scatter of islands and beyond them steep, green slopes marked by scree. The sun had not yet cleared the high ridges to the east but already a golden glow suffused the sky. Seabirds dipped and wheeled, filling the air with their cries. He felt his heart lift. For perhaps the first time in a year he touched contentment. He glanced over at Josephus and smiled.

"I think I'm ready for some horizons, old friend," he said.

Josephus smiled back. "Those at least I can promise you."

He pointed to the north where the mountains started, rank on rank. Some still showed traces of snow around their peaks.

"We'll be turning for the coast before we reach those but they and their like will be our constant companions for many a mile."

'Mountains', thought Lucius. "Do you know," he said out loud, a wistful note in his voice, "I had no idea how much I missed mountains."

"Of course," said Josephus. "I should not be extolling such mole hills to a man of Tarraconensis. Then tell me as we walk of the mountains of your youth."

Lucius let his mind float back a dozen years.

"Ah but they were *real* mountains, Josephus. They could kill the unwary and yet, to us who lived amongst them, they were our friends."

His thoughts returned to his home valley; the endless gulfs of blue leading the eye ever higher and onward. He told his friend of sheer walls of rock and how he had learned to climb them.

"They called it the trial by rock and water. All of us boys had to take the trial during our twelfth summer. It made sense. A man who cannot ford a mountain torrent or climb safely is a danger to himself and his kin in those parts. So we were set a circuit. We had three days to complete it, finding our own food and making our own shelter."

He thought back to how it had felt. "I own that I saw it much as a game yet one of my friends lost his footing in a stream and broke his arm. Another fell to his death from El Muro. He was buried with much wailing but those of us who survived all, I'm sure, felt our superiority."

He was speaking of the high pastures, carpeted with wild flowers in the spring when he suddenly fell silent, stopping in his tracks.

"Into the trees," he hissed, waving the slaves towards the woods close on their left.

"What is it?" asked Josephus.

"Listen."

Clear on the southerly breeze came the sound of running feet, many of them.

The mules were quickly hidden in the underbrush. "Take cover Josephus."

Lucius tugged at his friend's arm but he stayed where he was.

"No, Lucius. This has gone far enough. It must be faced down. I will not have this trip dogged by fear."

Emotions warred in Lucius's mind. The events of Channelkirk were still vivid yet the trader had seemed quite clear that he could handle robbers without resort to violence. The problem was that Lucius had yet to see any evidence. All his instincts urged him either to run or fight yet he could do neither without denying his friend.

The tall figure of the Syrian exuded calm. He stood in the middle of the road gazing south. Against all his instincts Lucius took up station ten paces behind the Jew and slightly to the right so that he could watch what happened. With a great effort of will he kept his hand away from his sword.

At that moment a tall warrior carrying a war spear came skidding into view fifty yards down the track. Without checking his pace he let out a wild whoop. Apparently unconcerned, Josephus stood his ground, raising both hands, palms outward in the universal sign of peace. The warrior raced on, now levelling his spear at the old man. At the last minute he swerved aside, one brawny arm casually sweeping the trader off his feet.

Lucius drew his sword. The spear point moved to seek his belly. Koun broke into a continuous yell, sure now of his quarry. The Roman would die and Callum would be proud of him. Seconds slowed into minutes. He had time to note the fall of each foot, where it was positioned. He altered the point of aim slightly as the Roman moved his stance. He watched his spear being swept aside. Now the Roman was pirouetting away from him and he braked, ready to turn and counter attack. His brain just had time to detect a numbing blow across the small of his back. Strangely he was now looking at the sky, now the path behind him...

From their hiding place in the trees the slaves barely had time to understand what they had seen. At one moment the young warrior was set to run the Roman through, at the next the Roman had swung his great sword in a glittering arc and taken the other across his back. The dull *thunk* of the breaking backbone had carried clear to them. For a few moments their fascinated eyes watched the warrior's legs continue to run while his body folded backwards. Finally the whole assemblage of skin and bone fell in ruin, skidding along the earth.

* * *

Koun was somewhere in the lead. He was young and ran well. Gareth and Lug were just about to round the corner. Discipline played no part in Celtic warfare. It was every man for himself. The prize was death to the enemy or a place in the harper's repertoire of a winter's evening.

Callum had heard Koun's war cry. The lad was keen enough, give him that. Couldn't fight to save hisself but still…Now more yelling came from around the bend. Iron rang upon iron. Callum put on a spurt. Cabal leapt along at his side, his lithe body at full stretch.

* * *

Lucius had grabbed up the fallen spear, shifting the sword to his left hand. Now he turned and ran to bestride Josephus. The old trader made to sit up.

"Crawl clear, Josephus," he shouted, eyes fixed on the near corner.

Josephus clambered to his feet. "Nay, my friend. Give me the sword," he said, his voice even.

Lucius turned to his companion in disbelief. "Josephus this is no time…"

"No more it is," came the calm reply, "but I'm thinking that you could do with someone to guard your flank."

Lucius suddenly felt alive with the hot joy of battle. Grinning he lofted the sword to Josephus who, catching it effortlessly by its hilt, took up position five paces to his right.

Two more warriors rounded the corner. Again, without pause, they screamed and charged. Lucius levelled his spear at the hulking figure on the left. From the corner of his eye he saw the Syrian crouch, hands extended, balancing the sword. He could spare no more attention for the old man but, just before he engaged his opponent, he heard the strong, clear cry of "Judah Maccabee!"

* * *

Callum rounded the corner. Gareth and Lug were engaging two figures. One was the Roman. He slowed, waving down those behind him. Time to let the heart slow, the hand steady. Gareth and Lug would keep them busy while they prepared for the slaughter. He walked forward, bringing his breathing under control. A sharp word brought Cabal to heel. There was elation in the knowledge that he had out-thought his prey. Then he saw the huddled corpse beyond the fighting. Koun! The Hag help us. Morag would have his guts for this.

Callum gestured his men into line. There were five to his right, six on his left. Each of them levelled their brutal war spears as they advanced. Lug was down, a spear in his groin. The Roman was twisting the blade. Now he pulled it clear, the bright arterial blood fountaining.

"Gareth," Callum shouted. "Come back!"

In the brief moment of distraction as Gareth heard his name, his opponent's sword took him in the face, carving out a great flap of skin from his right temple to his jaw. Snarling in disbelief he sprang forward only to come up all standing with Lucius's spear lodged in his belly. He went down, snapping the haft of the spear as he fell. The Roman snatched up Gareth's spear.

"Oh you bastards," muttered Callum in reluctant admiration. "Oh, but you are goin' to die hard for that."

Taking its time from Callum the line of warriors and a small dog moved relentlessly forward towards the two men. At Callum's gesture the ends of the line advanced, creating a loose semi-circle.

"Back slowly, Josephus," said Lucius, never taking his eyes off the big man in the centre of the line. He had last seen him by moonlight with ropes of saliva hanging from his jaws. Now he knew what this was about.

"Josephus," he said out of the corner of his mouth. "It's me they want. Move away into the trees now. Take the slaves and get out of here."

He heard a wry chuckle. "Did you run when I was lying on the ground?" asked the Syrian. "Nay, Lucius: it has been a good life. I will not end it by abandoning a comrade."

Lucius felt a rush of affection for the old man. "Thank you, my friend," he said. "There is one more throw of the dice. I'm going to challenge the leader. Win or lose, they may let you go."

Lucius grounded the butt of Gareth's spear and stood upright. When he spoke his voice was loud, his speech near-fluent Selgovaen.

"I am Lucius Terentius Aquilina. Who seeks my death?"

At Callum's signal, the line of warriors stopped. He stood forward two paces. This kind of thing he understood. Advancing one foot in the declamatory mode, he thumped his chest and growled, "I am Callum MacCallum, Laird of Craigneuk. It is me wot seeks your death."

Callum: yes that had been the name. This was the brute who had thought he owned Aithne.

"Then, Callum MacCallum of Craigneuk, let us settle this in fair fight, man to man but let this worthy old man and his slaves go free. You have no quarrel with them."

Callum thought about this. He knew he could beat the Roman but why bother. The lads wanted a bit of the action and he certainly wasn't letting anyone go free.

"Nah," he snarled. "Nah: might 'ave done but you see that dead un near your foot?" Lucius didn't look. That was an old trick but he was aware that he had backed as far as the body of the first warrior. "Well," Callum went on, "that's my sister Morag's son. Nah she's going to give me gyp about that. So wot we're goin' ter do is ter butcher yer mates so's you can watch 'an then we're goin' ter butcher you slowly, Roman, all on yer own." Callum paused then started to laugh, a strange, rusty noise. He had thought of a joke. "Might save the mules though," he choked. For some moments his bulk heaved with laughter. His men joined in but the tips of their spears never wavered. Cabal barked twice.

Suddenly the laughter ended. "Take 'em!" he commanded. The warriors started forward.

Lucius crouched and levelled his spear. Josephus hefted the sword. "It was a noble try, Lucius. Thank you for your friendship."

Lucius was about to reply when a voice cut across the scene.

"Mine," it said. The word was not shouted but something in the quality of the voice caused everyone to stop and look towards its source. Unnoticed a small man, naked to the waist, his body covered in whorls of blue, had emerged from the woods.

He strode forwards between the two groups then stopped. Keeping his eyes on the Selgovae he gestured towards the Jew and the Roman saying again, "Mine." The word was spoken in Selgovaen.

'Oh fuck,' thought Callum. 'Picts'. Still, he wasn't about to lose face so he stepped forward, glaring down at the little man. "No, little man, they ain't yours; they're mine. Nah get outa the way an' we won't say nuffin' more about it."

Only Josephus who spoke Pictish understood what the little man said when he turned and called into the wood. Freely translated it went, "Ach, by the Paps o' the Hag; why can they no speak a proper language. Hamish, now, do ye know any more of their heathen cant?"

Hamish emerged from the trees, a hunting bow in his hands, an arrow nocked to the string. "Nay, Alaistair. Ah can manage t'say 'beer' an' 'woman' but that's aboot all."

"I wonder, Alaistair son of Clayne, son of Manas if I may be of assistance?" All eyes turned once more, this time to the old trader.

The little man turned his back on Callum and wandered over. "Ach, o' course. I niver thought to remember that ye had the true speech, Josephus. Weel now; will yer tell yon lummox that he is surrounded by four times his number o' Pictish lads an' if he wants to die easy then he an' his gooks lays doon their spears."

The little man paused.

"Mind you," he added reflectively, "Ah'm no fussed either way. Will ye tell him that now?"

"With pleasure," said the Syrian. Turning to Callum he translated.

The Celt replied with a loud guffaw. "Tell 'im we ain't goin' nowhere. Tell 'im if he doesn't get outa my way, I'm going to rip his lights out an' feed 'em to the fishes."

Alaistair held up his hand to save Josephus the trouble of translating. He shouted something into the woods. Josephus flinched. Moments later a flight of arrows came whistling from all directions and transfixed Gol, the biggest man there. Gol fell with a mighty crash. The Celts scattered only to be herded back by a line of Picts, armed to the teeth, who emerged from the trees. Only Cabal escaped. Carefully Callum laid down his spear. The others followed suit.

"Weel now," said Alaistair, "that all seems verra satisfactory."

He paced over to where the Syrian stood and grasped his wrist. "Welcome again to Pictland, Josephus. And what ha' ye done to bring yon foreigners doon on our heeds?"

"A million thanks, Alaistair, for your timely intervention," replied Josephus, "and a million apologies for being the cause of this unpleasantness. The Celts have a personal quarrel with my partner here. Alaistair MacClayne may I name Lucius Terentius Aquilina, a trader from a far land who has come to learn about your bountiful country."

Lucius, who had understood nothing of this interchange, recognized that he was being introduced and grasped the little man's wrist when it was offered, looking straight into his eyes. The Pict gazed long and deep then, releasing Lucius's arm, turned back to Josephus.

"Now I may not ha' much of yon's heathen tongue but did I no hear the big yin call this man a Roman?"

With the smoothness of long experience Josephus explained, "He is indeed a Roman citizen by virtue of his birth but that is all. His home is amongst mountains, not unlike your own but much smaller, in far Tarraconensis."

Alaistair looked from one to the other, weighing up what he had heard. "Aye, weel; there's a story here I ken fine an' I doot but ye'll tell it when you're ready. But for now I must deal with yon," he said, jerking his thumb at the Selgovae.

Gareth who had lain unconscious since he fell let out a groan and tried to turn over. Alaistair clicked his fingers towards Hamish and pointed at the fallen Celt. Unsheathing a long, sharp knife, Hamish knelt beside Gareth and cut his throat.

"Alaistair," asked Josephus. "What do you plan for the others?"

"Aye, weel," said the Pict with no visible emotion. "We'll fill them wi' arrows and toss them in the loch."

"May I crave a boon?" asked the trader. "Will you allow me to speak with my partner before you kill them?"

"Aye," said Alaistair. Take your time. Yon's going nowhere."
With that he turned and walked with Hamish towards the Celts.

Chapter 22

(Messenger)

Aurelio lay back against a beech trunk, chewing a grass stalk. The river drew close to the road here where a wide lawn swept down to the water. It created a sun-filled bay, ideal for the noon break. He opened one eye to check on the mules. They were cropping grass beneath the trees, each with a hobbled forefoot. Cadmus and Marcellus leaned on their elbows nearby in the shadow of the wagon, talking quietly. Tadg would be away hunting for the pot. The small Celt could never be still.

Silvery laughter came from his right. Aurelio raised himself on one elbow to find its source. The river, maybe a hundred yards wide at this point, flexed lazy muscles between wide sandbanks. Near at hand Adolphus was wading with Trista in the shallows, her small hand engulfed in his great fist. The girl laughed again causing Aurelio to smile. She wore a chain of daisies on her head, evidently the product of the big man's calloused hands.

'Strange', he thought. Adolphus rarely spoke unless spoken to yet it was obvious that the two were chattering away as they paddled, he with his halting, Germanic accent, she in bright, clear Gallic. Aurelio smiled at the unlikely scene. He had been worried by Trista's reticence. His few attempts to engage her in conversation had elicited mostly one-word responses. Perhaps Adolphus, with his child-like simplicity, was less threatening, more sympathetic to her.

Marcellus padded over. "Would you like anything else to eat, Aurelio?" he asked.

"No," replied the trader. "Let's start packing up. We've a few miles yet to do today."

Marcellus gathered up the dishes and took them to the water's edge. He spoke briefly to Adolphus who relinquished

Trista's hand and waded ashore. Trista continued to paddle slowly, dredging the sand with her feet and crooning to herself. Aurelio stood up, brushing crumbs from his tunic. He fell in beside Adolphus as the big German came level.

"Thank you for getting our little companion talking, Adolphus," he said.

Adolphus looked at him shyly and blushed.

"She nice," he said. "But she very sad."

Casually, Aurelio asked, "Why is she sad, Adolphus?"

The German scratched his head. Slowly he replied, "Her mother, father die. She all alone." Then, without pausing, he plodded on to where Cadmus was freeing the mules.

Aurelio mused. Strange that no one had taken the girl in. Middle Gaul was as civilized as any area in the Empire. He would have thought that some kindly person would have looked after her. He made a mental note to try to find out whether she had any relatives.

While Cadmus and Adolphus harnessed the draught mules he untied the hobble on one of the pack animals. He was just fitting its blanket, prior to loading the panniers, when he heard hoof beats coming from the west. He turned to look. Cantering along the further grass verge came the unmistakable figure of an Imperial courier.

The Imperial Post was part of the glue of the Empire. Established by Caesar Augustus, it allowed the central government to maintain touch with the furthest corners of the provinces. To facilitate this, Rome maintained a network of posting stations along the trunk roads where strings of the finest horses were kept. Their riders, the Corps of Imperial Couriers formed an elite.

They were required to ride at least fifty miles a day, days on end, to take news, edicts and important orders to and from the centre. Such a punishing regime called for superb horsemen who were both fit and intelligent. Aurelio had heard stories of couriers covering up to one hundred and sixty miles in a day although he didn't know whether to believe them.

He raised a hand in greeting to the passing horseman. To his surprise, on seeing him, the courier reined in and walked his horse across the road. "Greetings," said the trader.

"Greetings," returned the courier. The horse, a fine black stallion, was sweating. It sidled, clearly ready to run again. The courier's fingers played with the reins as the horse mouthed its bit. He was a young man wearing light, leather half-armour and a short sword. He leaned forward and patted the horse's neck, looking keenly at the trader. "I am seeking Gaius Gnollus Brocchus. I wondered whether you might have seen him," he said."

A thoughtful expression crossed Aurelio's face. He appeared to be thinking. At length he shook his head. "No, my friend. I once knew a Gnaeus Gnollus Brutus but I doubt he is the man you are looking for."

The courier sat back in his saddle, taking up the reins. "Ah well," he said, "it was worth a try. I will wait for him at the next post house. It's only another three miles up the road."

With that he squeezed the horse's flanks. The stallion bounded forward, his hipposandals striking sparks from the stone setts. Aurelio marvelled at the young man, sitting so tall and unmoved by the animal's gait. Like many things, Aurelio reflected, it was a skill worth the watching but that didn't mean he would wish to do it himself. He turned back to the mule.

* * *

An hour later they drew level with the posting station. It was a large, brick building with a red tiled roof and wide eaves. The stables were in two wings at the rear, accessed through a tall, square door.

"We'll rest here," Aurelio called to his team. "Half an hour, perhaps; I have business within."

As he walked towards the door he put a hand within his tunic and removed a light, silver chain from around his neck. Within the main entry he turned right into a smaller door. All post stations were built on the same pattern. This door gave access to the inn where travellers, as well as couriers, might find food and drink.

After the bright sunlight outside he had difficulty making out the interior. Then, in a far corner, beyond the bar, he saw the courier alone at a table, eating. There was a scattering of other travellers taking their ease. Aurelio made his way to the bar and ordered a tankard of beer. With this in his hand he crossed to where the courier sat. The young man looked up at his approach.

"Gaius Gnollus Brocchus," the trader said. "Didn't he come from Vicus Leudicus?"

The courier finished his mouthful and took a gulp of wine. "Nay, the one I seek lives in Sunuci but come, my friend. Sit with me and pass an idle few minutes."

Aurelio sat, placing his beer tankard on the table and beside it the silver chain from around his neck. The courier picked up the chain. He studied the seal hanging from it.

"A pretty thing," he said. "Amethyst, is it not?"

He placed it back on the table, his eyes flicking briefly around the room. Apparently satisfied he leaned closer, lowering his voice.

"I am charged with telling you that your orders have been changed. You are to make your way to Borbetomagus on the German frontier, trading as you go. You should arrive no later then the end of Junius. When you arrive you will make clandestine contact with Decimus Villius, the head of intelligence to the civil administration. He will be expecting you. Your recognition sign will be *saxum candidum*. His will be *cervus rufus*. That is all the information I have."

Aurelio took a draught of beer and wiped his mouth with the

back of his hand. "You will know the routes, friend. How should I proceed from Avaricon?"

The courier thought for a moment. "Head for Nancy first. When you leave Avaricon, take the small road east to Le Charité. There you can cross the Loire. Head north up the river valley to Montargis. From there, take the trunk road to Nancy. After that, seek directions to Mannheim and, as I remember, you will find Borbetomagus a short distance to the north."

"And how far would you say that was altogether?"

The young man pursed his lips. "Perhaps four hundred miles, give or take a little. You will have to cross mountains in the latter stages but it will be high summer and the roads are good."

Aurelio did some calculations. It should be possible allowing for trading, rest days and accidents. There might even be some days to spare. "Do you report back to someone," he asked.

The courier nodded.

"Tell them I will be there in the last two weeks of Junius." He tipped a little beer onto the floor in libation to Mercury, god of travel and communications.

"I must go," he said, standing and draining his tankard. Curiosity overcame him. "How did you find us?"

Smiling the courier said, "We knew your route and the time of your departure. I simply went to Caesarodunum and followed the road."

'So much for secrecy,' thought Aurelio.

He bade the young man goodbye and went out again into the spring sunshine. Marcellus and Cadmus arose from the grass verge as they saw him. Trista was clinging to the back of a mule being led by Adolphus. She was shouting to go faster. It almost seemed a shame to head onwards but the sun was starting to wester and there were at least seven miles to go to the next village where Tadg would have accommodation ready for them.

Once they were under way he walked alone, deep in thought. Dacia had been a general strategic objective. He had expected to receive instructions once he had arrived there next year. These new instructions indicated some specific employment. What might it be?

He knew the German frontier; which legionary did not? It was there, in the Teutonburg Forest, more than a century ago, that the Germans had wiped out three legions under Publius Quinctilius Varus. Aurelio still found the fact staggering. Sixteen thousand trained infantrymen overrun by untrained barbarians: three legions out of a total strength of twenty-eight. Since that time the Roman army had been wary of the deep, dark forests across the River Rhenus.

Would he, he wondered, be invited to cross the river and enter the forests. He shuddered and made the sign against evil. Still, he had once felt the same about crossing into Pictish Caledonia and look how that had been.

* * *

As the Pict leader had walked away, Josephus turned to Lucius, searching the younger man's eyes. "Well, Lucius?" was all he said.

Lucius drove the spear he was carrying into the ground and folded his arms. He looked down, his right foot tapping, then up at his friend. After a further pause he said, "You want me to say that we should let them go, don't you Josephus?"

The trader sighed. "No, Lucius; you are wrong. This is not about what I want. I have no say in this. The quarrel is between you and the Celt. If I have a need in this matter it is to see my good friend Lucius walk away unscathed by the experience."

Lucius gazed at the Syrian, his mind a turmoil of conflicting emotions. The evening at the Channelkirk inn was still fresh in his mind. Josephus had said that he sensed a potential for good in him. Not so long ago the Old One had said something similar. He trusted this man, admired his dignity and calm, yet was he right that violence perpetuated violence?

"You fought them, Josephus," he said. "You fought to kill."

"I did, Lucius, but nothing I have told you means that you must die needlessly. I do not counsel you to go blindly to death following someone else's rule. Those warriors looked on us with the Dark Eye. They saw not people, merely victims. Only a human contact could have changed that and there was not time."

He turned to look at where the Celts were now sitting on the ground, surrounded by Pictish spears. The Picts were systematically looting what little the Celts had. Josephus pointed towards them.

"Three lie dead while another dozen live. I put it to you that the living and the dead represent two separate problems, one in the past, one in the present."

Lucius cast round towards the lake, seeking inspiration. He stooped to pick up a pebble, skimming it at the water. It bounced once and sank. He gazed at the ripples.

Still with his eyes on the water he said, "Josephus, if we let them go, who's to say that they won't come after us again?" He turned. "If it was just me, then perhaps yes, but you are involved. They would kill you without a thought."

"As to that," replied the Syrian, "I am at ease. Who is to say what will happen? Maybe the Celts will die on the way back. Maybe I will be killed by a wild boar in the coming weeks. It is not for us to know the future and even if we did, who is to say what is good and what evil."

The old man placed his hands on the other's shoulders. "But this, Lucius, mark this; anything begun in blood will end in more blood; of that you may be sure."

Lucius drew a deep breath. He was not at all sure about this. To a soldier there was only one answer: kill them. Yet he had wondered in the last week when his conscience had died. Was it yet possible to lead a principled life; to become a centre of calm like Josephus? Suddenly, unbidden, there came to his mind the clearest picture of the fox cub; of Aithne holding it; of the two of them leaving it at the mouth of a fox's earth. Perhaps there was yet hope.

"Will the Picts let them go?" he asked.

"I believe it can be arranged but Lucius, is this what you want?"

Lucius waited a moment longer then nodded. "Yes, Josephus; it is what I want."

The trader smiled and slapped his friend gently on the upper arms.

"I cannot, in all conscience, tell you that you will not regret this but...you will not, ultimately, regret it. Now, will you leave the negotiations to me?"

Lucius, in his turn, smiled. "Yes, old friend."

* * *

The mechanics of the deal were not clear to him because he didn't have the Pictish but he was able to appreciate how Josephus worked his audience. At the start there was muttering from the Picts, the occasional voice raised in protest. Gradually, though, there were nods. The turning point came when a warrior complained, indignantly, that Cabal had bitten him as he tried to steal him away. Grins turned to laughter. Finally, spears were held aloft as the small warriors cheered.

Josephus beckoned Marcellus to him and gave instructions. Shortly afterwards the slaves appeared from the woods rolling two small casks. Marcellus placed something in his master's hand. With a great show of ceremony, Josephus handed it to Alaistair who held it up to the light. Lucius saw that it was one of the fine opals in an intricate copper setting.

Negotiations completed, the old trader came and stood by his side watching the gleeful Picts take possession of the kegs. "The brooch is a gift for Mairead, his woman. I believe it was that which finally swayed him."

Josephus turned his level gaze upon his friend. "Now, Lucius, with your agreement I suggest that you be the one to tell Callum that he is free to go. Alaistair wishes him to understand that he and his band have until the sun touches the western hills to leave the valley of the Long Lake. If they tarry, he says, they will be killed out of hand."

He beckoned Cadmus over. The slave carried Lucius's sword, now cleaned of blood. Cadmus handed it, pommel-first, to Lucius who accepted it, sliding it home in its sheath. With a nod to Josephus he set off to where the Celts sat, stopping a few paces in front of their leader.

"Laird Callum of Craigneuk, I would speak with you," he said.

Wordlessly Callum stood, Cabal clutched in one massive fist. He topped Lucius by half a head. Hate bruised his eyes.

"Lord Callum," said Lucius, "upon the advice and by the good offices of my colleague here, we have prevailed upon the Pictish leader to let you go free."

Callum's eyes did not so much as flicker.

"You are to leave the valley of the Long Lake by the time the sun touches the western hills. Any that remain at that time will be killed. Do you understand?"

The black eyes continued to bore into him, unblinking. Callum made as if to spit then, glancing at the Picts, appeared to think better of it. In a low, rumbling voice he said, "Don't think this'll save you, Roman. I'm going to kill you if I 'ave to follow you to the ends of the bloody earth."

He turned his back upon Lucius. His men looked up at him expectantly. "Get up real slow," he said. "Turn around and walk slowly back darn the track. This may work. It may not. Only way to find out is to try it."

The warriors started to get up. One reached tentatively for his spear. A grinning Pict jabbed at his hand. The Celt quickly withdrew it and stood. Turning like men in a dream they started to walk southwards. A wave of jeering and insults arose from the Picts. It finished only when the Celts rounded the corner and disappeared from view.

Chapter 23

(Caledonia)

And so began Josephus' last trading trip.

That first day Alaistair and his band bore them north up the Long Lake to Glenfalloch, a settlement on the narrow alluvial plain at the head of the waters. Lucius looked back. The setting sun stained the eastern hills. He wondered whether Callum and his band had made their escape. It would have been a close thing, he knew, involving a ferocious forced march.

Had it been a sensible decision? There was no way of knowing but he noted that his heart was lighter for having made it. He resolved to put it from his mind. Around him torches were being lit. In the central space between the huts, a fire was built. Sparks rose into the still evening air of the deep valley. An eerie wail arose as a piper inflated his instrument. A drummer tapped his drums, listening intently to their tuning.

Lucius had another thought: these were the very people who had fought the Fifth the year before and here he was, if not a valued guest, at least accepted into their midst. He didn't know what to make of that, nor the fact that he found himself rather liking these noisy, contentious people.

Despite the exigencies of the day, Josephus had put the slaves to setting out their wares. He could do little else. It was evident that their arrival had been anticipated. Indeed it seemed, from what Josephus had told him, that the Picts had watched their progress towards the Long Lake for at least five days.

Trestles had been found from somewhere. Marcellus and Cadmus were spreading the black cloths while Adolphus unloaded the mules. As they worked, Josephus held the growing crowd spellbound with descriptions of the hidden treasures about to be revealed. Excitement built as the shadows deepened. Men had set up the first of the casks on a saw-horse. With the reverence of ritual, they prepared to tap it and draw off a sample of its contents. Savoury smells wafted from the cooking pits.

Lucius stood in the shadows, watching the old trader at work. He had known the Syrian was a master of his craft but, nevertheless, he was seeing a new side of him here. Josephus wove magic. He was providing a show for the little people, something over and above the crude business of trading. Later the old man explained.

"The point is, you mustn't let the customers see the stall too early. If they do, some of the magic, some of the authority of the business is dissipated. All too easily it can become a crude melee, especially with an audience as excited as last night's. Normally we maintain the mystique by being at the market early. In cases like last night, however, it is up to the trader to keep the people distracted until a critical mass of wares is on display. What constitutes that mass, I cannot tell you. You just know it when you see it."

By the time Marcellus gave his master a hidden signal, the crowd seemed almost reluctant to approach the stall, almost in awe of it. Lucius watched the trader change from magician into welcoming host, beckoning the crowd forward. But once the trading started, business was furious. Lucius was pressed into service, fetching, carrying and displaying. Fuelled by raw spirits, the bagpipes and drums, the evening quickly turned into a celebration. Small bands of Picts came down from the hills in the darkness, summoned by the sounds and distant lights. Dancing started and not a few fights.

It was well after midnight before business slackened. Josephus suddenly looked exhausted. The slaves were stretching backs and arms. There was much yawning. Josephus took Lucius's arm.

"Well, my friend," he said, "what did you make of your first night's trading?"

Although tired, Lucius thought he had never felt more alive unless it had been in the hard, bright joy of battle.

"It...it was amazing, Josephus. I would never have thought that selling things could be so exciting. Tell me, how much did we profit?"

"Ah, my friend," said the trader, shaking his head, "that is part of the mystery. It will be revealed tomorrow. For now just revel in the joy of the trading. It is four parts being appreciated; five parts bringing joy to others and only one part making profit."

Lucius smiled. "That wasn't what you said to the ship's captain."

Josephus clapped his arm. "Oft times I tell people what they want to hear. Why bother the honest fellow with concepts which might prove beyond him?"

* * *

They followed the sun on its northward journey, travelling by easy stages through deep glens, first north and then west, setting up the stall wherever they stopped. So passed Crianlarich, Tyndrum and Dalmally. In each place Josephus taught Lucius a little of the art of trading. In Crianlarich it was the importance of detail; of how clean, black cloths are the best background for display. At Tyndrum he invited Marcellus to expound further upon the secrets of display; of the grouping of like objects; of the rhythm of height and colour. In Dalmally where an old woman bargained with him for twenty minutes over a single ribbon, Lucius began to learn patience and respect.

Beyond Dalmally they encountered the tang of kelp and salt water. The track ran westwards along the shores of Loch Etive, a landlocked arm of the sea. In due time they came to Dunbeg, a strong hill fort overlooking a great harbour where trading ships and fishing boats lay at anchor. Lucius stood upon the cliffs and looked beyond the Firth of Lorne to the mountains of the Inner Islands. To the southwest an archipelago drew his eye to the rim of the world. He breathed deeply and felt a bittersweet longing.

That night they were housed in the chieftain's hut. Josephus spoke long with the chieftain after the evening meal. He went to bed thoughtful. In the morning he sought out Lucius and together they consulted the trader's map of Caledonia. It was little more than a sketch with large blank areas in the centre and to the north and west.

"Ieuan has been telling me about the Inner Islands and the complex of peninsulae which lie to the west. Previously I have turned north here and travelled up the coast of the mainland. Yet I am minded to visit new lands. Ieuan has promised me a ship to ferry us across the Firth should we wish to go."

The decision was Josephus' but he sought Lucius' opinion as an equal. They discussed the merits of established markets and new ones; the importance of opening new markets weighed against the servicing of old ones. In the end the decision was made. The long-suffering mules were hoisted aboard one of the chieftain's sleek galleys and the company was rowed across the sparkling waters of the Firth of Lorne with Lucius hanging fast to a rope, willing the further shore to come closer. The galley was carefully beached in the harbour of Lochaline in Morven so that travellers and mules arrived ashore almost dry-shod.

Whenever, afterwards, he thought of those summer days, they took on the semblance of a dream. It seemed that the sun always shone although he had distinct memories of miserable nights sheltering under rocky overhangs, while rain lashed the darkness. From settlement to village they journeyed along sheep tracks. Their world was one of muted colour – sea pink and saxifrage, purple heather and yellow gorse.

For two days, while the company rested, Lucius borrowed a mule and made his way by heather track to the great Mull of Ardnamurchan where the Western Ocean broke in ruin on towering granite cliffs. He shaded his eyes, looking westward to where distant mountains broke the horizon. That night he lay awake under the stars. He thought of Aithne. He found his memories, once so painful, now sweetened with love and gratitude. When at last he slept, lulled by the booming of the waves, there lingered a smile upon his lips.

Onward they went, turning their stock into silver and gold, transmuting it back into other goods – hides, furs, jewellery, dried fish. In a deep valley at the junction of two lochs, they stayed to help in the erection of a standing stone. The entire population of the village, men, women and children, turned out to help. Here the massive strength of Adolphus came into its own as he supported the granite monolith while the Picts wedged it into place. That night, his face split from ear to ear with a grin, he sat in the place of honour and was toasted in heather beer.

On Midsummer's Eve, at the mouth of the Great Glen, Lucius danced once more. He danced to the rhythm of harp and drum with a raven-haired woman. After a whispered consultation with the Harper the vibrant notes of a Tarraconensis dancing tune took the air. In the lingering northern twilight the two bodies stamped and whirled, the crowd clapping out the rhythm. The woman would have shared his bed but Lucius took her by the hand and together they joined the crowds climbing Druim Fada to the stone circle. There they merged their voices in the paean to the Undying Sun as the rose-light of dawn backlit the bulk of Ben Nevis.

And on and on. Now tormented by midges in the summer heat until a woman versed in herbs traded a pot of noxious grease for three needles and a quantity of dyed linen thread. Their way lay northeast, now, up Glen Mor, the great valley that split the land from side to side like a knife wound. Lucius' confidence grew. He now carried the value of each item of stock in his head. The cant of the trader, that semi-humorous rhetoric which invited participation, came easy to his lips.

On the lonely road between Laggan and Aberchalder, one

cloudy evening, Lucius watched, heart in mouth, as Josephus faced down three vagrant Picts, intent on robbery. Never once did the old man raise his voice. He leaned on his staff, a centre of calm, and spoke with the men, asking about their lives and their needs. Quite soon they were speaking as old friends. Marcellus was invited to put up a generous bundle of food for them and after maybe thirty minutes, the two groups parted with expressions of mutual esteem.

At Inchnacardoch they came out of the hills at one end of the longest, thinnest lake they had yet seen. The stillness of the deep valley seemed fraught with portent. Trading was poor. There was much subdued talk about cattle and a monster in the lake. That evening the local spirit man advised Josephus not to set out the following morning until certain rites had been conducted, said rites costing one silver coin.

In the hour before dawn Lucius awoke to the sound of hooves passing his hut. A cow lowed and was silent. He had almost nodded off when the air was rent by bellows of terror, suddenly cut off, somewhere down by the lake. The spirit man, smiling with satisfaction, made an early visit to collect his due and the trading party set off but always with one eye on the still grey depths to their left.

As July became August they arrived on the shores of the Eastern Sea. The mountains fell back on their right while to their left opened a broad estuary. Josephus had planned to stay in the prosperous settlement of Inverness for a week, trading, mending harness and buying stock. However it soon became clear that Inverness was an armed camp, awaiting assault from the north. With so many warriors gathered in one place trade was brisk but, after consulting with Lucius, Josephus cut short their stay. Thus they journeyed on across a wide coastal plain, sand dunes on their left and fields ripe for harvest on their right. On the second day distant smoke rose to their rear. They increased their pace.

Two days later all was peaceful once more as they moved

away from the conflict. On either side of the road families, intent upon the time-hallowed business of harvest, toiled in the fields. Then, on a lonely stretch through the Wood of Ordiequish, Cadmus collapsed. Josephus and Lucius had watched him through the previous day, noting his high colour and increasing confusion. The Syrian called a halt while Lucius examined the slave.

"He's red hot," was his verdict. "We'll need to get him comfortable under cover."

They drew aside into a glade where they constructed a shelter of hazel wands, thatched with heather. Cadmus was carried within and laid on a bed of heather. Then, at Lucius' insistence, he took over the slave's care, bidding the others camp at a distance.

"We cannot be sure that this is not infectious," he told Josephus. "It makes little sense for all of us to catch it."

So for a week they tarried, content to mend and clean in the drowsy summer days. In truth it was a welcome break after the strains of the journey. Josephus was quietly amazed, seeing a new side of his friend. He watched from a distance as Lucius spooned broth into Cadmus' lips and sponged his brow with cool water. The ex-soldier seemed totally focused on his task.

During the second night the others dozed fitfully, kept awake by the thrashing and groans coming from the shelter. Beneath the cries of the slave ran the steady counterpoint of Lucius' soothing voice. In the dawn he emerged from the shelter, his hair lank upon his forehead, and accepted the cup of wine offered him be Marcellus. He drank deep.

"How is he, Master?" enquired Marcellus, hesitantly. Cadmus had been his close friend for several years and he was deeply concerned. Good friendship between slaves was a treasure to be valued.

Lucius seemed not to hear for a moment. Marcellus noticed the dark shadows beneath his eyes. Dragging a hand down his face he turned to the slave, smiling wanly. "He'll do," he said. "The fever broke last night. All he needs now is rest and good food."

Joining them, Josephus saw his friend swaying, evidently with fatigue. "Right, young man: off to bed with you," he said. "We'll take over now."

Lucius slept for twelve hours and awoke none the worse. Four days later Cadmus, although hollow eyed, was again able to travel. From time to time Marcellus saw the eyes of his fellow slave fixed upon Lucius. His expression seemed speculative. Later Cadmus confided in his friend.

"I can't really explain it but when the fever was at its worst; when I didn't know up from down; when I could feel the Old Hag's claws fastening into my skin, he called me." Cadmus shook his head, as if in disbelief. "I swear I could hear his voice telling me to come back; that it wasn't my time yet."

He paused, struggling for words.

"See, I don't know that I believe it now but it seemed so real to me then. He, like...he contended with the Hag for me. I can't rightly say that he fought her but he brought in bright light; sort of violet, blinding light..." His voice trailed away. His eyes sought something beyond sight. He gave a little laugh, his embarrassment clear.

"So what happened?" prompted Marcellus.

Cadmus gestured helplessly with his hand. "Well it was like the Hag was being battered by a strong wind. Her hair was streaming backwards and her features all sort of...smeared. Slowly she released me, claws coming out of my flesh one by one. Then she, I don't know, *bowed* to him, if you can believe that, and just sort of blew away like dust."

He shook his head, playing with the bridle he had been mending.

"Thing is, Marcellus, who is he? I mean, I thought he was just a soldier, retired before his time 'cos of the drink. Now, well...I dunno. It's like he's some kind of wizard or something."

* * *

They arrived at no conclusions but the events of Cadmus' illness drew the already close-knit group even closer. Josephus had never known a happier or more fruitful journey. The slaves, ever privileged compared to their fellows under Imperial rule, worked with a will. Frequently now he heard laughter. As for Lucius, the Syrian remembered the gaunt cheekbones and haunted eyes of a year ago. Now there was a spring in his friend's step; a new purpose in his eyes.

The settlement of Keith came and went with feasts and dancing in honour of the harvest gods. The emphasis of trade now was on converting their remaining stock into portable valuables. Josephus explained that the nearer they came to Devana, the more they would encounter people used to Roman currency. The ideal was to arrive at the military base with mules unburdened but for sacks of money, gold and silver. Since they would increasingly be coming within the orbit of military patrols, this should not lead to additional fears about robbers and thieves.

And so as the sun appeared fractionally lower each noon and set a little earlier each evening, they journeyed through Strathbogie with mountains still showing far to their right. Already, by the Crofts of Shanquhar, they were able to free one lame mule from its load. In the Glens of Foudland, beside the infant River Don, they woke to a morning of mist. Moisture decked the blackberries and the first plangent scent of autumn pervaded the air.

And on and on...

They left the hills for the broad coastal plain of Formartine heading ever to the south and east. The Don, tamed by summer's drought, dawdled peaty brown between rocks. At Inverurie there was a great autumn fair. Josephus watched Lucius directing the setting up of the stall in the dawn light. The movements of the young Roman were unconsciously choreographed with those of the slaves. Little was said. Little needed to be said but Lucius clearly imprinted his growing style on proceedings.

With a sense of release Josephus walked across to his friend and touched him on his arm. Lucius turned, smiling when he saw the old trader.

"You're in charge today," said Josephus.

Lucius stood, open-mouthed. In charge? He wasn't ready. It wasn't his stall.

Josephus was talking. "I'm going for a stroll. Might have a lazy noon meal at the inn. Get what you can; emphasis on sale prices; discount for coins but I don't need to tell you all that. I'll see you at sunset."

With that the Syrian hefted his staff and made off across the market place.

Lucius looked from his retreating back towards the slaves. They continued to arrange stock with studious concentration. 'I can't do this,' was all he could think.

"What would you wish as centrepiece, Master?" Marcellus at his most bland stood back, chin in hand, considering. Hearing and understanding, he now made shift to ease the Roman into his new role. "The cairngorm necklace would look well but so would the larger of the Goddess statues."

Lucius jerked out of his brown study. He mused for a moment then, taking a coin from his pocket he tossed it to Adolphus. "Slip over to the flower stall. Get me a bunch – reds and yellows – as much as the coin will buy." Then to Marcellus: "We'll build the Goddess a bower and incorporate the necklace. See if you can weave the stems through the beads. You know the sort of thing. Cadmus, let's have the wine amphorae prominent on the ground to the left then get you dressed and out you go. Mingle until I pull my right ear."

After that the day passed in a blur. Lucius, dressed in his market costume – tweed cloak fastened with a silver brooch over a fur-trimmed russet tunic, the whole topped by a tall hat bearing a feather – dealt with lairds and farmers, hill-men and their wives. The dealing was hardheaded; everyone knew that the trading year was coming to its close – and while he let many items go as bargains, he scored some notable triumphs.

The amethyst geode from Cyrenaica, a constant, heavy companion for five months, was carried off in triumph by a laird's wife for a price that satisfied both parties. The Goddess was placed with reverence into the arms of an old woman while the flowers were scooped up and given to her granddaughter. On a whim Lucius bought the cairngorm necklace with his own money and gave it to a bonny young woman who had looked at it wistfully. Josephus would have frowned at such fecklessness; indeed Marcellus looked askance. Lucius, however, wanted someone to share his joy and the look in her eye as she fastened the stones around her neck, more than recompensed him.

The prolonged packing up as the shadows lengthened brought in a flurry of last-minute purchasers so that by the time Josephus returned it was to a stall almost devoid of stock. Josephus looked around him at the aftermath of overturned boxes and packing straw.

"A good day, I surmise?" he enquired, one eyebrow raised.

Marcellus and Cadmus looked as though they had run a long race. Adolphus stood massive as ever, waiting for the next instruction. Lucius rose from the crate where he had been sitting. He removed his hat and fanned his face, looking around, slightly bemused.

"I just don't know where they all came from," he said. "There can't be that many people in the whole of Caledonia." He looked to Josephus. "I hope you'll think we were successful. We certainly pleased a lot of people and it was so much..." he flapped his arms, now smiling "fun!"

He laid a hand on the Syrian's arm. "Thank you, Josephus. Thank you for your trust. I'm sure you could have done better but it was one of the most magnificent days of my life."

Josephus placed his hand on his friend's. "As to doing better, well I doubt it." Then, "Adolphus," he called. "Let me see you lift the strong box with one hand."

The big slave came forward and grasped the handle of the box with his big fist. Sinews stood out as his arm took the strain. Slowly the box rose from the ground. "It heavy," was his verdict as he replaced it. Laughter greeted his comment and he smiled his big, slow smile, not certain what he had said but delighted nevertheless.

Josephus clapped his hands. "Well, my friends, you have done well. Now pack everything and bring the mules to the inn. I have bespoke a roast sheep in the yard at the back and it will be cooked to a turn in half an hour. Cadmus, bring an amphora. I believe we have earned it."

The evening was long and convivial. They had to feast in the inn's backyard since slaves did not eat with their masters. Still, the management knew a profit when they saw one. As long as they stayed behind the bushes at the far end there was no problem. Josephus was a past master of these occasions. They only happened once a trip and although master spoke to slave as equal for the length of that evening, it was understood that the normal dispensation would apply on the morrow.

Much later, as the moon stood towards its zenith, Lucius kept a tryst in the market square.

Chapter 24

(Going Home)

Devana was a sizeable fort at the mouth of the River Don. Outside its high, turf walls clustered a settlement of thatched huts. Beyond the huts rose the masts of three trading vessels gently rocking beside a wooden jetty. Grey clouds scudded low from the west. The light was starting to fail as they led the mule strings up the final half-mile slope to the gates of the rest house.

It had been a wet two days march from Inverurie. At the start, despite a few sore heads and a misty drizzle, there had been a holiday mood among the group. Now everyone was tired as well as soaked to the skin. Lucius found himself in a strange mood. His thoughts kept harking back to the summer just past: the sights, the people, the achievements. At the same time he found himself looking forward to the next market, only to realize that there were no more, for this year at least. He felt deflated.

From their conversation it was plain that the slaves were looking forward to their winter quarters at Trimontium. Josephus had been careful not to say as much but Lucius had little doubt that he too yearned for his snug villa in the Northern Vicus with its fire of apple logs and its elegant furniture. Yet Lucius was not at all sure he too wanted to return to Trimontium. How would that first sight of the Eildons affect him? How would it be to visit Aithne's lonely hillside grave? Did he really wish to meet again his old colleagues?

His orders were to complete this year's trading trip and then report to Sixth Legion headquarters at Eboracum. There he would receive discrete briefing as well as assistance in setting up as a trader. Common sense would indicate bypassing Trimontium and heading straight for headquarters yet he was still, nominally at least, Josephus' guard. The Syrian was heading home with a small fortune in precious metals and coin. He would be at his most vulnerable on this last leg of the journey and the slaves would be little protection. Adolphus, who had the strength to take on ten men, lacked any aggressive instinct and, in any case, slaves were not allowed arms more dangerous than a stout staff.

No, it seemed that he must deliver the rest of the party to Trimontium. Perhaps he could make his stay as short as possible but, then, he would have to visit Aithne. Yet what could he say to her? Although logic told him otherwise his heart told him that he had betrayed her.

Josephus and Lucius stood in the shelter of the entrance to the guesthouse while the slaves led the mules through to the stables. The Syrian had noted his friend's withdrawn expression. So here was the crisis. The hawk was nearly ready to fly. Well, so be it. He, Josephus, would do his part.

After they had eaten and he had seen the slaves bedded down, Josephus sat once again with Lucius in front of a log fire. The Roman had maintained some conversation during the meal but now he leaned forward, elbows on knees, staring into the flames. Between his hands he cupped a goblet of wine.

Josephus studied his map of Caledonia by the light of an oil lamp. The map, a little more complete than last year, was spread across his knees. He angled it to catch the lamp's yellow light. Now he tapped the map with his index finger.

"What do you think, Lucius? We could travel back down the trunk road. That'd take, say, ten days. It would be quicker if we could ride the mules but the mule hasn't been born yet that can carry Adolphus, so there it is. Or we could take ship to the mouth of the Tweed and walk back to Trimontium along the valley. At best that would be two days by ship and another two on foot. Of course, if the weather turns foul it could take for ever."

Lucius, who had been jerked back from his own thoughts at the words of the trader, raised his goblet to his lips then took the near edge of the map in his hand, the better to study it. After a moment's thought he smiled wryly. "Really, Josephus, I'm the last person to ask if you want an honest answer. Two days in a ship; in the open sea; in October? Can you imagine it?"

The trader smiled too, encouraged to hear his friend jest.

"We would put you under the half deck on a couch of lamb's fleece. I have a draught distilled from the seed of the poppy. You would know nothing until we carried you ashore," he replied.

Lucius put down his goblet and traced the length of the Via Domitiana with his finger, studying the lie of the land. At length he said, "If it was just me, I would walk the road. At least I would know that the ten days was indeed ten days. If the winds turn foul the sea journey could be open ended. Indeed, we might never even put into the Tweed."

He stood and leaned one hand on the massive beam over the hearth, gazing into the fire.

"On the other hand," he continued, "if I were to think only of your security, it would have to be the ship. The Via's patrolled but no-one could call it entirely safe this far north." He did not mention the small but heavy chests hidden within the mules' panniers. Even in a government guesthouse, discretion was the rule.

He turned to the Syrian with a grimace. "On balance, I'd have to recommend the ship although the gods know that I don't look forward to the prospect."

Josephus nodded thoughtfully. He began to roll the map. "Of course," he said as if musing out loud, "there's no requirement for you to come with us now, Lucius. Perhaps you have plans of your own?"

Lucius waved one hand vaguely, looking back at the flames. "Plans," he said, "well…" He trailed off then squatted down and began to prod at the fire with a branch from the log basket.

Josephus allowed the silence to build. Finally, when Lucius said nothing, he sighed.

"My friend," he said, "may I speak openly?"

Lucius looked over his shoulder at Josephus. He studied the familiar features of the Syrian: the deep eyes, the hooked nose, the long, grey beard. In the mellow lamp light they seemed the epitome of calm and wisdom, as if Josephus were a revenant of a former age. He tossed the branch onto the fire, stood and returned to his seat.

Facing the trader he said, "Of course you can, Josephus."

Josephus hitched his robes at the shoulders. He looked around the common room. There were several other guests but none near them. The general murmur of conversation was enough to cover anything he said but, nevertheless, he leaned closer and lowered his voice.

"Lucius, my friend," he began, "I was glad to have you with me on this journey for several reasons. For myself, you have provided excellent company and a sense of security. For you…well, I was glad to offer you a period of healing. And it seems to me that the healing has at least begun, wouldn't you say my friend?"

Lucius nodded. "It has, Josephus. I shall ever be in your debt."

Josephus waved away the thanks with a smile. He paused again before continuing.

"Forgive me, Lucius, if this is no business of mine, but I have never understood why you resigned your vine staff. I can understand that the death of Aithne hit you hard but the Fifth was your life; your support. You may tell me that your drinking meant that you had to leave. Indeed, I had supposed that I would have to wrestle with you on the journey, trying to wean you away from Bacchus, but never once since we started out have you shown the least sign of addiction."

Josephus looked at his fingernails and then back at his friend.

"Tell me, Lucius, might you not, even now, petition to resume your former rank?"

Lucius looked uncomfortable. "Nay Josephus," he said, "you do not treat the Legion like that. Once you're gone, you're gone and the skin heals as if you had never been."

The landlord's dog, a hound of indeterminate breed, waddled over in search of leavings. Lucius stroked its head absently. The dog looked soulfully into his face for some moments and then, when no food was forthcoming, waddled away again.

Josephus felt his way forward, carefully.

"Have you ever thought of being a trader, Lucius? I ask because I believe you have it in you to be a good trader, perhaps even a great one. By no means everyone has this skill. It seems to me that it might be a shame to waste it."

More than anything Lucius wished not to lie to his friend. Now he sensed the possibility of continuing this conversation with the truth.

"It's funny you should ask that, Josephus," he said. "I have given increasing thought to it over the last months. I have a small gratuity from the State. It was in my mind to buy some trade goods and maybe set up in a small way, perhaps in southern Britannia."

Josephus reached for the wine flask. He filled Lucius' goblet first, then his own, nodding thoughtfully the while. He set the flask down again, wiping a few drops of wine from the table with his finger.

"Then listen, my friend for I have a proposition to put to you." He paused, stroking his beard, the firelight dancing in his eyes. "Lucius, I never had a son, or at least," he looked aside into the fire, "not one that I know of." He turned again to his friend, his gaze deep and serious. "But if I had had one, I could wish that he had been like you, unlikely as that may seem," he smiled, "between a Syrian Jew and a mountaineer of Tarraconensis."

"I am old," he continued. "There are only a few more journeys left in these old bones."

He dismissed Lucius' protest with a wave.

"The horizon still calls but soon it will be that greater horizon and, in truth, I am curious to know what lies beyond it. I become weary. But before I cross that horizon I would like to know that what I have built here on earth will be in safe hands."

He managed a self-deprecatory chuckle. "There are the slaves, you see. I wouldn't have them sold to just anyone. And then there are the mules and the villa, quite apart from a tidy sum of treasure I have put away."

He paused, then went on in a measured tone. "Lucius, would you be my partner? Would you come with me on my last few trading journeys? After that it is in my mind to return to Latakia, to rest these old bones in warm sand. Perhaps I may even find my way to Q'mran again. I see myself seated at the mouth of a cave, disputing the Torah with young disciples agog at my learning. I would take with me a comfortable sum to see my through my final years. All the rest I would leave to you"

All the while, as he spoke, he had studied his friend's face. Although Lucius struggled to maintain his composure, Josephus had caught the flicker of agony in his eyes when he had mentioned partnership. 'It is as I surmised,' he thought to himself. 'There is nothing to be done.'

He clapped a hand on his friend's arm and made to get up. "It is late, Lucius. Sleep on it. There is no urgency. Give me your answer when you are ready."

Chapter 25

(Tweed)

"Pull, you whoreson bastards!"

The shipmaster's snarling cry cuts across the thunder of the waves. Even in the foetid gloom of the half-deck it carries enough force to waken Lucius from his stupor. Clinging with reflexive hopelessness to one of the pillars supporting the steering deck, he opens gummy eyes.

"Put your fucking backs into it unless you want the crabs to eat your useless guts!"

The deck is falling away beneath his legs. Lucius watches with dull curiosity as his bed, the foul nest of sheepskin which has sheltered him for three days, slides away into the gloom. He dry retches. Where his stomach ought to be is an aching void. Misery fills his thoughts.

The deck suddenly reverses direction. Things unseen cannon past him in the gloom together with a quantity of filthy water. The leather curtain protecting the entrance to the half-deck is swept abruptly back.

"Let's 'ave you, mister."

The mate, a grotesque, simian creature with long arms and bandy legs, stands silhouetted in the half-light. Despite the extravagant pitch and roll of the ship, he swings from one handhold to another, neatly avoiding the bales and boxes lying tumbled in the darkness.

"Gotta job for you, we 'as," he growls taking hold of Lucius' arm. Even over the odour of the half-deck, the acrid stench of the man assaults Lucius' nostrils. He dry retches again. With remorseless power the mate detaches Lucius' hold on the wooden upright before half dragging him into the open air. From forward, where they are penned, comes the frenzied braying of the mules.

"'ere," the mate says, thrusting a leather bucket into his hands. The ship which has been presenting its stern to the sky, suddenly reversed its pitch. Lucius sits down abruptly. A wave of filthy water sluices around him, enveloping him to his armpits. A liberal dollop hits him in the face.

The mate reaches down one powerful arm and hoists him to his feet.

"No time for playing silly bastards," he says. "Fucking bail unless you wants to swim ashore."

The word 'bail' means nothing to the soldier but the mate waves one hairy arm towards the bows where, amidst the spindrift, three sodden figures are scooping up water with buckets and emptying them from the rowing ports. Lucius staggers forward to join them, eliciting curses where he bounces off the crewmen pulling on the heavy sweeps. One of the bailers, robe kilted above bony knees, pauses briefly, wiping lank hair out of his eyes.

"Welcome to the Tweed," says Josephus, before bending to scoop and empty another bucketful. Beyond him Marcellus and Cadmus work without pause.

"Might I suggest you join us in our efforts?" says the trader. "Only I fear you are offending the mate with your lack of industry."

Lucius turns to see the mate swinging towards him on prehensile arms. Hurriedly he bends and scoops with the others. Strangely, as he works, he starts to feel almost human. The vice-like headache which had been his for days evaporates. Were it not for the threat of impending death, he would feel almost well.

All around are huge, yellow waves. From time to time one breaks explosively in a welter of spray. Others simply rise and collapse. Through the spray ahead of the ship, Lucius catches occasional glimpses of a low, wooded headland. To his left, for perhaps half a mile, lies a field of boiling white water. Occasionally a patch clears long enough to show sand before another great comber breaks in ruin.

What, to Lucius, appears to be the end of the world is, in fact, a carefully calculated piece of risk-taking by the shipmaster, in pursuit of a fat payment promised him by Josephus. The wind is foul for the entrance. This means shipping the great sweeps and rowing into the river mouth. However the Tweed is in mild spate after autumnal rains making it impossible for the ship's crew to row against the current without assistance. The shipmaster, who knows these waters well, has therefore elected to enter the river on the third hour of the flood tide when tidal stream and river current will roughly cancel each other out.

Which would have been fine except for the maelstrom where river and tide meet over the shallow bar at the river mouth and which now bids fair to overwhelm them. Huge standing waves rise and collapse. Others roar up behind the ship, forcing it bodily forward, the surf tumbling and crashing over the bulwarks. At these moments the steering oar is useless. Only the strength of the crewmen on the sweeps keep the ship from broaching broadside on to the waves and capsizing.

The shipmaster is currently wondering whether he had seriously miscalculated in his pursuit of profit. There is nothing to be done, of course. There is no question of putting about in this sea. Nor can they anchor. They are committed. Heaving on the steering oar with all his strength to counteract the slewing of the ship, he sends up a brief prayer to Poseidon.

"Pull, you bastards!"

They'd better had. Just over two hours of flood left and they are tiring. Two men to each of the eight sweeps, except for the bow sweep to starboard. There the huge German slave pulls on his own. Twice he has seen the mate shouting in his ear, telling him to pull less strongly. If his great strength breaks the sweep, unbalancing the effort, they will die.

Lucius staggers and bails. Sometimes they seem to gain on the water. Then a wave crest will crash inboard, making nothing of their efforts. His muscles ache. Salt water encrusts his eyes. Yet, slowly he becomes aware that they are gaining. Over the last half hour the motion of the ship has become less violent. He risks a look over the bulwark. The scene has changed. Out to the right waves crash over black rocks and onto a broad beach. The low, wooded headland is nearer and passing slowly down their side.

He dips a few more buckets-ful before glancing astern. He shudders. A wall of yellowy-white water cuts off the view to seaward. That's what they have come through. He swears to himself, not for the first time, that he will never take ship again. Then, in a guilty after-thought, he gives silent thanks to Mithras and Mercurius for his deliverance.

During the next hour, with the blissful ignorance of the landsman, Lucius is unaware of the prodigies of seamanship unfolding before him as the ship crabs upriver. Twice they touch bottom on the shifting sandbanks as the shipmaster seeks out the weaker currents. Then there is a mad race across the tumbling river, dodging tree trunks and sea wrack. Finally the anchor stone is dropped, the ship slams into the jetty and the mate swings ashore to drop a heavy leather hawser onto a bollard.

Crewmen collapse groaning where they sit. Adolphus lumbers to his feet looking dazed. Lucius gazes at the shore: the beautiful, solid shore. From a path through the trees appear four legionaries and a pair of slaves. There is a fort on the hill above, built to protect the harbour and give warning of sea borne enemies. Lucius has patrolled here on occasion. Two of the men, a decurion and what Lucius takes to be a clerk, come out onto the jetty while the others stay at the landward end.

"What ship?" asks the decurion, casting a disdainful eye over the filthy, sea-stained upper-works and the jumbled, sodden deck.

"Sea Beauty," replies the shipmaster with no hint of irony.

"Sea Pig, more like," comes the laconic reply. "That'll be five sestertii landing fee and," he casts a theatrical look to left and right, "two more for damaging the jetty."

'It's good to be home,' thinks Lucius.

Chapter 26

(Death)

Tadg ran. He ran and ran until he thought his heart would burst.

"Cinnie, I'm coming," he gasped, unaware.

Bracken caught at his feet. From time to time he fell but always he clambered up again and ran on. The sun was almost down but he would continue as long as the light lasted. Ahead of him the three hills stood clear against the westering sun. Just a matter of finding bastard Callum now – find him and make sure that Cinnie and the bairns were safe.

For two months on Callum's orders, Tadg had become part of the fishing community in its mean little settlement at the mouth of the Tweed. At first he had demurred. After the brutal murder of Rhodri following his leadership challenge, most of the remaining warriors had deserted Callum. Tadg had thought him weak enough to defy. What a fool he'd been.

"'s all right, Tadg." Callum had seemed all affability. "'f I woz you I wouldn't go neither." He picked up Cabal and stroked his head reflectively. The little dog licked his nose. "Nice little woman like your Cinnie," he continued. "Wouldn't want to go away in case anyfink happened to 'er. And then there's the bairns. Delicate fings bairns. They get hurt dead easy."

He turned his massive head towards Tadg. His eyes were half-closed. A salacious leer parted his lips. Tadg had shivered. The message was clear.

Callum had done his homework. Josephus's movements were an open secret around Trimontium – away in May, back early October. Only doubt was whether he'd come back by road or sea. He'd done both in the past. Callum's answer was to send Tadg to the mouth of the Tweed. Cadhir he had sent to the vicinity of Camelon where the Via Domitiana, coming from the north, crossed the Eastern River. Having seen what had happened to

Tadg's mild revolt, Cadhir kept silent. Nevertheless Callum made reference to the small Celt's white-haired old mother. Callum believed in motivation.

* * *

It was the night before the parting of the ways. Tomorrow Lucius would turn south on moorland paths to Cappuck and thence to Eboracum. Josephus had reassured him that he and his party would be safe on the last day's march into Trimontium.

"After all, I've done it before and these last miles are well-patrolled. No, my friend: I understand some of your reluctance to return to Trimontium. You must follow the dictates of your own heart."

Lucius had tried to explain what he was about to do, without lying, but even to his own ears his words sounded false. When he finally fell silent, Josephus reached for the satchel in which he kept his documents. They were camped in a wooded glade. It was a clear, chill night. The stars hung low, coruscating. Josephus rummaged. He brought out a parchment, rolled and tied with a ribbon.

"My will, Lucius," he said, holding the document up so that the firelight illuminated it. "I had it drawn up and witnessed by the clerk at Devana. It is a proper will, executed in Latin. In it I leave everything to you."

"Josephus…" Lucius began.

The old Jew held up his hand.

"You are going to become a trader, Lucius. It is right that you should face your own problems so that the lessons you learn are equally your own. In the fullness of time, however, you will need investment. It is inevitable. When that time comes I want you to be my inheritor. In that way you will carry on my work in Malkuth, the Plane of Earth."

Lucius felt tears very near. All this from a man he was

deceiving.

"Josephus...I don't know what to say," he began. "You do me too much honour."

"No, my son." The Syrian's voice was measured and calm. "Not too much honour, I assure you."

He placed the palms of his hands together beneath his chin. The night became very quiet. In his stillness, lit by the flickering flames, he reminded Lucius of the sandstone statues in the Syrian Desert, remains of ancient Chaldea.

"There is much you will learn as you travel. For now let me just tell you this: there is a Divine Spark in all of us. In some it is buried deeper than in others. In you, my son, it is barely veiled. What I have done here is merely to embody what is written in the Akashic Record; the record of all that was and is and will be. Had I wished I could have done no other. As it is, you are to all intents and purposes my son. Thus what I do, I do with the heartiest delight."

He raised his hands to shoulder level, shrugging extravagantly. The spell was broken. His face creased into lines of laughter.

"Come, my boy; enough of this. If this is to be our last night together for a while, let it be one of joy and laughter. Cadmus," he called, "an amphora, if you please and come you all to the fireside. We will celebrate."

* * *

A chill little breeze heralded the morning. Mist wreathed fitfully among the beech trees, where a few yellow leaves yet fluttered. Josephus had insisted that Lucius take one of the mules and a proportion of the year's takings. With a full heart, the Roman loaded his belongings into the panniers until there was nothing left but farewells.

The slaves gathered round. Lucius gave them each ten denarii.

In turn, they bowed and murmured his thanks. Adolphus looked first with amazement at the money in his vast paw, then at his benefactor until Cadmus took the coins and placed them in the purse at the giant's belt.

Lucius turned to Josephus. He had wondered what he would say at this moment. When the words came it was as if someone else spoke.

"Would you give me your blessing, Rabboni?" Where the Hebrew word for teacher came from he didn't know. Perhaps he had heard it somewhere. He knelt.

The old trader stood before him, placing his hands upon his head. With eyes closed he raised his face to the sky. Lucius did not understand the words of the blessing. Some were chanted in a strong monotone, producing a powerful effect. Waves of heat seemed to emanate from the Syrian's hands and Lucius felt his heart leaping in his breast. Now the old man was taking him by the elbows and raising him. He planted a kiss on each of the Roman's cheeks then the two men embraced. Finally they stood apart, Josephus with his hands on the other's upper arms.

"Go well, young friend," was all he said.

Lucius nodded mutely. There was nothing left to say. He turned, unhitched his mule and set off to the south.

* * *

Lucius walks southwards, downhill, along the muddy sheep track, the bridle of the mule loose in his hand. He is tempted to turn. Perhaps his companions will still be standing at the edge of the wood on the hillside, watching him. Instead he picks up his pace, facing resolutely towards his new life. Tears are coursing down his face now but he is unaware of them. The mule baulks, equally unhappy at leaving its friends. Lucius yanks on the rope and on they go.

Ten minutes now since the parting. Lucius lifts his head. He cuffs angrily at the tears and looks around him. A terrible cry rents the air. He turns, his eyes wide with shock. The mule blunders into him then skitters aside. The initial cry is followed by a barely-heard bubbling groan of agony and then the braying of frightened mules.

Lucius drops the bridle and starts running, running back towards his friends. The way is steep and muddy yet he moves as fast as he can, steel-shod sandals throwing up gobbets of mud, the great sword thumping on his back. At the main track he turns left, along the borders of the wood, hurrying on. The way continues to rise along the rim of a small quarry, to the left, used for road-building material.

Now he slows. Whatever he is to face, he must have his breathing under control. He reaches over his shoulder and draws the great sword from its sheath, holding it before him in both hands. The bubbling cry comes again, much closer, somewhere just ahead. Lucius moves into the shelter of the trees, gliding silently over the fallen leaves and beech mast. There! Twenty yards ahead. Lucius eases behind a tree trunk the better to take in the scene. When he makes his move there must be no room for error.

Nearest to him, just off the track, within the margin of the wood, cluster the mules. They have been tethered to a bush. Partly masked by them he sees the slaves. Marcellus and Cadmus are sitting on the ground. Adolphus lies nearby. Blood seeps from a wound to his head. Beyond them again stand two Celtic warriors, apparently meant to be guarding the slaves. In fact their attention is focused some yards beyond them and slightly to their left.

Following the direction of their gaze, Lucius' feels his heart falter. Josephus hangs from the branch of a tree. A length of rope tied to both his wrists has been passed over the branch so that his toes just touch the ground. His head is slumped. Blood drips from his face.

In front of him stands Callum. He has sliced the old man with his spear from shoulder to hipbone. Now the Celt is working the point of the spear into his stomach. The old man writhes and groans weakly. Lucius is barely aware of another man, a slight figure, watching from the other side of Callum. He is not dressed for war and Lucius dismisses him. Lastly, incongruously, a small dog sits near Callum, watching proceedings with evident interest and wagging its tail.

Callum speaks. "Nah, trust me, I can keep yer alive all day, old man." He waggles the spear haft and Josephus thrashes. "So just tell me where 'e's gone an' it'll be a nice, clean thrust to the heart, you hearin' me?"

The plan is formed. Not many options. Aim: save Josephus. Method: kill the Celts. He needs fighting room. He needs to get closer. Both mean moving to the left onto the path. He glides slowly in that direction, noting that the lip of the quarry lies beyond the path. Callum and the guards are still intent. He is behind their line of vision. Fifteen yards; ten. He is partially shielded by the mules. He looks up. The small man beyond Callum is looking straight at him, his eyes round as plates. Without thinking Lucius raises his finger to his lips and glides on. Amazingly the small man nods and relaxes.

Five yards and the dog whirls, yapping. Lucius springs. The nearest guard is turning as the great sword takes him in the neck. He topples taking the sword with him. His dying cry gurgles and is choked off by blood. The second guard has half-turned and is bringing up his spear as Lucius leaps the falling body, drawing the short, stabbing sword. Ignoring the spear he crashes into the second man, taking him off balance. He thrusts upwards with both hands and all his strength. The man grunts and starts to fall. The short sword too is jammed.

Lucius leaves the swords and catches up the guard's spear before it can fall. He whirls towards Callum, just in time. Fast as a snake the Celt is upon him in a crouching run, the bloody spear blade flickering like a tongue. Lucius parries and thrusts, moving to his right.

"See to your master," he shouts at the slaves.

Then the fight is on. Adrenaline slows time so that each engagement seems to take minutes. There is time to read the flicker of an eyebrow, to watch the opening of a bloody seam in the flesh. Callum fights with a cruel grin on his prognathus features. He fights with a frightening intensity. Being a Celt he can't resist taunting his opponent.

"Was she good, then, Roman? Did you enjoy 'er? Only I 'ad 'er years ago so she was spoiled goods, wasn't she?"

Lucius fights with measured skill but he is aware of the guile and strength of his opponent. Callum is turning him, trying to force him back towards the lip of the quarry. Lucius parries. He slips under Callum's spear. The quarry edge is ten feet away; plenty of room.

A needle-sharp pain in his ankle causes him to look down involuntarily. Growling and snarling, the little dog has fastened onto him. He kicks out, sending it flying, howling, into the woods. He falls backwards in the process. Callum's spear hisses past him, carving a shallow wound across his upper chest and left shoulder. Lucius loses his spear as he hits the ground. Callum is upon him, stabbing downwards again and again while Lucius rolls and scrabbles among the leaves. His hand finds a rock and he hurls it at Callum. By luck it glances off the Celt's brow, distracting him long enough for Lucius to scramble to his feet.

Callum pauses, breathing heavily. He cuffs blood from his forehead and grins his evil grin.

"Oh dear, little soldier boy," he sneers. "Has youse lost your little spear then?"

Keeping his blade aimed at the Roman's stomach he bends down and picks up the fallen spear. He seems to consider for a moment.

"Fair fight, eh? I'll let you have it back, shall I?"

Lucius pays little attention. It's just words. He glances beyond the Celt. Marcellus and Cadmus have released Josephus, are tending to him. Adolphus is sitting up, swaying. He sees the bloodied body of his master and lets out a howl of grief. Callum is distracted for a moment and Lucius springs forward but the blade is there, jabbing at his chest and he moves back.

"Nah," says Callum. "Don't fink I wants a fair fight."

Deliberately he throws the spear behind him. In the same moment he springs forward. Lucius dodges right, hears a squeal of outrage as he trips over the terrier and falls. The fall goes on longer than it should. It ends with a numbing impact and unbelievable pain. Consciousness recedes. When it returns, it brings back the pain – hideous grinding agony.

He is looking upwards towards the green lip of the quarry face. There, looking down at him, are the faces of Callum and the terrier. The latter is whining. The former is bellowing with laughter. After a while he manages to choke out some words.

"Just wait, Roman; just wait 'til my fucking harper gets to sing about this." Laughter overtakes him again, then: "You're goin' t'be so fucking *famous*!" He howls with mirth for some seconds then starts to calm.

"Right," he says. "Three man-lengths straight down. Shouldn't be able to miss an' even if I do, there's plenty of spears up 'ere."

He brings his spear into view and raises it. Lucius gazes at the razor sharp point, dulled by Josephus' blood, then closes his eyes. He begins the incantation to Mithras, god of the Legions. He has barely started when he hears an animal howl followed by a hollow impact. He opens his eyes as something heavy crashes past him, peppering him with rocks and dirt. Painfully he turns his head. He is looking into the bloodshot eyes of the Celt at a distance of five paces. Callum's skull is crushed and leaking. He is dead.

Wearily, Lucius turns his face back to the quarry edge.

Adolphus, a large branch in his hand, gazes downwards in dulled surprise. Marcellus and Cadmus stand on either side of him, faces blanched with shock.

Lucius licks dried lips. When he speaks his voice comes out as a croak.

"Does your master still live?"

"He does, Lucius," replies Marcellus.

Lucius takes several deep breathes. The pain throbs terribly. He locates it in his right leg – probably broken. He feels consciousness slipping away and brings it back by sheer willpower.

"Marcellus," he croaks, "tend to your master. Cadmus: use Adolphus to bring me to your master."

Either then or when they come to move him he loses consciousness. It is a mercy. Somewhere he has a jumbled memory of the little dog skittering down the sheer cliff. It noses its master's face. When there is no response, it lies down and places its head on its paws, whining quietly.

* * *

When consciousness returned, he was lying near Josephus. Marcellus had propped his master's head on a bundle of clothes and was smoothing his brow with a damp cloth. Lucius craned round to look at the Syrian. His eyes were closed and his breathing shallow and ragged. He groped for his friend's hand and grasped it but the healing power was gone, overwhelmed by the bolts of pain consuming his body. In any case the old man's aura was near extinction. He squeezed the hand and Josephus' eyes flickered open.

He gazed at Lucius, at first without recognition. Then awareness returned. A fond smile formed on his lips.

"Marcellus," he whispered. "Cadmus, Adolphus, leave us please. We must talk."

Reluctantly the slaves rose and moved off a short distance into the woods.

Josephus gazed at Lucius' face, taking in his features.

"So, my son," he said, his voice barely audible. "It seems that you will inherit sooner than we thought." He coughed weakly.

"Josephus," said Lucius, riding the waves of pain. "We will get you to a surgeon. We will make you well."

The Syrian rolled his head briefly in negation.

"Nay, my son; you know better. Now listen; there is very little time." He licked his lips, then continued.

"Marcellus will say Kaddish for me. He is a Judaean Jew. Leave the funeral rites to him."

He breathed hoarsely for a few moments.

"As for you, you go to serve your Emperor – no, don't ask me how I know, my son. I have many sources of information. You are a good man and true. You will serve him well. Take the slaves and the rest. No one will question your inheritance. The will is foolproof. The slaves are discreet and need a master. It will be the most natural thing in the world when you journey forth as my heir; better, I would hazard, than anything imperial clerks could put together."

He flinched, grasping Lucius' hand convulsively. The next cough brought blood to his lips. He was silent for a while. Lucius gazed on him with deepest sorrow. He had not realized before how much he had come to love this man.

"Lucius." The voice was weaker now. He had to strain to hear. "There is a greater story of which you are a part. You will catch glimpses of it as you journey on. Stay true to that story. Shine in the darkness my son."

The old man fell silent. Lucius thought that he was gone but he opened his eyes once more. Lucius crawled closer to hear his words, fighting the pain.

"Go to Q'mran for me, my son, when you may." The voice came soft as falling leaves. "Tell them how Josephus ben Judah died. Tell them that I kept the faith."

His head fell sideways. Lucius gazed through tears at his friend, his father. He reached out and closed Josephus' eyes, eyes that now beheld the Greater Horizon.

* * *

Later, when Marcellus had intoned Kaddish and prepared the body, while Cadmus and Adolphus made two litters to sling between the mules, Lucius looked up to see the small Celt standing near. In his hand he held the bridle of Lucius' mule.

"Saw him wandering down in the valley. Thought you might want 'im."

Tadg tied the bridle to a bush and made to leave.

"No, stay," called Lucius. Loss of blood and pain had weakened him severely but his mind was lucid.

The Celt turned back and knelt by the injured man.

"Why did you not betray me when you saw me?" asked Lucius.

Tadg pursed his lips and looked around the glade, embarrassed. Finally he looked back at the Roman.

"'e 'ad it coming did Callum. Said 'e'd rape my woman an' kill me bairns if I didn't spy on you. I might have told on you but then I fort, I can't kill 'im; maybe the Roman can. An' you did, didn't you?" His gap-toothed smile was engaging.

"Tell me your name," said Lucius.

"Tadg," replied the other, "Tadg of...Well, I ain't Tadg of anywhere no more. But that's good too."

"Well, Tadg of Nowhere, I am Lucius Terentius Aquilina and I want you to do something for me. Go to the mule. Unload everything from the panniers and lay it on the grass. Near the bottom you will find a heavy, leather bag. Bring that to me."

Hesitatingly, Tadg did as he had been bade. Two minutes later he laid the bagful of coins beside Lucius.

"This," Lucius indicated the bag – he felt too weak to lift it, "is for you, Tadg. Take it and the mule with my blessing."

Tadg was speechless. He reached a hand towards the bag then stopped. "Do you mean it, Master? It ain't no trick?"

"No, it's not a trick, Tadg. It's a thank offering."

The little Celt's eyes sparkled. He grasped the bag and stood looking down at Lucius.

After a moment's reflection he said, "You ain't 'alf bad for a Roman. Tell you what, you ever get any trouble round Selgovae lands, you just send for Tadg."

With that he turned, slipped the bag into the pannier and untied the mule. He led the beast as far as the edge of the quarry where he peered downwards. Lucius heard him give a sharp whistle. After a few moments the small form of the terrier appeared, belly close to the ground, tail between its legs.

"Come on youse," said Tadg and man, mule and dog set off into the trees.

Chapter 27

(Aftermath)

'Nancy, 30 miles'

The granite milestone stood proud of the weeds on the far side of the fosse, the ditch that bordered the road. Aurelio gazed at the wooded hills surrounding them. They were lofty hills, clad with fir trees. He took in a deep breath of pine-scented air. Far to the east now, just above the treetops, rose the peaks of mountains, blue and hazy in the distance. Soon, in the next day or two, they would be amongst them and his heart was glad.

It was a little under a month since he had received his orders. They had made good time despite a broken wheel. It had been repaired at Augustobona and they had carried on through the fragrant heat of early summer. The market takings had been good. The Imperial Treasury would be proud of him, he thought wryly.

This was plentiful land and peaceful. He had never travelled it before but was struck by its ordered beauty; its rich farmland and prosperous farms. There was an air of settled tranquillity about it – not what they'd find once they were through the mountains. In theory the German tribes were at peace in their forests across the Rhenus but, unless things had changed, the near bank, where the Legions waited, would be a watchful military zone. The ghost of Publius Quinctilius Varus still dogged the Rhenish frontier.

"Aurelio, what will you have for your supper?"

Trista had come dancing up from the wagon. In her hand she held a hazel switch with which she artlessly decapitated the roadside cow parsley.

"Marcellus says that there is the smoked ham we bought in Doulevant or the trout me and Adolphus caught this morning. I think," she lowered her voice confidentially, "we should have the trout. Adolphus would be so pleased. It was the first one he's ever tickled and anyway, it'll go off in this heat if we keep it 'til tomorrow."

This was a different Trista from the skinny, verminous thief they had first encountered four weeks ago. Good food had filled her out. Exercise and fresh air had brought a glow to her person, a glow no longer hidden by grime. "The man likes clean girls," the woman had said and Trista didn't need to be told twice. In truth she still didn't completely believe that the man was on her side but in the absence of any proof to the contrary she would keep her side of any bargain.

Aurelio made a show of judicious consideration, stroking his jaw. "Then I believe we must have the trout," he announced. "And what part are you going to play in its preparation?" Aurelio had made good his intention of employing Trista. She had proved apt. The mules had never before been so well-groomed. Ribbons, evidently purloined from stock, were plaited into their manes. On Trista's insistence, Cadmus had shown her how to prepare hoof oil. Aurelio could have sworn that the mules themselves now stepped out with a new pride.

Progress had not been so rapid on the cooking front. Trista's efforts could best be termed enthusiastic. Trista frowned.

"Marcellus is going to show me again how to gut and clean them." She looked up at Aurelio with large, serious eyes. "He says that it wasn't my fault, last time. He says he should have been watching me more carefully." She switched the head off a passing dandelion. "Anyway, he says that fish gut is a delicacy in some places and it didn't do Cadmus any real harm."

Aurelio suppressed a smile. Trista started skipping along beside him. A blue dragonfly danced across their path. She tried to touch it with her hazel wand but it jerked swiftly away.

"Aurelio," she asked, "why do you walk with a stick?"

Aurelio was used to being questioned in this manner. Trista was no respecter of privacy but, then, it seemed that no one had ever taught her social niceties. They now knew a little about her background; just a little, though, because she only talked freely to Adolphus. If questioned Adolphus would volunteer a version of what he had heard but forgot most of the details.

They knew that her parents had been moderately well to do, that they had lived in a town on the banks of the Loire and that both had died suddenly some time ago. Since then it was evident that Trista had lived on her wits. Aurelio was no nearer discovering if there were any other near relations. Although in general she was as bright as a button, any attempt at questioning met with downcast eyes and a stubborn silence.

Aurelio came back from his thoughts to see Trista still gazing at him, awaiting an answer.

"I fought a very bad man," he said, "and broke my leg."

Trista considered this for a while.

"Did you kill him?" she asked, flicking the head off another dandelion.

"No," he replied. He wouldn't tell her that the killing had been done by Adolphus, that gentle giant, her friend. "No, he was killed by someone else. I just fell over a cliff, that's all."

Trista looked at him, shocked, for a moment, then giggled. "You were very clumsy then, weren't you?"

Aurelio took a mock swipe at her with his stick. "Cheeky girl," he said with an attempt at severity. "Go and tell Marcellus I'll have the trout."

Away she danced, back to the wagon where Marcellus would be making preparations for the evening meal. Aurelio followed her progress fondly for a moment then returned his gaze to the road.

Clumsy indeed! Still, the result had been the same. The ride in the mule litter had been agony made worse by the grief of knowing that the body of Josephus was being carried close by. He remembered little of the details. After some hours they had reached the Via Domitiana and fallen in with a patrol. The decurion had sent a runner on to Trimontium to alert the surgeon. A medical orderly met them a few miles short of the camp and administered poppy to alleviate the pain.

Later, in the hospital he had woken to a moment of lucidity. The surgeon, a Greek trained in Alexandria, was tutting over his leg.

"Comminuted, do you see?" he was saying to the orderlies. "That and compound. Blood loss of three pints or so but that is to be expected. Only lucky there was no arterial rupture. Well, we must set about reduction though I doubt but we'll end up with a short leg."

A flask of poppy juice was raised to Lucius' lips and he swam away on a dreamy tide cut short by unconsciousness when the surgeon made a start.

The surgeon had been right, of course. The leg was only slightly shorter than the other but the difference felt enormous. His convalescence had been a struggle. The hospital was built round a courtyard and it was here that other convalescents lay in the weak spring sunlight – but not Lucius. Daily he had worked hard on rehabilitating the leg, swinging away with the aid of a crutch, teeth gritted with determination not to give in to the pain. He could be seen, even on the worst of winter days, hobbling around Trimontium camp. Even the surgeon, a wintry man, inured to the folly of mankind, showed guarded pleasure at his progress.

"Gratifying," had been his verdict when the plaster was removed. "Take care of it and you will walk almost normally. I would suggest a stout cane. There will undoubtedly be some pain in damp weather but it can't be helped. Now we need your bed so I would be grateful if you would make other arrangements as soon as possible."

'Other arrangements' had meant sharing the modest quarters of Quintus Fabricius for a week or so as he waited for wheeled transport to take him to Eboracum. During that time, with the aid of his friend and seated on a mule, he had climbed to the lonely northern shoulder of Eildon. There Quintus left him in the sea of heather beside Aithne's small grave.

Lucius had sat silently for a while. He had no proper sense that she was here. After a period of time, however, he looked around him at the wooded vistas, heard the song of the lark, felt the gentle westerly breeze on his cheek. If she was anywhere, he reasoned, it must be here, a part of the surroundings she had loved so much. He placed an offering, a small bunch of bluebells and campion, on the stone slab.

Gradually he began to speak, telling her of all that had happened since he had set out from Trimontium the previous year. He told her of the markets and the adventures, finishing with the death of Callum. Finally, haltingly, he told her about the woman with whom he had lain in Inverurie. Then he fell silent. Small white clouds hurried by on the breeze. Heather bloom scented the air. The sun sparkled on the distant Tweed. After a while there stole over him a sense of peace; of being cherished. He had the strongest feeling of wholeness. Forgiveness was his, he discovered, but with it came the recognition that he hadn't needed it. He returned to the camp much more nearly at ease with himself.

The Chief Clerk, a master of legal administration, undertook to prove the will before the military magistrate and then executed it. It seemed that Lucius was now a wealthy man although he could take no pleasure in the fact. The beasts, slaves and stock came to him of course but there was also a small fortune in specie and precious stones lodged with one Mordecai, the nearest the eastern Vicus had to a banker.

Then there was the small but exquisite villa in the Northern Vicus. Lucius had considered keeping it but knew in his heart that he would never return to Trimontium. In the end it was sold to a civil engineer, contracted by the government to survey and initiate repairs to the Via Domitiana. He would make good use of it on his regular tips up and down the road.

Later, on the eve of his departure, Flòraidh had sought an audience with him. He had seen her from time to time about the camp. She was now the property of a Brigantean merchant.

"Flòraidh," he said. "How good to see you. How is life treating you?"

Flòraidh raised her eyes timidly for a moment then looked down at the floor again. How thin he looked. How pale and drawn. She longed to take him in her arms; to comfort him; to take away the pain. But that could never be – not now. He was gone from her and she belonged to another master.

"I am very well, thank you, my Lord," she replied.

There was an embarrassed lull in the conversation. Neither knew how to speak to the other.

"I trust your new master treats you well," he managed at last.

"Oh...oh yes, my Lord," she responded, thankful that her shawl covered the bruises.

There was another pause then Flòraidh cleared her throat. "This woman would speak, Lord."

"Yes, of course, Flòraidh; speak away," said Lucius with an attempt at heartiness.

"My Lord," she said, "I was asked by a man in the market place to bring you something. May I give it to you please?"

"Certainly," Lucius replied, his curiosity piqued.

Flòraidh, retreated through the curtain at the entrance of the quarters. She returned carrying a walking stick. It was of black-thorn and handsomely carved. The handle was in the shape of an eagle's head, emblem of the Legions and symbol of Lucius' cognomina, Aquilina. She handed it to Lucius.

"Why, it's beautiful," he said, turning it this way and that.

"My Lord, I was told to tell you that Tadg made it. He said that he hopes it will help you and that you'll remember him kindly by it."

Lucius was lost for words. For her part Flòraidh knew that in another moment she would be in tears.

In a breathless rush she said, "May it please you, my Lord, may I go? I must prepare my master's meal."

Without waiting for a response she turned and fled, stopping in the safety of a narrow alley behind the barracks. There she wept as though there were no end to her tears.

* * *

The next day a supply train for Eboracum gathered in the Western Vicus. Lucius's mules were to be incorporated in the mule strings under the care of his slaves. Lucius climbed onto the seat of one of the wagons. He fully intended to walk as much as possible but would wait until the train had sorted itself out on the road.

Mules brayed and men shouted. There was much pushing and shoving as the military escort attempted to bring order. Lucius gazed around. A crowd had gathered to watch their departure; well-wishers and tearful wives, people with last minute messages and mere gawkers. A slight figure stood at the edge of the crowd. Lucius thought he recognized it. The man looked up then down quickly as he saw the Centurion's gaze upon him.

"Tadg?"

Tadg looked up again.

"Tadg: come here man," called Lucius.

Reluctantly Tadg sidled across to stand by the wagon. Lucius looked down at the Celt, wondering at his shyness. He picked up the blackthorn cane.

"Tadg, I have to thank you for this. It is beautiful and I will keep it by me always."

The little man looked embarrassed. "'s alright," he muttered. "Thought you might need something...after what happened like."

There was an awkward silence.

"So why are you not at home?" asked Lucius at last. "I imagined the money would set you up as a man of substance; that you would be fathering children and buying cattle."

Tadg traced a pattern in the dust with his foot. He cleared his throat. After a while he spoke. Lucius had to lean down to hear him.

"Ah well: the money: yes. Thing is I took it 'ome an' gave it to Cinnie, 'er being my woman." He paused and heaved a deep sigh. "Only seems I'd been away too long an' Cinnie had took another man." He kicked at a stone. "She...she didn't tell me when she took the money an' the mule. I didn't know 'til 'er new man threw me out of the village."

He spat. "Big bugger 'e was too an', anyway, I didn't think it was worth fighting about. So me an' Cabal, that bein' Callum's dog, we set out wandering."

He faltered to a stop.

"But where is Cabal?" asked Lucius, looking around.

Tadg looked out at the crowd. A tear trickled down his cheek. Angrily he cuffed it away.

"Wolf took him, didn't it?" he murmured. He gazed into the distance.

A degree of calm had fallen upon the scene as the supply train finally took shape. The last mule was pushed into place. The Optio in charge of the escort walked towards the head of the train, checking beast and man.

"Tadg?" Lucius found himself talking without knowing what he was going to say. "Tadg, I'm setting up as a merchant. I may need help. Would you like to come with me?"

The little man dragged his gazed away from the distance. He looked up at Lucius, his eyes red with unshed tears.

"Yus," he said. "I'd like that."

* * *

The journey was relatively uneventful – the usual broken wheels and lame animals. Any robbers lay low, intimidated by the military escort, awaiting more vulnerable prey.

When he finally arrived at military headquarters, it seemed that no one knew anything about him. Lucius, however, with long experience of military administration, exercised patience. Eventually, after three days, he was grudgingly admitted to the office of a clerk in the Intelligence Section.

"This is all very irregular," was the clerk's opening gambit. He peered at a clay file. "It seems that you were meant to have reported here in October of last year." Marking his place with one finger he looked up, his features set in disapproval.

"And where, may I ask, have you been in the interim?"

"In hospital at Trimontium recovering from a broken leg," replied Lucius, evenly.

The clerk sniffed. He looked back down at the file.

"That's all very well but funding has been withdrawn. The decision is quite clear. The Imperial Treasury cannot be expected to wait upon your convenience."

Lucius leaned forward, placing both hands on top of his black-thorn stick. He smiled benevolently at the clerk. The clerk became nervous.

"Now, we both know, you because you have read the file and I because I was there, that I was personally recruited for this task by the Emperor with the knowledge of Legate Metellus. We also know that if I walk from here to the Legate's office and explain to him that you are refusing to facilitate the Emperor's instructions, he or his representative will come here and flatten you."

The clerk did his best to look outraged. Lucius merely leaned back in his chair and smiled with even greater benevolence.

"So, what I propose is that we avoid the pain and inconvenience of involving the Legate and start this conversation again. Good afternoon, my name is Lucius Terentius Aquilina."

The clerk drew a hissing breath. For several seconds he

shuffled files around his desk then looked up again, his finger again marking a place.

"It seems that there is a sub-clause allowing for additional subventions in the event of unplanned contingencies. You will, however, be fully responsible for all purchases, contracts, indemnities and remunerations however incurred and notwithstanding any verbal agreements heretofore entered into by any or either party. Furthermore the Imperial Treasury can take no responsibility for any liens, torts or arrogations pre-dating or post-dating this memorandum of understanding. You will, of course, provide clear and unambiguous receipts for all disbursements to this office along with a full, clear, written explanation of each and every such disbursement. Is that clear?"

Slowly, with the aid of his stick, Lucius rose to his feet. He limped to the desk, placed both hands on it and leaned forward. The clerk found himself the close focus of two incredibly hard, unblinking blue eyes. His face became pale. He leaned back as far as he could in his chair. It was not far enough.

"If by that you mean I am to spend my own money preparing to execute the Emperor's express wishes, then so be it. If, in order to reclaim my expenses, you expect me to justify them to you, then I won't. If you fail to reimburse me or place any further impediment in my way, I will have you sacked and enslaved. Subsequently I shall purchase you. I will then rip off one of your arms and beat your head into a bloody pulp with it. Is *that* clear?"

At no time did Lucius raise his voice, a fact that the clerk found deeply intimidating. Weakly he nodded. There would be ways of frustrating this creature later but for now he just wanted him to go away.

"I said, is that *clear*?" repeated Lucius.

"'es," croaked the clerk, then, gathering what saliva remained in his mouth, "Yes."

"Good," said Lucius, standing up. "Good. Well, as it happens

I shall be providing the slaves and the pack animals from my own pocket. I would be grateful if you would make a note of that now because any attempt to reclaim them as government property will be met with violence. I shall return in three days having bought a wagon and trade goods. At that time I shall require full recompense. At the same time I shall require a proper briefing by someone considerably senior to you. See to it."

With that Lucius turned and limped from the office.

* * *

Now he looked around him with a strong proprietorial feeling.

Of the eight mules, each now trailing a lengthy shadow, five were originals. One had broken a leg at a difficult river crossing and been put down. Two others had been retired.

The wagon was still the one he had bought in Eboracum. Floored with larch, its ash frame was strong enough to take almost any punishment. With its tarred canvas cover over iron hoops, it held the most perishable stock. On really wet nights it could shelter the whole crew in some discomfort. The wagon had been expensive but he considered it a sound investment for the Imperial Treasury.

Expensive too was the harness. The yolks were of hornbeam while the leather harness was the finest the Brigantean tanners of Eboracum could provide. That would need replacing in a year or two but not until then.

Yes, it had all served him well. So far, of course, the Emperor had received no return on his investment in terms of intelligence but that, it seemed, was about to change. In purely financial terms the team was starting to show a profit, all of which, it had been made clear to him, was his to reinvest as he saw fit.

Marcellus swung down from the wagon. He walked briskly up the line of march to join his master.

"Will we be stopping before long, Aurelio," he asked as he

drew level. "Supper will be ready as soon as we can get it to a fire."

Aurelio looked ahead, shading his eyes. "We should see Tadg soon," he replied.

Tadg was a free spirit and Aurelio made use of him by sending him ahead hunting, finding news and arranging campsites where there were no villages. The road ran gently downhill. As if on cue a small figure stepped out of the trees and waved.

"Yes, there he is," he said, pointing. "Where the road crosses the stream. Let's see what he's got for us."

Tadg trotted up to meet them.

"Seems like a regular camping place, just off the road to the left," he reported.

A minute later the road crossed over a culvert and a grassy bay amongst the trees opened to their view to the left of the road. The fosse had been bridged with heavy planks. Aurelio turned and signalled to Cadmus and Adolphus then crossed the plank bridge with Marcellus and Tadg.

Marcellus took charge of making camp. Adolphus unloaded the pack mules while Cadmus freed the draught animals. Tadg helped him lead the beasts to the stream to drink before hobbling them. Trista prepared their nosebags from the feed bins in the wagon. She sang as she carried them one by one to the mules. One expressed its impatience by nudging her and received a slap on the muzzle.

"Shame on you, Nero," came her piping treble. "For that you will be fed last."

Nero responded with a mournful braying whinny. It had been Trista's fancy to name each of the mules after an emperor. Thus, in addition to Nero, there were Tiberius, Claudius, Galba, Vespasian and Titus. Domitian and Nerva pulled the wagon. Trista had wanted to call Nerva Trajan but Aurelio had vetoed this on the grounds of public sensibilities. Trajan had only been dead eight years and there were many, notably veteran legionaries, who still venerated him.

Marcellus had built a stone grate and now the pungent smell of wood smoke wafted across the clearing. This spoke so much of large meals in the fresh air that Aurelio found himself salivating. 'Soon,' he thought. There was no point in hurrying Marcellus. Cooking was just one of the slave's talents. Aurelio had no doubt that he could have held a position in the kitchens of any patrician's household. The meal would be worth waiting for.

He made his way over to the bank of the stream, removed his sandals and waded into the cool water. The sun had now declined behind the trees but the air was still warm. Crickets called from the long grass. Aurelio eyed the still water under the tree shadows near the opposite bank. Surely there would be trout rising with the twilight. He would fetch out his rod after supper and try his luck.

"There you are!"

Trista was fond of sounding like an exasperated mother, especially when engaged in her self-appointed task of chivvying Aurelio. He turned to see her standing on the bank, hands on hips, a look of long-suffering patience about her face.

"Supper's ready and will spoil if you don't come this minute. Here, give me your hand."

She held out an imperious hand to him. Smiling, Aurelio waded to the bank and allowed himself to be helped from the water.

"Now dry your feet and come along."

With that she turned and flounced off towards the campsite. As he buckled his sandals Aurelio wondered, not for the first time, at the natural moral ascendancy of woman over man, no matter their respective ages.

The meal was good. Marcellus carried with him in the wagon an iron oven made to his design by a blacksmith. This he incorporated into the open hearth, covering it with clay in such a way that hot fumes heated the interior without burning the contents. Thus they were treated to baked trout with almonds followed by a pie containing apples dried and stored since last harvest.

At length they reclined, replete, around the fire. Aurelio finished off the last of his wine with a runny cheese, bought at the last market.

"Thank you, Marcellus. That was excellent," he said, climbing to his feet. "Now I'm going to try for an hour's fishing before it gets dark."

As he crossed to the wagon to collect his gear Trista was disputing with Cadmus whose turn it was to clean the dishes. There seemed little doubt that it was Trista's. Her objections were merely routine. As he climbed down from the wagon with his rod, she was heading for the stream with an armful of plates and cups.

"Trista," he said, "would you do that downstream and round the corner please." He pointed towards the trees at the back of the clearing, farthest from the road. "Then you won't disturb the fish."

Trista gave him a look, tossed her braids and changed direction. She disappeared among the trees. Silence settled over the glade but for the gentle murmur of the stream and the slaves' quiet conversation as Aurelio took his stance, shin deep in the water. However, his hour of contemplation was not to be.

"Master, horses."

Tadg stood on the bank pointing to the road. Yes; now he too could hear hoof beats above the noise of the stream. There was nothing strange in this. The road was well-frequented yet it was late and the cadence of the sound indicated horses being ridden rather than pulling a cart. Aurelio wondered why he felt a measure of foreboding. He glanced at Tadg. What he saw in the Celt's face confirmed his anxiety.

"Go to Trista. She's downstream, through the trees." He pointed. "Tell her to hide. Stay with her."

Tadg needed no further instructions. He left at a fast lope. Aurelio climbed barefoot onto the bank and stood, rod in hand, waiting to see what the twilight would bring. He did not have long to wait. Six auxiliary cavalrymen trotted over the culvert, causing it to echo. As they came abreast the campsite, they slowed to a walk before turning across the plank bridge into the glade. The leader raised his hand and the troop halted. He dismounted, handing his reins to another, then strode towards the fire. He was broad rather than big but his helmet and leather armour gave him presence.

By now the twilight was well advanced. The edges of the glade were lost to shadow. He stopped in front of the fire, surveying the scene with a look of mild contempt.

"Where is your master?" he demanded in a harsh voice. It was evident by their garb as well as their manner that Marcellus, Cadmus and Adolphus were slaves. Marcellus stood, about to speak, but Aurelio forestalled him, stepping forward into the edge of the firelight, his rod upon his shoulder.

"I am here," he said quietly.

The man turned swiftly, his hand on his sword. Then he relaxed. He strode towards Aurelio, removing his leather gauntlets as he went. Two paces from Aurelio he stopped and looked him up and down, slapping the gauntlets rhythmically into his right hand. Apparently satisfied he held out the hand.

"Duplicarius Ulpius, Eighth *Augusta* Lancearii. We would share your campsite if you have no objection."

Aurelio took the proffered hand smoothly, without pause. Normally he would welcome company but his unease remained. Still, there was nothing to be done. The cavalryman's request was no more than a courtesy.

"Be welcome, Duplicarius. We have finished our supper but please feel free to use the fire."

Releasing the man's hand he noted, peripherally, Tadg emerging from the trees, adjusting his clothes.

"Marcellus," he called, "make room for our friends at the fire."

He turned, as if seeing Tadg for the first time. "Tadg, you good-for-nothing, have you not yet finished the dishes?" he cried.

He limped rapidly away towards the small man in a display of anger. Closing with Tadg he took him by the shoulder and shook him, meanwhile leaning close.

"While they're busy with their horses, take a blanket and her sack of clothes to Trista," he whispered. "Tell her to stay where she is for the night. See her comfortable then return with the dishes. Now I'm going to hit you. I'm sorry."

He fetched Tadg a convincing blow around his ear shouting, "And when I tell you to do a thing I mean now, not next week. Now get about your duties."

He thrust Tadg from him then returned to the fire where the cavalrymen, now dismounted, were unsaddling their horses.

"Slaves!" he said to the Duplicarius. "Where do you go to get good ones?"

The soldier smiled. The tension was broken. Everyone understood the problem of slaves – lazy, shiftless, ungrateful. Marcellus and Cadmus watched him carefully from lowered eyelids. They would realize that something was wrong. Never in three years had their master behaved thus. Adolphus, stolid as ever, appeared not to have noticed anything. Aurelio sent them away to their rest under the wagon. He could rely on Tadg to explain the situation regarding Trista. His main worry was Adolphus. The big man was incapable of dissembling.

The soldiers settled around the fire. They produced their rations and began to eat. When Tadg returned Aurelio told him to bring an amphora of ordinary wine then sent him away as well. He settled down to learn what he could.

There were the normal questions – where bound, where from – then the Duplicarius, with what he probably thought was a casual manner, said, "Funny, running into you. We were told to look out for a set up just like yours – trader, wagon, mule string, four slaves. Thing is they're supposed to have a young girl with him and she's wanted by the magistrates in Lutetia. Wouldn't know anything about that I suppose?"

Once Aurelio had made a poor liar but since his association with markets, dissembling came to his lips with practiced ease. He gave a bark of laughter.

"Tadg," he called, "another amphora."

He turned to the Duplicarius.

"This story deserves more wine." He busied himself putting more wood on the fire, buying time until the Celt should hear what he said. Tadg bustled up with an amphora.

"Pour," he ordered, indicating the cups of the troopers. Tadg started round the circle.

"That girl!" he began. "Took me for a right soft-hearted fool. Saved her from a mob, we did, weeks back. She'd been thieving. The crowd were going to hang her." He spat into the fire. "Well, I thought, waste of fresh, young woman flesh, I thought. Gave them five sestertii for her. They were glad enough to take it."

Working himself up into righteous indignation, he continued.

"So we saved her life, gave her good food and a place to lie her head and how do you think she repaid us? How?"

He shook his head in disgust, almost shouting now. "Took off with my purse and a sack of dates from Arabia Petraea, that's how. Now I wouldn't mind about the money but have you any idea, any idea at all how much dates cost?"

One of the troopers exploded with laughter. As if given permission, the others joined in. Aurelio allowed the look of disgust to linger for a moment then joined their laughter ruefully. He glanced at Tadg who nodded slightly and retired to the shadows.

When the laughter had run its course the Duplicarius asked, "Where did this happen and how long ago?"

Aurelio pretended to think. "Must have been two weeks back, somewhere around Augustobona, I suppose. Here," he said, brightening, "if you find her, remember the figs belong to Aurelio of Tarraconensis, Purveyor of Fine Goods to the Discerning."

This elicited another and louder round of mirth. When he could make himself heard he continued, "We'll be stopping in Argentoratum so if you hear anything..."

Shortly afterwards, satisfied that he had sown as much disinformation as was safe, he excused himself and retired to his bed near the wagon. There he lay wakeful but still. The troopers remained by the fire for a while longer before retiring in their turn. Aurelio listened. The coughs and splashing of urine stilled. Soon there was silence but for the occasional stamp of a hoof and the calls of night birds. Still Aurelio waited.

About an hour later he heard stealthy movement. In the faint backwash of starlight he could just make out a figure climbing over the tailgate of the wagon. Whoever it was he was very good. Aurelio heard nothing more until perhaps fifteen minutes later when the figure rolled silently off the tailgate and crept back towards the sleeping troopers beyond the embers of the fire.

In the dawn light the camp stirred as the slaves began their morning preparations. Tadg was nowhere to be seen. Aurelio watched as one of the cavalrymen squatted by the hearth and engaged Cadmus in conversation as the slave brought the fire to life. Another, apparently taking in the scene across the stream, spoke to Marcellus as he collected water. Aurelio noted that Marcellus kept Adolphus close by him. Soon breakfast was completed and the cavalrymen began tacking up their horses.

"Will you be starting out straight away?" asked the Duplicarius as his men mounted.

"Not straight away," replied the trader. "I had it in mind to try casting some fly for trout while it is still cool."

It transpired that the Duplicarius was a keen angler too. There was a brief but spirited exchange of views: flies, best for which conditions: rods, flexibility versus strength; fishes, caught, seen and lost. Finally they parted with genuine expressions of mutual esteem. The detachment walked in file across the bridge and then, increasing to a trot, disappeared to the east.

Aurelio turned. The slaves were all watching him. He gave a slight shake of his head.

"Clear up here," he said. "I'm going to try for a fish."

The slaves returned to their tasks. Aurelio fetched his rod from the wagon and took up his stance in the stream. Half an hour passed before there was a clatter of hooves on the road. He turned as two troopers cantered into view. They slowed to a walk and crossed the plank bridge.

"The boss left his knife behind," said one of them. "Lose his arse, that one would, if it wasn't tacked on tight." He dismounted. All the time his eyes darted around the glade. His mate's horse appeared intent on sidling across to where its rider could get a clear view of the back of the wagon. Finally the dismounted trooper bent and picked up a knife from the long grass.

"There it is," he said. "We can get back now Aulus," he called to his mate.

He mounted with the characteristic leap of the cavalryman. Gathering his reins he nodded at the stream. "Any good?" he asked.

Aurelio held up a piece of twine threaded through the gills of two small trout.

"Take them," he said, "with my compliments to the noble Duplicarius."

The trooper urged his horse forward to the edge of the stream. He took the fish, nodding his thanks, then wheeled away. Together the two riders crossed the plank bridge before spurring into a canter and disappearing up the road.

Aurelio crossed to the wagon. He stowed his rod then turned.

"Marcellus, prepare the mules but keep an eye out on the road." He turned towards the trees. Tadg materialized from the shadows.

"Show me," said Aurelio.

As they entered the wood. Tadg put his fingers in his mouth and gave the warbling call of a chaffinch. A little deeper into the trees he called out quietly, "It's alright. You can come out Trista."

From a dense clump of alder a face appeared. It was crumpled either from sleep or lack of it. There were leaves in her hair and a smudge of something on her cheek. Aurelio helped her out of the thicket while Tadg recovered her sack and blanket.

"They were looking for me, weren't they?" said Trista in a small voice then she hurled herself at Aurelio and burst into tears. He held her close while her small body convulsed with sobs. Across her head he gazed helplessly at Tadg. After a while the tears subsided.

"Come, little one," he said, wiping her cheeks with the sleeve of his tunic. "Let's get you some food."

At the edge of the glade, screened from the road by shrubs, the slaves gathered round. Trista clung to Aurelio. He sat with his back to a tree trunk, his bad leg stretched out in front of him, holding her within the crook of his arm. Cadmus cleaned her face with a damp cloth. Marcellus offered her food kept back from breakfast but she wouldn't eat. Adolphus merely towered in the background, a picture of anxiety. "I didn't tell," he kept repeating until Cadmus bade him sit down and be quiet.

Aurelio knew that he had to get to the bottom of this. He considered sending the slaves away but didn't. He reasoned that Trista was more likely to speak with her other friends present and, anyway, he felt that they had a right to know what they were getting into. Taking the girl by her shoulders he gently turned her until they were facing each other. Trista looked at her hands.

"Trista," he said, "look at me."

Reluctantly she raised her eyes to his face for a moment before looking down again.

"Trista, my dear, you know that you are safe with us, don't you?"

Trista sniffed and nodded her head. So far, so good, he thought.

"We're all of us your friends, Trista, and we will protect you but we can only do that if we know what's going on, do you understand?"

She looked up at him and held his eyes for a long moment before nodding again.

"You knew those soldiers were looking for you, didn't you? Can you tell me why?"

There was a long pause then she whispered something that he didn't catch, her hands fluttering like moths in her lap.

"Can you say it again a little louder please, my dear?"

"I said Sertorius sent them," she whispered.

He glanced at the others. Marcellus and Cadmus shrugged. Tadg shook his head. It wasn't a name any of them knew. He took a deep breath.

"Help us, Trista. Tell us who is Sertorius?"

Trista looked up again, her eyes full of unshed tears. She took a shuddering breath and wiped the back of her hand across her nose. With a visible effort she fought back the tears. Aurelio's heart went out to her.

"He killed my p-parents and...and now he wants to k-kill me," she stammered.

Time was moving on. Aurelio knew he had decisions to make. He weighed the information he had gleaned. Sertorius could command imperial troops and he wanted this girl dead. Apparently he wanted her dead so badly that he would send patrols out over a wide area on the off-chance of finding her. Either that or he knew roughly where to find her. That was really worrying. If he knew that then there was a chance that the mission was compromised.

"Tadg, go silently four hundred paces up the road on this side, within the trees. Take care not to be seen. Look to see if they've left a picket. Take your time. Make a thorough job then return. If no one is watching we will set out to the west. There is a track leading north half a mile back. We will take it. My guess is that if we make for Nancy we will find them waiting on the road so we will make for Mediomatrici. Marcellus, you and the others, move the stock in the wagon. Make a hiding place for Trista. Make it as comfortable as possible. She may be in there for some time. Trista, I want you to be very brave. Do as Marcellus says. We will look after you."

Chapter 28

(Fugitives)

The track was unpaved, rutted. In winter it would be impassable to wheeled traffic but now in high summer it gave a firm, dusty, footing. Tension dogged their journey, everyone casting glances over their shoulders. Walking at the rear of the column, Aurelio reviewed his decisions. It was not a comfortable process.

Certainly they could not have gone on towards Nancy. The Duplicarius was clearly suspicious. There would have been another meeting and this time a thorough search. By turning back and away from the main road, however, they had as good as admitted their guilt.

Aurelio tried to put himself in the cavalryman's shoes. No point in pretending another chance meeting nor would he risk a confrontation in Nancy. No: it would happen somewhere on the main road. They would be, what, five miles up the road? Time enough for the trader's party to relax. So the question was, how soon would it be before the Duplicarius became suspicious when they didn't appear? Two hours he thought, possibly three.

Aurelio put his fingers to his mouth and whistled. As Cadmus's face appeared around the canvas cover of the wagon Aurelio held his arms up, crossed at the wrist. Cadmus reined in the mules. Marcellus and Adolphus came to a halt with their mule strings. Everyone stood still and listened. A growing breeze soughed in the treetops. A jay scolded then fell silent. No hoof beats; no voices. Judging by the sun an hour or so had passed since they had started out so perhaps they had two hours more.

Tadg appeared around the bend of the road, running in the relaxed lope he could keep up all day. He slowed and stopped, barely breathing heavily.

"Nothing," he said.

Aurelio gestured forward with his arm. The wagon creaked

into motion. The pack mules resisted the tug of their lead reins for a second before they too moved. Tadg melted into the trees. Aurelio resumed his thoughts.

Six men; how would he deploy them? Probably in pairs. Yes; it would have to be pairs. So – one pair to follow the main road westwards for, what, ten miles? That left two pairs to search side roads. How many side roads? He had no way of knowing. Was the one they were on an obvious choice? Probably, yes. Then consider command and control: where would they rendezvous and when?

His head ached. There were just too many imponderables. All they could do was to keep plodding northwards and meet problems as they arose.

Marcellus handed his lead rein to Adolphus. He came back to walk beside Aurelio.

"I have spoken to him but he really doesn't remember much. Her home was by the River Loire. Her family were Gauls, probably Roman citizens, I think, and in some way important. He talks about fire but can't explain and he has no idea who Sertorius may be."

Aurelio nodded. Most of this they already knew although fire was a new element.

"Would anything be gained by my questioning him?" he asked.

Marcellus considered. "Honestly, Master? No. He will likely become tongue-tied and even more confused."

He hesitated for a moment.

"Speak," said Aurelio, tired and irritated.

Marcellus licked his lips. "What are the chances of them finding us?"

Aurelio laughed; short, bitter. "I wish I knew. We understand so little of this, Marcellus. Sertorius is the key. If he is acting with government approval then he can deploy any number of troops and, sure as daylight, we will be found. If, as I guess, he is acting unofficially, it comes down to how many troops he controls. Those Lancearii were from the Eighth. The Eighth is stationed beyond the mountains on the Rhenus. That alone is strange because they are a long way from home."

"If I had to guess I'd say that something illegal is afoot; that Sertorius is using troops through personal influence. That probably means that he only has a limited number at his disposal. If that is so, they will only be covering the main roads."

He stopped and turned towards the rear, leaning on his stick. The sun, now high in its morning ascent, dappled the path behind them. Fatigue and worry were warping his judgement, he knew that. Still no sound from the rear. He sighed. "That means that we can expect to see more of them after we head for Mediomatrici on the next main road."

Turning he began hobbling briskly after the others. "Somewhere in the next hour we need a place to hide."

* * *

"I must relieve myself," whispered Trista. Her face was pale and unhappy.

"Go back into the trees, then," breathed Aurelio. "But not too far and be as quiet as possible."

The girl crept silently into the undergrowth.

It had been hard work hauling the wagon into its current resting place. They dared not follow a proper track so it had been a matter of forcing a way in through an area of less dense scrub and trees. For the final phase they had unloaded two of the pack animals and roped them in tandem with Domitian and Nerva, much to the latter's disgust. They had pulled the wagon over a small rise, Adolphus adding his weight, and into a shallow gully. Cadmus and Aurelio had gone back to cover tracks, as best they could, and remove broken branches. The result would not fool a trained tracker but Aurelio was banking on a cursory inspection by bored troopers. Now Cadmus was hidden near the road, watching. Tadg was still somewhere out in the woods, down the road.

"Food, Aurelio?"

Marcellus offered a heel of bread, a slab of cheese and a cup of watered wine. Aurelio took them, absently poured a libation and began to eat. The sun was beyond its zenith. The next couple of hours would be the danger time. Perhaps it would be best to stay here for the night. After all, he had no way of knowing how the Duplicarius would plan the search. Anyway, the pause would give him time to question Trista; see whether he could make any more sense of what they were up against.

Trista. How long had she been gone? Surely too long. He craned round towards the undergrowth where she had disappeared. Nothing.

"Marcellus," he called quietly, "has Trista come back?"

The slave shook his head. He too peered around him. He crept over towards Aurelio.

"She should have been back by now, certainly. Shall I go and look for her?" he whispered.

Aurelio nodded. Marcellus crept into the undergrowth. Within minutes he returned. Putting his mouth close to his master's ear he said, "No sign at all, master. I called quietly but there was no answer."

"Jupiter's teeth," he muttered savagely. This was all they needed.

He crawled over to Adolphus. "Adolphus," he whispered. "Stay here. Whatever happens keep the beasts quiet."

Adolphus nodded, solemnly. Adolphus had a way with animals. With any luck the mules would stay quiet for him even if other animals passed on the road.

He crawled back towards the undergrowth, motioning Marcellus to join him. Once through the barrier of elder and broom they stood and listened. The wind soughed in the topmost branches and a few birds sang but apart from that there was silence. Long, irregular rows of pine trunks disappeared into the distance. Aurelio was reminded of the columns of a vast temple.

He took Marcellus' arm and leaned close to his ear. "Listen: the one thing that'll make this worse is if we get lost," he whispered. "So, you go that way," he pointed half to their left, "for three hundred paces, then return the same way. I'm going that way." He pointed half to their right. "We meet back here."

Marcellus nodded and set off. Fifteen minutes later they returned. Each shook his head. Aurelio bit his lip. The stupid young fool. He understood why she had gone; would have done the same himself in her place but oh the silly, brave girl.

"Marcellus," he said at length, "go and relieve Cadmus. Tell him what's happened.

Stay on watch until nightfall then return. Don't light a fire. Assume that you're being watched. I'm going to hide here in the bushes. After dark I'll be heading out into the trees. No one is to come back here unless there is an emergency. Is that clear?"

"Shall I bring you food and drink before I go?" whispered the slave.

Aurelio nodded. It would be a long watch.

* * *

Gods, it was dark and he was tired. He shifted slightly, straining to hear anything above the noise of the wind in the trees. Earlier a fox had gone by a short distance upwind without noticing him. Apart from that and the call of the occasional night bird there had been silence.

Using the skills taught him as a youth he had, with infinite care, crawled a hundred paces into the wood as soon as it was wholly dark. Since then he had lain amongst the pine needles, unmoving even when insects crawled across his exposed skin.

Despite the warmth of the night he was cold from inaction.

For the hundredth time he cursed Trista. He no longer had any idea of how long he had been here. The realization was gradually being borne in upon him that this was futile. He racked his brains to think of another way of finding her but could think of nothing. He cursed himself. He had no right to be doing this. Only the mission mattered. Trista was endangering that mission. She had offered him the opportunity to go on without her. It was his clear duty to take that opportunity.

All he had to do was stand up and walk back to the camp. He could catch a few hours' sleep and in the morning be on his way – no more worries about patrols; just the mission, just a simple life.

Still he waited.

Finally his exhaustion turned to anger. Damn the girl. She was none of his business. He would leave her.

He was tensing his muscles ready to stand when he heard the branch snap over to his left. He moved his head slowly in the direction of the noise, careful to look with the edge of his eyes for the best night vision. Nothing. No – there was a slight scraping, somewhere above ground level. And there! A white blur, barely seen against the darkness. Someone was climbing down a tree.

He came to his knees, wincing as his right leg protested, then to his feet. With infinite care he moved forward, testing each footfall, until he was a few yards from the tree he had marked. The descending figure had stopped. He realized that it was caught on a branch moments before there was a ripping noise and a quiet curse. He was waiting as Trista tumbled to the ground.

"Trista."

There was a muffled gasp.

He tensed, ready to grab her if she should run but instead she stood, her arms slack against her sides.

"Aurelio," she said, "I knew you would come."

* * *

It was morning. Slanting sunlight filtered through the trees. The dawn chorus had subsided into the work-a-day voice of bird life. Marcellus prepared breakfast while Adolphus fed and groomed the mules. Cadmus was back on watch at the edge of the road. Aurelio sat thinking deeply, his back against a tree. Beside him Trista, wrapped in her blanket, slept on. She had been exhausted and frozen when he had brought her back to the camp the night before. The slaves could not hide their delight at her return. She had hugged Cadmus and Marcellus then clung to Adolphus, crying quietly but with desperation. Adolphus had stroked her hair with his great hand and, at length, she had quieted.

Marcellus was at his elbow. "Breakfast is ready, Aurelio. Shall I wake her?"

Aurelio nodded. She would be rested now. He needed her fed and then he would have to question her. Too much was at stake now. He needed answers before he could decide how to proceed. He rasped a hand across his unshaven jaw. Mithras, but he was tired. His body ached with lack of sleep.

Marcellus gently shook her shoulder. "Trista, time to wake, my love."

Trista stirred sleepily then sat up. She yawned and stretched, looking about her, only gradually remembering where she was. She turned to look at Aurelio.

"Oh, Aurelio I'm…I'm so sorry," she said.

"Peace, child," he replied. "I understand. Eat now. Then you and I must talk.

Trista rose and went into the trees. Aurelio found himself involuntarily looking at Marcellus. The slave looked apprehensive. Aurelio shook his head slightly. They had to know if they could trust her. Nevertheless, there was a distinct slackening of tension when she returned a few minutes later. Oblivious of the atmosphere she sat and fell upon the food.

Marcellus went to relieve Cadmus. Adolphus, his duties completed, sat on a shaft of the wagon, his moon face vacant. Trista finished the last of her watered wine, licked her fingers and turned to the trader.

"I'm ready, Aurelio," she said.

He cleared his throat, suppressing the irritation he still felt for last night's antics. He chose his words. "Trista, what you did last night was very brave but there was no need for it. You are part of our team now. We look after each other. Neither I nor the others will give you up without a fight so you have nothing to fear. Do you understand?"

Trista nodded solemnly, running her fingers through her unbound hair.

"I understand, Aurelio, but you would be better without me. I am a danger to you."

Aurelio felt like agreeing. Instead he reached out and took her hand.

"Trista, do you trust me?" he asked.

Again she nodded. He pressed her hand, then let it go.

"Then understand that whatever trouble you're in, we can make it go away. But first you must tell me what this is all about. Then I can make a plan. Will you do that for me? Will you tell me what I need to know?"

Looking into his eyes Trista drew a deep sniff, then nodded once more. She looked down at her hands where they plucked at her skirt. After a pause she began in a small voice.

"It was the window made me do it, that and Nurse. She was snoring like a hog..."

* * *

The sun was halfway up the sky, now, glittering through the leaves into the clearing.

"I don't remember much more. The men must have gone

because the next thing I knew it was getting light. People from the village had come. Some of them were throwing water from the river onto the fire but it was no good. The house was just a grey, smoking wreck by then."

"I must have climbed down. I remember standing under the Granfer tree in my nightdress. I should have gone to the people in the village earlier but I was so afraid. I didn't know who I could trust. I wasn't really thinking at all. My hands were burnt so I suppose I must have tried to find my family..."

She was quiet for a moment, wiping her eyes with the back of her hand.

"The villagers were kind but I could see they were afraid. They put salves on my hands and sent me off to the Præfect in Aurelianum but the man who went with me disappeared when we heard horses and I...I just wandered off. I suppose I should have died but I didn't. It was late spring and warm at night. I stole clothes and food and kept on moving."

She looked up at Aurelio. "That's all, really. By the time you met me I was able to keep myself alive but it wasn't much fun. When you found me I didn't know whether to trust you either. I still didn't know until yesterday, I suppose..."

She leaned over and hugged the trader, burying her face in his chest. Then she sat up.

"I'm ever so glad I did meet you, though but I'm so, so sorry, Aurelio. It feels like I've brought my bad luck with me. Please, if it's easier, I'll just go. I won't mind; really."

She looked down. The curtain of auburn hair fell forward, hiding her face.

'Gods!' thought Aurelio, 'how can I be so weak?' In truth, in his deepest heart, he knew it was his loneliness. He craved affection like anybody else but what price duty?

He forced himself to smile. "You're not going anywhere without us." He smoothed her hair. "And I tell you solemnly that together we can solve this problem. Now I'm going to ask you some questions and then we'll work out what we're going to do."

She nodded, looking very relieved. She began to braid her hair.

"First of all, have you any idea who Sertorius is?"

Trista frowned, thinking, then shook her head.

"Father was a Præfect. He knew many important people in the government. Sertorius could be one of them."

The next question was harsh. "Have you any idea why your parents were killed; why anyone would want your whole family dead?"

He needn't have worried. Trista had been living with their deaths for two years. She considered then replied, "Not really but you know all kinds of things like this happen in powerful families. Vibius, my tutor told me about it. He said that anyone who aspired to power should wear an armoured back plate."

He marvelled at her insouciance.

"Last question for now: do you have any close family or is there somewhere where you can be safe?"

Trista smiled wistfully. "Well, Uncle Tuccius commands the Twenty Second Legion at Moguntiacum but I don't know whether he would want to be bothered with me."

Suddenly Aurelio saw light through the darkness. Where better for the girl's safety than in the heart of a Legion? Not only that but Moguntiacum was a short distance north of Borbetomagus, their destination.

At that moment Tadg came running through the trees from the direction of the road with Marcellus stumbling behind him.

"They're coming," Tadg said in a low voice.

Aurelio hauled himself up using a branch, ignoring the pain in his leg. He beckoned Cadmus to him.

"Marcellus, stay here. Make sure Adolphus keeps the beasts quiet at all costs. Tadg, back to the road. Make ready to follow them if they go by. Cadmus with me to the road, quiet as you like."

He selected his stabbing sword from where it leant against the tree and handed it to Cadmus. The slave's eyes widened. "Master…" he began.

"No time for that," whispered Aurelio, hefting his longsword. Cadmus had been a man at arms. Aurelio had expected more courage. Perhaps slavery…He thrust the thought away. None of the others had the necessary skills. It would have to be Cadmus.

Moments later they were established in shadow behind trees within sight of the track. Hoof beats came loud from the left, then the jangle of bits. Into their line of vision at a brisk trot came two horses carrying lancearii. The troopers mostly looked ahead but cast occasional glances at the ground. They passed. Nothing about them indicated that they had seen anything amiss. The hoof beats died away, heading north. Aurelio crept across to Cadmus.

"Stay here. Give us the chaffinch when you hear them return. I'll come." The slave's face was pallid. He licked his lips nervously then nodded.

Aurelio limped back to the wagon. Adolphus was holding the bridles of the mules, his face near theirs as if he was talking to them. The others looked mute questions at Aurelio. He shook his head.

"They were lancearii but they passed by. They will be back, though. By then I want us to be ready to leave quickly. We have preparations to make."

He set Adolphus to harnessing the mules then turned to Marcellus and Trista.

"Trista," he said, "we are going to have to diguise you." He paused. This was not going to be popular. "You are going to become a boy."

Trista looked disgusted.

"I'm afraid we're going to have to cut off your hair."

Trista gasped. Automatically she pulled both braids forward and held them to her chest with crossed arms. She looked at him with horror.

"Aurelio, must you?"

He crouched down in front of her.

"Listen, Trista: those men out there will kill you if they can. Your hair will grow again. You won't. I'm sorry but we have to do this. There isn't time to argue."

Eyes downcast, she nodded rebelliously, scuffing her foot back and forwards in the pine needles.

"Marcellus," he said, "fetch the shears. Cut her hair off."

He turned to the mules. What next? His mind felt heavy. Stray irrelevancies gleamed and disappeared. Yes, the panniers. He must select what they needed. Two minutes later he looked up. Marcellus crouched in front of Trista who appeared to be pleading with him. In three strides Aurelio crossed the clearing. He grabbed the shears from the slave's hand.

"Gods, do I have to do everything?" His whisper was hoarse with anger. Marcellus fell back, raising one hand as if to ward off a blow.

"Get a tunic and breeches out of stock." He pointed at the wagon. "Use your needle and thread to make them fit the girl. Do you think you can do that without a problem?"

Marcellus backed off awkwardly, using his hands and feet. He stood, nodded miserably and set off for the wagon. Trista, meanwhile had, unbidden, loosed her hair. It hung about her shoulder in auburn profusion.

* * *

The deed was done; the hair collected carefully in a canvas bag when Aurelio heard the call of the chaffinch. Raising his finger to his lips he glanced at the others then started towards the road. Once hidden he looked across at Cadmus. The slave pointed to the north. Yes: here came hoof beats but the horses were now walking. Master and slave crouched lower. The two Lancearii came into view, one of them leaning forward over his horse's withers.

"See, it's got to be around here, Fulke." Aurelio could clearly hear the one studying the ground. "Mules shit an' there were eight of 'em an' you got to admit there was shit up to here but none further on. Stands to reason they're holed up hereabouts."

Aurelio cursed. What had he been thinking of? Even a raw recruit would have done better.

The trooper reined in and sat back in his saddle looking around.

"Look, mate," said Fulke, halting too, "you may be right, you may not. It could have been other mules. Who knows? All I'm saying is we gets back to the boss an' lets him decide."

The first trooper wasn't convinced. He pointed right between Aurelio and Cadmus.

"See, look, there's a broken branch here." Without warning the man dismounted. Aurelio tensed. Handing his horse's reins to his mate the trooper came forward. Aurelio looked across at Cadmus. Using only his fingers he indicated the dismounted trooper and then pointed at Cadmus. Cadmus, his face white as a shroud, nodded. If it came to killing Aurelio had given him the easier of two difficult targets. Aurelio himself would be going up against an armed, mounted man without the element of surprise.

The first trooper examined the broken branch.

"Looks recent to me, Fulke." He peered into the shadows among the trees, fingering his sword hilt.

Fulke made a disgusted sound and spat.

"Well, if you're going in there, Kai, you're going without me. That trader looked like an ex-soldier and did you see the size of that evil brute he had with him? He'd likely rip you in two. Nah," he said, "we ain't paid enough to make decisions let alone get killed. Let's get back to the boss. It's going to be bloody dark by the time we get there even at the trot."

His horse whickered. The harsh bray of a mule answered from

the wood.

Kai drew his sword in one fluid motion. Fulke slid from his horse, all arguments forgotten. As the trooper knotted the reins round a branch, Cadmus broke. With a strangled cry he threw aside his sword, leapt to his feet and fled into the wood. Kai gave a shout and leapt after him. Fulke drew his sword and followed.

For a moment Aurelio's tired brain was paralysed. Fulke was past him before he reacted. Then he was three paces behind the trooper, closing the distance and raising his broadsword. As he brought the sword down it glanced off a branch, taking the man in the shoulder, almost severing his left arm. The soldier turned, blood pumped down his side, drenching his tunic. He raised his sword. There was a brief swish followed by a thud. A small arrow quivered in his throat. The man dropped his sword and fell to one knee, clutching at the shaft of the arrow.

"Please," he croaked, blood flooding from his mouth. The sword too took him in the throat. Aurelio forced it clear of the falling body with his foot and ran on.

Before reaching the glade he slowed and caught his breath. Tadg came from the trees on his left, nocking another arrow to his bow. They could hear voices. Silently they crept forwards. Through a thin screen of leaves they took in the tableau. Cadmus cowered on the ground behind Adolphus who stood stolidly beside the mules. Marcellus lay sprawled on the ground apparently unconscious. Nearer, with his back to Aurelio and Tadg, Kai backed towards them. Aurelio could make out Trista's head over the man's shoulder. He was dragging her while holding a knife to her throat.

Tadg held up his bow. He raised an enquiring eyebrow. Aurelio shook his head: too much danger to Trista.

"Just stay where you are and no one gets hurt," the lancearii was saying to the slaves.

Then he shouted, "Fulke, where are you? Get yourself over here."

Aurelio stepped through the undergrowth. "I am here, Kai," he said. Kai just had time to realize that the voice was wrong when a sword appeared briefly in his vision. Before he could react he felt the warm trickle of blood as its cutting edge broke the skin over his Adam's apple. A voice spoke in his ear.

"Put the knife down, Kai, then the girl. Then you can walk out of here. If you don't, I'll kill you. Do it now."

Kai hesitated then dropped the knife as the sword cut deeper. He let the girl go, watched her scramble away, sobbing. There was just this one thin chance to live. His last thought was 'Bugger' as his Universe filled with pain. The sword cut through cartilage and flesh. He died.

* * *

The logic was unassailable. The soldiers were hunting Trista. They believed she was travelling with five men, a wagon and six pack mules. They had to split up.

If the Duplicarius had accepted his lie, they would be expected to turn south for Argentoratum after Mediomatrici. In fact they would continue east towards Mannheim then north to Borbetomagus. Thus it should be safe for the party to join up again some distance after Argentoratum. Mannheim seemed the obvious place. This, for want of a better, was the plan Aurelio had adopted.

He looked around him. By the Wolf's teats they were a sorry crew. Cadmus, shocked and ashamed, could barely control his limbs. Marcellus lay slumped against a tree, a blood-stained bandage around his head. Huddled against his side, Trista shivered and sobbed. Only Adolphus seemed unaffected by what had happened. He gazed around the glade, a puzzled expression on his face. Tadg was already away down the road, keeping watch.

As for himself, now that the killing lust had left him, he felt only self-disgust and depression. Exhaustion wrapped his mind like a dirty blanket. He must think for them all now, otherwise the deaths and the time they had bought would have been for nothing.

"Adolphus," he said. "There are two horses on the track. Make sure they are properly tied and safe then return here."

He turned, beckoned Cadmus and followed Adolphus. When they reached the first corpse Cadmus vomited. As he wiped his mouth he started to mutter, "I'm sorry, Master," over and over again until Aurelio rounded on him savagely. Together they dragged the body back into the woods then returned for the second one. There was no time to bury them so Aurelio set the slave to covering them with branches and leaves.

Back in the glade Marcellus was on his feet, leaning groggily against a tree.

"I'm sorry, Master…" he began before Aurelio cut him short.

"If any one else tells me they're fucking sorry they'll be coughing up teeth for the next fucking week. Is that clear?"

He glared round the company meeting the fearful eyes of the others.

"Now we have just a little time to get out of here with our lives. Let's get to it!"

* * *

Marcellus had been plainly shocked when Aurelio had explained to him that he would be going on north with Adolphus, the wagon and four pack mules. They had just spent a sweaty hour manoeuvring the wagon back onto the road. The afternoon was far advanced.

"Master," said Marcellus, "we are slaves. We will be at everyone's mercy. Any freeman can call us to account; steal the wagon if they so wish. There would be no redress open to us."

Controlling his temper with difficulty, Aurelio clapped a

hand to the slave's shoulder. He even managed a wolfish grin.

"Then you are not a slave. From this moment I grant you your manumission. When we arrive in Borbetomagus I will arrange it officially and you will have it in writing. From henceforth you are Marcellus of Judaea, Purveyor of Fine Goods to the Discerning. Adolphus is your slave. Is that understood?"

Marcellus's face, beneath the dirty bandage, was an almost comical display of mixed emotions. In the Roman Empire slaves had no rights but with a master like Aurelio conditions were remarkably pleasant. Food and keep was provided along with a stimulating life which was to all intents and purposes, free. After fully five seconds Marcellus stammered, "Th-thank you, M-Master."

Aurelio went on. "From now on you must start to think like a freeman. You will take one of my costumes to wear and three quarters of the money. I want you to trade enough to make any watcher believe that you are what you appear to be. At the same time you will make your best speed to Mannheim. That is where we will rendezvous."

He did not explain that, originally, he had planned to send Cadmus with Marcellus on the basis that Adolphus could so easily give away their identity. Since the events of this morning, however, Cadmus had all but gone to pieces. He doubted that the slave could be trusted to act a part. Thus, though it wasn't ideal, he would have to come with Tadg, Trista and himself.

"And what of you, Master?" asked Marcellus.

"We will head north with you now. As soon as we find a track heading east, we will leave you, Trista, Tadg, Cadmus and I, along with the horses and our two mules. From then on you will be relatively safe. We shall make our way over the mountains by tracks and by-ways to Mannheim. My guess is we shall be there in three weeks. Whoever arrives first will leave word of their whereabouts at the government rest house."

Much as he hated to admit it, the horses would make life

much easier. In any case they couldn't be left behind.

They had made their way five miles northwards with one or other walking behind carrying a shovel, scooping up droppings and flinging them far into the undergrowth. Now, in the cool of early evening, they had stopped where a fairly well-used track branched off to the right. Tadg, tireless as ever, had been waiting for them.

The six of them stood in a loose group, unwilling, yet, to part. Aurelio looked at them one by one. He was ashamed of his earlier outbursts yet pride prevented him from saying so. The three slaves – more friends than servants – had been with him through Caledonia, the death of Josephus and all that had followed – Marcellus, the resourceful trader and cook; Cadmus, usually so quick and lively, cheerful in the darkest moments; Adolphus, the gentlest of people despite his great strength, a giant who understood beasts better than his fellow men.

Tadg…well Tadg was just Tadg: a force of Nature, a law unto himself but faithful, having given his word. Aurelio had come to depend on him as his strong right arm.

Then Trista. There had never really been any doubt that they would go to all this trouble for their young vagrant. Indeed, Aurelio was aware that he would have faced the nearest his companions could muster to a mutiny had he made any other decision. In a few short weeks her youthful zest had found its way into all their hearts. Life on the road without her would be intolerably dull.

"Well," he said at last, "we must part for a short while. We meet at again at Mannheim."

Marcellus and Cadmus exchanged glances. Marcellus cleared his throat. "Master – Aurelio, that is, Cadmus and I wanted to tell you something." He looked at Cadmus again. The latter nodded. Marcellus continued.

"We understand something of your, er, mission. It's not that anyone said anything, certainly not Josephus," he added hurriedly, "We just, well, sort of picked it up."

He hesitated, trying to gauge the effect of his words on the trader. Aurelio wondered, not for the first time, quite how secret his mission actually was but simply nodded.

"Well," Marcellus continued, "we just wanted you to know that we are with you. We won't fail you."

He petered off into embarrassed silence.

Aurelio suddenly found his heart very full. There was something here to ponder at length: how men held in slavery could yet owe this degree of loyalty to a master. He took Marcellus's right hand in both of his. Looking into his eyes he said, "It was well said. Go well, my friend." He turned, taking Adolphus's great paw in his own. "Go well, my friend." Adolphus shuffled his feet. His face went very red.

Aurelio paused, searching for a parting word. "If things become really bad for you, remember this," he said to Marcellus. "Trista is doing our cooking."

The men laughed, louder and longer than the sally deserved, Adolphus with a puzzled expression on his face. Trista, who had been almost silent, shrieked and beat at Aurelio's arm in mock fury. Then it was time to go.

Cadmus helped Aurelio onto his horse. Trista went first to Marcellus then to Adolphus, hugging them both. Marcellus whispered something in her ear and gave her a small package. "Go now, little one," Aurelio heard him say. "The gods be with you." Cadmus lifted Trista up and placed her in front of Aurelio then, gathering up the lead reins of the mules, he scrambled onto his own mount. Tadg was already off up the road, questing the growing shadows like a hound.

Together they set off. Trista peered around Aurelio and waved at her friends until the wagon creaked out of sight followed by Adolphus leading the mules.

Aurelio felt her small hand creep into his larger one.

Chapter 29

(Mountains)

This was travel to Aurelio's taste. Were it not his for worries about Marcellus and Adolphus, Trista (answering, when she remembered, to the name Tristan) and the mission, he would have been truly happy. As it was he breathed in the pure air of the high foothills with relish. These were not true mountains – they were passing south of the Haunsrück and north of the Vosges ranges – yet to Aurelio they were a joy. Generally the steep slopes were heavily wooded with trees of all kinds. The main human activities involved logging, woodcutting and charcoal burning.

At irregular distances were clearances supporting small villages and fields. Some nights, when it was dry, they slept out in the open. On the whole this was preferable to the insect-ridden huts where accommodation would be grudgingly offered at a price. Occasionally there were inns where they lay soft for a night.

They did a little trading in order to explain their presence but, on the whole, they kept up the pace of their eastward journey. Trista proved an asset to the business of selling. Her pert face and cheeky self-confidence found chinks in the hardest hearts. There were times when Aurelio worried about the calculating looks cast her way but when the chief of one village leaned confidentially close over a mug of ale and asked whether he might buy the 'pretty boy' his fears abated.

Along the way Aurelio and Tadg who acted as scout, asked, casually, after the name Sertorius. They were met with shaken heads until one night, a week into the journey, when they were staying at an inn on the banks of a large lake.

"Would that be Gaius Sertorius Bassus?" asked the landlord. "Has big estates over Niederbronn way? Something high in the government, so I'm told. Don't know what but he's rich as Croesus. Owns half the countryside over there. Wagons going in and out all times of the day and night, so I'm told."

The landlord removed their plates, wiping the table down with his cloth. He stood back, hand on hip, thinking.

"Tell you what, though, old Edgard worked out that way before he retired. Woodsman if I remember aright. Should be in later." He chuckled. "That is unless the sky's fallen by then. I'll send him over, yer Honour, if you'd like."

Aurelio thanked the man. When the landlord was gone he turned to Trista.

"Gaius Sertorius Bassus: ring any bells?" he asked quietly.

Trista thought then shook her head.

"No," she said, "but Father travelled all over Gaul and knew many important people. It could be him."

"Well," said Aurelio, "I will stay and talk to this Edgard. Let's see you to bed and, remember, try to stride."

To his mind there was no better indication of gender than the way a person walked. For seven days now, he had been trying to persuade Trista to adopt a straight-legged stride but with small success. She found it difficult to maintain and, as soon as her attention wandered, she was back to her normal graceful gait.

They went out into the courtyard. He stood guard outside the communal privy while Trista went within then they turned into the stables. Aurelio led the way up to the hayloft where, in the gloom, Cadmus nested in the straw. His snores came, deep and slow. As usual, Tadg was off somewhere about his own business.

"Goodnight, Aurelio," said Trista. She stood on tiptoe, put her arms around his neck and kissed him on the cheek. Aurelio had tried to stop her doing this too but with no success. In truth, his heart was not really in it anyway.

"Goodnight," he replied before climbing down the ladder and returning to the communal room.

An hour later, as he sat nursing a pot of ale near the door, he looked up to find a gnome-like, old man at his elbow.

"'ears you wants ter know about the Sertorius estates. Who you be anyway?"

Ignoring the man's surly manner, Aurelio invited him to sit down.

"I am Aurelio, a trader, travelling the road to the east. I understand that Gaius Sertorius Bassus is a rich man, has estates along the way. I wondered whether it might be to my advantage to stop there and offer my wares."

Edgard guffawed into his ale pot. "Doubt you'd have anything he'd want," was his opinion. "Ol' Gaius, 'e owns half of Germania Inferior. Owns jewels an' vineyards an' chariot teams and fings. Nah; 'f I was you I'd keep goin' ter Sarrabrucca. Buy anything there they will." He spat into the rushes.

As a trader, Aurelio was used to dealing with rude people. Rather than take offence he called for more ale and set himself to become the butt of the old man's ill nature for the evening. Edgard contradicted everything Aurelio said and poured scorn on all his opinions but in the interstices the trader was able to build up a picture of Gaius Sertorius Bassus.

It seemed that he was a well-connected Roman patrician who chose to live out here on the edge of the Empire. He held no government appointments although he had done in the past. Indeed, he had for a while been a Tribune with the Eighth Legion. There was nothing unusual in this. Most young patricians served with the army, usually for as brief a period as possible. It was a prerequisite for a political career. As Aurelio had cause to know, many of them were ineffectual if not downright dangerous as officers.

The main estate was called Cruorsilva, Bloody Wood in the vernacular. A part of it had been in the family for years. Sertorius had inherited it in his thirties. Since then he had added a great deal of farmland and tracts of forests. It seemed that he guarded his property with a private army mostly made up of exlegionaries. The source of his wealth was not altogether clear and Edgard became suspicious at the direction of Aurelio's questions at this point.

"What you want to know all this for, anyway?" he asked, slurring his words. He had drunk a prodigious amount of ale at Aurelio's expense. "You just a small-time trader or what? Sound more like a spy to me."

"It's just passing interest, my friend," said Aurelio. "A trader needs to know who may buy from him. It's always worth knowing about rich men."

He took a denari from his purse and slid it across the table. The old man swayed to his feet.

"Well, piss on you and yer trading and yer fucking money he said," scooping up the coin and biting it. He pointed a dirty finger at Aurelio. "You wants ter watch yersel'. We has ways with foreigners round 'ere."

With that he belched prodigiously and weaved off towards the bar. The landlord who had watched all this made his way across to Aurelio.

"I'm truly sorry, yer Honour," he said. "I knew him for a mean old bastard but if I'd known he was going to be that rude I'd never have sent him to you."

Aurelio reassured the man, paid his tally and then, yawning, went to bed.

* * *

Two days later they crested a rise. Across their front in the valley below ran the trunk road from Argentoratum to Metis. Their own road crossed it before coming down to a ford in a small river. Beyond that again in the distance they could make out a line of heavy wagons turning off up a metalled road to the left. The road wound up a hillside before disappearing through a fortified gatehouse in a well-built wall that stretched off to left and right without break.

As they began their descent Tadg appeared from among the trees at the side of the road.

"That's Cruorsiva," he said, jerking his thumb. "Had a word with one of the waggoners. 'e said the big 'ouse is the other side of the hill, about a mile."

Aurelio gazed at the opposite side of the valley. So here it was at last although he ruefully admitted that it didn't change anything. The place would be well-guarded. Indeed, he could see half a dozen guards checking the wagons in at the gate. It would be altogether best just to hurry on by.

They crossed the trunk road. Clear, brown water hurried across the gravel bed of the ford. As they emerged on the other bank a group of uniformed men mounted and on foot, came into view from around a bend in the road. In the centre of the group was a rich, curtained litter, carried by slaves. Aurelio beckoned the others off the road onto the grass verge to make way for the other party. Armed escorts could be tricky, sometimes reflecting the whims of their owner.

Before coming up with them the group turned off towards Cruorsilva. They hadn't gone far before there was a slight commotion and the litter swayed to a stop. A mounted man, helmeted and crested, the guard commander perhaps, manoeuvred his horse next to the litter. He bent down, apparently speaking to the passenger, darting occasional glances at Aurelio's party. Finally he saluted, straightened and urged his horse into a trot towards them. He stopped, the horse snorting and fidgeting.

"Are you in charge?" The man looked down his nose at Aurelio.

Aurelio bowed.

"Claudio of Baetica, at your service."

The armed man looked him up and down with disfavour.

"My Lady commands you to bring your best wares to

Cruorsilva." He pointed up the road towards the gatehouse. "Be there in two hours; you alone. Leave these...others...here."

He turned his horse in a swirl of dust and cantered back to the litter. Once again he bent down and exchanged a few words with his mistress before taking his place again at the head of the escort. Litter and escort started up the hill towards the gatehouse.

"You'll not go?"

Tadg was looking up at him enquiringly. Aurelio raised his cane to his chin and considered for a moment.

"Well, it's difficult to know how not to," he replied. "Whoever owns this place makes the rules and they aren't going to take kindly to having their desires set at naught."

Trista and Cadmus looked at each other, then at Aurelio. Cadmus cleared his throat but said nothing. Trista had no such scruples.

"Aurelio, you can't, you mustn't. That's where Sertorius lives. You said so. It's too dangerous. Let's just hurry on...please."

Aurelio turned to her.

"Trista," he said. "Think about it. If I don't go they will likely send a mounted patrol after us to drag me back and what will we have gained?"

Trista glared at him, furious.

"On the other hand," he continued, "here is an opportunity to find out why we have been followed. All I'm going to do is go in there and do a little trading, because I have no other option. Then I'll come out. With any luck I may be able to discover something."

Trista gave him one last glare then turned and flounced off.

"And don't flounce," he shouted after her but to no effect. She stopped on the riverbank arms folded, her back radiating outraged disapproval.

Aurelio turned to the others.

"So, do you have any free advice," he asked.

Cadmus looked at his feet, shaking his head unhappily. "No, Master," was all he said.

"You, Tadg?"

The Celt shook his head once.

"Thank Jupiter for small mercies. Right: I'm going to take Galba. You take Vespasian and the horses. Find yourselves a place out of sight in the trees and prepare a meal for my return."

With that, Aurelio took up the mule's lead rein and stalked up the road towards the gatehouse.

* * *

"Yeah?"

The black-browed spearman lounged out of the guardhouse. Even from a distance of four paces his breath smelt foul. Aurelio noted the man's bulging gut. So...an ex-legionary, perhaps, but very much gone to seed. Nevertheless, there was a shining edge on the spearhead.

"Claudio is my name. I am a trader from Baetica. I am bidden by the Lady of the house to bring my wares for her perusal. See here, I have this fine wine from Narbonensis."

He took a small amphora from one of the panniers and offered it to the guard.

"I would value your opinion and that of your companions. Take it. Drink. Enjoy."

The guard stepped forward, keeping a leery eye on the trader. He grasped the amphora, uncorked it and took a swig. Wiping his mouth with the back of his hand he belched and spat.

"Horse piss," was his verdict. "Hans," he called over his shoulder, still looking at Aurelio from under the overhang of his brow, "come an' have some horse piss."

Another man emerged from the guardhouse, this one tall and thin. Blond hair hung lank across his forehead. The first guard handed across the wine.

"Woss he want, anyway?" said Hans, taking a pull at the amphora.

"Wants ter go trading up the 'ouse," came the reply.

A slow smile crossed Hans's face.

"Thirsty work, guarding," he said, "'specially when you gotter check all the stuff goin' in."

Aurelio smiled in his turn. He produced another amphora from the pannier and a large, succulent sausage.

"Belgican," he explained, handing across the food. "Finest you will taste this side of the Rhenus."

The two guards exchanged glances.

"Garn then," said the first. "Go on in. See whether Cruorsilva's gonna make yer rich. Ask for Creperum. He'll see yer right."

He looked at Hans. The two of them started laughing. They were still laughing as the man and mule turned the first corner.

* * *

Aurelio walked for half an hour. The road wound gently upwards between pine trees. Then, abruptly, the trees ended as the road turned to the left. He found himself standing at the top of an escarpment, gazing down across wide parkland. Below him, beside a lake, sprawled a huge, single storey building. It was a palace rather than a villa. The features – red pantiled roof surrounding a central courtyard with pillared porticoes – were unmistakably Roman.

Beyond it, in an area of churned mud and fallen trees, stood a dozen or more crude, wooden barns. As he watched, an empty wagon emerged from one while a loaded one eased forwards to take its place. Clear across the distance he heard the creak of the wheels, the crack of a whip and the complaint of the oxen.

Aurelio leant on his stick. On the face of it the scene was one of rural peace yet something was not quite right. He tried to place what it was. It was something to do with the proportions of the buildings, perhaps. For a moment he felt strangely faint. The building seemed suddenly very close, every detail stark. Then it was far away and indistinct. He closed his eyes and shook his head. When he opened his eyes the scene had returned to normal.

Still shaking his head he tugged on Galba's lead rein and continued down the road. After a while he became aware of the silence. There was nothing strange about silence out here in the countryside but he suddenly realized there was no birdsong. As the thought formed, a cock pheasant exploded from the undergrowth, whirring across his front. Galba baulked for a moment then came on. Aurelio had taken perhaps a dozen paces when he realized that birds were singing all around him. He frowned. Had he been wrong? Had they been singing all along? He shook his head again.

For another fifteen minutes he followed the road as it wound down the scarp face. Where it levelled off there were fields on his left running back to vine covered slopes. He began to see workers in the fields but when he waved and called out they merely straightened from their tasks and looked at him silently. Faint on the wind came the baying of dogs – big dogs. The house was now hidden by a low crest. As he breasted the rise the red pantiles came slowly into sight, much closer than he had expected.

Galba chose this moment to plant her feet and refuse to continue. She let out her coughing bray. Pull as he might Aurelio couldn't move her. He had to resort to the goad carried in the pannier but seldom used. Finally she moved forward, defecating and passing wind loudly.

As he approached the porticoed entrance, apprehension, almost panic, gripped him. The temptation to turn and flee was very strong. He might have given in to it had not a tall figure wearing a long robe appeared from the door at the top of the steps. The man paused, looking towards Aurelio, then began a sedate descent. As he drew closer Aurelio saw that he was an albino. He was tall and well-made, his face composed in a smile.

"Welcome," the man said, his voice curiously high-pitched. "I am steward here. How may I help you?"

Aurelio forced a smile. "I am Claudio of Baetica; itinerant trader. I was bidden by the Lady of the house to bring my wares here for her perusal. The guard told me to ask for Creperum."

The steward's nostril flared. His eyes narrowed. Then he relaxed with a visible effort.

"The gate guards: yes. 'Darkness': it is a stupid little name they call me in order to give offence. I will see about them. My name, in fact, is Minicius."

He gestured courteously to the right.

"Come," he said. "The stable yard will be the place. I will have the slaves bring trestles for you."

In the stable yard Aurelio spread his cloths on two trestle tables and unloaded the panniers. When Minicius came back to check his progress, Aurelio gave him a brooch of Corsican origin. "For your troubles," he said. Minicius inclined his head.

Aurelio stooped. He picked a small jewelled dagger and handed it hilt-first to the steward.

"And perhaps you would give this to your master, with my respects?"

Minicius accepted the weapon.

"I'm sure he will be delighted," he said in his fluting tones.

"May I know his name?" asked Aurelio.

The steward frowned.

"Is it not strange that you should know of Cruorsilva but not of its master?" he said.

Aurelio shrugged. "There are many roads and many names. I mean no disrespect. This is my first time in this province."

Minicius nodded thoughtfully, tapping the dagger in the palm of his hand.

"Well, my master's name is Gaius Sertorius Bassus. You would do well to remember it."

At that moment there was a commotion at the far side of the stable yard. Somehow Galba had jerked her lead-rein free. She whirled around seeking the entrance to the yard, her hooves clattering on the cobbles. Then she was away, accelerating into a canter. She disappeared out of the gate. Aurelio started after her but Minicius called after him.

"Leave her, trader. I will have my men recover her."

Aurelio stopped and returned to his wares. Why was Galba behaving like this? She was normally the most biddable of beasts. And why had no one tried to stop her? Several grooms had been lounging near the gate, close enough to head her off but they had simply stared with a curious lack of interest.

With an effort Aurelio returned his attention to setting out his stall. A few servants drifted by, giving his wares a cursory look. Aurelio tried to engage them in conversation but his efforts failed. He gave an involuntary shiver. Something wasn't right here. There was no sign of the Lady. He began to consider packing and leaving but Galba had not yet been returned. 'Another half hour', he thought.

Then there was a flurry of movement at the door of the house. A group of women was descending the steps into the yard. Their coloured chitons and elaborate hairstyles marked them out as more than servants. Together they advanced across the cobbles, laughing and chattering. Aurelius was reminded of a flock of starlings.

In the midst of the group walked a striking, tall woman. Her chiton was flame-coloured, belted at the waist with gold. The group parted as it reached the cloths upon which the wares were placed. The chattering increased in volume. First one, then another bent to handle items. Aurelio noted that the tall woman did not bend. She pointed and one of the others would hand her what she wanted. First she studied a pair of red, soft leather slippers, then an elaborately ornamented hand mirror.

Despite the ingrained instinct not to stare at potential

customers, Aurelio found his eyes drawn to her. He became aware that he was staring. Rarely had he seen such a well-formed female body, or one so elegant. The folds of the chiton seemed to enhance, rather than hide the firm roundness of her breasts and the length of her legs. As she stood in thought, one leg advanced, he studied the slight convexity of the front of her thigh.

He looked up to find her eyes upon him. They were dark eyes, preternaturally large. She paused, gazing at him, then, without breaking the contact, handed the mirror to one of her companions. She came towards him. He was aware of the sway of her hips, the susurrus of silk about her limbs but was unable to remove his eyes from hers. She stopped less than a pace away. He felt her warmth.

She studied him, her head on one side. Her eyes were green and almond-shaped, framed by kohl. The corner of her full lips lifted briefly then she spoke, her voice low, her words extending in a drawl.

"What name do you go by, trader?"

Aurelio licked dry lips.

"Why, Claudio, my Lady; Claudio of Baetica."

She smiled, running the tip of her tongue along her lips.

"Baetica; a beautiful province, by all accounts, full of beautiful women. Tell me, Claudio of Baetica, how could you bear to tear yourself away from your raven-haired beauties?"

Silk swished as she gently moved her hips.

"My Lady," he began, his mouth dry. "My Lady, I...I would venture that there are none more comely in Baetica than could be found here in Cruorsilva."

Her smile widened showing perfect teeth. She turned her head and looked at him from the corner of her eyes.

"Such gallantry," she said, touching him lightly on the shoulder. "You will stay and eat with us."

She turned in a swirl of silk. Over her shoulder she said, "And now we will make your fortune, Claudio of Baetica."

She swayed back to where her women chattered, comparing clothing and jewellery. Aurelio followed her, his gaze fixed on the movement of her hips. The woman beckoned Minicius. She whispered to him. Purchases were enumerated and tallied. Minicius brought out a large purse and paid Aurelio in full. Then, without a backwards glance, the group of women formed up, moved off and re-entered the house.

Minicius put away the purse. He gazed speculatively at Aurelio.

"My Lady Tiberia tells me that you will be dining here this evening," he said, one eyebrow delicately raised.

Aurelio passed a hand across his face. He felt that he had awakened from a dream. He gazed around him then back at the steward.

"Er…it was kindly meant but really I must be about my business," he replied.

Minicius looked at the trader.

"In Cruorsilva, the wishes of my Lady Tiberia are not the subject of debate, trader," he said. "Besides," he continued, his tone slightly more emollient, "my men have had difficulty catching your mule. No doubt it will be available later. If it is not then we will replace it for you."

"Now, if you would be so good as to pack your goods, you can leave them in the stables. Enter the house through that door," he pointed, "and you will be shown to the baths."

With that he turned and made his way back to the house.

Aurelio stood, undecided. He looked to the south where the others would be waiting. They would worry when he didn't return but, then, there was nothing to be done. He was being presented with a chance to learn useful intelligence. In any case, he could not carry the stock without a mule. He shrugged his shoulders and bent to collect his wares.

* * *

Later, bathed and dressed in a borrowed tunic, Aurelio was shown into a large room. Despite the warmth of the summer's evening, heavy tapestries were drawn across the windows. Torches burnt in sconces adding to the heat.

At his entrance the babble of conversation stopped. All eyes turned to him.

"Ah, the trader."

An enormously fat man lounged on a couch. He wore the purple *toga picta*, heavily embroidered with intricate patterns. This was the dress of triumphant generals or consuls, emperors even on special occasions. Either this man was very important or thought he was.

He waved a beringed hand at an empty couch beside him.

"Be seated. Be welcome. Let the Bacchanalia commence."

His voice was deep, mellow and sonorous. As he spoke his jowls wobbled.

Aurelio bowed.

"My Lord, Gaius Sertorius Bassus," he said on a rising inflexion, making of it a question.

"Indeed," said the man, showing carious teeth in a smile. "And you, I am given to understand, are Claudio of Baetica." He too used the rising inflexion.

Aurelio bowed again.

As he made his way to his place he took in the rest of the room. In the centre was a long, low table, covered with dishes, flagons and cups. Aurelio had attended few formal feasts in his life and none this elaborate. The luxury and abundance of meat and fowl, confection and fruit was almost overwhelming, the savoury fragrances mouth-watering.

There were about a dozen guests, men and women. In the dim light it was difficult to make out details. It seemed that some, in the shadows at the end of the table, were wearing masks. He became aware of the Lady Tiberia reclining on the couch next to his. She wore a chiton, sumptuous in green and blue. Her eyes followed him as he crossed the room. Aurelio took his seat and reclined. A slave stepped out of the shadows and filled his crystal goblet. Conversation began again but not at its previous level. Aurelio had the impression that everyone was listening.

"So, Claudio of Baetica." Sertorius laid emphasis on the name and the province. "I hear that you have *satisfied* the ladies of my humble home."

There were titters from the shadows. All eyes were again upon him. Sertorius gazed unwinkingly from under heavy lids, a small smile pulling up one corner of his mouth.

Aurelio took a sip of wine, gauging the temper of the gathering.

"Ah, my Lord: my luck lies in trading but I would trade all to be the bringer of such *satisfaction*."

Laughter greeted his sally yet there was an edge to it as though the company was laughing at another joke. Sertorius's smile broadened but did not touch his eyes. They, nestling in rolls of fat, gazed steadily, calculating, untouched by emotion.

"I do declare: a wit. We are honoured." He inclined his head slightly and raised his left hand palm upwards.

Conversation became general. Sizzling joints were borne in and placed on the table. Aurelio watched how the others pointed at food, leaving it to slaves to heap their plates. He followed suit. His goblet was kept full.

"Claudio." It was Tiberia. She was presenting him with a choice gobbet of meat. He went to take it from her.

"No," she said. "Open."

Obediently he opened his mouth. She placed the meat in his mouth and he began to chew.

"Lick." She held out tapered fingers. Aurelio glanced at her. She smiled lazily at him. He licked her fingers. Before he had finished she removed her hand and turned to the man on her other side, talking to him as if continuing an interrupted conversation. Aurelio felt a pang of pure jealousy, compounded by the realization that he was thoroughly aroused. From his left came a deep chuckle.

"You must not mind the Lady Tiberia," said Sertorius. "Otherwise she will drive you mad."

"She is your wife?" asked Aurelio.

Sertorius chuckled longer and louder; yet, again, the humour did not touch his eyes. Other guests watched the exchange.

"No, Claudio of Baetica. My tastes run in different channels. And even if they did not and she were not my sister, I would not risk my welfare with such a one."

He paused to cram a handful of food into his mouth. Some of it fell on his toga. Yet more remained smeared around his lower face. He raised his goblet to his lips, taking a massive swig before wiping his mouth with the back of his hand.

"So," he said, when he was once again able to speak, "where is your current journey taking you?"

Aurelio had his answer ready.

"Once out of the hills, I thought I would turn south and make for Argentoratum. Maybe I will winter there. I have not yet thought that far ahead."

"Ah," replied his host, "Augusta Trebecorum, to give it its formal title: a deadly dull and proper place. I cannot recommend it. No," he appeared to think, looking the length of the dining table. "No, I would have thought you would have fared better by heading for Mannheim and then, perhaps, wintering in Borbetomagus."

Again, Sertorius finished on an upward inflexion. The room had fallen silent. Aurelio schooled himself not to look round. Instead he took a long pull at his goblet, thinking furiously. Was it just a coincidence that Sertorius had named the towns towards which he was making or did he know? Either way his only course was to maintain his bluff, however transparent.

"Well, my Lord," he began, "I am willing to be advised by you. Since I have never travelled in this province before, one town seems much like another to me. Does Borbetomagus have much to recommend it as winter quarters?"

Sertorius raised his sparse eyebrows, apparently in surprise at Aurelio's ignorance.

"But did you not know? Borbetomagus is the headquarters of the Twenty Second Primigenia. You would have a captive market all winter. And, of course, the Emperor and his court will be arriving there within the month. No, my friend, if you would make your fortune, you must certainly travel to Borbetomagus."

* * *

It was some hours later. Aurelio had lost track of time. His stomach was distended with rich food. Several of the guests had summoned slaves to help them to the *vomatorium* before returning and attacking the food again. Feeling self-conscious he finally went himself. On his return, his head noticeably clearer, he schooled himself to eat little and drink less.

He had been aware of the proximity of the Lady Tiberia all evening. From time to time he allowed his eyes to linger on the shape of her limbs. Whenever he did, he felt his body become aroused. She, however, had largely ignored him since feeding him the gobbet of meat. Now she turned. In her hand was a goblet of wine. She brought her face close to his. Her perfume enveloped him.

"Claudio," she whispered. "Take the goblet and drink while I speak."

Looking deeply into her eyes, he drank. The wine was spicy and warm.

"I would talk with you privately," she went on. "I shall leave the table shortly. Wait ten minutes, then follow me. My maid will be waiting outside the door to show you the way."

He nodded but she had already turned away. She snapped her fingers. Two female slaves came forward and aided her to her feet although, to Aurelio's eyes, she needed no help. Looking at the state of the other guests, most of whom were uproariously drunk, he wondered how much wine she had taken. She made her way towards the top of the table, pausing to whisper something to Sertorius before leaving the room.

Aurelio looked around for someone to talk to but everyone else seemed to be engaged in the kind of deep philosphical discource which only wine generates. *In vino philosophus,* he thought. Instead he made a show of taking more food although he only toyed with it. When he judged that ten minutes had passed, he too snapped his fingers and was helped to his feet. He stood waiting for a break in the conversation Sertorius was having with the woman on his other side.

After a minute or so Sertorius turned, affecting surprise.

"Why, trader," he said. "How long have you been standing there?"

"But a moment, my Lord," he replied.

"Have you had enough?" asked Sertorius.

"My Lord, I would love to stay but I fear that I must make an early start in the morning. But I wished to thank you for your excellent hospitality. It is seldom that one eats so well on the road. Even less frequently is one admitted to such, ah, august company."

"A pretty speech," said Sertorius waving a hand. He sounded bored.

"Go, then. No doubt *someone* will find you a bed." He broke into muffled guffaws. The woman next to him joined her treble giggle to his. In a moment the whole room was laughing. Aurelio left with what dignity he could command.

* * *

"But we must do something?" Trista's voice was sharp with anxiety. "We can't just leave him in there. Anything might have happened to him."

Cadmus looked unhappy. He had contributed little to the discussion. Tadg squatted near the fire whittling flakes of bark from a stick into the flames. Trista held Galba's head, stroking the mule's neck. Galba had found her way back to their camp in the woods at twilight without her harness. Since then Trista had been sick with worry, urging action.

"Peace, little one," said Tadg. "Aurelio can look after 'isself. 'e's held up for some reason. If we go blundering in there in the dark we may miss him or we may get caught ourselves."

He tested the point of the stick with his finger.

"But Tadg..." Trista began.

"Hush," he said. "Look: if 'e's not back by tomorrer we'll think again. For now we just wait. Now get some sleep girl."

Looking miserable and rebellious Trista rose and fetched her blanket from one of the panniers. Wrapping herself in its folds she curled up with her back to the fire and the two men. Tadg rose, beckoning Cadmus. Together they went a little way into the trees.

Tadg put his head close to the slave's ear. "We keeps watch tonight. I'll go first. Keep an eye on 'er ladyship. Give 'er 'alf a chance and she'll be off after him."

Chapter 30

(Darkness)

The maid was a plump and comely Gaul. She led the way down several corridors and across a courtyard, stopping at a pair of cedar doors. She knocked. Without waiting for an answer she opened one and motioned him within, closing it behind him.

Inside, the room was warm and dark, lit by a single lamp behind a red shade. The atmosphere was heavy with perfume; frankincense Aurelio thought. His senses were strangely heightened. He felt the individual fibres of the curtain within the door brush against his hand, heard the rush of blood in his arteries.

There was a swish of silk. Tiberia stood before him clad in a loose robe. He gazed, transfixed as she reached out and ran one hand down his chest. The response of his body was immediate and massive. His last cogent thought was one of embarrassed lust.

* * *

"Lucius."

He was running through a great building searching every room.

"Lucius."

He must find her. She was in here somewhere.

"Lucius, wake up. Lucius…"

The building swam before his eyes, then, like mist, dispersed. He was looking up into Tiberia's face. Her long, black hair hung down, enclosing him as in a tent. Pain beat at his temples. He had no idea how many times they had made love; only that he was ready again. A tiny corner of his mind wondered at this…

He cupped one of her breasts and kissed the nipple. Tiberia

took his hand, folding it in both of hers.

"No, Lucius," she said. "Now we must talk."

He tried to nuzzle her breast again but she took a grip on his hair, pulling him away.

"Talk, Lucius. Then you shall have me again."

Sulkily he sat up, wincing at the fresh scratches on his back. Tiberia plumped up a pillow and sat close against him, her lips next to his ear.

"Lucius," she began, "I need your help. I am frightened. My brother is mad, quite mad."

Too late he realized that he was meant to be Claudio.

"My...My Lady," he began, "you have me wrong. I am Claudio of Baetica, a humble trader..."

Angrily, Tiberia punched his shoulder. "No time," she snapped, then in a gentler voice, "there is no time."

She reached across him to where his clothes lay heaped by the bed. She rummaged amongst them for a moment then sat back up

"This," she said, holding out her hand. "How do you explain this?"

Hanging from her fingers by its silver chain was the amethyst seal.

"This is the Imperial seal, Lucius."

"It...it is just a trinket. I won it at dice. That's all, I swear."

Tiberia grasped the seal in her fist. Her face became cold.

"Lucius Terentius Aquilina," she said, enunciating each syllable slowly and distinctly. "Or would you prefer Aurelio Silvio Trio? You see, my brother's tentacles penetrate the farthest corners of the Empire. Do you still deny me?"

Then her face crumpled, her head went down and she began to sob against his chest. All he could think to do was put his arm around her and stroke her hair. After a minute the sobs began to subside. She sat up, cuffing tears from her kohl-smudged eyes. When she spoke her words were punctuated by shuddering breaths until she had herself under control.

"Sertorius he...he plans to overthrow the Emperor."

Lucius was stunned.

"Lucius." She put her arms around his chest and clung to him. "I don't want to die. You must help me."

"Help you?" he said. "How?"

She looked up at him, biting her lip. Although her make-up was smudged and her hair tousled, she looked very beautiful.

"It is known that you are an Imperial agent...no, my lover." She placed a finger on his lips as he opened them to deny her words. "No, there is no time. Sertorius knows everything. In the morning he plans to torture you. You must flee tonight but please take me with you. Please protect me, I beg of you. If Sertorius goes ahead with his plans and fails, the Emperor will take a terrible revenge upon our family."

She took both his hands in hers. "Take me with you to Borbetomagus, to Hadrian. Explain to him that I had no part in these plottings. He will listen to you."

Lucius' thoughts were in turmoil. There were things he needed to know here but his mind was clouded and slow.

"But how will he overthrow the Emperor?" he asked at length.

"Oh," she said, "it is something to do with the German tribes. He has been stirring them up; promising them spoils. The barns behind the house, they are filled with weapons for the Germans and gold; lots of gold. Somehow he plans to betray the Legions on the frontier so that they are defeated and Hadrian taken. Then Sertorius will proclaim himself Emperor."

Lucius shook his head.

"But who will follow him?" he asked.

"You don't understand." She spoke impatiently. "My brother is immensely rich. His influence stretches far and wide. He has suborned whole Legions elsewhere. When the time comes they will back him. Hadrian must be warned."

Again she clung to him, crying. He held her, gazing across her head to the wall beyond. There was just too much here to take in. What she said made sense but could he trust her? And if he trusted her, could he really leave her here and run? Was it not possible to take her with him?

He made his decision. After all, she knew much more about this than he did. She would make a much better witness before Hadrian. Taking her by the shoulders, he gently held her away so that he could look down into her face. With his thumb he wiped away the tears that hung trembling on her lower eyelids. Then he kissed her gently on the lips.

"Shush, my dear one," he whispered. "You shall come with me."

Tiberia sat perfectly still for a moment then reached for him. Her arms went round his neck and she kissed him deep and long, her tongue probing his.

"Oh, Lucius," she said at last, loosening her grip on his neck. "I knew you wouldn't let me down."

As if by accident her hand brushed his manhood. She bit her lower lip with her small, white teeth and blushed.

"Lucius," she said, her voice low and seductive, "may I tell you something?"

Her hand settled on the throbbing member. "Yes," Lucius groaned, pressing her backwards into the pillows.

She giggled. "The wine I gave you before we left the feast? It contained a tincture of belladonna. It is the plant of Venus. She has seen to it that your little man stands so tall, so often."

"Hades," muttered Lucius. A small part of his mind told him that he should be preparing to flee but the power of Priapus was abroad in his blood. He entered her.

"Well, perhaps just once more," she murmured, driving her nails into his bare buttocks.

* * *

Later she pushed his body off hers. He muttered something incoherent in his sleep. She leant on one elbow looking down at him, a secretive smile on her lips. Sweat and other bodily fluids glistened across his muscles. She traced the lines of old scars with her eyes. 'What a shame,' she thought. She could have had such fun with him. But, faugh: she would have become bored, sooner rather than later. He was too prim for her tastes although it would have been enjoyable to pervert him, to turn him into a lap dog whining for her favours. Perhaps Sertorius could be prevailed upon to let her have him for a little longer.

She reached behind the drapes at the head of the bed and pulled a hidden bell rope. A moment later the door opened silently. Her maid glided into the room carrying a goblet, soft slippers silent on the tiled floor. She gazed at her mistress, questioning. Tiberia nodded.

"Tell your master that this is the one," she whispered.

The maid nodded, placed the goblet on the table beside the bed and left as silently as she had arrived.

Careful not to awaken Lucius, Tiberia slipped off the bed. She went to a chest and selected clothes suitable for riding. Quickly and silently she dressed.

"Lucius." The name wove its way into a voluptuous dream.

"Not Lucius – Claudio," he muttered.

"Lucius, my love. It is time to start moving." She shook his shoulder.

Reluctantly he opened his eyes. Tiberia was smiling down at him. In her hand she held a goblet.

"We have to get ready, Lucius. There are only a few hours to dawn and we must be far away by then. Here, I have prepared a draught to cleanse the belladonna from your system. It will also clear your mind."

Lucius struggled into a sitting position. Tiberia folded the goblet into his hand. He took a sip and grimaced.

"No," she said, "it is not very pleasant but you must drink it all. Take it down in one swallow, then lay back while it works."

Lucius did as he was told, almost retching at the bitter taste. She took the goblet from his hand, placing it back on the table. Lucius was still opening and closing his mouth in disgust. Placing a hand on his forehead she eased him back against the pillows.

She gazed at him for a moment then leant forward and kissed him on the lips. "There now," she said. "Rest easy for a few minutes while I arrange for horses and food. When I return you must be ready to leave."

With that she turned and left the room.

Lucius lay amidst the wreckage of silken sheets trying to think clearly. Despite the draught his thoughts kept returning to Tiberia's voluptuous body. Petulantly he wished her to return. The aftertaste of the draught was foul on his tongue. Sweat was breaking out all over his body. He raised a hand to wipe his brow. It felt enormously heavy. Instead of moving upwards, it wavered and fell sideways back to the sheet. He tried to move it again but succeeded only in fluttering the fingers…

* * *

Panic stirs. He tries to move his other limbs but they are too heavy. His head moves slightly from side to side but, even as he tries, the movement slows and dies. With a huge effort of will he calms himself. Something strange is happening but this will not do. He is alive. His heart still beats. His lungs still function. He tells himself that panic is the least useful emotion in a paralysed body. It seems to help a little.

The door crashes open. From the corner of his eye Lucius watches four figures in black robes enter the room. He realizes that they are wearing masks – not the masks of feast and fete but animal masks, real and frightening. They come to the bed. Two of them, a pig and a leering fox, grasp his ankles and pull his legs roughly off the mattress. The other two, seemingly a cat and a weasel, take his wrists. Spread-eagled he is swung from the bed.

He is very frightened now. Never before has he experienced such a total surrender of control. With fear comes the sapping realization that this is the Lady Tiberia's doing. She has been false all along. He has allowed himself to be betrayed. Darkness enters his mind. What use is he? He has failed his Emperor. He has failed his companions. He thinks of Cadmus, Tadg and Trista out there in the dark, waiting, worrying. He longs to be with them with every fibre of his being.

Instead he is carried along darkened corridors, his back and occasionally his head scraping on the floor, being bounced off the walls as the group rounds corners, his manhood flopping flaccidly. After some minutes the four carriers stop. Inches in front of his inverted face tower black double doors. The weasel knocks loudly three times and the doors open.

Lucius is immediately aware of a noxious smell; compounded, it seems, of vomit, faeces and decay. He gags as he is carried into the chamber beyond, into a dank and oppressive darkness. The doors slam shut. He is lifted and dumped on a flat, stone surface, banging his head sharply in the process. There is a period of shufflings and mutterings then silence. Lucius lays supine, his nerves strung to breaking point, awaiting what is to come.

A mask swims into his view. It is fashioned in the shape of a he-goat with great horns curling towards the ceiling. Lucius guesses it to be Sertorius by the obesity swaddled in the black robe. The figure speaks in deep sonorous tones.

"So, Centurion Terentius," it says. "You have had your...diversion. Now it is time to pay."

From the folds of his robe Sertorius brings forth the small, jewelled dagger Lucius had given to Minicius for his master. He brings the point of the blade slowly to within half an inch of Lucius's right eye. Lucius, unable to blink, is forced to stare in horror. The point is so close that he cannot focus on it. As he waits for the thrust that will remove his eye he feels his sanity strain at its moorings.

"You recognize it, I see." Sertorius removes the blade, holding it up, seeming to study it. "A pretty bauble. You will be pleased to know that it has been dedicated into the service of the Darkness. For a gift freely given then perverted is a powerful weapon, especially against the giver."

He turns and waddles to the foot of the table where he stands, studying the prone figure for some seconds. At length he raises his hands and speaks, his voice taking on the singsong note of incantation.

"Shortly you will join us in a rite. It is an ancient rite which will channel the power of this gathering against one person. That person is Publius Aelius Hadrianus," he spits the names, "so-called Emperor of Rome."

"It is fitting that, as the Chosen One, you should know the nature of your sacrifice, for thus, with your fear and despair, will it become more potent. This night you will donate a quantity of your blood to the making of a mannequin representing your lord and master. Again, it is fitting that the blood so used should be taken from a devoted servant of the impostor. The perversion is thus complete."

Sertorius brings both hands forwards, index fingers pointing at Lucius. When he speaks again his voice is as implacable as winter.

"Tomorrow, at the dark of the moon, as the mannequin is dedicated, your heart will be torn from your living breast and sacrificed to the Darkness. Your soul will be ripped from your etheric body and banished into everlasting oblivion. Thus will the potency of the curse be ensured. Thus will both impostors die."

Lucius knows despair. After all that had gone before – all the battles, all the dangers – that he should die in this squalid manner, as the plaything of these perverts. Tears well. They fill his eye sockets, blurring his vision. In his extremity, unbidden, the words of the Invocation of Mithras, the Undying Sun, come to his mind. A spark of resistance arises in his breast. He cannot speak the words out loud but he can think them. Surely Mithras will listen.

"Oh noble Lord Mithras, Sun that ever lives, vouchsafe now thy Light to we who struggle in shadow…"

Around him arises the harsh bedlam of the Black rite but he does not hear it. He has passed within. When the blade punctures the vein in his arm he feels nothing.

* * *

The awakening was slow. For a long while he could not distinguish waking from the turgid dreams which clung to him. Eventually he recognized a tendril of consciousness and clung to it with all his will. Slowly he followed it upwards. Thirst was the first reality followed by a pounding in his head. His body was a bundle of pains, the worst being in the crook of his right arm.

His eyes were closed and crusted, otherwise he would have opened them. As consciousness increased, and, with it, memories, he willed himself to lie still. He listened. Faintly he heard birdsong and then a distant voice raised in tuneless song. Apart from that there was silence. He was lying on a soft, yielding surface. Something else prodded his memory. A scent? Yes; of course, the lingering perfume of frankincense. Could he be back in the Lady Tiberia's room?

Encouraged by the silence he attempted to open one eye. It hurt and would not budge at first, however the pain produced tears which must have dissolved some of the crust for suddenly he could see. It took a moment for his labouring brain to note that he had control of his muscles again. Tentatively he tried waggling one finger. Yes, it worked but the arm would only move a slight distance before stopping. He realized that he was spread-eagled on the bed with his arms and legs tied. Nevertheless his was a functioning body again.

His spirits rose very slightly. Then the full weight of the previous night's events came back and they fell again.

The door opened. He lay quite still. There were footsteps. They stopped by the bed. Someone said, "Tsk, tsk; the state of you."

He lay quite still, pretending unconsciousness.

"By Demeter's Paps, what you people do get up to." The accent was that of rural Gaul.

"Hot water an' rags, that's what we'll need, though how I'm to clean you properly while you're tied up like that, gods only know."

Footsteps receded.

Lucius thought rapidly. This was a servant sent to clean him. Would she be a part of the evil operating in this house? He thought not. That had had all the hallmarks of a group of patrician initiates. Gallic peasants would have their own rites and superstitions but they would tend towards witchcraft. The perversion to which he had been subjected last night was an altogether more intellectual business.

Might she help him? Probably not. A household servant going against the interests of her master risked dismissal and, where Sertorius was concerned, quite possibly death. However, he had to make the attempt.

He heard the footsteps once more. The door opened and closed. There was the clatter of a wooden bucket being put down by the bed.

"Well, let's see what the damage is."

Lucius groaned and opened his operable eye. A well-built, middle-aged woman bent over him with her sleeves rolled up. She looked to be a merry soul although she looked at him askance.

"Oh, awake, are you? How's the head?"

"Bad," he croaked.

"An' no surprise, I'm sure," came the reply. "The rate you lot was carrying on last night, it's a wonder you're awake at all."

Lucius was comforted by her matter-of-fact approach.

"If you could just lift your arse up a ways it'd help," she said.

Lucius arched his back as best he could.

"Bedding'll have to go," said the woman.

Her brawny arms bunched as she slid the sheet out from under him. She seemed quite unfazed by her task. He became aware that he was sadly mired in excrement and dried urine. He felt ashamed.

"Right," she said. "Let's get you cleaned up."

Wringing a rag out in the bucket, she began to wipe him down with warm water. Lucius cleared his throat.

"Might I have a drink do you think? I am very thirsty."

The woman paused in her task.

"Dunno about that. 'er Ladyship didn't say nothing about that an' she's very particular when she has a gentleman friend in, so ter speak."

Lucius attempted a winning smile, knowing that he probably looked like a fugitive from battle. "I think Her Ladyship may have forgotten about it in the, er, exigencies of the night but I really would count it a great favour if you could get me just a little water. I certainly won't tell her."

The woman considered. "Well, I s'pose it can't do no harm. But mind you *do* keep quiet about it. 'er Ladyship can be a right barbarian when she gets going." She giggled. "But I s'pose I don't have to tell you that, do I?"

She rose and moved towards the window. There was the sound of pottery on glass then of water being poured. Lucius found himself swallowing involuntarily. The woman came back, lifted his head and held a cup to his lips. He drank greedily. Nothing, he thought, had ever tasted so good. When he had drunk his fill the woman lay his head back on the pillow.

"Close yer eyes," she said.

Lucius obeyed. The damp rag was gently wiped across his eyelids. This, he thought, was definitely not a bad woman. His hopes kindled.

"You can open them now."

He opened his eyes. Apart from a slight granular feeling his eyelids were clear.

"My thanks," he said. "You are indeed sent from the Goddess. Might I know your name?"

She gave him an arch look. "Not that you needs to know but I'm Bonduca, one of the house maids. Now let's get on 'cos she likely be along soon an' it won't do if you're still covered in shit an' piss."

Lucius noted that she seemed quite incurious about how he came to be in this condition. Presumably she had cleaned up on similar occasions. But, if Tiberia was about to make an appearance he must make his play.

"Bonduca," he said, "if you could just loose my limbs, it would make your task much simpler."

Bonduca concentrated on her task, wiping away diligently in all his most private parts.

"Likely it would," she replied, "but I knows better than to get involved. When 'er Ladyship ties up one of 'er guests, 't ain't up to me to untie them. You just lie still."

Lucius lay still. He tried not to let his disappointment overwhelm him. He resolved to try again.

"Bonduca, how would you like to earn yourself a hundred sestercii?"

The woman snorted. "The last one offered me a thousand." She wrung her rag out in the bucket. "Didn't make no difference though." She paused and fixed him with a jaundiced eye. "See, it's one thing for you to run off. You might even give me the money but you wouldn't care what would happen to me after you'd gone, would you?"

She turned away and went on with her washing.

"I've got a good position here. You wants to ask yourself what would happen when they found you was gone. Think they wouldn't work out who let you go? Think they'd pat me on the head an' say, 'Well done, Bonduca: you done the right thing there'?"

She shuddered. "I'll tell you: it wouldn't just be flogging. The master don't believe in leniency."

Bonduca threw the rag into the bucket. Taking up a towel she dried him then dabbed perfume on chest and stomach.

"Gotter make you smell nice for the Lady haven't we?" she remarked.

She went to a chest and came back to the bed with fresh sheets.

"Move your arse again," she ordered.

Lucius arched his back. He decided to make one more attempt to win the woman's support.

"Bonduca," he said. "I am an imperial agent. It is vital that I reach the Emperor. If you will help me escape you will be richly rewarded and protected."

Bonduca said nothing as she smoothed the sheets and tucked them in. Finally she stood up with a slight groan, one hand in the small of her back. She turned to him.

"Listen, mister: it ain't for me to judge, but if you gets yourself into these positions it's your own fault, ain't it? You had your fun and the Lady had hers. Likely she'll have a bit more fun an' then she'll let you go. Look on the bright side. She don't normally do anything worse than flesh wounds."

With that she picked up her bucket and left the room.

Left alone, Lucius strained at his bonds with no result other than hurting himself. He craned his head to look at them. The cords were stout linen, pulled tight. They were anchored to the bed frame which was solid oak. He felt panic lurking at the edge of his mind and forced it down. There must be a way...

Footsteps sounded in the corridor. The door opened. There in the doorway, one hand on the doorknob, stood the Lady Tiberia, cool as the morning, her hair freshly curled, her blue chiton falling gracefully to the floor.

"So, my lover, you are awake and clean."

She walked slowly towards the bed, smiling, looking up and down his naked body. She sighed.

"Such a waste," she said, "but perhaps we can use a little more of you in the short time you have left. In the meantime, Sertorius has ordered that you be humiliated and brought to despair as much as possible. He sees such things in the same light as baiting a bull before it is slaughtered: it softens the tissues and makes for much better eating."

She laughed. Her laughter was musical. Lucius wondered that such a beautiful body could contain such a treacherous personality.

"So, I have a visitor for you," she continued. "You might even say an old friend." She raised her voice. "Heliodoros," she called.

Lucius turned his head towards the door. A man entered. He was slim, of medium height with black hair. He looked vaguely familiar but Lucius could not place him. He stopped near the bed and struck a pose, smiling expectantly. When Lucius said nothing, the smile faded.

"Well really," said the man, his voice petulant, "my big entrance and you don't even remember me, do you?"

Lucius shook his head. "Should I?"

The man stamped his foot. "Heliodoros, sometime courtier to his Imperial Pomposity Hadrian the Hispanian. We met in that ghastly, damp hole in Britannia. You were unkind to me; very unkind."

Lucius remembered. Heliodoros, the Greek actor who had made unwanted advances to him in Trimontium in the process of choosing him a new identity. His hair then had been blond. Now it was black yet the features were entirely familiar. The dawning realization must have shown in his face.

"Yes, you remember *now* don't you?" He loomed over the bed. Tiberia restrained him with one slim hand.

"Gently, now, Helio," she said. "He is not to be hurt – yet – remember? Why don't you just tell our guest what you are about to do? He will enjoy that."

Heliodoros relaxed.

"Yes, indeed," he smirked. He turned away from the bed, paused for a moment then whirled back, crashing one foot to the floor, his right fist to his chest.

"Hastatus Prior, Second Cohort, Sixth (*Victrix*) Legion reporting for duty, sir!"

Lucius marvelled at the transformation. The Greek was, for the moment, every inch a seasoned centurion positively exuding martial zeal. Heliodoros seemed pleased with the effect.

"Or would you prefer..."

He seemed to shrink in size. His back bent slightly and he leant on a non-existent stick.

"...Aurelio Silvio Trio, Purveyor of Fine Goods to the Discerning, at your service."

He flourished his free hand to underscore his words.

Lucius nodded. So this was why his disguise had been so flawed; why his whereabouts seemed to have been an open secret. The Greek had been a spy in the Imperial court.

As if reading his thought Heliodoros said, "Yes, my uncouth military friend, your every move has been known these three years. And in all that time you have been like a little mouse, scampering towards the cat. And now the cat is going to eat you, after playing with you, of course."

He paused to titter.

"Oh, but you mustn't worry," he went on. "Your usefulness will not die with you tonight. No, not indeed. Within the hour your identity will take horse for Borbetomagus in the person of your humble servant."

Heliodoros bowed elaborately.

"There I – you – will warn his Imperial Pomposity of certain imminent threats from the barbarian hordes across the Rhenus. It will be," he declaimed, "my greatest part. So serious will those threats be that the Legions will deploy in forward positions. Which is a shame." He looked at his finger nails, frowning slightly, then looked up again, his face wreathed in smiles.

"It is a shame because they will be facing in *quite* the wrong direction. You see, the Germans will fall upon their unguarded flank and, quite simply, destroy them." His face turned wistful. "All those lovely soldier boys, gone, quite gone, in one great bloodbath."

Despite himself, Lucius was fascinated. So this was the scheme in which he had been unwittingly involved. He sought for ways to dint the Greek's confidence.

"And what makes you think that they will believe that you are me?" was all he could find to say.

Heliodoros smiled, condescendingly.

"Why, because I shall arrive in a cart with mules and slaves, all provided by my beloved patron, Sertorius. And, of course, I shall show the appropriate officials this."

From within his tunic he withdrew the amethyst seal on the silver chain. Lucius had known but the dismay he felt was real.

"And don't worry for me, as I know you will. I shall not expose myself to Hadrian or that dullard Meridius. Mine will be a flying visit by night made to the Legion's intelligence chief. I will return unflinchingly to danger to find out more of the barbarians' plans, pausing only to deliver some immortal words which I will work out between now and then."

"And now," he struck a pose, "I go. We shall not meet again."

He turned and marched from the room, leaving Lucius to digest his words.

"So..."

Lucius turned his head. He had forgotten Tiberia's presence.

"So, you have been duped by your own foolishness; your body has been used and shortly your very essence will be used against your beloved Emperor. Tell me,

how do you feel now that you understand the depths of your betrayal?" she asked, smiling down at him.

Lucius glared at her. Anger grew in his heart but he husbanded it, refusing her the pleasure of seeing it.

"Gladly will I tell you how it feels," he replied. "It feels as if I have done my best against overwhelming odds. It feels as if I have not once betrayed the trust place in me by the Emperor. It feels as if I have done my duty. Now, will you tell me how it feels to wallow in the pit of depravity, perversion and faithlessness that you call a soul?"

The slap rocked his head. It stung but Lucius felt a small spring of pleasure to have elicited even such a slight victory. He turned his head back towards the woman. Her long nails were inches from his face.

"Know this, spy;" she hissed, "were it not for Sertorius, I would rip your eyes out here and now. What do you know of the trials and indignities our family has had to suffer? You understand nothing, slave, *nothing.*"

With an effort she stood upright. She was panting.

"But I tell you this, your death and degradation tonight were always going to be hideously painful. Now I will make it my business to extend the pain and suffering as long as possible and the last thing you will see as you die will be my face smiling at your agony."

Her voice had risen to a shout. In the silence that followed she turned on her heel and left the room, slamming the door.

Lucius's spirits were quite uplifted for a while, following this exchange. Once again he struggled against his bonds, trying to free just one limb but he had to admit that there was little chance of success. After some minutes he lay still again. How long until nightfall? Some hours, he thought. There was almost no hope of escape. He thought about the moment when they would take him from here. Would they drug him? Possibly, but that would mean him drinking something. He resolved to resist to the last moment and, if it was at all possible, to kill himself or be killed before his ceremonial execution.

With that decision made he found a strange sense of peace. He relaxed and closed his eyes. Almost immediately he slipped into an exhausted sleep.

Chapter 31

(Escape)

Tadg came awake instantly.

"Nearly dawn," said Cadmus.

Tadg threw aside his blanket.

"Anything?" he asked.

"Her ladyship tried to escape an hour or two back. Said she was going to relieve herself but we know that trick. She came back meek enough when I followed her. Apart from that there were wagons on the road, heavy ones. Sounded like they came down from the estate and went east. No sign of the boss," he finished.

Tadg took a strip of dried meat from his pack. He chewed it reflectively.

After a few moments he said, "I'm goin' in there then."

Cadmus did not argue. He was only glad that someone was taking action. He no longer believed in his own courage.

"How'll you do it?" he asked.

Tadg thought.

"Front door, I think. If I go over the wall an' get caught there's no chance of blagging me way out. No: soon as it gets light we gather firewood an' load Vespasian. I'll go in as a peasant delivering firewood to the kitchen. It's not perfect but it'll have to do."

"I'm coming with you."

Both men turned. Trista was struggling out of her blanket.

"Listen, girl..." began Tadg.

"No, you listen." Trista's colour was high, the look of combat in her eyes. The two men tensed. They had seen this mood before.

"You know your Gallic is terrible, Tadg. If you open your mouth, they'll know you're not a peasant. I c'n do local, see," she demonstrated, dropping into the patois. "Besides," she went on as Tadg started to protest, "what could be more innocent than a boy leading his stupid father? And I know big houses. I grew up in one. I'll be much better able to find my way around. So I'm coming."

Tadg and Cadmus exchanged glances. The decision was up to Tadg but both men knew the destructive power of Trista in a bate. They would probably have to tie her to a tree to keep her out of it.

"If you come, will you do exactly what I say," asked Tadg.

Trista became big eyes and dimples. "Of course, dear Tadg."

Tadg shook his head. He spat into the fire. Look at it how you would, the girl was trouble.

"C'mon then. We go as soon as it gets full light."

* * *

For the gate guards it had been a long night. Apart from the wagons there had been nothing. In half an hour they would be relieved and the only one more or less awake couldn't wait. He leant on his spear, eyes heavy with weariness.

"'scuse me, mister."

The guard jerked awake.

"Wot!"

He looked up then down to where a grubby child was pulling at his sleeve.

"Wot d'yer fink yer doin' sneaking up on people like that?"

The child wiped a grubby hand across its nose.

"Didn't creep up an' you woz asleep." It glared at the guard accusingly.

"Well wotta yer want, then?"

"Me an' me Da'," she jerked a thumb at a small man holding the lead rein of a mule, "we've got to take this firewood down ter the 'ouse. C'n we go in?"

The guard scratched his head.

"Can't yer ol' man speak for hisself then?" he prevaricated.

Decisions were not his forte.

"nah, 'e's thick, see. 's why I do all the talking."

The guard pondered. He could wake Variatrix, ask him, but he had a wicked tongue on him first thing; was as likely to bawl him out as anything.

"Well I dunno nuffink about no firewood." He struggled for a grip on the situation. "Who sent for it, then?" Yes; that seemed like a sound gambit.

"It woz that steward bloke, you know, Wossisname," replied the urchin.

"Wot, ol' Creperum, big bloke, all white?"

"Yeah, that's him. Sent this bloke ter me Da'. 'Lug,' 'e said, on account a that's me Da's name (only I did the listening on account of him being thick). 'Lug,' 'e sez, 'we needs firewood down the kitchen. We needs it termorrer, early. That Wossisname, that Creepyum, he says yer the man for firewood. We're counting on yer.'"

The child fell silent, staring at the guard. He wanted to tell it to stop staring. It was making him feel uncomfortable.

"Orl right then," he said at length. "Yer can go in but...but." He sought for a parting shot which would imprint his status as a guard. "But don' you go walking on the grass," he said. "The master's most partic'lar about 'is grass."

The child continued to look at the guard as the small cavalcade entered the gate. The guard thought that it was shaking its head at him as if in disbelief. He didn't do anything about it, though. He doubted he'd come off best.

* * *

Around the back of the house the kitchens were busy. The field workers and servants were being fed. Emphasis was upon cauldrons of bland, sustaining food. Peacocks stuffed with honeyed dormice were for their betters, later in the day. Slaves came and went carrying provisions in one direction and rubbish in the other.

Tadg and Trista mingled with the crowd. They had unloaded Vespasian and left her hobbled, grazing in a copse beyond the lake. Tadg reasoned that since the house had not ordered any firewood, they would be straining credulity by arriving with a load. In any case, Vespasian had become increasingly unsettled the closer they had drawn to the house and Tadg believed deeply in animal instincts. Their plan now was to join the crowd in the refectory, pretending to be field workers, and see what they could learn from the gossip.

They shuffled along in the queue, collecting bowls of steaming stew and a hunk of bread each. Tadg nodded towards a table where a dozen servants were eating. The pair sat at one end of a long bench and applied themselves to their breakfast, listening.

At first the talk was of people and activities on the estate which meant nothing to them. Then one of the women looked over her shoulder, leant forward and said in a low voice, "Bel's Bunions but that were a rare old party they had last night. Gerd's been in the vomitorium since dawn. Baling it out by the bucket load, she says."

"Aye," said another, leaning forward in his turn. "Seems as the Lady got 'er 'ooks into that trader. Poor bugger: bet 'e wishes 'e'd never come to Cruorsilva."

There were some muffled sniggers.

"Wot's she done to 'im?" asked someone down the table.

"What ain't she done," said the other. "Bonduca says she's got 'im tied to her bed. Says he was in a right ol' state this morning." His voice fell to a whisper. "I think his Nibs…" He looked to right and left, significantly. The others nodded and fell silent. After a while, someone ventured that the grapes had caught downy mildew. With evident relief the others fell upon the topic and soon the conversation was off in another direction.

Tadg nudged Trista. The two of them stood and moved to a quiet corner. Tadg leant down. "Ask someone to point out Bonduca to you," he said.

Trista looked around then made her way to the serving table where the queue had all but gone. She selected one of the cooks who looked less surly than the others.

"'scuse me," she said, "only I'm new here and I've gotter talk to Bonduca. Could you point her out to me, mister?"

The cook looked around then pointed with his wooden ladle. "Big woman, brown hair, shaped like a mountain: end table by the door," he said.

Trista thanked the man and made her way back to Tadg. She pointed out the woman to him.

"Right," he said, "you go and look around outside; get your bearings but look innocent an' remember you're a boy. I'll see you in the stable yard in half an hour."

* * *

"Beautiful morning," said Tadg.

Bonduca had just emerged from the door of the refectory. She paused.

"Do I know you?" she asked, looking with what she imagined to be hauteur at the small man who had addressed her. By his speech he was a foreigner of some sort and rather small. He lounged against the wall outside the refectory as if he owned the courtyard at least. Evidently not of high status yet there was something about him that made her linger.

"Nah," said Tadg. "Field worker, me. Took on yesterday. Just trying to get my bearings, like. Then I seen you. Tadg I fort – that being my name – Tadg, that's one fine piece o' womanhood there. Could do worse than say 'allo I fort. So 'ere I am an' ain't it a beautiful morning."

Having made an early start, Bonduca had a small amount of

time to spare and no pressing engagements. She decided to indulge herself.

"Might be a beautiful morning for some if they've nothing better to do. *Some* of us have important work to be getting on with."

Not in the least put out Tadg said, "Arr; I fort to myself that's a smart woman. She'll be important, like, around 'ere. I bet this 'ousehold couldn't run without 'er. I woz right, wozn't I? Tell me, wot sort of important work do you do then?"

He does have a rather nice smile she thought...

* * *

"South wing; bed chamber off the atrium. Can you find it?"

"South wing." Trista turned on her toes, pointing uncertainly. "Is that south?" she asked.

Tadg nodded.

"Follow me, then."

She led the way through the doorway of the stable yard and turned left. Tadg followed her. He noted with mild dismay that no one would take her for a boy any longer. Her hair had grown over the last weeks. It was nearly shoulder length and lustrous as well as being far too fine for a boy's. And, again; Trista wasn't striding. Her movements were graceful in a way which could never be masculine. He sighed, inwardly. It really was the least of their troubles, he supposed.

Trista led the way around the outside wall of the house, across well-scythed turf, dotted with rose beds. The perfume from the flowers was sweet on the morning air.

Apart from a few distant gardeners they saw no one.

After a few minutes they rounded a corner. Here was a sheltered cove made up of three outer walls of the house. Wisteria grew on the walls. A pair of white rowans gave shade. Trista pointed across beyond the trees.

"There," she whispered.

Three windows, their shutters open, pierced the single-storey wall of honey-coloured brick. Tadg looked around. No one was in sight. The morning was peaceful and clear yet to his Celtic senses there was an unmistakable air of brooding. Something unpleasant lurked around here. He shivered. Still, there was work to be done.

"Stay here and whistle if you see anybody, alright?"

Trista nodded.

Tadg strode across the grass as if he had every right to be there. Trista watched him stop by the first window, his back to the wall, listening. After a moment he turned and slid along the wall so that he could glimpse the interior. He moved to the second window where he repeated the procedure, then to the third. Finally he came back across the grass.

"In the middle one," he said, "tied to the bed. I'm going in. You move across to the flowerbed by the wall. Pretend you're weeding. Look natural. Whistle if anyone comes then amble off 's if you're just one of the staff. No sense in two of us getting caught."

The two drifted across the grass, looking around them as they went. Trista knelt down, her face towards the gardens. She began pulling up plants indiscriminately. Tadg took one last look around before opening the shutters fully. With his hands on the window sill and one foot on the brickwork he hoisted himself up and disappeared inside.

* * *

Lucius came awake at the creak of the shutters. He lay with his eyes closed, disorientated. What now, he thought? There was the light scuffle of footsteps. He tensed.

"Master!"

The voice was low but not a whisper. Scouts learnt early on

that the sibilants of a whisper carried much further than quiet, ordinary speech. Lucius opened his eyes.

"Tadg! Thanks be to Jupiter. I'd all but given up hope."

"Are you hurt?" asked Tadg, nodding at the bandage around the crook of Lucius's right arm, as he worked at the knots binding his right leg.

A shadow passed over Lucius's face.

"No. Nothing serious," he said. "Just get me free."

He sat up, massaging his wrists as the last rope came loose.

"Right," said Tadg. "Out the window and we'll make it up from there. We've got Vespasian in a copse down by the lake. If you can walk that far we'll get you aboard her and find a way over the wall."

Lucius shook his head. "No, Tadg. You go now. Wait for me at the copse. There's something I have to do before I leave and I can't involve you."

Tadg swore quietly. "Master, they ain't goin' to let you go if they catches you again. You'll only get one chance to get out of here an' that's now. So come along, please."

Lucius stood up, one hand steadying himself upon the wall.

"Tadg, you're your own man. I cannot order you but there's no point in both of us dying. Now go."

'Stiff-necked bloody Roman,' thought Tadg. He sheathed his knife.

"Well, whatever you have to do, I'm coming too."

"So am I."

The two men turned. There was a scrabbling outside and Trista fell through the window in a flurry of limbs.

"Trista?" said Lucius. Tadg groaned.

"Can't you ever do what you're told?" he asked.

Trista stood then ran across the room and flung her arms around Lucius.

"I was so worried about you," she cried.

Trista seemed unaware that Lucius was naked. Lucius was

not. Despite himself, he stroked her hair. He was just about to renew the argument when footsteps sounded from the corridor outside. Tadg drew his knife, gesturing the others to the corner where they would not be seen from the door. He took up position flat against the wall on the opening side of the door. The door opened, hiding the little Celt from Lucius. In a blur of movement, Tiberia fell into view followed by Tadg holding her wrist.

Before she could utter, Tadg's hand was over her mouth, his knife at her throat.

"Gently," he whispered in her ear. "Gently or you die."

Lucius moved to the door. He looked out. The passage was empty. He entered the room, closing the door.

Tiberia's eyes locked with Lucius's, glittering with hate. He crouched down beside her.

"Tadg," he said, "I'm going to ask the Lady some questions. If she should cry out or even talk loudly, don't wait for my order. Cut her throat."

Tadg nodded.

"Now move your hand from her mouth."

Tadg did as he was bidden. Tiberia turned her head with quiet deliberation, despite the knife, and spat. Then she looked back at Lucius.

"There are few things more ridiculous than a naked man," she said.

Involuntarily, Lucius looked down. He felt the initiative slipping away from him. With a conscious effort he ignored her jibe.

"Answer my questions, Tiberia, and you will not be harmed. Fail to do so and you will be killed. Do you understand?"

Tiberia smiled lazily. "At your orders, my lover," she said.

Lucius was conscious of Trista's shocked gaze. Again he exercised his self-control.

"Trista," he said. "Look in the chest over there. See if you can find me some clothes."

"Trista!"

The knife point left a surface cut on her neck as Tiberia jerked her head sideways to look at the girl. Red beads of blood formed along the cut. Tadg, on a hair trigger, looked for an order from Lucius, willing him to tell him to cut. Lucius shook his head.

"You? Here?" hissed Tiberia, apparently unaware of the blood running down her throat. "We hoped you were dead."

Trista stood uncertain. Her fingers played with the girdle at her waist.

"Fetch the clothes, child," said Lucius gently then to Tiberia, "Why is she important to you?"

Tiberia returned her gaze to Lucius, her eyes hooded.

"That," she said calmly, "I will not tell you and you may kill me."

Lucius considered.

"Then tell me this: has Heliodoros left for Borbetomagus yet?"

"Yes," said Tiberia. "He left on a fleet horse. You cannot hope to catch him. He will use your identity to change mounts at the posting stables. He will arrive at Borbetomagus in two days, three, no more."

"To whom is the temple dedicated?"

"Why, the Dark Apollo, but..."

Her eyes darkened. "You fool. You wouldn't."

Tadg tightened his grip as she struggled, his hand once again over her mouth. Blood stained the neck of her tunic. After a few moments she lay still again.

"Here, Lucius."

Trista, blushing now at his nakedness, handed him a bundle of clothes. He began to dress. "Find something to use as a gag," he ordered as he pulled a tunic over his head.

It took the combined efforts of all three of them to gag the Lady Tiberia and secure her on the bed: not that she struggled but rather refused to co-operate, hanging like a deadweight.

Finally it was done. Lucius turned to the others.

"What I must do now is dangerous; more dangerous than I can easily explain. Please will you both now leave by the window and wait for me with the mule?"

Tadg was willing to go but Trista asked, "Can't you tell us what you're going to do? I'm sure we could help."

Lucius crouched down before her.

"Trista, there is an evil temple in this place. Within it is a doll, made in the likeness of the Emperor. Sertorius and the others of his chapter will use the doll to harm Hadrian. The doll must be removed and taken safely to the Emperor. Only there can it be neutralized. I am going to take it. I know how to do this but you don't. If you came with me you would be in more than mortal danger. It is best if I go on my own."

The Lady Tiberia writhed against her bonds, shaking her head furiously and making grunts. Tadg stirred uneasily. As a Celt he had a deep respect for things of the spirit. This was what he had felt approaching the house. There was evil here. Trista had turned pale yet her face expressed determination.

"I don't know much of what you are speaking but tell me honestly: will you be in more than mortal danger before you enter the temple?"

Lucius thought for a moment. Tiberia had fallen silent.

"Honestly?" he said. "No: no more danger than we are in now."

"Then I will come with you and keep watch," said Trista quietly.

"Aye," Tadg found himself saying. "And I suppose I will too."

Trista added, "I think I know where the temple is too."

Lucius sighed, slapped his knees and stood up.

"Well, there's no time to spare for arguing, I suppose. Come."

He opened the door and looked out. All was quiet but for muffled grunts from Tiberia. Lucius beckoned. Trista pointed to the left. In single file the three set out along the corridor. At the end of it they came into an empty courtyard where a fig tree leaned over a pond. Trista pointed to the right.

After several more twists and turns they came to a corridor which ended in tall, black doors. Tadg was sweating freely. He felt as if he had the start of a fever. His hands were shaking.

"Master," he gasped, "I don't think I can go any nearer. I'll stay here and guard."

Lucius nodded.

"Trista, stay here with Tadg. I must make preparations. Whatever happens once I have entered the doors, no matter what you hear, you must not follow me. Count to a hundred slowly and if I have not returned by then, go."

Tadg wiped his lower lip with the back of his hand and nodded. Trista said nothing. Taking this for assent, Lucius moved towards the doors. When he was five paces in front of them he stopped and became quite still. Trista watched from the corner of her eye. Lucius remained still for some minutes. Then his arms moved in a series of gestures. She was reminded of the old priest of Jupiter at her home. He made a series of gestures like this when he was invoking the god. She wondered what god Lucius was invoking. She hoped it was a strong one.

Now Lucius was looking upwards, his arms open as if in supplication. His jaw was moving as if he was addressing some unseen presence. Finally he made a complicated sign in front of him, squared his shoulders and moved towards the doors. Trista watched as he grasped one of the handles. He opened the door and slipped inside. Trista started to count.

* * *

Lucius stands inside the doors, breathing slowly to calm his heartbeat. One part of his mind accepts that the Undying Sun surrounds him with protection. Another more earthly part is terrified. It is dark yet, as his eyes adapt to the gloom, he sees that oil lamps burn with a sickly blue flame on either side of the threshold. The stench is less than it had been the night before but it is still noxious.

He probes the shadows with his senses. There is an overwhelming sense of baleful watchfulness. Chitinous wings seem to rub slyly in the shadows. His palms are slippery with sweat. With an effort of will he begins the ritual of *Lux Repurgo*. Taking up one of the oil lamps he moves forward. In the feeble light of the lamp he can make out the black altar and before it a brazier full of glowing charcoal. It seems an enormous distance ahead of him. Still he walks towards it, every step a great effort.

"Veni Mithra. Ave Mithra..."

It becomes icy cold but still he moves forward, slowly, slowly. He holds the lamp aloft. Yes; there on the altar lolls the doll, its face turned towards him grinning. Onward now, apparently forcing his way through invisible cobwebs, their filthy, gritty strands caressing his face.

"Lux invictus, Lux æternus..."

Sounds – the prolonged hollow scraping of the closing tomb; now a crepitant slithering from somewhere close behind him. He forces himself not to look back. The walls of the temple have receded into darkness. He toils across an endless floor towards a diminishing altar. Fear croons.

"Puer laurifer..."

From the dark there materializes first one and then more succubi, rotting horrors of faces on voluptuous bodies. They float close whispering invitations of profound depravity. His manhood comes erect. Thoughts of coupling fill his mind. He stumbles then forces himself onwards, fumbling for the words that will protect him.

"Mithra...Mithra..."

A succubus attaches itself to him, moulding its body to his. He feels its breasts crushed against him, its leg forcing its way between his. His body suffuses with tumescence, overwhelming all other sensations. The maggot-filled pit of its mouth seeks his lips. With a supreme effort he forces it away. The demon falls to the floor, shrieking and dissolves into a writhing mass of serpents which hiss at him before gliding off into the gloom.

"*Mithra...Lux...*"

Suddenly a peal of deep, suggestive laughter rolls around the darkness, booming and fading then returning. He comes to a halt, his heart labouring, his breath ragged. His head feels enormously heavy but, with an effort, he drags his gaze up from the floor. There ahead of him beside the altar stands an enormous slug-like figure bearing the mask of a goat. The great body oozes slime which pools on the floor, steaming and bubbling. Its smell, compounded of death and corruption, wafts over Lucius. He vomits then stands swaying, shivering, wet with cold sweat, staring at the abomination before him.

"Mithra..." The voice of the Beast drips with distain. It echoes in the void. "Pitiful child god of the Persian barbarian. Do you seek protection there, hopeless fool?"

Laughter detonates like thunder.

"For he cannot save you. He cannot even hear you for you stand in the House of the Dark One; *Apollo Acerbus*, Lord of Despair. Kneel now, forsaken by-blow. Kneel and worship the Darkness before you die."

It seems that a great weight presses upon Lucius's shoulders. He fights against it but his knees buckle. He is forced to the floor. He feels weak and ill. Deep loneliness floods his being. Despair envelopes him. He had sought to challenge the Dark Power but he has been unbelievably foolish. It is so much stronger than him: stronger than the Light. It will triumph. Unseen the oil lamp falls from his nerveless finger and rolls into the shadows.

He makes one last effort to speak the name of his god but his tongue cleaves to the roof of his mouth. He becomes dumb.

"And now come to me," orders the great voice. "Come to sacrifice for though outside this temple it lacks an hour or two before the null of the moon, here time has no meaning. Here your death is timeless."

The goat-masked monstrosity holds forth a finger. It gestures upwards. Lucius feels himself stand without volition. His jaw hangs slack. He watches in horror as first one foot, then the other moves forward, betraying him; carrying him towards the altar.

* * *

Trista has been restive. She crouches beside Tadg at the corner of the corridor. She has been counting slowly and steadily – *seventy-nine, eighty, eighty-one*. She looks behind her at the black doors. Surely he ought to be out by now. She has heard nothing since he went in and the door swung shut; just his receding footsteps, then silence.

"Tadg," she whispers. There is no answer. Tadg is staring straight ahead, his face beaded with sweat.

"Tadg." She pulls at his sleeve.

"Let be," murmurs the Celt, jerking his sleeve free, still staring straight ahead. There will be no help from him.

Trista fears for Lucius. She sees with the eyes of a child. Lucius is blind to his own weaknesses. That makes him vulnerable. She realizes she has stopped counting. How far had she got? She guesses. *Eighty-three, eighty-four...*

Her head jerks round. What was that? It seemed she heard a faint thump and a tinkle from inside the temple. *Eighty-five, eighty-six...*He said not to go in whatever they heard but she never promised. *Eighty-seven, eighty-eight...*Without realizing it she is counting faster.

A crash! That was definitely a crash although muffled as if by distance. What should she do? She looks again at Tadg but his eyes are glazed. He is shaking like a man with the ague. Rivulets of sweat are running down his face.

Ninety-two, ninety-three, ninety-four...

He's not going to come out; she knows it deep within. She creeps away from Tadg down the corridor towards the doors. It doesn't smell very nice. The doors are very intimidating like there might be something nasty behind them. She is reminded of the pig sty at home. When she was little she used to be so afraid of Llywd the great boar who lurked behind its walls.

Ninety-seven, ninety-eight, ninety-nine...

She takes a deep breath...*a hundred.*

She glances back at Tadg. Poor Tadg: he is, after all, only a peasant full of superstitions, not a patrician like her. She accepts that, in the end, responsibility will fall on her shoulders. It is the way of the world. Blithely ignoring Lucius's instructions, she grasps one of the door handle and opens the door very quietly.

Oh, what an awful smell? Llywd was never this bad. She peers within. It's quite a big room. There are black curtains all the way around the walls. She can see this in a dancing light. It comes from somewhere over to the right where a patch of black carpet is burning. She wonders why.

Then her attention is drawn to the far end of the room. It's Lucius! He is lying on a big, black table. At its head stands an immensely fat man who holds a curved dagger in his hands. He has the dagger raised above Lucius and he is muttering to himself.

"No!" she shouts although she is not aware of doing so. Not my Lucius she thinks. You're not going to hurt my Lucius. She looks around for a weapon but sees nothing. When she looks back at the altar the fat man is looking at her.

"You!" he shouts, pointing a great, fat finger at her. "You brat. You Spawn of Hades."

He starts towards her. Frantically she looks around again for a weapon. All she finds is an oil lamp on a table by the door. She snatches it up as the man bears down on her and throws it at his face. Then, without stopping or thinking she runs to where Lucius is sitting up, staring about him, as though he had been in a trance. She grabs his arm and turns, ready to fight the man in the mask to the death.

What she sees is the man trying to tear off the mask. It is burning and so is the top of his robe. As he wrestles with the mask he roars curses and threats.

"Come *on*, Lucius," she says, tugging at his arm.

Lucius swings his legs over the edge of the altar, shaking his head.

"Trista," he begins, "I *told* you..."

"Oh shut up, do," she cries, pulling him off the altar, onto his feet. He turns and gathers the doll in his arms, then follows her towards the door. Trista stops opposite the burning figure. He has managed to pull the mask half off and is beating at the burning robes with blistered hands. Trista's nostrils flare with hate.

"You murdered my parents," she says. "You burned my house," she shouts. Then with an access of strength beyond her years she places both hands on the enormous stomach and pushes. She pushes Sertorius backwards into the charcoal brazier. He trips and fall, taking the brazier with him. He screams and rolls from side to side among the burning coals. His oil-soaked robes burst into flame. He screams and flails at the flames.

"I hate you," she screams.

A hand grasps her arm and pulls her away.

"Come on, Trista. That's enough."

Lucius drags her from the room and closes the door on the screams within.

* * *

Cadmus paced to and fro in the clearing, gnawing at his thumb. Where were they? What would he do if they didn't return? He had been a slave for so long that he couldn't easily answer this question. He must return to his master. If he didn't then everyone's hand would be against him. But if his master was dead...he would be without protection of any kind.

Galloping hooves: they were coming towards him through the trees. Galba lifted her head and gave her croaking neigh. Damn, thought Cadmus as he hurled himself into the undergrowth. The mule had given him away. He peered between stems of plants, trying to stay still despite the thorns which had punctured his skin. Then he saw Vespasian, minus her bridle and panniers, cantering into the clearing. She trotted up to Galba. They stood nose to nose while they snuffled at each other.

He stood. What did this mean? He went over to Vespasian and ran a hand down her withers. She looked well enough but where was her harness. More to the point, where were the others. The two horses leaned forward and sniffed at Vespasian. She snapped at them but without malice.

"Cadmus."

He whipped round, his hand going to his knife. It was Tadg. Across his shoulders and in his hands were Vespasian's gear.

"What's happened? Where are they?"

"They're coming," said Tadg. He was barely breathing heavily although he had evidently been running. "I come ahead to see that the horses were ready. We're going to have to light out of here quick."

The horses were already tacked up. Now Cadmus put bridle and panniers on Vespasian.

In answer to his questions he said, "It was 'orrible – Dark Stuff; don't want to say no more. They had the master. We got him out once then Trista, bless her, had to get him out again. That's a plucky 'un, I don't mind telling you. Set the place afire. I was scared shitless. Well, we got out, came up towards the gate fast as we could then I whispered in Vespasian's ear, told 'er to get home fast an' let her go. She shot through the gate while we were getting over the wall. Worked perfect."

Just then Lucius and Trista came crashing through the undergrowth. Both were blown. Cadmus noticed that Lucius carried a cloth-covered bundle in his arms which he placed on the ground. He also noticed that Tadg kept a wary distance from it. Lucius bent, heaving for breath, as did Trista.

When he could finally speak he said, "We must leave, fast. Tadg: find us the best way so that they won't find us."

The small Celt looked away through the trees, his nostrils twitching. He was not happy with his performance in the big house. He sought redemption.

"Ford the stream here in the woods." He pointed. "Head west 'til you're out of sight of the gatehouse then strike north into the hills. I'll come with you to the stream then I'll backtrack: wipe out your trail then lay a false one. Once you start north, keep moving. I'll find you."

They mounted; Lucius on one horse with Trista in front of him, Cadmus on the other holding Galba's lead rein and Tadg, leading Vespasian. Tadg led them in single file through the trees until they came to the stream. There he stood with Vespasian, one hand held aloft in farewell as the others crossed. Trista looked back once but the small tracker was already lost in the shadows.

Chapter 32

(Borbetomagus)

When afterwards Tadg looked back on the road from Cruorsilva to Borbetomagus, he remembered it as one of the most frustrating journeys he had even made. First of all, against all odds, he missed the trail left by the others and failed to catch up with them for four days.

Having laid a false trail to the east, he had led Vespasian back westwards along the road in clear view of the world. The area around Cruorsilva was like an ants' nest, stirred with a stick: patrols heading out in all directions. He was stopped at the bridge over the stream below the gatehouse and questioned. However, by pretending to be slow-witted, he was assessed as harmless and allowed on his way again in a few minutes.

How he came to miss the trail left by the others, he was unable to say. They had been at pains not to leave any obvious mark of their passing but even so, an experienced tracker like Tadg, alerted to the approximate course of their trail, should not have missed it. He would have been ashamed had he not felt that other forces were at work.

By the time he found them again, they had been forced well to the westward by patrols, Cadmus's horse had become badly lame and the wound in Lucius's right arm was infected and poisoned. Lucius had become so ill that they were laid up in a hollow in the hills when he found them. Cadmus had done what he could for Lucius but neither he nor Trista had any real medical knowledge.

Tadg examined the arm as Lucius tossed in delirious sleep. It was locked solid by the swelling at the joint. The skin was hot to the touch and flushed crimson. Red lines ran away up and down the arm while evil-smelling pus oozed from the unhealed wound.

Tadg hissed through his teeth as he examined it: a dirty blade if not actually poisoned he thought. Lucius cried out as the Celt ran his fingers around the swelling. Putting the arm gently down he stood and beckoned the others to the far side of the fire.

"I'm going to use a hot knife on him and then drain it down." Cadmus winced.

"Yes," said Tadg, "it'll not be pretty but the wound's gone bad and next thing you know he'll lose his arm if not his life. So, Trista, start boiling water and look out some clean rags for afterwards. Cadmus, dig out one of those cheap daggers from stock. I'll not use my own for this. It'll ruin the temper. Cut me a wedge from the spare sheet of leather too. That'll be for his mouth. Then you'll have to hold him down while I work."

The next half hour was distressing for all of them. Trista couldn't bear to watch as Tadg went to work. She concentrated on making the fire as hot as possible and boiled water in every container she could find. Cadmus was white as a sheet as he struggled to keep a hold on Lucius's twisting body. When the smell of burning flesh came, it was all he could do to keep from vomiting.

Eventually the deed was done. Tadg threw a bundle of pus-soaked rags onto the fire before taking a deep draught of wine. Lucius mumbled and tossed fitfully while Trista soothed his brow with a wet cloth. Cadmus finished smoothing balm on the wound and knotted a loose bandage over it.

"What about the horse?" asked Tadg.

"Well," said Cadmus, "the rest'll have done her good but I'm doubting she'll be up for riding for a while yet."

Tadg grunted. "Way this journey's going I doubt we'll be moving for a couple of days anyway." He jerked his head at Lucius. "He'll not be fit to move yet a while."

The two men exchanged a meaningful glance. Cadmus lowered his voice.

"Seems like there's a curse on us," he murmured. "Seems like ever since we came to Cruorsilva it's all gone wrong."

Tadg nodded.

Cadmus licked his lips. "What's he got in that bundle; the one in his saddle bag?"

Tadg took another swig of wine. He squinted at the sun before answering.

"That bundle?" he said. "That there's a mannequin of the Emperor, done by them Dark Ones in the big house."

Cadmus made the sign against evil. The whites of his eyes showed.

"That'll be it, then. That'll be why all this bad luck's following us." His voice fell to a whisper. "We should burn it."

"No!" Trista sprang up and came towards them.

"Lucius risked his life to rescue that doll," she said. She turned to Tadg. "You were there. You heard what he said. It must be taken safely to the Emperor. Only the Emperor can dispose of it without causing his own death."

She paused, hands on hips, looking from one to another, scorn written large. "I'm ashamed of you both. You're talking superstitious nonsense. If either of you lays one finger on that doll, you'll have me to answer to, do you understand?"

Such was her moral force that both men nodded automatically. Trista was a Roman aristocrat. Age didn't come into it. As a slave, Cadmus was conditioned to obey her. Tadg, though a free Celt, was imbued with the ethos of the Woman Leader. It would go very much against the grain to gainsay her, young though she was.

"Right," she said. "Let's hear no more of it. We'll settle in and make the best of things until Lucius is fit to travel. Cadmus, tidy this place up. Make us a camp fit to live in for a few days and gather fodder for the animals. Tadg, as soon as you're rested, I want fresh meat and herbs. Lucius is going to need to eat well."

* * *

They stayed there for a further four days as Lucius slowly returned to health. By then the swelling had gone. A solid diet of fresh stews and choice vegetables had brought colour back to his face. Nevertheless he fretted. Heliodoros now had a week's lead on them. Lucius was aware of the mischief the Greek could wreak in that time.

The night before they planned to set off again there was a sudden, intense thunderstorm with torrential rain. The campsite was swamped by a flash flood. In the ensuing confusion, the animals broke free and ran into the night. The humans clawed their way to the shelter of a small copse, there to wait the coming of a miserable dawn. First light showed a scene of desolation, their belongings spread over half a mile between pools of standing water. Prominent among the wreckage lay the lame horse, whinnying piteously. Somehow it had broken a leg. Tadg dispatched it with his knife.

It was near noon before they had recovered all that they could and found the remaining animals. The day was overcast, a small, northerly wind driving drizzle. With Lucius on the remaining horse and the others on foot, they set their faces to the wind and made for Mannheim. Lucius reckoned it was forty miles away, perhaps three days at the speed they could expect to travel. Their way lay through high, wooded hills. Tracks were few and, more than once, they found themselves retracing their steps from dead ends.

A black bear entered the camp on the first night, scenting the newly slaughtered carcase of a deer which Tadg had hung from a tree. Unable to reach the meat, the bear had blundered around the campsite until it stepped in the embers of the fire and went howling into the night. Although it did little damage, the horse and mules broke free once more, running into the dense trees. In the morning it took two hours to find them and continue on the journey.

Finally, on the third day, they came down out of the hills onto the flood plain of the Rhenus. Below them stretched cultivated land dotted with farms and villages. In the middle distance rose smoke which could only be Mannheim. The rain which had dogged them for three days finally cleared and, as they found their first firm track, their spirits started to rise. By late afternoon they were travelling through the outlying slums of the city, approaching the western gate.

"The rest house?" said the gate guard. "You goes down to the centre then right an' out the south gate. You'll find it there by the bathhouse. Big place. Red roof. Can't miss it."

The rest house was not too busy and Lucius was able to take rooms for himself and Trista as well as space in the stables for the others and the animals.

"Are there any messages for Aurelio of Tarraconensis?" he asked the host. The man allowed as there might be and went off to consult his wife. The latter bustled up to the bar and told Lucius that a pleasant, cultured person by the name of Marcellus had been in just that morning as he had for over a week, asking for news of one Aurelio. She gave directions to the inn outside the north gate where he was staying. (It wasn't an approved one. Lucius could tell by her expression). Tadg undertook to find it while the others bathed. Tadg didn't hold with bathing.

Wallowing in the warm water, Lucius felt as near happy as he had in a month. Then he sat up in alarm. He called to one of the bath slaves, "What is the date?"

"Maius, Tenth day before Calends," came the reply.

Lucius slumped back into the water: ten days before the deadline for his arrival in Borbetomagus. With only twelve miles left to travel, he could afford to relax.

When, washed scraped and shaved, he emerged from the bathhouse, wrapped in a towel, Marcellus was there to greet him with an armful of clean clothes. The man's pleasure at seeing him again warmed Lucius's heart. For the first minute there was a confused flurry of half-finished sentences as each sought to learn what the other had been doing whilst responding to the last question. In the end, having ascertained that the inn in which Marcellus and Adolphus stayed was not too particular about slaves eating with freemen, Lucius sent Marcellus on ahead to order a meal with wine.

Trista's small face appeared round the partition dividing the men's and women's changing rooms, her hair tied on top of her face.

"Lucius," she asked, "must I dress as a boy," she screwed up her nose, "or a girl." She dimpled winsomely, putting her head on one side.

Lucius pretended to think for a moment. "Well...I suppose...oh, alright. Be a girl again. You weren't a very convincing boy anyway." Trista let out a whoop and disappeared.

Lucius dressed and went to wait for her in the common room. Some time later he looked up. In the half-light he saw a slender woman making her graceful way across the room towards him. It was only as she neared him that he realized this was Trista. When had she become so tall and...and feminine?

Her hair fell in auburn waves almost to her shoulders, held up in some way at the back. Her plain chiton, secured at the shoulders by enamelled broaches, displayed curves he had never before noticed. Lucius found himself gaping. He stood, not knowing quite what to say. She smiled at him.

"Well," she said, "will I do?

* * *

The meal at the other inn was a joyous affair. Marcellus recounted the journey they had made, Adolphus grinning and nodding beside him. They had met no inquisitive patrols on the way but had played the part of travelling traders, gaining confidence as they went. Lucius was amused to see how much stature Marcellus had gained.

"At Kaiserslautern there was a big May Fair. We stayed and traded for two days." He looked anxiously at Lucius. "I hope that was acceptable, Master."

Lucius nodded and smiled. "You did well, Marcellus. As it turned out you could have spent a week there and still have been here before us."

Marcellus looked relieved. "Anyway, there were many Germans in the crowds. It helped a lot that Adolphus was able to speak to them. We benefited greatly and I took the liberty of buying a large number of good quality furs with some of the takings." Again, a hint of worry touched his features. "I think you will find that we have made a healthy profit."

"I'm sure I will," said Lucius. He paused. "But now, my friends, we must take counsel." He looked around the circle of expectant faces – Tadg sharp as a native sheepdog, Marcellus and Cadmus, serious, anxious; Adolphus with a puzzled frown and Trista, her chin cupped in one small hand, looking on with a small smile. "It seems that you all now understand what my mission is. Indeed, as it turns out it is probably the worst-guarded secret in history."

There were smiles around the circle.

Lucius went on. "I have told you how things now lie. My identity has been stolen and our enemies will, by now, almost certainly, have fed false intelligence about German intentions to legionary headquarters at Borbetomagus. If I go there, it is likely that I will be taken for an impostor and quite possibly imprisoned. In any case I can give them no firm intelligence to refute what Heliodoros has told them. It seems to me that my best course is to cross the Rhenus into Germania Superior and try to find out what the German tribes intend. Thus armed I can return to Borbetomagus with something to tell the authorities."

He paused, looking around the circle. "Since whatever decision I make will affect you all, I would welcome your observations."

There was silence for some seconds.

"Do we have any idea when the Germans are going to attack?" asked Tadg.

Lucius shook his head. "None," he said. "I have no idea how much time we have except that I am supposed to report to Borbetomagus within the next ten days. It is possible that, having made himself known to the authorities, Heliodoros will cross the Rhenus, returning just before the attack in order to sow maximum confusion."

Trista piped up. "Could I go to Uncle Tuccius and explain what has happened," she asked.

Lucius rubbed his chin.

"When did you last see him?"

Trista looked doubtful. "I'm not really sure. I was very little. I remember him tossing me up in the air..." She trailed off.

"Trista," said Lucius, "it is a good idea but why should your uncle believe that it is you. Even more, why should he believe that I am who I say I am and not an opportunistic fake?"

Trista looked crestfallen. "I don't know," she whispered.

Tadg, who was sitting beside her, placed his hand on her shoulder in consolation.

There was another short period of silence.

"Could we find and stop this Greek?" asked Marcellus.

Lucius pursed his lips. "That would only be possible if we waited for him around Borbetomagus. I have been across the river and it is a deep, dark country, covered with forest. There are small communities nestling in clearings. It would be sheer luck if we ran into Heliodoros over there. If we were to hang around Legion headquarters waiting for him we would, at best, learn no intelligence about the Germans."

He paused again in thought. "No," he said, "the more I think about it, the more I believe that we have to find out what the Germans are doing. We must cross the Rhenus and, I think, make our way northwards on the far bank, gleaning what intelligence we can."

There was silence again, everyone absorbed in his or her thoughts.

"We could visit my Mum."

All eyes turned to Adolphus. The big man, realizing he was the centre of attention, turned bright red and hung his head.

Lucius recovered first. "Your Mum ? Does your Mum live over the river, Adolphus?"

The big man looked up and nodded, evidently confused. He said nothing.

Lucius tried once more. "Where does your Mum live, Adolphus?"

Again there was confused silence.

"By your leave," said Marcellus, looking at Adolphus, then at Lucius, jerking his head towards the door. Lucius nodded. Marcellus took Adolphus by the arm and led him outside. The others waited expectantly.

A few minutes later the two returned and sat down.

"It seems that Adolphus's home village is across the river and one day's journey north of here," said Marcellus. "He says it's called Bensheim. As I understand it, it is a peaceful place, not really part of the confederation of warlike tribes. They live deeper in the forests." Marcellus smiled. "Adolphus says his Mum cooks the best boar's tripes in Germania Superior and he wouldn't half like to eat a plateful."

There was a general easing of tension around the table.

"Well," said Lucius, "it seems we have a plan. Tomorrow we cross the Rhenus and sample the delights of Bensheim."

He raised his goblet. "To Adolphus's Mum's boar's tripes."

* * *

Lucius stood with the others watching with amused disbelief. Sunlight fell between massive trees into a clearing in the forest.

A few dozen huts stood amongst a patchwork of cultivated plots. In front of the nearest hut a tiny woman with a bent back was berating Adolphus. Whatever she was saying, it was finding its mark. The big man looked a picture of anxious misery. He stood, downcast, wringing his old felt hat in his hands. Other Germans, some leaning on their hoes, had gathered round to enjoy the spectacle.

With a final pronouncement from the woman, which sounded like a curse, Adolphus bent down. The woman straightened as far as she could and planted a kiss on his cheek. Then, without looking at them, she beckoned the others forward with an imperious gesture, setting off across the clearing. As they approached Adolphus he looked up sheepishly.

"My Mum ," he explained.

The crossing of the Rhenus had been easy enough. Whatever the state of relations between Rome and the German nation across the river, trade went on. Thus they had boarded the big, flat-bottomed ferry that crossed from Mannheim and started their journey north. Now, a day and a night later, they had found Bensheim in its clearing close to the east bank of the great river. Lucius fretted that he still didn't have a plan. By default they would go on trading for the moment and see what turned up.

Now Adolphus's mother was indicating an area of beaten earth, evidently the meeting place of the small community. A large man with a bushy, white beard joined them. In broken Latin he introduced himself as the Dorfmeister and bade them welcome. Lucius thanked him, explained that they would be ready for trading in one hour and asked him if he could keep the people clear until that time.

In truth their stall, designed for trading in provincial towns, was altogether too luxurious for the little place. However, in rapid discussion with the others, Lucius scaled it down and halved the prices. He determined to do Adolphus honour in his home village. To the Dorfmeister he gave two amphorae of fine wine; to Adolphus's Mum, a piece of amber containing an insect, the whole mounted on a silver chain. He too received a kiss.

Then, seeing that the populace were abandoning their fields despite the efforts of the Dorfmeister, he donned his trader's outfit – long, green velvet tunic trimmed with fur and a tall hat marked with signs and sigils – and began the Words. The people gathered round. It mattered not that he spoke in Latin. Enough of them knew sufficient to translate for the others but, rather more, it was the wonders he displayed that held them spellbound.

To Trista fell the task of selecting ever more exotic items and relaying them to Lucius while the others laboured to set up the stall behind the cart. She used her imagination, seeking what might be of interest to their clientele. Thus he exhibited in turn a hunting bow, a glass jug shaped like a fish, a clay likeness of the Goddess and a set of wooden farm animals. A small tapestry of a wild boar embroidered on a black background drew gasps of admiration. Trista had just arrived at his elbow with a small donkey stuffed with straw when Marcellus arrived, breathless, with the news that they were ready.

Lucius held up his hand for silence. He looked slowly from left to right, catching the eye of each individual then proclaimed, "The market is open."

There was a carnival atmosphere about the following hours. Adolphus, grinning hugely, nodded and bowed to all and sundry. Men came and clapped him on the shoulder. To his embarrassment, an increasing number of young women, giggling, dared each other to kiss him. Trade was as brisk as anything they had experienced. Once the pricing was known, word went out and an increasing number of people emerged from the trees, some herding animals, others carrying axes.

Towards the middle of the afternoon, Lucius noted a group of large, muscular men joining the crowd. Although they weren't armed their studded leather jerkins and arm torques marked them out as warriors. With only one German-speaker and that Adolphus, Lucius was limited to watching. It wouldn't do to suggest to the big man that he speak with the warriors. Lucius had no illusions about Adolphus's ability to dissemble. Instead he nudged Tadg.

"Can you follow them without being seen?" he asked.

"'course I can," came the reply.

"Do it then. Tell me where they go."

Tadg nodded. Half an hour later, Lucius realized that he had gone.

Late in the afternoon trade had begun to slacken when six warriors, each carrying a war spear entered the clearing. Evidently they had not come to trade. They made purposefully for the stall, brushing aside villagers who failed to get out of their way. The leader, a big man with a long, blonde moustache, stopped in front of Lucius. The trader took in the man's bulging muscles and arrogant stance. He imagined meeting an army of such men at the shield wall.

"You – komm."

The warrior's sweeping gesture took in the stall then jerked over his shoulder to the north. Lucius scented danger. He decided to prevaricate.

"I'm sorry; I don't unders—"

"You – komm!" The gesture was repeated. The voice rose in pitch and volume.

Just then the Dorfmeister came hurrying over. He bowed obsequiously to the warrior before addressing some words to him in German. The leader fixed the old man with a sardonic eye and spat out a reply. The Dorfmeister turned to Lucius.

"You are required at the Waldfest," he said. Then, in a lower voice, "It is useless to resist. You must go."

Lucius glanced from the warriors to the Dorfmeister.

"What is the Waldfest, old man?" he asked.

"It is a great gathering in the forest; a celebration for the gods.

It seems the Festmeister has heard of your coming and requires that you go and trade at the Fest."

"Will we be safe?" asked Lucius.

The old man shrugged his shoulders.

"What is safe?" he asked. "This is Waldfest."

The leader of the warriors was becoming restless. He grasped the Dorfmeister's shoulder and bellowed at him while the old man cringed. When he had finished, the Dorfmeister turned to Lucius and whispered.

"He says if you do not go now they will spear you all and take the stall. You must go – go now."

The villagers had drawn back from the stall, watching proceedings anxiously. The team stood, waiting Lucius's word, each of them holding an item of stock, ready to start packing.

"Pack," he ordered.

Articles were thrust into boxes and on to the wagon. Cadmus fetched the mules, harnessing them in a flurry of leather. The well-rehearsed routine was completed in less than half an hour. Wagon and mules stood loaded and ready. The warriors took station, two ahead of the traders and four behind.

"Komm," shouted the leader, gesturing forward.

The villagers stood silent. Just as the group was about to enter the forest a small figure thrust its way through the crowd. Ignoring the warriors, Adolphus's mother hobbled to where her son led his string of mules. She placed a bundle in his free hand. Dutifully, the big man bent down and the woman kissed his cheek. Then she stood watching him walk away from her, tears streaming down her cheek until one of the warriors pushed her out of his way. She fell to her knees.

Dolefully, Adolphus looked at Lucius, holding up the bundle.

"Mum's boar tripes," he said.

* * *

They walked for over an hour. The sun was now well to the west. Beneath the trees shadows lengthened. Lucius thought about their position. If they were required to trade then they should be safe. The status of a trader was not unlike that of a herald or emissary. To a degree they stood aloof from factions and warring parties. Which was all well and good if one ignored the various heralds and emissaries who had been sent back to their masters in pieces.

Lucius had had dealings with the Germans during his military service. They could be courteous, even welcoming, but not far beneath the apparently civilized exterior there lurked a deep well of savagery, one which could burst forth without warning. It might be that they would trade. Equally, the stall might be pillaged and all of them killed.

He sighed. Time would tell. For the moment there was nothing to be done and they had a hidden resource. Tadg was still out there in the forest. Tadg would be watching and assessing. If worst came to worst he could be counted on to cross the river and tell the army whatever he had been able to glean.

Light was fading fast as they came to a tree trunk blocking the road. The leader of the escort shouted a command and a dozen big men emerged from the trees. Half of them laid down their spears, grasped the tree and moved it aside. The wagon and mules passed through. Lucius noted that neither the escort nor the picket spoke. He filed this away. It argued an advanced degree of discipline.

As darkness fell, firelight leapt some distance off to the right of the track. Lucius heard the deep, bell-like baying of dogs. More firelight twinkled off to the left and then as they moved on and night fell, the forest became alive with firelight, a hundred points of fire glimmering through the trees. There was more noise too: the whinny of a horse; deep male voices raised in song. Lucius felt the forest closing in on him. The gods, he thought, were very close.

Suddenly they came out of the trees into a wide clearing lit by bonfires. The contrast between the dark of the forest and the flickering shadows of the clearing was marked. Among the fires Lucius could make out figures engaged in various activities. There was a wrestling match and here a spear contest. There were several cooking pits and the clearing was full of the smell of roasting boar meat.

"Gehalten!"

The leader of the escort strode past Lucius, holding up his hand.

"Cadmus, stop," called Lucius. The slave hauled on the reins and the wagon came to a halt.

The German pointed at Lucius. "Kommen sie! Schnell!"

The tone of voice was clear. The warrior turned and strode across the clearing, Lucius, leaning on his stick, following as best he could. Within the circle of fires he could make out a kind of open-sided pavilion made of logs. Heavily armed warriors stood at the entrance. The escort leader stopped, waiting for Lucius to catch up. He pointed to the pavilion.

"Festmeister," he said. There were more words, delivered in emphatic German. Lucius wondered what he was failing to understand. Then the man gestured him forward and together they entered. Lamps lit the interior. Furs and skins hung from the walls and covered the floor. In the middle, upon a massive throne of tree boughs, sat a gnome-like old man clad in furs. On his head rested a crown of oak leaves. He leant forward, his hands resting on a cudgel of dark wood.

Lucius's escort grounded his spear with a crash and barked out a salute. The old man nodded at him then turned his saturnine gaze upon the trader. For several seconds he looked Lucius up and down then snapped his fingers. A slight figure limped forward and stood by the throne. Without taking his eyes off Lucius, the Festmeister spoke. When he had finished the other man translated.

"The Festmeister bids you welcome. You are to enjoy our hospitality. German peoples are known for their hospitalities. You will trade. You will enjoy yourself. This is the Waldfest. You say Forest Feast. German peoples make merry. You do good, you leave unharmed. You do bad, you die."

He paused. The Festmeister spoke again.

"Festmeister now do you great honours. You step forward."

Lucius stepped forward. The gnome man turned and took something from one of his attendants. He gestured for Lucius to bow his head. Not without apprehension, the trader did as he was bidden. A ribbon was passed over his head. Looking down Lucius saw that it was red and yellow. From it hung a wooden medallion. He looked up to see the Festmeister's dark eyes glittering on his. The old man spoke again.

"Festmeister say der Unmenschen don't eat your soul now when you are lost in forest."

The Festmeister started to laugh, a strange creaking sound. He slapped his thighs with glee. His attendants joined in. Evidently the joke was a good one. As the laughter died down, the old man spoke again briefly.

"Now you go trade good," said the translator.

Lucius bowed. He turned and, together with his escort, left the pavilion.

He found his team huddled around the wagon, surrounded by German warriors. Well, thought Lucius, this will either be a triumph or a total disaster.

"Marcellus," he said, "the black and silver outfit if you please. Trista, weapons and wine. I don't want to see the straw-filled donkey again. The rest of you, set up the stall."

* * *

It was a strange experience at first. Lucius found himself speaking to a largely silent audience who appeared not to understand him. However, after ten minutes he noticed whispered asides here and there and assumed that translation was taking place. Cleverly, Trista started with small items – knives and pieces of horse harness – then worked her way up through spearheads to swords. When he exhibited the great two-handed cutting sword forged in Baetica, a collective sigh went round the crowd.

A big, young warrior stepped forward and held his hand out. Lucius placed the pommel in the man's hand. The warrior hefted the blade then swung it, narrowly missing Trista. This brought forth laughter and comment. The spell of silence was broken as the blade was handed round.

Trista, looking aggrieved, whispered, "Do you want jewellery now?"

"Yes, let's have some torques and brooches," said Lucius.

He was still unsure of the mood of the crowd. They were big men of haughty mien, their eyes unreadable. He decided that nothing would be lost by testing them so, while he waited for Trista's return he walked into the crowd, his hand held out for the sword. The warrior who held it, testing the edge, looked up. For a moment dual emotions played on his brow. Lucius thought he was as likely to attack as to hand the sword back yet the trader persisted, his hand held out, eyes locked on the German's.

He saw the moment when the German relaxed, his decision made. Heavy though the sword was, he flipped it so that the pommel was towards Lucius, catching the flat of the blade without being cut. Lucius accepted the blade with a slight nod then slowly looked around him, gesturing the crowd back with his free arm. Slowly the warriors drew back. 'Now for it', thought Lucius.

He dropped into the stance of a sword fighter, the great blade held two-handed before him. Then, careful to favour his lame leg, he began the weapon exercises he had been taught by old Centurion Appius long ago. The blade began its low hum as he worked it in an S-shape to his front. Faster and faster he swung it. Now to the left; parry, slash. Now to the right, the blade singing now, his shoulder muscles starting to ache. Now to the rear, nearly losing balance on the bad leg – parry, thrust, swing – grunting now with the effort bringing the exercise to a halt with a shout and a downward blow that would have split an iron helm.

He stood panting and sweating as the warriors around him roared their approval. A leathern tankard was thrust into his hands and he drank deep of the ale, wiping his mouth with the back of his hand.

"When you've quite finished showing off."

Trista, one hand on her hip, the other loaded with jewellery, stood beside him. The Germans, noting her look of palpable disapproval, howled with laughter. Furious, Trista flung down her load, turned and flounced off to renewed mirth from the warriors.

Ruefully, Lucius sheathed the sword in its magnificent leather scabbard and attempted to re-establish the spell. He was only partially successful. Self-adornment was important to these men but not as important as swordplay. They continued to talk amongst themselves about the trader's unexpected skill with the sword and his castigation by the girl. Nevertheless, Lucius was aware that they were now well-disposed towards him and that was all that really mattered. In any case, five minutes later Marcellus came to report that the stall was ready. Lucius called for silence with partial success, and bade the crowd welcome.

It was soon clear that weapons were the main focus of trade. Had they the stock, they could have sold several wagonloads of swords and spear-heads. As it was, in the hours before midnight, they sold out of almost every weapon. Lucius brought out the other two Baetician two-handed swords and held an auction for two of them. The other went to an enormous man wearing a leathern kilt and breeks, his muscular torso tattooed with interlocking patterns. By the way the crowd fell back before him it was clear that he was a war leader of some standing.

He did not barter for the sword. Instead he pulled a thick, gold torque from his left arm and threw it onto the stall without a word. The crowd stood silent as Lucius handed him the sheathed sword, pommel first. The German pulled it from its scabbard, looked at the silky sheen of the blade reflecting firelight and made a short emphatic comment. Whatever he said found favour with the warriors crowded around the stall for they gave a great shout, waving weapons and tankards in the air.

The leader then turned to Lucius with a curiously gentle smile.

"It were good that thou left by the way thou came tomorrow, trader."

The words were framed in good Latin.

Lucius stared at the German for a moment then inclined his head. "As you suggest, my Lord, but may I ask why?"

The smile left the German's face. Lucius shivered within at the atavistic cruelty that replaced it. A scar pulled the corner of the man's lip downward.

"Your curiosity is dangerous, trader. Cross the river as soon as may be and then keep going. That is all I shall say."

With that he turned on his heel. The crowd parted before him. He strode across the clearing and into the darkness of the forest.

Trade slackened markedly after this incident. With their stock of weapons all but gone, such interest as remained was chiefly in amulets and charms of the kind which kept warriors safe in battle. Cadmus, dressed in suitable robes, dedicated the purchases in the name of the buyer's favoured god for a small additional fee. Such rituals were carried out in the privacy of the wagon lest any perceive a lack of ceremonial knowledge.

Lucius had time to ponder. He might have put the prominent purchase of weapons down to the sanguinary nature of the customers but the sale of amulets was another matter. Men didn't buy amulets until the reality of dying sometime in the near future, became real in their minds. Also he hadn't seen a single woman since coming to the Waldfest. There might be esoteric reasons for this to do with the sanctity of the event but, taken with the weapons and amulets as well as the warning from the war leader, Lucius reckoned he was looking at an army on the eve of battle. But putting this all together, he doubted he had enough information yet to be of use to the Roman army on the opposite bank.

"Trading good?"

Lucius looked around. It was Tadg. The small Celt stood relaxed, looking around the remaining customers. Lucius wasted no time asking how he came to be there. Tadg came and went where and when he wanted.

"What have you learnt?" he asked.

"Boats," said Tadg. "Lots of boats in the trees down by the river. Funny thing: they weren't well-hidden. I c'd see fires on the other bank where the Legion's camped. I'm pretty sure in daylight they could see some of the boats. Now that don't make sense, does it?"

"'nother thing: these fires in the clearings: all of the one's I looked at there wasn't more than one or two peasants there feeding the fires. What's that all about? I mean, if you woz to look through the trees, you'd think that there was a 'uge army 'ere, but there ain't, is there?"

Lucius rubbed his chin and pondered.

"Hear me, Tadg, and check my reasoning." He paused, collecting his thoughts.

"Here, in the forest opposite Borbetomagus, are warriors but not an army. Fires burn at night; lots of fires. To anyone watching from across the river, it will look like a big army. By day the same people will catch sight of poorly hidden boats: not many: just enough to make it look like carelessness."

Cadmus came by, the stars on his pointy hat catching the

sparkle of firelight. He made a sign over a leather bag on a thong and handed it to a young German in exchange for a handful of coins.

"To the Roman general, it will seem as if he is going to be attacked frontally from across the river. Heliodoros, masquerading as me, has reinforced this. We, returning to the to the west bank tomorrow, can be expected to do the same."

Tadg nodded. "Sounds good so far."

"Right ," said Lucius. "This means that the general will align the axis of his front to the river. But we know – we think that the Germans are going to fall on the flank of the army."

A fight broke out in front of the stall between two warriors, each intent upon buying a copper torque. The other customers gave them room and cheered them on. It didn't last long. The smaller antagonist kneed his opponent in the groin and then head butted him into unconsciousness. The crowd reformed over and around the body as the victor paid for the torque.

Turning back to Tadg, Lucius went on.

"That means there's another large force of warriors hidden north or south of here. We travelled here from the south, close to the river and saw nothing. Did you see anything?" he asked.

The Celt shook his head. "Nope," he said.

"Then they must lie to the north," said Lucius.

"So d'ye want me to take a look?" asked Tadg.

Lucius thought then shook his head. "We both need to go. No disrespect, Tadg, but what is needed here is a detailed military appreciation. Not only that but I need to pass on that information. On top of that we're running out of time. My guess is the attack will be tomorrow or the day after. They'll make a feint across the river here, just enough to make sure they have the Legion's attention. While they're doing that, a bigger force will cross downstream and fall on its left flank."

"We must go north, find out what we can and then cross the river somehow. And my bet is that if we're lucky we'll be doing it with a howling horde of German's on our heels."

He didn't say what would happen if they weren't lucky.

Chapter 33

(Crossing the Rhine)

The wagon swayed and bucketed over the ruts. Trista clung on to the seat as Cadmus whipped up the mules. She peered behind. Marcellus rode Nero with Tiberius and Claudius on a lead rein. Adolphus lumbered along leading Galba, Vespasian and Titus. Never before had she travelled at this speed with the team, but Lucius had been explicit.

"Off at dawn," he had said. "We act normally until we're clear of the roadblock. After that I'll slip away and you go as fast as you can to the ferry. If I'm right, no one will try to stop you. They'll want you to take the wrong information to the Legion."

Trista had wanted to go with Lucius and Tadg but had seen that she was the only one with a chance of talking to Uncle Tuccius, Legate of the Twenty Second (*Primigenia*). And so, as soon as the tree trunk had been dragged into place behind them and they had rounded the bend, Lucius raised his hand in farewell and disappeared into the trees.

Trista felt bereft. Since the incident at Cruorsilva she realized that Lucius was only mortal like the rest of them. He could die at any time. The only comfort she could take was in the fact that Tadg was with him. If anyone could see him through safely it was Tadg.

They had paused briefly at Bensheim to rest the mules. The villagers had come out and given them cool water. Adolphus's Mum had thrown up her hands, disappeared into her hut and emerged with a leaf-wrapped bundle of boar's tripes, sufficient for all of them. Trista thanked her gravely and assured her, through the Dorfmeister, that they would eat them at their noon break.

Noon was now close and, thanks to the progress they had made, Mannheim was visible on the other bank, one of the ferries making its beetle-like way across the water towards the east bank. There was perhaps a mile to the landing place and Cadmus urged the mules on to make sure that they reached it before the ferry.

How would Uncle Tuccius receive her, she wondered. What would be her best approach? It was years since she had seen him. Would he remember her?

Now the landing place was in sight. Beside her, Cadmus groaned. A queue of ox carts and wagons awaited the ferry; more than enough to fill it. They would have to wait perhaps an extra two hours before they were able to embark.

"Go to the front of the queue," said Trista.

"But Trista…" he began.

"Do as you are told!" There was no mistaking the command in her voice.

As the ferry drew in towards the shore the trading wagon followed by its mule strings pulled past the queue. A crescendo of complaints followed it. They came to a halt at the water's edge. A fat teamster, leather apron flapping against his legs, whip held in one large hand, bustled up to them.

"Now see here," he said, shaking his whip.

Trista turned towards him. She gazed at him down her nose for fully three seconds from the high ground of the driving seat.

"No, you see here, my man," she drawled. "I am the Princess Trista of Aurelianum and this is my train. I am summoned, summoned I say, to attend upon the Emperor Hadrian at Borbetomagus. We are already late. If you have any complaint, you and your fellows, you may address it to His Imperial Highness. In the meantime I and my retinue are going to board this ferry and this," she leant back into the wagon, "is for your trouble."

She sat forward again and held out a linen purse which clinked suggestively.

The teamster scratched his head. A small crowd had gathered

around him by now.

"G'arn, Emil. What's yer 'urry," someone cried. "Let's us go an' drink to 'er 'ighness while we wait for the next boat."

There were growls of agreement as well as sundry nods towards the inn by the landing stage.

"Well, 'tis an 'ot day, yer 'ighness," agreed Emil. He reached upwards and took the purse. "'an wot I say is them that's in a 'urry should be allowed to get on wiv it."

"An' the gods bless you," he added as an afterthought, bobbing his head.

The ferry had by now emptied. Cadmus urged the mules forward onto the timber deck. The ferry master peered towards the shore. A line of abandoned ox teams stood on the slip while a small crowd of drivers and teamsters straggled up the slope to the inn.

"Where're they goin' then?" asked the ferry master.

Trista came to stand beside him.

"I'm sure I don't know," she replied in her best little girl voice. "But my Daddy is waiting for me across the river and he'll be ever so anxious." The sailor looked down into large blue eyes. "Please may we go now?"

Trista believed in never beating one trick to death.

* * *

Miles to the north Lucius and Tadg crept through the forest. The trees here were huge and ancient, their lichen-covered trunks rising sheer fifty feet to the canopy. Together they had skirted the area of the Waldfest. Most of the outlying clearings were abandoned. In some, peasants dozed in the sun while in a few others branches were being stacked near the ashes of last night's fires. From this Lucius deduced that the fire subterfuge would be used for at least one more night.

It was cool under the trees. The noonday sun thrust its beams between the leaves here and there but the overall atmosphere was one of damp stillness. Tadg who was in the lead held up a hand and crouched behind a bush. Lucius joined him. A hundred yards ahead the upper works of an ox wagon could be seen moving from right to left beyond a screen of bushes. As the first one moved out of sight a second one appeared and then a third.

"Reckon that's a supply road. Follow that an' we'll likely find the camp," said Tadg.

"This side or the other?" asked Lucius. They would have to parallel the road keeping to the trees. Tadg was the expert on this.

"Sun's from the south – reckon this side. It'll be darker."

They set off westwards, keeping the wagons in view to their right.

* * *

Borbetomagus was an armed camp. The small provincial town, standing to the west of a wide flood plain, sloping gently down to the Rhenus, usually dozed through the summer heat. Now, however, the Twenty Second *(Primigenia)* Legion had moved south from its permanent headquarters at Moguntiacum in response to strong rumours of a German attack across the river. To add to the activity, the town was preparing for the imminent arrival of the Emperor Hadrian.

The Emperor was engaged in his continued study of the Imperial frontiers. This summer he was travelling south through Germania Inferior, seeing for himself the state of the defences as well as judging the effectiveness of the administration. Being continually updated about the perceived German threat, he had timed his journey to coincide with the deployment of the Twenty Second. As an ex-soldier as well as Commander-in-Chief he was keen to see the Legion in a full-scale action.

For Quintus Tuccius Bassus, Legate of the *Primigenia*, the Imperial visit was a complication he could do without. It was not often that the Legion, or a large part of it, deployed tactically for battle rather than for exercise. His staff was fully stretched organizing accommodation, logistics, movements and intelligence. He was fully stretched making decisions, signing orders and checking the excesses of his less intelligent Tribunes. Yet, all the time he was looking over his shoulder, awaiting word of the Emperor's approach along the road from Colonia Agrippinensium.

Tuccius was only glad that the Emperor had acceded to his request that he come by road. The original plan had been for the Imperial progress to have taken place by galley down the Rhenus. The Legate shuddered to think of the risk he had averted. Imagine the galley overwhelmed by Germans; the Emperor taken.

He returned his attention to the clay tablet before him.

"No, no, *no*, Publius. The axis of the formation must be at right angles to the threat. Now from whence is the threat, Publius?"

The young Tribune leaned uncertainly over his commander's desk, unnerved by the close scrutiny of the Legate. Tuccius tried to restrain his irritability. Part of his job was to bring on these young men but this adolescent's lack of chin and conspicuous acne generated little confidence.

"Er, would it be here, sir?" asked the Tribune, sketching a vague line with one bitten finger.

Tuccius closed his eyes and breathed deeply for a moment.

"No, Publius, it is not. Intelligence puts the enemy's main force here below the bend in the river. That's backed up by our own observation of poorly hidden boats and fires at night. So you must turn the axis of our formation forty degrees thus, so that it is facing the threat, do you see?"

Publius nodded uncertainly.

"Redraw the plan, run it by the Senior Tribune and have markers placed for my inspection by the ninth hour. Dismiss."

The Tribune picked up the deployment plan, saluted awkwardly and left the tent. Tuccius took a deep breath rubbed his face and shouted, "Next!"

"Tribune Marius, sir." The Senior Tribune entered and saluted.

"What can I do for you Marius? Word from the scouts?"

The Legate was expecting to hear of the Emperor's approach at any minute.

"No word yet, sir. Sir, sorry to bother you with this, but there is a young person here wishing to see you. Arrived on a trader's wagon with slaves and mules. Says it's a family matter. I can make her go away but only if we use force. Thought I'd just run it by you first."

"A girl, d'you say?" The Legate was suddenly all attention. "Did she give a name?"

"She says her name is Trista, sir."

"By Jupiter," exclaimed the Legate. "It can't be."

He leapt up, brushing by the Tribune, and threw back the canvas tent flap.

"Uncle Tuccius?"

The young woman took a hesitant step towards the tall, forbidding figure. The Legate looked her up and down.

"By all the gods, it is! Trista!"

He held wide his arms. Trista ran to him then, throwing her arms around him. Tribune and guards looked on in bemusement as the pair hugged each other. Finally the Legate stood and held his niece by her shoulders at arms' length.

"Trista." He stared at her in wonder. "But we thought you were dead. There is a story here. But come in, come in." He gestured towards the tent. "Wine and, and cakes," he called to his orderly.

"Uncle," said Trista. "May someone please look after my people?"

Tuccius looked round. Some yards away, under the watchful eye of two guards, stood a battered mule wagon with a canvas cover on hoops. Around it crowded mules interspersed by three men. All of them looked worried but especially an enormous individual who looked unmistakably German.

"These – ah – are your people?" asked the Legate.

"Yes, Uncle. Might they have food and somewhere to camp? We have come far and very fast with news for you."

"News, d'you say?" The Legate raised his eyebrows. "Well, well. Marius, see to them will you?"

The Tribune saluted. "At your command, sir."

* * *

Lucius and Tadg lay between the roots of gorse bushes growing along the top of a low ridge. The ridge faced the river, half a mile away, but the dense trees cut off any view of the water. Below them was a large clearing into which filed warriors and wagons from various directions. Lucius estimated that the clearing already contained some ten thousand men with more arriving by the minute.

The wagons, hundreds of them, were parked in rows to one side. Groups of slaves, supervised by warriors, were unloading them and distributing their contents. To Lucius, the most impressive thing was the relative silence which lay over the clearing. A slave who dropped a crate had been relentlessly beaten, apparently for the noise he had made.

"Silent, do you see?" he murmured to Tadg. "Across the river they won't hear a thing even if there is anyone there to listen. We must be a good five miles upstream from the Legion."

Tadg nodded. "D'you get the feeling they're waiting for something?"

"Mmm," replied Lucius. "Someone or something."

They were silent for a while. The flow of warriors into the clearing was slowing. Not far short of twenty thousand, thought Lucius, all big men and well-armed.

"What d'you make of the stone then?" murmured Tadg.

They had noted when they had arrived in their hiding place that a rough-hewn granite pillar some four feet high stood in the centre of the clearing. Now, the thousands of warriors had formed up in a great circle with the pillar at its centre, silent, waiting. The circle was complete except for a wide opening to the southwest.

"It's an omphalos of some kind," said Lucius. "You know: the centre of somewhere: the place where the luck resides." He paused for a moment. "Yet there is something familiar about it," he continued. "Do you see that hollow in the top? Obviously designed to take something but I wonder what."

Below them all was silent but for the collective breathing of twenty thousand men, sounding like distant surf. Then from the right, coming closer, the two men heard hoof beats and the jingle of harness. An elaborate coach pulled by matching black horses came into view. As it drew to a halt, a pair of Numidian footman sprang to the ground. One opened the coach's door while the other unfolded steps. Then both held up their hands to help the occupant descend.

"Sertorius!" breathed Lucius.

The obese figure slowly descended. They could hear the squeaking of the steps. Sertorius was clad in a black robe. Beneath the matching headdress they could make out bandages. As he reached the ground he leaned heavily on both slaves, limping whenever his left foot touched the ground. He stopped before the stone pillar.

From the crowd of warriors a tall figure stepped forth. It was the man who had told Lucius to leave at dawn, the war leader. With measured step, he walked towards Sertorius, carrying something. Arriving at the pillar he stopped and lifted high the object before placing it in the Roman's hands. It was a sphere of crystal perhaps nine inches in diameter.

"Of course!" Lucius could barely contain his excitement. Tadg looked at him.

"What?" he whispered.

"Watch," came the reply.

Sertorius held the ball up. They could just hear his words, an incantation. Then he brought the sphere downwards fitting it into the hollow on top of the pillar. A brief sigh rose from the crowd.

Lucius placed his mouth close to Tadg's ear.

"He is altering the geomantic flow, the natural energy of the place. I saw it done once when I was a boy. There was a village where nothing prospered. Livestock died, crops failed. In the end the local lord sent for a geomancer. He dowsed the place: said they had a black flow. The lord paid him to alter it so he had a pillar set up like that one. Put a quartz crystal on top. As he turned it, he turned the energy flow."

He was silent, watching Sertorius incanting, hands raised heavenwards.

"Did it work?" prompted Tadg.

"Oh yes. The place took off like never before. Population grew: harvests were wonderful. Trouble was..."

"What?"

"Trouble was the following month a village in the next valley was destroyed by an earthquake. Seems he'd turned the black flow onto them."

He paused again, scrutinizing the scene before them. Sertorius had taken up a position behind the stone, facing southwest towards the open sector of the crowd. He was silent now, his hands still raised. Now he lowered them, placing them on the crystal sphere. As they watched he slowly revolved the sphere, chanting all the while.

"What d'you think is down there to the south west, where the break in the crowd is?" breathed Lucius.

Tadg thought for a moment then light dawned. "Borbetomagus."

"And ...?" asked Lucius.

Tadg thought again. "The Legion?" he asked.

"Yes, the Legion," agreed Lucius, looking thoughtful.

* * *

"But Uncle..."

Trista was exasperated.

"No, no, my dear. Allow your old Uncle some sense when it comes to military matters. Your Imperial spy – your Aurelio is already working for us; has been for over a week. Valiant chap: he's been back and forth across the river with no thought for his own safety."

"But Uncle!" Trista almost shouted. "He's an impostor."

"Oh, I don't think so," replied Tuccius, kindly. "We have ways of recognizing these people you know. Absolutely no doubt he's the genuine article."

Before Trista could renew her attack, the sentry outside the tent flap crashed to attention.

"Senior Tribune, sir," he announced.

"Come," called the Legate.

Marius bent to enter, his helmet under his arm. He saluted. "Emperor sighted, sir. Reckon he'll be with us within the hour."

"Right," said Tuccius, standing and brushing cake crumbs from his tunic. "Alert the Quartermaster and the guard, standard bearers and all that. Bring my horse round. I'll meet the Emperor half way. Now where's that address of welcome?" He bent to search among the documents on his desk.

"Ah," he said, straightening, "here it is. Trista, my dear, Marius will find you quarters. May not be luxurious but we've little room what with the Imperial retinue. We'll speak again later."

With that he hurried from the tent followed by his orderly brushing ineffectually at the Legate's tunic.

"Yes, Uncle," sighed Trista.

* * *

"If you're going down there, I'm going too."

Night had fallen. In the warm summer darkness, twenty thousand warriors were settling down for the night. Such sounds as filtered up to the ridge were muted.

Lucius pondered. "Alright but stay at least fifty yards clear of the stone. There'll be real energy running there and it won't be nice. And stay behind me. That way you won't get in the flow when I turn it."

"Right," said Tadg.

"Afterwards we head for the river," continued Lucius. He was smearing his face with mud created from earth and spit. Tadg did the same.

They had already located the sentries between whom they would creep. On this side of the camp, away from the river, they were widely spaced. As if to help, a strong breeze had risen. The soughing in the treetops would cover any noise they made.

"Ready?"

"Aye."

The pair slipped into the darkness.

* * *

"Germania Inferior, nay, the entire Latin-speaking world rises as one to salute your beneficent Majesty..."

Hadrian gazed into the middle distance trying to maintain an expression of mild enjoyment. In truth he hated these moments; couldn't think why he allowed them to perpetuate. The thing he couldn't do was to stop Tuccius in mid-flow. Wouldn't be good for discipline – or the Imperial Image. Mustn't damage that. If that went by the board, so did everything else. Still, poor old pompous Tuccius. Sound enough soldier. He really shouldn't be put in the position of having to spout this stuff though.

"...and with one accord we greet your Imperial Majesty. Hail Caesar."

The surrounding courtiers, tired from the day's journey, replied "Hail Caesar" with whatever energy they could muster.

"Thank you, Legate Tuccius. It is gratifying, indeed, to make the acquaintance of the *Primigenia* once more and, indeed, you, old friend."

Hadrian and Tuccius had been Tribunes together in the Second *(Adjutrix)* many years before.

"And now, my Lord, may I show you to the quarters set aside for you?" said the Legate.

"Yes, indeed, Tuccius. And you will join me in a light snack and tell me about the military situation. You need not worry," the Emperor smiled. "I shall not keep you long. We both know what the night before battle is like."

* * *

They move through the sentry line like wraiths, stomachs to the ground, testing for twigs and dried leaves. Once on level ground, the last of the sentries behind them, Lucius touches Tadg's arm. They rise to their feet and stroll forward, attempting nonchalance. All around them in a great arc, warriors sleep. Some toss and turn. Others snore or cry out but the overall effect, beneath the noise of the wind, is one of silence. It is dark – no moon tonight and clouds have streamed in to cover the stars. As they cross the centre of the clearing it is as if they are swimming in the Void.

Lucius gestures, palm outward. Tadg stops and squats down. Ahead of them he can just make out the pillar. He shivers. His Celtic blood tells him that darkness, more than the night, is abroad. He looks sideways at the pillar. It is as if a corona of black light hangs over it. He feels borne down by a weight of depression, a realization of the hopelessness of all things.

Lucius, meanwhile, stands apart, running his hands from his head downwards, shaking his fingers. Tadg recognizes it as the rite of purification but knows that it will be useless. Darkness will triumph. Now the Roman holds his hands before him, palms up. He looks to the sky invoking the protection of Mithras, Apollo and Mars.

Dully, without hope, Tadg watches Lucius move forward. The darkness over the stone seems to rise, forming two huge arms which hover above his friend. They threaten to engulf him but seem unable to move. Against the dark background, Tadg senses an aura of light, flickering around Lucius.

Lucius stands before the pillar, pausing once more to invoke the gods. Now he lifts his hands and deliberately brings them down to lay on the crystal sphere. There is a spurt of actinic light. Tadg hears Lucius hiss with pain but his hands remain on the crystal. Simultaneously there is a commotion off to Tadg's right.

He looks that way. There is a tent. It rocks from side to side. An enormous white grub emerges, crawling from the entrance. Tadg recognizes it as Sertorius, wrapped in a flapping night gown. As he watches the Numidians emerge too. "Get me up, fools!" wheezes the obese man. The Numidians bend to obey but find themselves struggling with the great weight.

"Move, Tadg!"

The Celt looks to his left. Apparently struggling against enormous resistance, Lucius is turning the crystal, turning it to the right.

"Behind me, man!"

Tadg scuttles to the left, keeping a wary eye on Sertorius. The Numidians have him half way to his feet but lose their grip.

"Fools!" Sertorius tries to shout but lacks the breath. The thrashing of the wind in the trees covers his voice. For now the warriors sleep on.

Tadg turns his attention back to Lucius. Inch by inch, his feet digging into the forest earth, he is heaving the crystal around. For the first time Tadg realizes that wherever the crystal points, the trees break into a frenzy some ten feet above the ground. He hears small branches ripping away and thrashing into the undergrowth. He watches, mesmerized, as the damaging arc moves further and further to the right, away from Borbetomagus, back into the forest.

Sertorius is now on his feet, supported by his two slaves. His nightgown billows around him. Raising his hands towards Lucius he starts an incantation. He weaves darkness. A skein of deeper night hovers above his head. Small jags of lightening detonate around it. Tadg looks back at Lucius. The man is straining every muscle to keep the crystal moving. Tadg wonders if he should help him. As if reading his mind Lucius says, "Stay back; behind me Tadg, behind me." The words tear from his throat.

Now Sertorius raises his right hand, whirling it in a circle, faster and faster. The blackness swirls with it, a vortex of deeper night. Suddenly, he brings his hand forward and down towards Lucius. The black whirlwind leaps forward. It falls upon the Roman. Tadg watches helplessly as the bright aura dims. Darnkess surrounds his friend until he can barely see him. Despair engulfs the small Celt. He falls to his knees, his chin upon his chest.

Yet, after a moment he drags his gaze back up to Lucius. The trader is down on his knees but retains his grip on the crystal. The aura has not been extinguished but is growing again, pulsing with energy. Sertorius gives out a croaking wheeze. One of the Numidians turns and runs. The other cannot support his master. The two crash to the ground. Sertorius raises one hand and starts another incantation but the crystal continues to turn inexorably.

Lucius is back on his feet. The arc of destruction closes on Sertorius. Suddenly the tent is whipped away into the dark.

Sertorius begins to wail. He brings his hand down towards Lucius but nothing happens. The other Numidian leaps to his feet and runs after his mate. Sertorius wriggles his great mass, trying for a sitting position but as he strains to raise his torso from the ground, the energy beam is upon him.

With one last supreme effort, Lucius tilts the crystal so that the beam moves downwards towards the fallen man. Sertorius finds his voice. He starts to scream. Cries of alarm sound from around the clearing as guards realize that something is happening. With a burst of unearthly light, the beam touches Sertorius. His great body is galvanized, jerking in frenzied spasms. He half rises, screaming, then falls back. There is an explosion from the pillar as the crystal shatters, then utter darkness.

Chapter 34

(Betrayal)

"So, my man brought intelligence. Good, good. I had high hopes of him and I am glad to see that I was not wrong.

Hadrian cracked a walnut with a small hammer.

"Meridius – you remember him? Head of Intelligence? I could tell he doubted my judgement. Didn't feel that military men had the subtlety for this kind of work. Pity he's not here to see how wrong he was. Died, you know. Weak heart as it turned out. Tell me, Tuccius, do you ever wonder how you will die?"

The Legate chuckled. "In battle at the moment of victory for preference, my Lord, although I don't rule out the efforts of a jealous husband."

The Emperor laughed. He poked the fragments of shell with his finger, searching for the kernel.

"So we expect the Germans to mount a frontal assault across the river tomorrow at dawn?"

"Yes, my Lord. The intelligence was detailed and unequivocal. From our own positions we have detected boats hidden in the edge of the forest opposite." Tuccius allowed himself a chuckle. "I'm sure they thought themselves very clever but their camouflage leaves something to be desired."

He took a sip of wine.

"And as you can see for yourself, my Lord, they take little care to hide their campfires." He gestured towards the open window of the town house. The view, hidden by darkness, took in a sweep of water meadows running down to the river. From the forest on the east bank twinkled many pinpoints of light only partially hidden by the trees.

"We estimate a force of ten thousand, perhaps a few more," said the Legate. "With the cohorts to hand we deploy eight and a half thousand men. Thus they have nowhere near the three to one superiority needed to attack successfully on a well-found defensive position, especially as they have to cross the river to join with us."

He selected an orange and began to peel it with a small silver knife.

"So, with any luck, my Lord, I should be able to show you a textbook, if unexciting display of battle drill in the morning."

Hadrian withdrew his gaze from the window. He smiled. "I shall look forward to it, Tuccius. But now I shall not keep you from your preparations and, I hope, a good night's sleep. Perhaps you will join me for a small celebration after the battle tomorrow."

The Legate stood. "I shall be delighted, my Lord."

He saluted, turned, and left the room.

Hadrian swung round to the window again. He gazed into the darkness. For a while he tried to count the pinpricks of light but kept losing track. He yawned. 'Bed', he thought.

* * *

Tadg crawled through the darkness. There were shouts. A torch was lit only to be knocked to the ground and extinguished. A voice of command rang out. The shouting subsided. The same voice spoke again, clearly but not shouting. It was evidently giving orders – what orders, Tadg couldn't tell. All he knew was that it was time to find Lucius and get out of here.

His hand touched cloth.

"Lucius," he murmured.

There was a groan.

"My hands."

Tadg squatted behind Lucius, took him by the shoulders and lifted him to a sitting position. He felt stickiness on the tunic but it was too dark to see what it was.

"Tadg." Lucius's voice was filled with pain. "Somehow you

must get me across the river. The Legion must be warned." He took a shuddering breath. "I'd suggest you leave me and go alone but, gods help us, they'll need to hear it from me."

Tadg slipped his hands under Lucius's armpits.

"If I help you, can you stand?" asked Tadg.

"I don't know. Let's try."

As gently as possible, not knowing where his master was hurt, Tadg levered him up. Hissing with pain, Lucius assisted with his feet until he stood, leaning heavily on the pillar. They paused and listened. Bodies were moving through the night. From the direction of Sertorius's tent came an exclamation, then another. However, the discipline of the host held. Despite their numbers the clearing remained quiet except for the wind.

"Lean on me," said Tadg. "We'll head out through the gap in the circle, then to the river. I'm reckoning in this dark there's a good chance they ain't goin' to see us."

Together, Tadg's shoulder under Lucius's arm, they pushed off from the pillar and made their faltering way towards where they hoped the gap lay. Before they had gone more than a dozen paces further commands rang out in the dark. Voices from around the circle replied. Over the noise of the wind came the sound of men standing, picking up spear and shield.

The two men stopped.

"What d'you reckon?" asked Tadg.

Lucius listened.

"I may be wrong but I don't think they're after us – too many of them. They'd just fall over each other in the dark. My guess, and it's only a guess, the leader's sending his advanced guard across early. He may be worried that scouts across the river will have heard the noise. It may play to our advantage. Anyway, let's keep moving and see."

Painfully they moved across the dark clearing. Using the corners of his vision, Tadg picked up the mass of men lying on the ground, wrapped in their cloaks. He adjusted their course to the left, into the gap. It took another ten minutes for them to clear the gap before he eased round to the right, towards the river. Initially the way was clear but soon they found themselves stumbling through undergrowth. Once Lucius tripped and fell with a muffled cry of pain. It took more minutes for Tadg to raise him. They struggled on.

After another ten minutes, Tadg stopped.

"Listen," he said.

Ahead of them came muffled footsteps, crossing their front. They crept forward. Without warning a figure loomed into view from their right, barely ten feet away. Another followed and then another. A file of men was crossing ahead of them.

Lucius eased his mouth next to Tadg's ear.

"That'll be the way to the river. Wait 'til the last one's gone, then we follow."

Tadg nodded. In another minute a final shadowy figure passed them. They waited a few more seconds then started forward. A moment later, they found their way barred. Tadg used his free hand to feel in the dark.

"A rope," he said. "They were following a rope."

With some difficulty they ducked under the rope, finding themselves on a well-trodden path. Lucius was breathing heavily.

"Do you need to rest?" asked Tadg.

Lucius swallowed. "No, let's keep on. If I stop now I may not be able to start again. Besides, we don't know if more German's are coming."

They limped on. Both were tiring but the way was easier. Tadg began to wonder how they were going to cross the river. Steal a boat? Didn't seem likely if the German's were making a crossing. Swim? Easy to say but this was one big, cold, energetic river. It would have been difficult enough if they had both been fit but with Lucius in his present state…

Abruptly they came to edge of the trees. They stopped. Tadg

eased Lucius to the ground, propping him against a trunk. Ahead of them were noises of activity overlaying the night-sounds of the river. Tadg thought about scouting forward himself but was doubtful whether he could find Lucius again in the darkness. The Roman grasped his sleeve and pulled him near.

"Stay still and watch for the moment. We may see a pattern." His voice was weak, his breath ragged.

They watched for some moments. Gradually the picture clarified.

"See there," whispered Lucius. "Surely that is a group paying out rope."

Tadg squinted. "I think you're right," he replied. "Would they have a boat pulling across the river, do you think?"

Lucius was silent for some moments.

"Of course," he said. "Ropes to the river. Ropes across the river. D'you see? They've planned well. They had ropes rigged up to guide their warriors to the river in the dark. Now they're rigging ropes across the water. It's the only way to get a large number of men across a river quickly. You rig ropes and they pull themselves across in boats."

He paused again, breathing heavily.

"If they're doing that there will be a second rope for the journey back. There will be lots of ropes."

The hand with which he clutched Tadg's arm spasmed. Lucius gasped.

"Are you alright?" asked Tadg, placing his arm around Lucius's shoulder.

"Never...never better, old friend," gasped the Roman. "Now you must use all your guile. Scout out to the left. If I'm not mistaken we are on the edge of the force here. See if you can locate a boat."

Tadg swallowed his misgivings. "'ere," he said, "let's get you into a bit of cover then."

As gently as possible he helped Lucius into the undergrowth

then eased him to the ground. The Roman rolled onto his side and raised his knees up towards his chest.

"Quick as you can, Tadg," he hissed between his teeth. "The night marches on."

For a moment Tadg stood looking down at his friend. Then he turned and crept towards the river. At the last tree, some five yards from where Lucius lay, he took out his knife and cut a blaze in the bark of the trunk. It wasn't much but it would have to do. He turned left, flitting from shadow to shadow, counting his steps. Now that he knew where they were, he could clearly see the group of men handling the rope. He realized as well that, between him and them, a squad of warriors sat in lines on the ground, silently watching the river.

Tadg crept on then froze as he heard low voices ahead. There was grunting. Someone was moving a heavy weight, sliding it over the twigs and leaves on the river bank. Step by step he moved forward. There was the sound of the weight being left at the water's edge and now a group of men was coming back up the bank towards him, talking quietly among themselves. Tadg lay flat. In the dark the men passed close to either side of him.

He waited until the last one was clear then rose and followed them. Almost immediately he found himself on top of the group as they gathered round another boat, ready to lift it. Counting on darkness and confusion to hide his identity, Tadg went to the stern of the boat and grasped the rubbing strake. A quiet order and the boat was lifted: another, and they were heading back to the river.

At the river's edge they deposited the boat. As the others turned and plodded back, Tadg hid his small bulk behind the boat. Once he was alone he looked around him. He could make out four boats off to his right, upstream, all placed just above the water's edge. They were of all types and sizes, evidently brought together from up and down the river.

Checking that he was still alone, he selected a small skiff, saw that it contained oars, then placed his back against its stern He dug his feet into the earth and strained. For a moment nothing happened, then it moved a few inches towards the water.

'Right,' he thought.

* * *

"I don't care; I'm going,"

Trista offered the bit to Galba. The mule took it. Trista slid the crown over Galba's ears and buckled the nose band.

"But Trista..." began Marcellus.

"You must stay here and look after the wagon with Cadmus." Trista spoke matter-of-factly, as if it was agreed. "I will take Adolphus with me. I may need his strength and he is the only one of us who speaks German."

Cadmus tried. "Trista, what is going to happen to us when they find out you are gone?"

"You will tell them the truth that I ordered you to stay. Here, give me a leg up," she ordered.

Exasperated by her inability to persuade her uncle that he was being led by false intelligence, Trista had decided to head upriver. She knew that was where Lucius and Tadg had gone; knew that they would have to cross to this bank. With supreme confidence she believed that she would be able to find them in the dark and bring them back.

She took Tiberias' lead rein from Cadmus. Adolphus looked from Marcellus to Trista, shifting from foot to foot. His face was a picture of confusion. Marcellus sighed.

"Adolphus," he said, "you must go with Trista. You must keep her safe and help her to find the Master and Tadg. Do you understand?"

Adolphus thought for a moment then nodded his head several times.

"Yus," he said.

* * *

'Not exactly the bloody Tweed,' thought Tadg as he peered anxiously over his shoulder. Finding Lucius again and getting him to the boat had taken twenty minutes but had been accomplished without incident. Gambling with their luck and the darkness he had waited for a quiet moment before launching the boat and helping Lucius aboard. Now, however, he was beginning to understand that he had underestimated the mighty Rhenus.

It had started well. He had shipped his oar over the stern and begun sculling, pointing the skiff's bows well upstream. For the first few minutes as they cleared the shallows by the bank, he made good progress. Then, however, the boat began to feel the lazy power of the river. It wasn't that Tadg could see anything in the dark; rather that he could feel the boat was lifting and falling on long, sleek waves of turbulence.

He cursed and pointed the bows further upstream. This, he knew, would lengthen their journey but he was all too aware that somewhere close downstream were the ropes and a barbarian assault force crossing the river. Being swept into them would spell disaster.

"You're doing well, Tadg."

Lucius had benefitted from his rest by the river but Tadg had noticed him shivering – probably the onset of shock. Still, there was nothing for it but to go on.

"Don't know about that," he said through clenched teeth. "Be a bloody sight happier if I could see anything."

He didn't like the sense of being swept sideways.

Without warning there was a grating noise. The boat twisted to starboard and began to tip. Tadg turned, gaping.

"The rope, Tadg. We've hit a rope."

Tadg grabbed the gunwale, dropping his oar. He could just make out where the rope, taut with the weight of the boat, came out of the water ahead of them, water singing past it.

"Bel's Teeth," he swore. For a moment he thought about clearing the rope but the boat took another lurch. He stumbled towards Lucius, clinging to the gunwale. The noise of the water had risen to a roar. It was pouring in over the lower gunwale.

"Grab my belt," he shouted. "We're going into the water. Whatever happens, hang on."

He felt Lucius's hand go under his belt and steeled himself to ignore the cry of anguish as flayed skin scraped against leather. Together they crawled to the bows. The boat was now almost vertical. Tadg leaned round the bows, feeling for the rope. Nothing. He leaned further. His fingers found hempen fibres. Just an inch or two more. Suddenly the boat was going. The two men were pitched into the water. A long scraping and a splash and the boat was gone.

* * *

Most people would have admitted that they were lost but Trista knew where she was. She was here on the river bank, headed downstream. Admittedly she would have had difficulty relating her position to the rest of the world but, as her father used to say, "It is better to travel hopefully..."

The night was dark but her chosen path, keeping the water on her right, meant that she couldn't really be lost. Indeed, there was a well-trodden track used by travellers up and down the river for the very same reason. Still it was very dark. She took comfort from the solid bulk of Adolphus, felt rather than seen behind her.

She turned her head. "Once again, Adolphus: what are you to say if we meet Germans?"

Adolphus ducked his head then said, in a rush: "We is but poor fisher folk making our way to...to..."

"Moguntiacum," prompted Trista.

"Momdumdedumcum," continued Adolphus. "My wife 'ere

is…is…"

"Pregnant," helped Trista.

"Yus…that." The giant stumbled on, "An' we got to get 'er to 'er granma's ter 'ave the baby tonight…I fink."

Trista sighed. "Well done, Adolphus." She hoped that they wouldn't meet any Germans.

"And what language are you to say this in?"

Adolphus pondered. "German?" he hazarded.

"Well done, Adolphus," said Trista.

* * *

"I can feel the bottom," gasped Lucius.

'You might be able to,' thought Tadg, 'but I can't.'

Tadg's fingers had just closed over the rope as the boat disappeared. For an agonizing moment his one arm supported both their weights against the current before he brought his other hand forward. Freed from the boat the rope had risen above the water. Hand over hand, Tadg had dragged them both along towards the further shore. He was nearing exhaustion and very cold. Only grim determination kept him going.

Had he known it, they were out of the worst of the current here at the inside of a great bend in the river. The current, as it slowed, had deposited sand banks and it was upon one of these that Lucius now found footing. Tadg searched with his foot. Yes! Sand, at last. Now the question was whether or not this went all the way to the shore. They had to get out of this quickly. Lucius couldn't stand much more of it. He waited while the Roman slowly changed his grip so that his hands were clasped round his neck.

"Ready, Tadg," he muttered through chattering teeth.

Still holding onto the rope Tadg moved forward. The water level rose and fell. At one stage they lost the bottom again but the current was now minimal. Finally the water was down to their thighs, then their knees. Tadg began to feel Lucius's full weight again, without the support of the water. He forced one foot in front of another, too exhausted to care whether the shore was guarded. Finally he stood swaying on grass. Lucius let go his grasp and slid to the ground. Tadg fell to his knees.

"Bel's Teeth," he muttered. He was tired.

Off to his right a boat grounded in the shallows. There was splashing, warriors disembarking.

'Oh leave me alone,' thought Tadg.

"Lucius," he murmured, gently shaking his friend.

Lucius groaned. Tadg put his mouth close to Lucius's ear.

"We've got to get off the bank, into the trees. Can you help me?"

Weakly and with great effort Lucius replied, "I'm sorry, Tadg, I don't think I can stand."

Tadg looked downstream. Faintly he could see the warriors forming up. They disappeared into the trees. Now, if Lucius's theory was right, the boat would be brought over here to go back on their rope. No time for hanging about then. He turned Lucius onto his back, grasped him under his armpits and began dragging him. The effort was immense. At the first tree he propped Lucius up in a sitting position and knelt down beside him.

"I want to get you stood up leaning against the tree," he said. "Can you help me a bit with your feet?"

"Try…" whispered Lucius. Tadg lifted and Lucius scrabbled. It took them a minute but finally Tadg had him upright, pinned against the trunk. Taking a deep breath he bent, grasped the Roman around his waist and heaved himself upright. Something went in his back but he stood swaying.

"This is bloody silly," he muttered then, turning, he took one step and then another, heading south, heading for Borbetomagus.

* * *

The Cornicen whetted his lips. Not for the first time he cursed his rank which so often required that he be up before anybody else apart from the cooks. It was still pitch black, a good hour before dawn he reckoned. He watched the Signals Tribune out of the corner of his eye, blowing gently through the mouthpiece to warm the instrument. Now the Tribune's arm fell. Taking a deep breath, the Cornicen blew the first notes which would wake an army.

* * *

Tadg managed perhaps forty paces before his strength gave out. Clumsily he fell to his knees just off the path, behind a clump of brambles. Lucius's weight pressed him to the ground so that he had to crawl out from under. He straightened Lucius onto his back. The Roman's breath came harsh and ragged. He was shivering uncontrollably. Tadg chafed his hands.

'Leaves,' he thought. 'Bracken – have to make a bed, keep him warm.'

A scream came from up in the woods. 'Butchering the pickets,' thought Tadg. 'Butcher us if they find us.' Then he heard the hoof beats.

Animals! Now, if the gods only willed, this could be their salvation.

"Stay quiet," he murmured to Lucius then drew his knife and slipped into the night.

* * *

The cry when it came was short-lived. It ended in a bubbling groan. Trista stopped Galba and listened. It had come from somewhere up the slope among the trees. There was little to be heard above the thrashing of the wind in the trees. She thought they'd been going now for about two hours so she supposed that they might be somewhere near where the Germans would land.

For the first time her confidence began to falter. Somehow she had assumed that they would meet Lucius and Tadg coming towards them down the path. There would be hugs and greetings. They would mount the mules and arrive back in Borbetomagus in time to save the army. The night wasn't meant to be this dark. The world shouldn't have been so big. Certainly there shouldn't be bubbling cries in the night. Trista shivered.

'This won't do.' She squared her shoulders. "Adolphus," she said, "we shall continue on foot."

Only as she slid off the mule did it occur to her that Adolphus was already on foot. For a moment she chided herself for being so stupid but only for a moment. Taking Galba's reins she started forward. The mule followed, her ears pricked. Without warning she gave her hoarse, coughing neigh. Appalled, Trista turned placing her hand on Galba's muzzle. As she did so she felt an arm snake round her neck.

"Not a word," hissed someone in very bad Gaulish.

Chapter 35

(Battle)

The agent arrived in the hour before dawn. He was shown to the Legate's tent. Swaying with fatigue, clothes dirty and ragged, the man yet found the energy to straighten and salute.

"Well done, Terentius," said the Legate. "What have you to report?"

"My Lord, it is as I thought. They plan a frontal assault across the river." He paused for dramatic effect. "I had words with their war leader, Haimirich."

The Legate's eyebrows lifted in admiration.

"He has little idea of tactics," continued the agent. "He plans to throw them at you piecemeal, as they disembark, all ten thousand of them."

"Well done indeed," said the Legate. "And what of the flanks?"

"They are safe, my Lord. He has not the strength to mount a flank attack. Be at ease."

Tuccius sent the agent off to eat and rest. 'What a man,' he thought. 'Such military bearing; such...presence. What could I not do with ten thousand like him.'

As he rose his orderly entered carrying the Legate's best cloak and helmet.

The Legate smiled to himself.

"No supper tonight, Matteus. Victory feast with the Emperor, don't you know?"

* * *

The German attack came with the first grey of the dawn. A low mist lay in skeins across the water. The auxiliary skirmishers, waiting on the bank caught sight of the first boats briefly through a gap in the mist. They raised a shout and readied their spears.

Half a mile behind them, at the top of the slope, the Legate stood with the Emperor among the Praetorian Guard.

"As you will see, my Lord, the Legion is formed about an axis slightly west of north and facing east across the river."

The shout of the auxiliaries echoed up the slope.

"And there, if I'm not mistaken, is the enemy. Nothing if not punctual."

His staff laughed briefly, politely.

"And your flanks?" asked the Emperor.

"We have pickets and scouts out in each direction but your man, Terentius, brought final confirmation before dawn. This will be a frontal assault. They have not the force to open on two fronts."

"Ah, yes," said Hadrian. "Terentius. I would like to reaquaint myself with him. Please have him sent for."

* * *

Out on the left flank of the army the Primum Pilum strolled behind the front rank of the First Century. The First Cohort, an elite, reinforced cohort, always formed the left flank of the Legion in battle formation. The First Century formed on the front, left corner of the Cohort. The Primum Pilum, or First Spear, was the Centurion of the First Century. He was a battle-scarred veteran of many campaigns but also an intelligent man and a doughty fighter. The water carriers were scurrying along the ranks.

"Drink deep, lads. Never know where the next one's coming from."

The first sounds of combat were rising from the water's edge where the skirmishers had engaged the enemy. There was also the deep, bell-like baying of hounds. The Legions on the Rhenus made use of the great, brindled hounds bred for herding the Commissary cattle, to soften German attacks. It was reckoned a good way of preserving Roman lives.

With the river at its summer low, they couldn't see the fighting. There was a steep drop off down to the water's edge. The Primum Pilum was quite relaxed. No point in hefting shields for a good while yet. Best to have the men rested and relaxed when they formed the shield wall.

From up the hill a cornu sounded a complicated code. The Primum Pilum watched as two ala of cavalry, part of the auxiliary screen out beyond the First Cohort, detached and curved round in front of the army, ready to back up the skirmishers when the Germans broke through.

Because, break through they would. The skirmishers were only light troops. Their purpose was to harry and delay not to fight as such. The fighting would be done by the deadliest weapon yet known to the world; the heavy infantry of the Roman Legion in battle formation behind its shield wall.

"Helmet on, Legionary Drusus." Didn't do to let them get too casual.

Should be a walk-over from all he'd heard. Frontal attacks by great hairy Germans looked frightening but once they came up against the shields and the short stabbing swords, they'd be crying for their mummies.

The big man smiled. 'Why did they bother?' See, if he'd been the German war lord, he'd have mounted a flank attack. He looked up the grassy slope on their open, northern side. Pack the forest up there with even a small force then come streaming out when everyone was concentrating forwards.

He gauged the distance with his eye. What, half a mile? So three or four minutes at the run. There was only the auxiliary cavalry out there and they wouldn't be much use. No, three or four minutes and they'd be in the open end of the ranks. Unless we twigged in time and reformed. It was something they practiced but with this many men on sloping ground it wouldn't be that easy. Next thing you knew you'd opened your ranks to attack from the front and then where would you be? Butchered.

As he came to the end of the rank, before he turned to pass down between the next two, he stopped. There was movement up there on the treeline. He shaded his eyes. What in Hades? Two mules and a small group of people shambling towards them at a trot, waving and shouting. He wondered if the Tribune had seen them.

"Tribune, sir!"

The Tribune, mounted on his horse, turned towards the Primum's shout, following the line of his outstretched arm. He kicked his horse forward, winding round the flank of the Third Century to join the Centurion. The distant group were now stopped talking to an outlying cavalry picket. The picket was leaning from his saddle, listening. Now he pointed downslope to the First Cohort.

"What d'you make of it Primum?"

The Primum Pilum was comfortable with the staff officer. This one asked. Many didn't.

"Don't know, sir. May I suggest we go forward a little and meet them?"

"Optio," he called. "Take over here."

The Tribune urged his horse forward, the Centurion walking at his side. The group was closer now, coming on at an untidy trot. There was a girl on a mule in the lead, waving a shawl over her head. Behind her was another mule. The Primum was alert to the huge figure running along beside the mule apparently supporting the rider. A German, for sure. On the other side of the animal, also supporting the rider, ran a much smaller man.

The girl reined in her mule a few yards in front of the soldiers.

"We have news," she gasped. She turned to the others. The second mule came to an uneven stop. Its rider looked in a bad way. The Primum could see blood where the blanket wrapping him fell open. Deep into shock, he reckoned. The man would have fallen but for the supporting arms on either side.

"Lucius, tell them." The girl turned her mule, walking it back to the other.

The wounded man opened his eyes. Seeing the soldiers he made an effort to straighten, swaying in his saddle.

"Tribune." His voice cracked and died. The girl held a flask of water to his lips. He drank, water spilling down his front. He tried again. This time his voice was a little stronger.

"Tribune, you must look to your flank. I estimate twenty thousand German warriors not more than half an hour behind us."

He closed his eyes, slumping back against the big German.

Tribune and Centurion exchanged glances. The Tribune whetted his lips.

"Who are you?" he asked.

The man opened his eyes again. With an effort he said, "Lucius Terentius Aquilina, Centurion, late of the Sixth *(Victrix).*"

"Terentius?" said the Primum Pilum. "Not old Metellus Terentius's son?"

The rider smiled slightly and nodded. The Primum turned to his Tribune.

"I think this is the real thing, sir. Best get him to the Legate right away. By your leave, I'll call in the centurions. Get them thinking about changing axis."

"Very Good, Primum," said the Tribune.

The Primum Pilum marched away. "Centurions," he bawled, "on me!"

The Tribune beckoned one of his aides. He looked at the group before him, selecting the girl as being most obviously in charge.

"Will you vouch for the German?" he asked.

"With my life!" replied Trista, with rather more drama than was entirely necessary.

"Antonius," he turned to the aide, "see them to the Legate, fast as you can."

The aide saluted and, beckoning the group, set off up the slope.

* * *

Tribune Publius, he of the acne and receding chin, entered the mess tent. He looked around. Ah, there in the corner, reclining with a flask of wine. Publius had never known any spies but he felt an automatic distaste for them. Apparently this fellow was only a retired centurion anyway. The Tribune wove his way between benches and tables. He fixed the man with what he thought was a haughty gaze.

"Fellow," he said, "you are to come with me. The Legate wishes to see you." He paused, looking the man up and down. "And might I suggest you smarten yourself up a little."

Heliodoros put down his flask, smiling inwardly. 'Ah, young pup. Later today I'll see you spitted on a spear for that,' he thought. He stood.

"At your orders, sir," he replied, gravely.

He followed the young officer out of the tent. 'So, just one more performance,' he thought. What would it be? 'Give me a spear and let me join the front rank of battle?' Yes. They wouldn't let him, of course. Far too valuable. It made little difference anyway. He would be on a horse heading west as soon as he was free to do so. Friend looked too much like foe in the frenzy of battle and he had no intention of dying at the hands of his employers.

Tribune and impostor arrived at the top of the slope outside the city walls where the standards of the Twenty Second (*Primigenia*) glittered in the sun. Heliodoros took on his role. Exhausted hero: just a shade of a limp, a tiny bending of the back; just a hint of pain around the mouth. Then, behind the Legate, he saw the gilded armour of the Praetorian Guard. Pluto's Warts! There was the Emperor!

This would be a bravura performance indeed; a fitting end to a dazzling tour.

The Tribune saluted. "The spy Terentius, my Lord."

"Ah, Terentius," said the Legate. "The Emperor wishes to meet you."

The Legate was turning, beckoning him. Heliodoros, the Hero of the Rhenus, stepped forward.

"But that's not Terentius." The Emperor's voice was flat.

"But...but, my Lord," stuttered Tuccius, "he has the seal."

"Show me," ordered Hadrian, holding out his hand.

The Greek's hand went to the neck of his tunic. Whether he meant to take his own life or that of the Emperor was never clear for he died writhing upon the blades of two Praetorian spears, one in his stomach and one in his chest. The dagger slipped from his nerveless fingers as he died.

Slowly, calmly, for the Praetorians were dangerous with their Emperor threatened, Tuccius knelt. He slipped his hand into the neck of the corpse's tunic. The silver chain caught beneath the head. Tuccius jerked it free and slowly stood.

"You see, my Lord, he had the seal."

He held the amethyst on its chain out to Hadrian who took it.

Just then hoof beats approached from down the slope. Praetorians pressed forward spears levelled. The First Cohort aide stopped some distance from the group, eyeing the spears.

"My Lord, Tribune Naevius's compliments, he believes you will wish to question these, er, persons."

"Now *that's* Terentius." Hadrian pushed aside the Praetorians spears and came forward. He took in the blood-stained tunic, the crudely bandaged hands. "What have they done to you, Terentius?"

Lucius opened his eyes. He recognized the Emperor but thought he was dreaming. Neverthless, he tried to straighten up and deliver his report.

"My Lord, you must look to your left flank. Germans,

thousands of them..."

With that he fainted.

"Gaius, send for my physician." Hadrian barely raised his voice. One of his aides ran to obey.

"Set him down," ordered the Emperor.

Watched warily by the guard, Adolphus lifted Lucius from the mule and gently placed him on the ground.

"Now," said Hadrian, looking from Trista to Tadg, "can one of you tell me what this is all about?"

Trista turned to Tadg. "You tell the Emperor, Tadg," she said.

And so Tadg, son of Connell, of Black Hill in the Province of Caledonia addressed Publius Aelius Traianus Hadrianus, Emperor of Rome.

"Well, begging your pardon, sir, we come across the river last night with the German advanced guard. They had it all planned; murdering the pickets an' all. The master – Lucius, that is, or Aurelio as we calls him – he reckoned there was twenty thousand of them – counted them he did. Seems this bloke Sertorius – oh you knows him does you? Anyway, seems he plotted with them. 'e might be dead now; we dunno. An' they're about half an hour behind us we reckons. 'spect you'll see them coming out of them trees in a minute." He pointed to the north where the forest brooded at the top of the sloping meadows.

"By your leave, my Lord," said Tuccius. Hadrian nodded. The Legate turned.

"Aides, messengers to me. Orders group."

Tuccius, slightly pompous uncle of Trista, now showed his worth. The Second Cohort was ordered to withdraw from the line, passing behind the First, and establish a new front facing north, its left flank anchored by the city walls.

The right-wing cavalry were sent to reinforce the skirmishers who were told to hold for the time being. This would mean that many of them would die but it couldn't be helped. They would be ordered to withdraw by cornu signal. At that point all cavalry were to withdraw to the north where they would harry the attacking force's right flank, preventing them from passing behind the city and attacking from the rear.

The First Cohort, the elite of the Legion, reformed on the corner, facing north and east, left flank adjoining the Second, right flank on the Third. This was the crucial move, a complicated and ponderous evolution. Tuccius was pleasantly surprised when it happened with smooth precision.

"Well done, Primum Pilum," was the Tribune's verdict.

"That's what they pay me for, sir," came the terse reply.

It all happened not a moment too soon. "My Lord," cried one of the Tribunes, pointing.

The edge of the forest was suddenly alive. As they watched figures boiled from between the trees. Tuccius was reminded of an ants' nest stirred with a stick. War horns sounded and with a roar the first lines of warriors started down the slope.

"Signal the skirmish line to withdraw."

The cornus sounded their deep, bell-like notes. Down on the flat ground bordering the river centurions shouted their orders. Shields were lifted and linked. The short stabbing swords were drawn from their sheaths. The second rank prepared their *pilum*, the spears with soft iron heads, designed to lodge in the enemy's shields, making them useless.

* * *

As the skirmish line withdraws to the safety of the shield wall and the cavalry gallops clear to the north, the Germans surge up the river bank for the first time. Like a floodtide they come forward, roaring, axes and swords aloft. The sheer feral force of the great war band beats upon the Roman shield wall.

"*Pila* ready." The Germans come on: fifty yards, forty, thirty. "*Pila* throw!"

All along the line the long shafted spears fly. Some Germans fall. Many more cast away their encumbered shields. With a roar and an almighty crash the German horde falls upon the Legion. For a moment the straight shield wall buckles and bulges. Tuccius watches, ready to deploy reserves, but they are not needed – yet. The wall holds. The dying has started. Rank reinforces rank as decurions drag the dead and wounded to the rear. Romans are dying but many more Germans are falling to the deadly stabbing from within the shield wall.

He looks to the right of his line. Good. The Eighth Cohort is barely engaged.

"Signal the Eighth to change axis."

Again the cornus sound. Hinging on the Sixth, the Eighth begin to swing round to the north, like a great door closing. The few Germans at that end of the line are herded before the swords of the Eighth, back amongst their fellows. Taken in the flank, the Germans are now fighting on two fronts.

Tuccius grunts with satisfaction. A crescendo of sound ending in a mighty crash rolls down from the northern flank. He turns. The first wave of Germans have assaulted the First and Second. Beyond them the slope is black with warriors. More pour from the forest. Desperate though it looks, the German war leader would have done better to have gathered his forces and attacked with more weight, thinks Tuccius. Nevertheless, things look grim enough. Twenty thousand to the north, ten thousand to the east. He is outnumbered nearly four to one. Not good.

From the city walls the artillery, the manuballistae and catapults, hurl stones and bolts into the mass below, taking some of the pressure off the all-important left flank of the Second Cohort, where it abuts the wall. Beyond, *alæ* of cavalry wheel and attack in turn, funnelling the Germans in towards the Second and First.

The noise is intense as is the heat. It is mid-morning on a summer's day. The water bearers will be busy.

"My Lord?"

His orderly hands him a goblet of chilled wine.

"Thank you, Mattheus."

Yes, it will be a long day. He hums to himself, a melody he learnt in Macedonia. It would sound well played on a lyra – Phrygian Mode, he thinks. Below him, men continue to die.

* * *

"Remarkable, my Lord."

The physician extended his hand, palm upwards.

"As you see, we extracted a dozen or so pieces of crystal."

Hadrian frowned, peering at the small, bloody objects.

"They were embedded around the front of the torso, some quite deep. The pain would have been excruciating although they were not life-threatening in themselves. However, together with the burns to the hands they have induced considerable shock and dehydration. I am not altogether sanguine that he will survive, my Lord. The next twenty-four hours will be critical."

"Thank you, Achaikos. Keep me informed."

Hadrian turned back to the battle. It wasn't his habit to interfere although he knew the temptation. Tuccius was doing perfectly well. The Eighth had rolled up the initial attack from the river so that they, along with the Second and First, now held a short front from the city wall to the river, facing north. The riverbank was heaped with bodies, mostly German. They marked a hideous tide line showing the furthest extent of the assault.

Tuccius was now sending the disengaged cohorts round the city where they would concentrate before falling on the vulnerable flank of the Germans. It was a risk but, if it worked, it would clinch a victory. Hadrian had thought of sending the Praetorians to lend their weight but knew that he would meet resistance from the Legate. Of course the Legate would be right. As had already been proved an assassin's knife could find its mark even though he was surrounded by a Legion. But he would like to have seen how his guard would acquit itself in battle. Well, perhaps another day.

* * *

Late that night Lucius awoke. The first sensation was of pain, mostly from his hands. He tried to move them but couldn't. For a moment he thought himself back in Cruorsilva. He groaned. 'Not again,' he thought.

"Lucius." The voice was soft. He felt a cool dampness on his brow.

"Not Lucius," he whispered, "Aurelio…"

"No you're Lucius; my Lucius."

He opened his eyes. A face smiled down at him anxiously. In the small light of a single lamp the features were not clear.

"Aithne? Is it you?"

A tear squeezed from the corner of one grey eye, then another.

"No, Lucius. It's only Trista but I'm going to look after you just like Aithne would have done. You're going to get better, I promise."

Lucius gazed at the face before him. He smiled and smiling fell asleep.

* * *

It was three days later. The dead had been burnt – the Germans in great heaps; the Romans with due ceremony. The battle had lasted most of the day although the turning point, at noon, came when four cohorts had taken the Germans in the flank. Through the rest of the afternoon and early evening the war band had been pressed back towards the river until, without any obvious signal, men began streaming away, back into the forest. They had just had enough.

Tuccius forbade pursuit. It was always wise to leave the enemy an escape route. If he chose to use it then he would not be back in a hurry. Besides, the opportunities for ambush in the forest were too great and enough men had died as it was.

The Legate had joined the Emperor for the small, celebratory dinner that evening but there was little feeling of celebration. The fight had been too close to call and Tuccius felt humiliated for having believed false intelligence. Then there were the faces of friends with whom he would never march again. Men like the Primum Pilum, that doughty warrior, who had given his life when the corner of the First Cohort had threatened to collapse. There would be promotions to think about tomorrow as well as cremations. Life went on but in the flat aftermath of battle, depression was a reality.

Now the Emperor Hadrian sat behind a desk in his quarters. There was a knock at the double doors. "Come," he called.

A chamberlain opened the doors.

"Centurion Lucius Terentius Aquilina, my Lord."

Lucius was carried into the room on a litter borne by four slaves. Trista followed him carrying a box. The slaves put the litter down where the chamberlain indicated, beside a couch, and then left the room. The chamberlain placed a chair for Trista and then he too withdrew, closing the door.

Hadrian stood, came from behind his desk, and sat on the couch. He studied Lucius. The physician had thought that the Centurion would take pneumonia at one stage but the crisis had receded two nights ago. Lucius was pale, his face drawn but he was breathing evenly and his eyes seemed bright.

"Well, young man; I am glad to see you looking better. We feared for your life for a while there. How are you feeling?"

"There is pain, my Lord," replied Lucius, "but your physician doses me with the juice of the poppy. Mainly I just feel very weak."

"Well, that can be remedied with time, I have no doubt. Now, you requested this audience and, as you asked, a Magus skilled in the Mysteries waits in the antechamber, so pray tell me what this is about. I declare that I am full of curiosity."

Lucius swallowed.

"First, my Lord, may I ask if there has been any sign of Sertorius?"

The Emperor shook his head. "No sign and no news but, then, given what I have heard from your man Tadg, perhaps there is no news to be had any more."

Lucius placed the back of one bandaged hand across his mouth and thought for a moment.

"It may be so, my Lord. Indeed, I truly hope it is. Your Magus may need to know more. But I get ahead of myself."

A discreet knock brought a slave into the chamber carrying refreshments. He arranged a tray on a low table and left as silently as he had arrived.

"My Lord," said Lucius, "while I was prisoner in Sertorius's home, Cruorsilva, I was subjected to a Rite of Darkness. Thankfully, for all concerned, it was not completed."

He turned to Trista and nodded. She came forward, placed the box on the litter and released the catch.

"A mannequin was made, my Lord. It was a likeness of you, made with my blood."

Hadrian's eyes narrowed.

"During the escape, thanks largely to the Lady Trista, we were able to bring the mannequin with us."

Clumsily, with his bandaged hands, he opened the box.

"I suggest you do not touch it, my Lord."

Hadrian came forward and stared at the contents of the box. He shuddered.

"We have kept it safe, my Lord," Lucius went on. "I know a little of these things and I feared that if it was destroyed out of hand, you might be harmed. So I have brought it here in the hope that it can be made safe by someone skilled in the Arts."

Hadrian nodded thoughtfully. "Yes indeed," he said quietly after some moments. "Yes indeed. I see my debt to you – to both of you – is much greater than I had thought."

He stood and strode back and forth, one finger on his lips. He stopped before the litter.

"In a moment I shall bring the Magus in and you shall tell him all that you know. Then we will take counsel as to what may be done. We must not forget that your blood is in this mannequin – close the lid, by the way, there's a good fellow. Then you must get well and when you are well you will come and see me again, Terentius. There are things which we must discuss."

* * *

That night, in the crypt of the Temple of Jupiter, the Magus performed a complex ritual of cleansing. The mannequin was than disposed of using the Rite of the Five Elements. Hadrian woke from a dream in which he had been hurrying through a dark forest, stalked by a great beast. Sweat beaded his brow yet, as he lay there gazing into the dark, a feeling of deep peace stole over him. He turned over and was asleep without knowing it.

At the same moment Lucius too passed into a deep sleep. Trista, looking at him fondly, noted the change. She yawned as she smoothed his brow.

"Goodnight, my dear one," she whispered before rising and going to her chamber.

From that night Lucius prospered and steadily regained his strength.

Chapter 36

(Vale)

"So, Terentius, my physician tells me that you are well enough to travel."

Lucius and the Emperor sat in a rose arbour in the garden of a town house. The Twenty Second (*Primigenia*) had marched north to Moguntiacum, leaving behind four centuries to guard Borbetomagus. Now the court was busy packing for the Emperor would set off on his endless tour of the frontiers in two days' time.

"That is so, my Lord. I lack a little flexibility in my hands but the physician says that it will return given time."

"Just so," said the Emperor. "And now is the time for endings. It is in my mind to grant you some wishes for you have earned reward for the services you have done me."

Lucius made to protest but Hadrian waved him into silence.

"Terentius, I can't abide being obligated to anyone. You will tell me what things you need for yourself and your people and I will grant them. That will be an end of the matter. Now speak, man."

Lucius thought.

"Well, my Lord, for the Lady Trista I would ask that she be reinstated in the estates which Sertorius took from her parents. In all justice I would also ask that reparations be made to her from the estates of Sertorius for the murder of her parents."

Hadrian nodded. "That shall be done. I shall also appoint a guardian for her until she shall come of age or marry. The estates, after all, will need the attention of someone skilled in such matters."

Lucius nodded. "I am grateful, my Lord."

The Emperor sighed. "Poor Valerius. It would seem that he discovered Sertosius' plot; was coming to tell me. His mistake was telling the blackguard in advance. That's why he and his family had to die. We are only fortunate that Trista survived. Continue."

Lucius thought again. "My Lord, I shall come to myself last but one of the boons I shall ask is to be allowed to take leave of absence. Three slaves have given me exemplary service and deserve reward.

"I have set in train manumission for Marcellus and Cadmus. I shall give them the mules and wagon, which are mine, so that they may continue trading while I am away. The Imperial Treasury, however, originally provided the stock. May I ask that it be transferred to them?"

Hadrian smiled wryly. "If you knew the workings of the Imperial Treasury you would never have asked that. However I shall have my Chief Clerk look into it. There is, I am sure, some hope. What about the third slave?"

Lucius scratched his head. "Yes, Adolphus. He is the big German you will have seen. He would not be happy if he were freed. I doubt he'd even understand the concept."

He paused before speaking again, thinking out loud. "His mother lives over the river at Bensheim. She is reckoned the best maker of boar's tripes in Germania Superior."

He hesitated again.

"Come on man; out with it." Hadrian sounded impatient.

"Well it seems a strange thing to ask of your Imperial Highness, but would there be some way of providing her anonymously with a pair of breeding sows and a boar?"

The Emperor of Rome barked his laughter.

"Terentius, the finest minds in the Imperial Commissary will be set upon the task within the hour."

A cat jumped up onto the arm of the seat. It rubbed itself against Hadrian's arm. He scratched its ears absently.

"Then there is Tadg…"

"Ah, yes; the excellent Tadg. What of him?"

"Well, Tadg has expressed the intention of coming with me and I have been unable to persuade him otherwise. I asked him what he would like as a reward. He answered that he needs a new pair of boots and wonders whether he might have a legionary *scutum*. He was very impressed by the lethality of the stabbing blades that he saw during the battle."

The Emperor nodded. "They shall be provided with, perhaps, a little extra from me personally."

Hadrian took a sip of wine. The cat jumped to the ground and made off under the seat.

"And so we come to you, Terentius," said Hadrian. "You have served me beyond any reasonable expectations. You speak of leave of absence. I will happily grant this but I express the wish that you will come back and serve me in due time."

"My Lord," began Lucius, "I ask nothing more than to serve you again but I promised a friend, a very dear friend, before he died, that I would visit his homeland and tell his people how he died. If I may, I would tarry there a while for I believe that his people are especially wise and I wish to learn from them."

"And who are these people?" asked the Emperor.

"They are called Essenes."

Hadrian showed surprise.

"The Essenes of Judaea?" He fingered his chin.

"Well I am sure that you are aware that the Judaeans, that turbulent, contentious people, were scattered to the four winds years ago; their temple thrown down. Are you sure that these Essenes still live there?"

Lucius shrugged. "Josephus, my friend, believed they did. Apparently they inhabit caves near a great inland salt lake."

Hadrian nodded thoughtfully.

"This is what I will do. I will give you a letter to the Commander of the Imperial Squadron at Massilia. He will provide a galley to take you to Judaea. I shall give you another letter for the Legate of the Tenth. They have Judaea at the moment. He will give you all help you need. If anyone knows where the Essenes are, he will. As for the leave of absence, let us say one year in Judaea. Then I ask that you return and find me wherever I am travelling."

Lucius was overcome by the Emperor's generosity.

"My Lord," he said, "you have been more than generous. May I...there is..."

He trailed into silence.

"Out with it man. What do you want? Your weight in gold?"

Lucius steeled himself.

"When first you took me into your service as an intelligence agent, I asked you if you would keep my vine staff for me."

"I did. I've still got it. A promise is a promise."

"What I would ask, my Lord, is this: if there should come a time when you no longer have a need for my services, would you return my vine staff to me? May I become, once again, a centurion?"

Hadrian stared at the man before him. He deeply regretted his remark about the Centurion's weight in gold.

"A note will be placed on your file, Terentius. It will be open-ended."

He found himself with nothing more to say. The Centurion could not leave until dismissed.

"Carry on, Centurion Terentius."

Lucius stood. He saluted as if on parade.

"And, Terentius...thank you."

* * *

And so it was that some days before the calends of July, in the early morning, well before the heat of the day, Lucius and Tadg with Galba the mule passed through the south gate of Borbetomagus. Waiting outside were Marcellus, Cadmus and Adolphus. Lucius looked quickly around.

"No Trista, then?" he asked.

"Master...Lucius, she would not come," said Marcellus. "I don't think she could face it."

"It can't be helped," said Lucius, with a sigh, although in truth her absence hurt him more than a little.

"Anyway, my friends, let's not prolong this more than necessary. This is not goodbye. We meet again two years from now in high summer in Mediolanum. I expect the Emperor to have further employment for us then. In the meantime go well and look after each other. Remember, what profit you make between then and now is yours to keep, so trade wisely."

He clasped Marcellus's hand first.

"I cannot thank you enough, Lucius," said Marcellus. "I will strive to be worthy of you."

Cadmus said, "I don't feel that I deserve this freedom, Lucius. I don't feel that I always did as well as I could but I want to tell you that I feel different now. I'm going to try my best."

Lucius smiled and gave his hand an extra squeeze. He tensed, well-knowing the power of Adolphus's great paw. However, when the moment came, the grasp was barely painful. Lucius was unaware of the careful training for this moment, nor that Marcellus was staring meaningfully at Adolphus.

"Me Mum sent you this." He brought from behind his back a leaf-wrapped parcel. It smelt decidedly gamey. "She said I was to say thank you."

Lucius received the parcel. He turned to Tadg.

"Well, look at that, Tadg," he exclaimed, smiling manically, "enough boars' tripes to keep us going to the coast."

"Well, thank the gods," said Tadg, playing his part. He took the big man's hand. "You tell your Mum we'll think about her every time we eats them...

"...an' for quite a time afterwards, I shouldn't wonder," he muttered, as he turned away.

Tadg hefted Galba's lead rein. Lucius took one last look

through the gate but saw no one. He raised his hand. They chorused their final 'goodbyes'. The two men turned, setting their faces to the south.

Tadg sniffed the air. It was good to be on the road again. He fingered the Praetorian gorget, hanging around his neck on its chain. 'Nice bloke, the Emperor,' he thought. 'He didn't have to give me that.' The boots were good, too and he couldn't wait to try out the sword. Yes, all in all it had definitely been a satisfactory few weeks.

Just then there was a scatter of running footsteps. They stopped and turned. Trista came to a halt in a flurry of dust and skirts. Without looking at the two men she hugged Galba round the neck, kissing her muzzle.

"Don't you let them mistreat you," she said. "If things get too bad, just come back to me. I'll look after you."

She turned to Tadg, her back to Lucius. "I'll miss you so much Tadg." She hugged him and kissed his cheek then stood back to admire his gorget. "You look very smart."

She looked up solemnly into the Celt's eyes.

Quietly she said, "You'll look after...him, won't you Tadg? Only he's not very clever, you know. He'll fall into a hole or something if you're not there."

Tadg smiled. "Don't you worry, m'lady. I'll keep 'im out of 'oles."

Finally, hesitatingly, she turned to Lucius, her eyes downcast. They stood silently, facing each other. Tadg coughed. He tugged on Galba's rein and moved slowly off down the road.

After a few moments Trista looked up briefly and then down again.

"You will come back, won't you, Lucius?" she murmured.

Lucius moved towards her and took her hands. "You know I will, Trista."

She looked up at him again, her eyes large with tears.

"Only...only I'll miss you. Oh, Tutatis..."

She flung herself into his arms, sobbing.

Lucius held her to him, this girl woman who had come to mean so much to him. It was like losing a limb but he could not tell her; could not let any of this go any further. Trista had her life to lead.

He smoothed her hair until the tears started to recede. Trista stood back, knuckling her eyes.

"Will you write?" she asked.

"Of course," replied Lucius. "And you can write to me care of the Prefecture at Tiberius."

He reached out, taking her chin in his hand.

"I will never forget you, Trista." He smiled. "Look for me in the spring. Can't say when but I will come."

Trista tried to smile but the tears began to choke her again.

"Go on," she said. "I must look a sight. I don't want you to remember me like this."

Lucius caressed her cheek then let his hand fall. He looked deep into her eyes for the last time, turned and set off down the road to Massilia on the Middle Sea.

* * *

It was evening. The Emperor Hadrian was taking a final stroll in the rose garden attached to his quarters. I was a pleasant place. The evening was heavy with perfume. If ever he came to an end of travelling the frontier, he thought, perhaps he would grow roses.

He made his way down the stone path towards the rose arbour with its fine views of the Rhenus. As he neared the arbour he heard sobbing. He turned to his bodyguard. The Praetorian had heard it too and was sidling closer. The Emperor held up his hand then waved the man away. Reluctantly the guard moved back.

Hadrian stepped quietly forward and peered around the

wooden frame. There, lying on the bench, her face cradled in her arms, sobbed the Lady Trista. The Emperor paused. He thought he knew what this was about. Whether he wanted to get involved was another matter.

The Emperor did not value women greatly. For one thing his tastes ran in other directions. For another, the ladies at his court, almost the only women he came across with any regularity, were, for the most part, insipid. However, he had heard Trista's story; knew what she had done, albeit unwittingly, in his service. This woman had courage. Further, she was currently alone and undoubtedly in need of counsel. He made his decision, entered the arbour and sat on the bench.

"Sit up, my dear," he said in a matter-of-fact voice.

Trista turned her head. Seeing who had spoken, she tried to stop her sobs, only succeeding in producing a series of hiccups.

"Here," said Hadrian, handing her a square of clean, white linen. "Clean yourself up then tell me what ails you."

Trista sat up, took the linen square and dabbed at her eyes. Then she blew her nose. She went to hand the cloth back before realizing its condition. Instead she twisted it in her lap.

"Well, child?"

Trista sniffed.

"He wouldn't take me," she whispered. "I begged him and begged him to but he wouldn't take me with him."

Hadrian nodded. He placed an arm, stiff with lack of intimacy, around the girl's shoulders.

"We're talking of the Centurion Terentius," he stated.

"Yes; Lucius," she replied.

"You love him very much, don't you?"

Trista looked down at the scrap of linen in her lap. She nodded.

The Emperor was silent, choosing his words. Finally he spoke.

"When I was young, if you can believe it, I too was in love. He was a young man of good family although nowhere near as good as mine. To my eyes he was the kindest, wisest most wonderful person in the world. I truly believed that I would die if I did not have him. I loved him to distraction."

Hadrian gazed at the distant river, his brow furrowed as if he thought deeply.

"I believe he loved me too but not as much; not in the same way."

Trista, intent now, despite herself, upon the Emperor's story, relaxed into his arm, leaning against him.

"He wanted to be a soldier; would have had a brilliant career, I'm quite sure. But when he would have gone to join the Legions, I made it impossible for him."

He looked at Trista. "Even then I was very powerful."

He fell silent.

After some seconds Trista asked, "What happened, my Lord?"

The Emperor sighed.

"We were together for another six months but I could tell that he was not happy. At the end of that time a strange thing happened. I awoke one day and found a stranger lying beside me. Oh don't get me wrong; it was the same young man but I had changed him, the man I loved, into someone quite different, quite unlovable, by me at least."

He looked down at Trista. With his free hand he tipped her chin upwards.

"Trista, my dear, I can tell you as one who travels the length and breadth of this Empire, who has dominion over great and small, that the man you love is no ordinary man. In the whole Empire I doubt you would find more than a hundred to equal him. You have chosen well but understand this: if there were some way that you could bind your Lucius to you, you would kill the thing you love."

He let go of her chin but she remained looking up at him, her eyes wide, trying to understand.

"Fortunately for both of you," the Emperor continued, "he is wise. He understands the lesson I have just told you. He also knows that you have a life to lead. If it helps, my child, I believe that he loves you; not perhaps in the way you would want but in a manner much deeper; much more lasting."

He looked out across the Rhenus again, at the forests now void of lights.

"I do not say that you will never see him again. I believe that you will and I make no prognostications about what may or may not happen then, but this I counsel you: bury that thought deep in your mind. Until it comes to pass, imagine him as a bird, in the full vigour of its life, flying to somewhere wonderful."

He looked down at her with a grave smile.

"If you can do that, Trista, then your love will abide."

* * *

Many miles to the south, in a dell, in a wood, beside the great trunk road that runs arrow-straight to Massilia on the Middle Sea, two travellers sleep beside a small fire in the midst of the limitless dark.

Roundfire Books put simply, publish great stories. Whether it's literary or popular, a gentle tale or a pulsating thriller, the connecting theme in all Roundfire fiction titles is that once you pick them up you won't want to put them down.